Christmas in Chamonix

SASHA WAGSTAFF

Christmas
in
Chamonix

CANELO

First published in the United Kingdom in 2019 by Canelo

This edition published in the United Kingdom in 2020 by

Canelo Digital Publishing Limited
31 Helen Road
Oxford OX2 0DF
United Kingdom

Print ISBN 978 1 78863 979 8
Ebook ISBN 978 1 78863 320 8

Look for more great books at www.canelo.co

Printed and bound in Great Britain by Clays Ltd, Elcograf S.p.A.

For Ben. For the skiing but mostly, for us XX

Chapter One

November

Lily Jackson pushed her elbows into her client's incredibly hairy back and let out a deep sigh. It was more about Lily's state of mind than part of the treatment, but it seemed to help; her client let out an identically pleasurable sigh and relaxed visibly into the towelling-covered couch.

'So good,' he murmured into the face hole.

'Great,' Lily said, keeping one hand on the client's back as she reached for more oil. She was sure it was great for her client, but not so much for her, it had to be said. Massaging someone with such thick hair wasn't the most fun, however much she generally liked her job. Perhaps it was just that it was a little predictable. Lily was the sort of person who liked to feel safe and secure, but she also didn't like to stand still. And in her current job, she was definitely standing still.

Find a positive, find a positive, Lily intoned to herself. OK, so she loved the scent of the oil! Yes, she did. It contained juniper berry for detoxifying, rosemary to stimulate the circulation and warming black pepper. Her heart sank slightly. Was that all she could come up with? That she liked the smell of the oil? Good God. Maybe it was time for a change. Not that Lily particularly liked change.

She had only had one other job because she hated the disruption and having to adapt to new things.

'Is this pressure OK?' she asked, doing her best to fulfil her brief as a calming, professional masseuse.

'Perfect,' her client mumbled. 'My shoulder feels so much better.'

Lily felt gratified by that and momentarily considered her client. Kieran was a professional rugby player and might even be a famous one, but Lily wasn't really sure because rugby wasn't her thing. He had the chunky thighs, on reflection, but his face was... meh. And Lily was all about the face. And the eyes. And the voice.

She mentally pulled herself back into the room and accepted his compliment.

'Fantastic. Just relax into the couch and I'll make sure all these knots under the shoulder blade disappear.'

Lily focused her attention on the massage. This was a sports massage, meaning the emphasis was on the manipulation of a certain muscle's soft tissue in order to treat an injury and help prevent any further injury. Unlike a deep tissue massage, which focuses on putting pressure on the layers of tissue in the body, a sports massage relies upon safely and skilfully manipulating the damaged, fragile tissue to heal it. It was complicated, but Lily had been doing this job for ten years, so she was – if not an expert – shit hot. Ish. Totally in her comfort zone.

Thoughts of Jamie drifted into Lily's head and she allowed herself to indulge in them while the other half of her mind made sure the massage was perfectly executed. Her and Jamie on holiday in the Maldives. A water cottage with its own decking area for meals, a glass floor to watch the fish weaving through the aquamarine water beneath it and… and a curved slide to enter the water with a whoop and a splash! Lily felt a beaming smile spread across her face. Cocktails she'd never heard of because they were so cool and unique, both of them seated on velvet thrones in a swanky Mayfair bar with her favourite canapés. Shellfish-based, if she was allowed to choose. Which she was, because it was her fantasy. What else? Oh yes. A weekend away in a country hotel with a roaring fire and brisk walks with a dog. The French bulldog they had chosen together called Hugo. They would dress Hugo in a bow tie and bowler hat, if the whim took them, and he would 'complete them' before they decided to have a gorgeous little baby. Once they were married, natch. And it was about time she got married, or at the very least got together with the man of her dreams, because she was thirty-two. And as everyone knew, being thirty-two was brilliant in many ways, but not if one was single and didn't have a 'proper plan', as Lily's best friend Imogen called it, for acquiring a man and a future that involved marriage and babies. Which Lily wasn't entirely sure she wanted, but she would very much like to be in a relationship. She had been single for longer than she cared to remember, even though it was probably actually less than six months.

Lily had had boyfriends. Four serious ones, a few not-so-serious ones and what she felt was an adequate but not slutty number of casual flings. Why hadn't those relation-ships worked out? The serious ones, at least. She supposed it was because she had always felt as though something was missing. A special connection. Sizzling chemistry. Friendship. Something.

Lily sighed again, but this time, not so pleasurably. The problem was, none of these delicious thoughts she had about Jamie were memories; they were fantasies.

The actual memories were almost as good, they just didn't involve Jamie and Lily being a couple. But the memories of hanging out after school listening to music, picnics and rounders in the park, sharing Oreo milkshakes and discussing who they both fancied were still lovely. Jamie had fancied far more girls than Lily had boys and that had always jarred slightly, but still. Lily had always acted chilled about it, no matter who Jamie was fixated on. The point was, Jamie had been a huge part of Lily's childhood and beyond that. Thinking of their friendship developing into something else almost felt like a natural step. Not to mention how fantastic she assumed the kissing would be. And the sex…

Oh yes, the sex. This was something Lily fantasised about far more than she probably should. It was just *so* much fun thinking about Jamie and what he'd be like in bed. She had built him up into a veritable sex god, capable of slow, achingly romantic love-making all the way to hot, thrusting quickies and everything in between.

Why hadn't they ever got together? It was a question Lily had asked herself on and off through the years. They had friendship and a special connection borne out of all of the years they had been close. Was it the lack of chemistry? No, there was chemistry. Timing? Bad timing. Perhaps that was the answer.

Lily relaxed deeply into the massage, making sure all the shoulder knots had gone. Kieran groaned and moaned into his towelling hole as if he was enjoying the massage very much indeed. Lily finished up and walked back into

4

the room some time later with a glass of iced water, finding Kieran wrapped in the fluffy, navy towelling robe all clients were given, seated in one of the small armchairs in the corner of the room. His face was bright red from the massage and he sat with his gigantic thighs spread far apart, clearly unaware that he was showing off all of his rugby tackle. Again.

Lily averted her eyes and wondered if she should mention to her client that his scrotum was on show for the fifteenth time. The spa was very keen to maintain a professional stance at every turn, but Lily felt it might be helpful for Kieran to know that he was displaying his wares every time he came to the spa.

'Brilliant massage,' Kieran commented, accepting the glass of water. He checked out the smooth, navy-hued walls, the piles of thick towels and the on-trend, rose gold cushions and vases as he pushed his feet into navy mules – thus exposing himself even more.

'Thank you. I'm glad it was beneficial for you,' Lily replied with a polite smile, keeping her eyes on his gaze and away from his tackle.

'My favourite thing in the world, massages,' Kieran commented, looking in no hurry to leave. He scratched his balls and Lily winced.

'I do really love Christmas, though. And that will be here before we know it! What do you think… er, Lily, is it? Are you excited about Christmas?'

Lily chewed her lip and tried not to smile. She adored Christmas. She could wax lyrical about Christmas for a long time, and she had this fantasy about what she thought the perfect Christmas should be like. A non-commercial, snowy, steeped-in-tradition type of thing.

'I love it, actually,' she answered blandly, knowing she had to respond in some fashion. 'Not that I find it that Christmassy here, to be fair.' London was so busy in December and full of tourists. It just felt so commercial.

'Really? Oh, I disagree,' Kieran enthused, finally getting to his feet and thankfully taking his balls out of sight. 'I think it's beautiful in December. All the lights and the decorations.'

Showing Kieran and his premature Christmas musings out, Lily wandered around the health club to while away the last half hour before finishing her shift.

The health club in Wimbledon was essentially a spa with a gym attached to it. The spa was the star attraction, featuring the standard sauna and steam rooms, an impressive plunge pool and a hydrotherapy pool with multiple jets. It also had a Hammam area, with 'relaxed, heated seating', an ice fountain and Turkish baths with hot, hotter and hottest rooms. And the massage therapies the spa offered were both extensive and intensive: Bamboo, Deep Tissue, Ayurvedic with Shea Butter, Hot Stone, Swedish, Lava Shell, Himalayan Salt Stone, Indian and Tibetan Head. And Sports, which was Lily's area of expertise, even though she was also qualified in most of the others as well, not to mention elements of Tui Na, a Chinese massage which was all about releasing the flow of energy around the body.

Lily loved her job. At least, she loved being a massage therapist. She just wasn't sure she loved working at this particular health club anymore. She often used the facilities, particularly the gym, but for work all she was ever booked to do were sports massages, which became so formulaic after a while. Even the clients seemed formulaic: people who went to the gym a lot, and the odd, genuine sportsman like Kieran. Balls may or may not be included.

The other issue was that the health club also over-booked clients, so Lily carried out massages back to back without much of a break and it could be strenuous work. The workload was heavy and it had become a drudge, carrying out the same massage after the same massage with no challenge or fresh spark whatsoever.

Lily suddenly felt guilty. Who was she to complain? It was a good job and she was lucky to have it. Deep down, Lily knew she was more dissatisfied with other areas of her life than her job, but it was still a super-strict environment and she'd had enough of looking at a stranger's scrotum.

'You can go when the clock hits six pm exactly,' Karen, her boss, said from reception. 'But only if you've folded all the towels and topped all the oils up.'

'Of course,' Lily said while thinking about placing a large custard tart on Karen's head so all the gooey stuff oozed all over her uniform. Lily kept her mouth shut, knowing she'd already completed all of her tasks, but she headed back to her area to make sure everything was in place. Mostly just for something to do.

'Go if you like,' her co-worker Libby said. 'I'll make sure everything is ship-shape.'

Libby was Lily's one and only friend at the spa because she was the only like-minded one there. She was younger than the others, but it wasn't really about age. Libby just seemed more sociable and more understanding about other things going on outside of work. She was Karen's supervisor, so she had responsibility at the spa, but Libby seemed more relaxed about everything in general. She also had a boyfriend she fancied the fuck out of and couldn't stop telling Lily all the sordid details every time she got a chance. It was a quid pro quo situation; Lily listened to Libby's fruity tales and Libby let her out early on occasion.

'Are you sure?' Lily immediately went to unbutton her navy uniform, but feeling rude, stopped herself.

Libby smiled. 'Yes, of course. It's Friday. Go have a cocktail – or ten. I'd come with you, but I'm meeting my fella tonight. Ooh, I can't wait! I'm going to try and tantric him up tonight. Sting will have nothing on us by the end of the weekend!'

Lily quickly headed to the changing area and grabbed her clothes. The health spa felt especially claustrophobic today for some reason. She removed her uniform, folded it neatly and placed it in her locker. Quickly shimmying into skinny jeans, short brown suede boots and a cream off-the-shoulder top, Lily grabbed her brown, fur-trimmed jacket and made her way out of the spa. She felt that she looked pretty good. Classy and sexy – her favourite vibe.

Taking a deep breath of chilly November air, she started walking and texting simultaneously. She texted Ivy so she knew to meet her earlier, her text crossing with one from good-friend-and-provider-of-fantasy-relationship-scenarios-Jamie at the same time. It said:

'*Hey you. How's work? Need a catch up with my bestie. Miss ya!*'

Lily sent a quick text back. '*Miss you too. Work is a bit pants. Meeting my sis tonight but fancy drinks next week?*'

Jamie responded immediately. '*Yussssss! I'm in, Red. Text me the location and I'll be there x.*'

Jamie was the only person who ever called her Red. Lily wasn't sure she'd like it if anyone else called her that because she was auburn rather than 'red' as such, but it was Jamie and she loved that he had a nickname for her. 'Red' made her feel cool and sexy and like she was special, as stupid as that might sound.

Fifteen minutes later, Lily found herself outside the cosy French bistro she had booked a week ago, the bistro that reminded her of her parents – well, her mum and stepdad, to be precise – and their love of France. They still hopped across to Le Touquet on occasion and hired a farmhouse in the Loire valley every year, so French food was very 'second home' to herself and Ivy. Heading inside the restaurant with its familiar brick walls and scrubbed oak tables, Lily looked around for her sister and soon caught sight of her waving from a corner table. Ivy was wearing a black, fitted suit with a pencil skirt, a cute belted jacket and shiny, high-heeled pumps.

'Sis!' Ivy stood up and gave Lily a hug. 'How come you're out early?'

'Karen wanted me to stay until the last minute, but Libby took pity on me.' Lily shrugged her arms out of her jacket and slid into a chair. 'I managed to escape before she launched into a detailed description of the tantric sex she has planned for the weekend.'

'Yikes. Sounds awful. Still fed up with your job then?' Ivy asked, sitting down again.

Lily sighed. 'I guess so. Although I'm not even sure it's about the job as such. I mean, the staff never want to go out for coffee or drinks or anything, but I don't know… I don't know if it's even that.'

Ivy pushed an espresso martini across the table. 'I ordered these for us. I know they're not French, strictly speaking – and the look they gave me in here when I ordered them, honestly – but I figured you might need one.'

'I really do. Thank you.' Lily sipped the martini. 'Oh, that's so good. Just the right mixture of bitter and creamy.'

'So what's going on in your life?' Ivy sat back.

Lily regarded her sister fondly as she enjoyed her drink. Ivy was three years older and, like Lily, had long, auburn hair, but that was where the similarity ended. Lily had slanting, jade-green eyes, freckles and a laid-back dress style, whereas Ivy had wide eyes that resembled olives, pale, freckle-free skin and she dressed like the smart business woman she was, even on her days off. Ivy was the CEO of a trendy, online meal plan company, the headquarters of which were in Kensington. She spent most of her time at the office or travelling around the country promoting the business elsewhere and she had been particularly busy of late.

Lily did always feel rather pale in comparison to Ivy who was such a high flyer. Lily was in control of herself most of the time and as such, she supposed she rarely stepped out of her comfort zone. Whereas Ivy seemed to do it on a regular basis.

'Tell me all the goss,' Ivy prompted supportively. 'We haven't caught up properly in months.'

Lily smiled. It was true. She and Ivy were close, but not close-close. They chatted every few days and stayed in touch with one another, but they didn't necessarily put the world to rights or go into intimate detail about anything. Which was why Lily hadn't ever confided in her about Jamie.

Jamie Miller. Lily's hand paused on the stem of her martini glass. He had been her friend for, what, more than twenty years? His parents had moved into the area when they were in year eight. He had joined her senior school and they had been allocated as partners in science class. From that point on, they had become firm friends, finding themselves in the same classes on and off and making sure they spent plenty of time together outside of school too. In a purely platonic fashion, of course. Jamie had nursed Lily through her break ups and vice versa and they had remained friends throughout. Mostly Lily hadn't ever seen Jamie as anything but a good friend because she knew that he was a bit of a tart.

Recently, Lily had begun to see Jamie differently and she had no idea why. He had always been fun and funny and impulsive, but lately, Lily had started to see him as *attractive*. And that had been a very surprising turn of events. She wondered if he had perhaps changed and grown up a little, and that she was sensing it. Lily assumed Jamie had no idea her feelings had changed, but maybe it was about time Lily told him. The thought of it made her stomach flip over, but if she didn't tell him, he might never know and life would pass them by and they wouldn't ever get to kiss or do the sex thing or get tantric like Sting…

'Lily?' Ivy leant forward, looking concerned. 'Are you OK?'

Lily came out of her reverie with a jolt. 'Sorry! I was just thinking about something.'

'Something work-related?'

'Not really. Well, kind of.' Lily frowned. 'Work is OK. I feel ungrateful for moaning about it, really, because it's a good job. The staff are lovely and the clients are all pretty nice, apart from a few constantly showing me their scrotum. It's just not…'

'Exciting?' Ivy offered. 'All jobs feel like that at times. Even mine.'

Lily scoffed. She couldn't imagine Ivy feeling that way about her job. She was practically a workaholic. Everything revolved around Ivy's job, from her early morning gym sessions (spliced with yoga for her 'emotional well-being') to the ready-prepared, healthy meals she slotted into her day at the correct intervals. Lily used to wonder if Ivy scheduled in time to have sex with whoever she was seeing at the time the way she did her yoga sessions. Ivy truly was that organised and premediated about certain things, even though she constantly took risks when it came to work.

'Maybe I need to do something drastic on the job front,' Lily mused, perusing the menu. She wasn't sure why she was even looking at it. She always ordered two starters: the spinach and mushroom crêpes (mouth-wateringly delicious and oozing with gruyere cheese) and the baked crottin – warmed goat cheese with walnuts, croutons and golden raisins. Ivy was always going on about Lily stepping out of her comfort zone, but Lily liked what she liked and she felt much safer when she surrounded herself with familiar things.

Ivy's eyes dropped to her menu and Lily knew she was searching for the most nutritious, low-fat options. 'Drastic? In what sense? And I'm not sure I can see that happening, but I would love to.' Ivy turned and spoke to the waiter. 'I'll have the asparagus without the hollandaise and the salmon and ratatouille please.' She handed her menu over and gave Lily her full attention.

Lily didn't blame her sister for thinking that. When did she do anything that could be described as 'drastic'? Jamie popped into Lily's head again and she felt a shiver inside. Could she really be thinking about telling him how she felt? No, that would be insane.

'I… have some news actually,' Ivy offered carefully.

Knowing this would be work news, Lily idly wondered what drink to order next. Prosecco? Sauvignon Blanc? A Porn Star Martini, if only to see the look of horror on the waitress's face? Lily felt disloyal to her sister momentarily. It wasn't that she wasn't interested in Ivy's work. Lily just wished Ivy would open up a bit more sometimes and perhaps talk about her personal life.

'So, I've met someone,' Ivy announced.

Lily's head snapped up, cocktails and wine list forgotten. 'What?'

Ivy's cheeks flushed instantly.

'You're blushing!' Lily said.

'God, am I?' Openly cringing, Ivy put her hands to her hot cheeks.

Lily was gobsmacked. She had never seen Ivy like this before. Ivy was usually so composed. The last time Lily had seen her sister blush was when they were at school and Ivy had walked through an entire assembly hall with her skirt tucked into the back of her knickers. Understandably, Ivy had turned beetroot and had been utterly mortified and she had been known as 'Wednesday' for a long while afterwards, due to the unusual etching of the days of the week on the back of her knickers.

Ivy recovered herself but flapped a hand in front of her face for good measure. 'Lordy. Don't let me do that again.'

'Ivy.' Lily leant forward. 'Do you have the feels?'

Ivy pulled a face. 'What sort of expression is that?' She gulped down some of her martini. 'But if you mean do I

13

have feelings for this person? Then... maybe. I mean only "maybe" at this stage. But yes. I like him.'

'Wow.' Lily stared at her sister. Ivy was exceptionally pretty and she had men chasing after her constantly. It had been that way since school. But Ivy was famously married to her job and apart from the odd, rather uptight boyfriend over the years, Ivy remained cool in the face of men hotly pursuing her. Lily wondered who had caught Ivy's attention enough to make her blush and act all flustered.

'So. Who's the guy? Anyone I know?'

'Thank you,' Ivy said to the waitress as her asparagus arrived. 'Mmmm, that smells good.'

'Not as good as mine,' Lily said, inhaling her spinach and mushroom crêpes. 'Look at all this gruyere... I'll have to go for a long gym session after work on Monday.'

'Hardly,' Ivy scoffed. 'You're lovely and slim. I have to watch my weight far more than you do. As soon as I hit my thirties, I started expanding. You'll be fine for years before you have to worry about that stuff.'

Lily rolled her eyes and attacked her crêpes. 'So who's the guy?'

Ivy look suspiciously like she might be blushing again. 'Shall we order some Sauvignon Blanc? I... don't want to say too much at this stage. It's early days.'

'How early?'

'Like... a few months. Three, four...' Ivy shrugged vaguely. 'It might come to nothing.'

'Well, you clearly think it's something,' Lily returned swiftly. 'Otherwise you wouldn't be acting like a big girl's blouse.'

Ivy recoiled at the accusation but said nothing, focusing herself on the wine order. Lily wondered why Ivy was being so cagey. Was the new man thirty years older? Was he a drug dealer? Did he… God forbid and Lily devoutly prayed *not* – wear corduroy at the weekends?

'I'll tell you about him in due course,' Ivy said, softening when she saw Lily's frown. 'I want to tell you more, really I do. I'm just being cautious. And silly, probably. But you might not… approve.'

'*Approve?*' Lily laughed. Now Ivy really was being silly. 'Since when do you need my approval for anything? I'm not judgemental. I just want you to be happy.'

'I'm being so secretive,' Ivy said apologetically. She reached across the table and squeezed Lily's hand. 'And maybe "approval" isn't the right word. I just haven't felt this way before and I'm being cautious because… well, I don't know why really. And once I know it's serious on both sides, I'll tell you more. OK?'

'OK.' Lily picked up the glass of sauvignon the waitress had just brought them. 'Well. Cheers. To love.'

'To… love,' Ivy agreed.

Lily sipped her wine. Now she felt even more strongly that she should tell Jamie how she felt about him. If Ivy – the devout commitment-phobe – could get herself into a relationship, maybe it was about time Lily took control of her own life and started the ball rolling.

Chapter Two

A Week Later

'Is this pressure all right for you?' Lily asked. She sighed, feeling exhausted. It was already the sixth massage of the day and this client was also very hairy – even hairier than Kieran. He was a lovely client, but he was so covered in hair it was like massaging a thick animal pelt. It didn't put Lily off as such; she was used to such things, but she could barely reach his skin and had to go deeper with her strokes to make sure she was getting the muscles.

Lily also felt distracted. The spa had put all their Christmas decorations up the day before with baubles and tinsel everywhere – all matching, all very tasteful. There was a large Christmas tree in the reception area with fake gift-wrapped presents underneath it and it was beautiful, but Lily ached for something more authentic.

She couldn't stop thinking about Ivy and her new boyfriend. She really wanted her sister to be happy and Lily wondered who the lucky man was, but Lily also couldn't stop thinking about Jamie. About telling Jamie how she felt about him. She wasn't sure she could pluck up the courage, but she knew she simply had to step out of her comfort zone.

God! She was seeing Jamie later tonight. Lily's hand glided over the thick hair on her client's back. She really should tell Jamie tonight. I mean, what did she have to lose? He was between girlfriends as far as she knew. In fact, he'd been rather quiet on that front for a while, so it might be the perfect time to tell him how she felt.

Lily gulped.

'Pressure's great,' her client mumbled into the couch.

Lily focused herself on the task at hand, using deep pressure and firm strokes. The scent from the warm oil drifted up and relaxed her; a mixture of sweet almond oil, Indian bay, clove bud and lavender. Finishing up, Lily placed a large glass of iced water on the side and left so her client could get dressed in his gown (hopefully with his balls hidden).

After checking him out at reception and showing him to the door, Lily perused the appointments schedule online. She had fifteen minutes before her next client was due to arrive, so she headed out through the back door to check her phone. She was just flipping through her messages when her phone started to ring. It was her best friend, Imogen.

'Is that Lilian Lil McLilbeth?'

Lily felt herself grin on the inside. Imogen was *that* kind of best friend – the kind who could always make you laugh even with the way they say hello.

'Ims. It is *so* good to hear your voice.'

'I know, right?' Imogen laughed. 'Likewise, my friend.'

Lily checked her watch and settled down on a bench in the calm area reserved for staff. The trees were losing the last of their autumnal leaves and the small, neat square of lawn was almost completely covered with a scattering of orange, yellow and red.

'How's the job?' Imogen asked.

Lily sighed. 'I mean, it's good. No, it's not. But it's a job and I'm lucky to have it and all that.'

'God. You really are in a bad way,' Imogen commented. 'I get why you don't want to sound ungrateful for having a job, but still. You should be doing something you love. Like me.'

'You sound like my sister. She loves her job too. And she has a new boyfriend.' Lily rolled her eyes. 'Is this the part where you tell me how amazing your life is and how wonderful your job in Chamonix is?'

'Yes. Yes, it is. Because it is, actually. Ivy has a boyfriend?'

'Apparently.'

'That's a turn up. Anyway, my job.'

Lily could hear Imogen chuckling happily down the phone.

'My job is snow and it's skiing and it's nights outs and it's great company and lovely food and a teeny, tiny bit of work and… and it'll be Christmas here soon as well and that will be heavenly!'

'Yes, yes. Well, you've got me with the Christmas bit. It sounds gorgeous.'

'It's gorgeous year-round here, Lil. Even in the summer it's stunning. But covered in snow, with all the decorations up…'

Lily smiled. 'It sounds wonderful. I mean, I've never skied before, so I have no idea if it's a good thing or not…'

'It really is, Lily! And you'd be a natural.'

'Irrelevant,' Lily commented. 'Seeing as I have no desire whatsoever to throw myself down a mountain anytime soon. I don't get it, but Jamie raves about it all the time. He loves skiing so much. But really, why, for fuck's sake?'

'Oh, so many reasons! I'm going to try and change your mind about the whole skiing thing.'

Lily changed the subject. 'In other news, I might tell Jamie how I feel about him.'

'What?!' Imogen was well aware that Lily had feelings for Jamie, but she had been listening to talk of it for months now and wasn't convinced it was ever going to be a thing. 'When?'

'Oh, I don't know.' Lily faltered. 'Er… soon? Tonight, maybe? I'm seeing him tonight.'

'Wowzers.' Imogen was momentarily silenced. 'Well, it's about time, isn't it? You've been going on about Jamie for so long now. It's about time he knew how you felt.'

'Yes.' Lily felt excited and scared at the same time. 'What if he doesn't feel the same?'

'Of course he will,' Imogen scoffed. 'You two hang out together all the time. You're those cheesy best friends who love each other and don't get together for years and then they do.'

Lily felt a smile lighting up her face and mentally slapped herself for being such a sap. 'We're not best friends, as such. But we're good friends.'

'Details, details. God, you'll have to stay in touch every half hour tonight so I know what's happening.' Imogen paused. 'Anyway, I had an actual reason for phoning you. Our sports masseuse has just resigned.'

Lily stood up, sure she was being called back into the spa. She could hear Karen's voice calling her like a shouty school marm.

'Oh?'

'Yes, and I wondered if you might fancy the job.'

'What?' Lily frowned. 'What job? The one in Chamonix?'

'Yes of course, the one in Chamonix!' Imogen sounded impatient. 'Come on, Lils. It would be amazing if we were here together. I could teach you to ski and you could do the massage thing and there are some really nice people here... really lovely boys here...'

Lily thought about it seriously for a moment. Snow she could cope with. Snow, she loved. Christmassy. But skiing was an unknown, so she couldn't comment on that. The Alps? Lily was sure they were beautiful. Chamonix – breathtaking, no doubt. But it was just too much. Too big a change. And there was far too much keeping her here. Lily would miss Jamie too much. And her sister.

She brought herself out of her reverie, certain she could hear her name being called. 'I have to go. It's a lovely thought, Ims, and I'd love to see more of you, but maybe I'll come for a visit? Moving to Chamonix is a bit too drastic, I think. And I have... stuff here I'm kinda attached to...'

'Boo! OK then. I have a ski lesson, so I'll let you get on. Tell me what happens with Jamie?'

'Of course.'

Lily ended the call and felt her stomach lurch again. She'd have to focus on work to take her mind off meeting Jamie tonight. Dashing inside the spa again, Lily put everything out of her mind apart from massages.

–

Hours later, Lily was fiddling with her hair in the upmarket toilets of a funky cocktail bar in Covent Garden that was way out, even for one of Jamie's choices. She had pinned the front of her auburn hair up with some tendrils hanging down and when she had left the spa, it had looked pretty good. A tube journey and some drizzle as she dashed through the cobbled streets later and her sophisticated half-up-do turned into a wet, droopy mess that made her look like a wet spaniel.

Giving up on her hair, Lily nervously checked her make-up. It wasn't too bad. Her professional Kardashian 'smoky eye' was still in place and her up-flick eyeliner was immaculate. Touching up her nude lip gloss, Lily decided it would have to do. She had made an effort with her outfit, but hopefully in a very casual way. Black leather trousers with zips at the ankles teamed with little tasselled suede boots, a cropped white top and a mock leopard skin coat.

Was she too old for a cropped top at her age? Lily thought she just about rocked it. She supposed she would have to lower the length of her tops at some point, but not just yet hopefully. Removing the coat and hanging it over her arm, Lily headed back out to the cocktail bar. It was Jamie's choice of venue and Lily couldn't help raising her eyebrows at her surroundings. Floral walls adorned with over-sized blooms clashing haphazardly with banquettes in garish prints and a cocktail list full of classics with some unique new offerings with comedy names and 'of the moment' ingredients. It wasn't quite her fantasy of cocktails in Mayfair on velvet thrones, but maybe it could come close. And at least they hadn't put their Christmas decorations up yet. Lily couldn't imagine what decorations wouldn't clash hideously with the décor in this place.

Maybe they just sprayed glitter over everything and called it festive.

Lily looked around for Jamie. He was nowhere to be seen, but he was notoriously late, so she wasn't too worried. Taking a seat at the bar – inelegantly because it was one of those silly stools no self-respecting person can climb onto with any degree of dignity – she ordered herself a 'Smooth Criminal' for Dutch courage. It was a shot containing chocolate liqueur, hazelnut liqueur, and spiced rum with cardamom seeds scattered on top. Necking it swiftly, Lily took a deep breath. She was doing this. She was actually doing this.

'Red!'

Turning, Lily felt herself blushing, rather like Ivy had the other week. It was his voice. Jamie had the most sexy, manly, knicker-twanging voice.

'Jamie!'

She kissed his cheek and found herself enveloped in his effusive hug. He smelt good. Always. Of the woody aftershave he always wore and just something that was so Jamie. Washing powder, hair gel and probably Lynx or something similar. But it all suited him and smells had always been so evocative to Lily. Jamie's smell reminded her of her youth and of happiness and she always felt at home when he was around her. He had come straight from work, so he was in a navy suit with the tie hanging out of his pocket and his shirt unbuttoned at the neck. To complete the look, Jamie wore pointy, shiny shoes. In short, he wore the uniform of the young and trendy in the City – but he wore it well.

'Have you started without me?' he asked, edging onto the chair next to her.

'Oh that.' Lily pushed the shot glass away, embarrassed. 'No, that was just…' Her voice tailed off. She couldn't tell him it was to give herself courage to tell him how she felt. She could do with another ten, but still. It was a start.

'No matter.' Jamie raked his hand through his dark, floppy hair. 'Let's get a bottle of something. Prosecco?'

Lily nodded. She loved that Jamie drank bubbles. Men so rarely did. Accepting a glass some minutes later, she chinked hers against his.

'To us,' she said, without thinking. She felt herself flush. What an idiot! 'Oh, I just meant…'

'To us!' Jamie echoed, tapping his glass to hers. 'Absolutely.'

'Friends,' Lily murmured.

'That's it.' He sat back and grinned at her. 'So, Red. What's happening with you?'

Lily relaxed. This was the lovely thing about Jamie – she could totally be herself with him. She knew she could talk about anything and he wouldn't judge. He would always have her back. She filled him in on the work situation, throwing in a few peppy anecdotes to make him laugh.

'Ewwwww!' he said, letting out a loud belly laugh. 'Stop it about all the hairy backs and stuff. It's gross!'

'I don't really mind the hairy ones,' Lily said, feeling disloyal to some of her lovely clients. 'It's more the spa itself… it's just so unfriendly and not… me, I guess. Even though I've been there for years. Ever since the new management took over a few years back, I haven't really enjoyed it…' Her voice trailed away.

Jamie regarded her. 'So what do you think then? Do you need to change jobs?' He ordered some more prosecco, even though they weren't ready for it yet.

Lily stared at him. He really did have the most gorgeous eyes. Dark, intense... she shook herself. She really had to stop gawping at him like that. It was just that Jamie was always there at just the right times. Right when she needed him. Well, she needed him now. But in a different way.

'Erm. I don't know. I just feel rather... unsettled at the moment.' Lily swallowed. Was this the right moment? Should she tell Jamie how she felt? She opened her mouth to speak without any thought about what words would be the most appropriate when Jamie's phone rang. Lily closed her mouth. Saved by the bell.

'I have to take this,' Jamie said apologetically. 'Back in a sec.' He slid off his bar stool – with some dignity, it had to be said – and headed outside.

Lily took a deep breath. Wow. She had nearly just gone headlong into that conversation without putting proper thought into it and without formulating any kind of words around her feelings. Lily took a sip of prosecco. What did she need to say? That she had been in love with him for... oh, probably years now. Or more accurately, that she had been friends with him for the longest time and that close, fun, meaningful friendship had made her develop feelings for him.

Lily faltered, feeling like a silly schoolgirl. What if Jamie didn't feel the same way? A wave of nausea threatened to overwhelm her, but it might be the Smooth Criminal and a bucketload of Prosecco. God. She hadn't even thought that far ahead – about how he felt! Which was really quite naive of her. She had simply thought of blurting out her feelings without a single thought about what Jamie might think and feel.

'You OK?' A barman interrupted her thoughts, collecting glasses as he paused at her space.

Lily turned to him and frowned. 'Yes. No. I don't know.'

'Something to do with that guy who just left?' The barman gestured over his shoulder.

'He hasn't gone… he just took a phone call. But yes. It's something to do with him.'

The barman smiled at her. 'Just tell him.'

'W-what?' Lily was taken aback. 'What do you mean?'

'Tell him how you feel.' The barman shrugged. 'I've seen this kind of thing quite a few times since I've been working in this bar. What have you got to lose?'

Lily picked her glass up and drained it as the barman left. What did she have to lose? Only her self-respect, her dignity and the friendship she had with Jamie. Lily swallowed. She hadn't even thought about that! What if saying how she felt ruined the friendship? Jamie might not feel the same and he might feel awkward… or he might feel the same and they might give it a try and then it might not work and then they wouldn't be able to have their late night chats and all their flirty text messages. That barman had clearly watched too many romcoms.

But at the same time, even though she had a lot to lose, didn't she also have a lot to gain? If it all worked out. Feeling sick to her stomach, Lily decided she had to go for it. She was going to channel the overly romantic barman and say something.

'Sorry about that,' Jamie slid back onto his bar stool. He raked his hand through his hair and picked up his glass of prosecco.

'Work?'

Jamie looked edgy for a moment. 'Er, no. Not work. But nothing to worry about.' He brightened and checked his watch. 'So where were we? We've talked about your work and we know you need to probably leave at some point. Am I right?'

Lily sighed. 'I guess you're right, yes. I probably need to leave at some point.' The thought of leaving her job and starting somewhere new was making her stomach feel crampy, but Lily did know that was probably where she was headed.

'Tune!' Jamie said as a disco track came on and he started chair dancing. 'So... what about boys?' he asked cheerfully.

'Boys?' Lily couldn't help breaking into a grin.

'Yes, boys.' Jamie stopped dancing and laughed. 'Well, men, I guess. What's happening on that front?'

Lily chewed her lip, feeling her stomach fizz and bubble like the prosecco in her glass. 'Ummm. Not much, really.'

'Why the devil not?' Jamie demanded, removing his jacket and throwing it onto the chair next to him. 'You're gorgeous and sexy and you must have boys... and men flocking round you.'

Lily couldn't help her heart racing slightly at Jamie's words. Gorgeous and sexy? Is that what he thought of her? She had no idea he thought of her that way. Maybe she should tell him how she felt after all. Yes! She was going to do it.

Say it, woman, she told herself sternly. Say it!

'Well?' Jamie leant in and put his hand over hers. 'I'd love to see you happy…'

'Would you?' Lily felt quite sick. Maybe she'd had too much prosecco.

'Of course,' Jamie said warmly, still clasping her hand.

Lily decided it was now or never. 'Right. So the thing is… we've been friends for a long time, haven't we?'

'Years,' Jamie replied cheerfully, giving her hand a lovely squeeze.

'But recently, I've started to think of you as…' Lily faltered.

'As what?' Jamie removed his hand from hers and held it up in the air. 'This place is playing some wicked music! I'm going to start wishing I'd put my dancing shoes on in a minute.'

Lily gulped down some more prosecco. God, this wasn't going how she'd hoped it would.

Jamie stopped jigging about in his seat and gave Lily his full attention again. 'Sorry, Red. Very sorry. I'm listening. You were talking about our friendship. And about thinking of… something. Not sure what.'

'I've started to think of you as something other than a friend,' Lily blurted out loudly. Oh dear. She was extremely drunk now. Not ideal. She plunged into her speech haplessly.

'As more than a friend. As… a boyfriend. Well.' She stopped, confused and cast her eyes to the floor. 'Not a boyfriend. Because we're not that. Girlfriend and boyfriend. But maybe… maybe I want that.'

She met Jamie's eyes. He stared back and then his mouth fell open.

'What did you just say?'

Lily lifted her head, taken aback at Jamie's tone. He sounded shocked. But was he annoyed or upset? Lily wasn't sure, but she didn't think so.

'I – I was saying that I think I like you,' she replied, feeling almost shy around Jamie for the first time since they'd met. 'That is… I've always liked you. I don't mean that. I mean, I really like you. Like…'

'I think I know what you mean,' Jamie interrupted, nodding his head slowly. 'Wow. I had no idea. Wow. I don't know what to say, Red. That's so… unexpected…'

Lily felt panic rising in her chest and she was certain she had turned as red as the vulgar scarlet blooms on the walls. Jamie didn't feel the same way. Judging by the look on his face, he didn't feel the same way and he felt awkward and weird about her blurting out her feelings. Sod it, sod it, sod it!

There was probably a good reason why they had never gotten together. It could just be the timing. Maybe he didn't feel the same, or he only saw her as a friend and that was why they had always just missed their moment. Even if Jamie had moments of wondering if it might work out between them, he had clearly pulled back now and decided it wasn't meant to be.

Oh God. Lily wanted to curl up and die. Literally. That expression she had always heard, 'I wanted the floor to swallow me up.' That. Just that. Lily had the most horrible feeling crawling all over her body – shame, embarrassment and regret. Regret that she had opened her mouth and said something so stupid. Where was that bloody, idealistic barman? Nothing to lose indeed. Bastard!

Lily took a deep breath. OK. So, damage limitation now. That was what was needed here. She would just bluff it out. Blame it on the prosecco.

'Listen.' Lily put her glass down and tried to adopt a dismissive tone. 'Just... just ignore what I said. I shouldn't have said anything, and I got carried away for a moment...'

'No, it's OK.' Jamie looked dazed.

'I'm very, *very* drunk,' Lily assured him firmly, her heart thumping in her chest. This was far worse than being caught with her skirt tucked into her Wednesday knickers. 'Take no notice *whatsoever*. Pretend that conversation never happened. Seriously.' She pulled a nonchalant face and shrugged for good measure, almost falling over because she was so drunk.

Jamie looked pained. 'But I can't. I can't just pretend that didn't happen, Red! You've... you've got feelings for me?'

Lily waved a hand in the air. 'No, not exactly. Just a crush, I reckon. Nothing major and I'm sure it will pass.' Feeling deeply uncomfortable but needing to change the subject, she started to dance about in her chair. 'You're so right about the tunes in here, J! Banging. Wicked!'

Jamie put his glass down clumsily on the bar. 'But this... this changes... bloody hell, Red. I can't believe you've chosen now to – bloody hell!' He shook his head and turned away from her as if he needed to collect his thoughts.

'It never happened!' Lily reminded him gaily, starting to feel rather desperate. Why was he acting so weird? She took her phone out and pretended to look at it. Firing off a quick, agonised text to Imogen, Lily put her phone away and turned back to Jamie. Turning back to her, he looked pale. He kept running his hand through his hair over and over again. If he carried on like that, he'd suffer from premature baldness and start looking like his dad. Who, to be fair, was actually very handsome, for an older dude.

'J, it's nothing to worry about. Honestly. Just forget it,' Lily added earnestly.

'How can I forget it?' Jamie asked, sounding upset. 'It's… if I'd had the first idea that you even…'

Lily frowned, then squinted past Jamie's head. Hang on. Was that…? No, it couldn't be. Why on earth would she be here now?

'Is that… Ivy over there?' she asked Jamie, puzzled. 'She didn't say anything about coming out tonight. I thought she was staying in.' She waved at her sister for a few seconds until Ivy noticed her. Waving back brightly, she headed their way.

Jamie appeared to wince. 'Ivy. Yes. OK. Brilliant. Oh man.' He visibly pulled himself together by straightening his shirt, flicking his hair one last time and rubbing his hands up and down his trousers. 'Yes, Ivy is meant to be here tonight. That was my phone call earlier actually…' He turned to Ivy as she arrived beside him. 'Hey.'

'Hey.' Ivy leant in and kissed Jamie's cheek before hugging Lily. 'Well, this place is unusual, isn't it? Funky.'

Lily stared at Ivy fuzzily. Then at Jamie. Her brow furrowed. What had Jamie just said? That Ivy was his phone call earlier? What on earth was going on? And since when did Ivy use words like 'funky'?

Jamie was doing this weird thing with his mouth, as though he was biting his lips and clenching his jaw at the same time. 'So… erm… here's the thing…'

'Shall I say it?' Ivy cut in. She turned to Lily. 'You know I said I was seeing someone?' She turned back to Jamie coyly. 'Well...'

Lily felt her stomach plummet to the floor like one of those rides at Alton Towers. Except it didn't stop when it got to the bottom. Instead, it threatened to shoot right through to the floor. Lily wondered vaguely when she had lost control of her faculties. Surely she was too young?

'It's Jamie,' Ivy announced, unnecessarily.

Jamie pulled a sheepish face at Lily and slid his arm around Ivy's shoulders.

Lily swallowed. Her prosecco fizzed in her throat. No way. Jamie and Ivy. Ivy and Jamie. The guy she was in love with and her sister. Together as a couple.

'Say something, Lil!' Ivy said, snuggling into Jamie. 'We didn't want to say anything until we were sure, but it's been... how long has it been, J?'

Jamie shuffled uncomfortably on his bar stool and fiddled with his collar as though he was hot.

Lily was beginning to feel extremely sick. So Ivy called him 'J' as well now, did she?

'Er... four months?' Jamie offered.

'Four and a half actually,' Ivy corrected, but gently.

Lily knew she should say something. She had no idea what she was going to say, but she opened her mouth anyway. Instead of words, an exceptionally long, loud burp came out.

'Lily!' Ivy giggled.

Jamie grinned then stopped suddenly.

Lily didn't know whether to laugh or cry. The only thing that could top that would be to fart as well. If that happened, Lily would force the ground to swallow her up because she would be so mortified she wouldn't even be able to function. She took a deep breath. She felt like such an *idiot*. Surely only a total wally could have missed this going on right under their nose.

For four and a half months, neither of them had said anything. All those texts and chats and drinks and lunches and late night calls with Jamie – which now felt inappropriate – and he hadn't said a single word. Not one. About seeing someone, about being in a relationship. Let alone that he was dating her sister, for God's sake! Lily felt betrayed and there was part of her that hated Jamie for hiding such a huge secret. Especially after her foolish confession.

And what about Ivy? Lily seethed, absurdly upset. All those times she could have said something and she said nothing. Only recently had she finally admitted to being with someone and all the time, the whole time – and behind her back even if they hadn't meant it – they had been seeing each other and talking intimately and kissing and having sex and…

Lily needed to get out of the bar. She was pretty sure she was going to be sick and then farting would be the least of her worries. Her Smooth Criminal was about to make a reappearance in front of two people Lily couldn't bear to look stupid in front of. More stupid, that is.

'I wasn't sure if you'd approve of Jamie and I being together,' Ivy was saying, raising her voice to be heard above the music. 'Seeing as you're such good friends and you always said he was such a tart! But we thought the time was right to tell you. Didn't we?'

Jamie nodded, not meeting Lily's eyes. 'Yes. Yes, we did.'

Knowing she needed to say something, Lily dug deep. This was her sister and her good friend. It was horrible and it was shit, but there was nothing she could do about it. She would look like a total bitch if she didn't say something wonderful.

'I'm... so happy for you,' she said, fighting the urge to cry. 'So happy for you. Really.'

'Oh, that's lovely of you.' Ivy let go of Jamie and hugged Lily again. 'I've been so worried about telling you. With you and J being such good friends and all that.'

'Yes. Yes, we are.' Lily pulled back and plastered a watery smile on her face. 'OK, listen. I'm going to have to go now. Love you and leave you and all that.'

'Oh no!' Ivy looked deeply disappointed. 'Must you?'

'Yes, I'm so sorry. I don't feel that great.' Lily swiftly gathered up her things. She couldn't even look at Jamie. Ridiculously, she felt more betrayed by him than she did Ivy, although she wasn't sure why. Maybe because he had been texting her at midnight as though he couldn't stop thinking about her when he was actually in a serious relationship with her sister.

Jamie got off his bar stool. 'Are you – shall I walk you out?'

'Gosh no, don't be silly.' Lily gave him another brief hug that felt unbearable and kissed Ivy's cheek. 'Have fun, you two and I'm sure I'll speak to both of you tomorrow. Bye!'

Pushing her way through the crowds of people dancing and drinking, Lily moved as quickly as she could. Once outside, she gulped the cold night air into her lungs and took a moment. It was no good. She couldn't just breeze this one out the way she usually did. Jamie and Ivy were a couple. And they were going to be amazing together and then they were probably going to get married on a perfect, sunny day in a barn with macarons for wedding favours and a cake adorned with fresh, summer blooms. Then they would have gorgeous babies – twins, one of each – dressed in Baby Boden outfits as they were wheeled around in their Silver Cross Pram.

All of that was really great because they both deserved to be happy. Lily wasn't the sort of person to hope it would rain on their wedding day or that their perfect twins wouldn't sleep properly for at least two years, but basically it was pretty much the most shit thing in the world right now. And it really, really hurt.

Bursting into tears, Lily leant over and heaved prosecco and heartache all over the pavement.

Chapter Three

Two Days Later

'That literally sounds like the most shit night ever,' Imogen said, her voice sounding tinny. Presumably it was from being up a mountain in France. 'I don't blame you for throwing up at the end of it. Nauseating, the whole thing.'

'Tell me about it,' Lily said, cradling her phone into her neck as she pulled the sleeves of her jumper over her hands. She was sitting shivering in the pretty back garden of her mum's house in Kent, having been invited over for Sunday lunch for her mum's birthday. It was a gloomy autumnal day and the heavy atmospheric weather suited her mood perfectly.

'So, what are you going to do?' Imogen asked, shifting into practical mode.

'Do?' Lily frowned. 'I'm not going to "do" anything, Ims. What can I do?'

'Leave the country?' Imogen promptly returned. 'That's what I'd do.'

'What, take the job at the ski place with you?' Lily surmised, rolling her eyes at her predictability.

'Er... yup. Why not? I certainly wouldn't sit around watching those two fawning all over each other.'

Lily sighed. She had to admit the thought of seeing Jamie and Ivy together was torturous and she wasn't sure she could cope with it. Maybe it would be better to just get away. Her job wasn't making her smile anymore and she had drunkenly told one of her closest friends that she was in love with him. Lily cringed. Could it get any worse?

'Lily!'

She looked up and saw her mum waving at her from inside the house. 'Ivy and Jamie are here! Come inside and say hi.'

'Oh bloody hell. Did you hear that?' Lily asked Imogen.

'What, the sound of you resigning from your job and packing your suitcase full of the cutest ski jumpers and salopettes ASAP?' Imogen said. 'Yes, I think I did.'

Lily couldn't help smiling. God, she would love to be around Imogen right now. That was just what she needed. Laughter and fun and just getting away from all of this stress and heartache – not to mention the intense embarrassment. Lily's cheeks felt hot just at the thought of Jamie's horrified face the other night.

'OK, here's my plan.' Imogen always had a plan for everything. 'I've already given your CV to my boss, Celine. Yes, yes, I know. I'm super-bossy and out of order, blah, blah. But she thinks you sound wonderful and all you'd need to do is have a phone interview with her. Then she'd send you a plane ticket. Trust me. So have a think about it and give me a nudge as soon as you want me to arrange the call.'

Lily got up and rubbed her bum, which had turned numb from the cold. 'I think you're getting ahead of yourself...'

'I think by the end of lunch you'll be on the blower to me, begging me for that job,' Imogen retorted. 'Godspeed and all that and I'll talk to you later.'

'Bye, Ims.' Lily ended the call. Taking a deep breath and berating herself for being a drama queen, she headed indoors.

'Isn't it wonderful that Ivy and Jamie are together?' Lily's mum, Sue, squawked like an excited parrot. A small, neat woman with one of those haircuts described as 'elfin'. Sue was dressed in a fluffy, somewhat cropped black jumper and some skinny jeans.

Lily had always thought of her mum as relatively trendy, but today she looked as though she'd been shopping in Top Shop and she was rocking it. She was drenched in her favourite Youth Dew perfume, as always, because she believed that only Estée Lauder made timeless perfumes.

'Wonderful,' Lily murmured by way of a response. She kissed Ivy's cheek and managed a half-hug with Jamie – who looked great in a crisp, white shirt with navy chinos and a smart houndstooth jacket. And who still smelt intoxicating.

This was no good, Lily realised despondently, roughly shoving her hands into her pockets. Nothing had changed. Not on the feelings front. She had bared her soul in a desperately cringy fashion, found out the person she was head over heels for was dating her sister, and she still wanted to snog Jamie's face off.

'I'd welcome you to the family, but you used to more or less live here!' Dave, Lily's stepdad guffawed, self-consciously pulling his new bright, cobalt-blue jumper away from his slightly rotund tummy. Lily hadn't seen it before and her mum and Dave were clearly making a huge effort because Jamie was Ivy's new man, even though they had known him for years.

Placing his hands on his waist like a comedian about to deliver his best punchline on stage, Dave continued with his theme. 'The thing is, you always used to be in Lily's room, rather than Ivy's… what an irony!' He laughed.

'Oh *yes!*' Sue exclaimed, as if she'd only just thought of it too. 'How *funny!*'

'Stop it, you two,' Ivy said, beaming from ear to ear. Lily thought her sister's whole face might crack from sheer joy if she wasn't careful.

Nasty, jealous *bitch*, Lily told herself sternly. Stop that. She could feel Jamie's eyes on her and she really wished he'd stop staring. Just because she'd told him about her stupid feelings didn't mean he got to gawp as if she were some kind of circus animal.

'Are you OK?' Jamie asked.

Lily turned to him. 'Er, yes. I'm fine, thanks.' She frowned. He looked concerned about her and she wasn't sure why. Hang on. Did he feel *sorry* for her? That she really couldn't take.

'I've cooked a lovely pork loin,' her mum said, drawing Jamie to the oven coquettishly. 'Look at it. Look at the crackling!'

'Ooh,' Jamie chorused dutifully. 'That looks amazing. Thanks, Sue. I'm starving. I can't wait to tuck in.'

'Well, sit down all of you. I'm about to serve. Dave, are you carving?'

Dave responded by doing a bizarre robot dance Lily had seen a gazillion times before. Personally, she thought he'd been watching too much Gavin and Stacey, but to be fair, he pulled it off with aplomb.

'I am carving, I am carving…' he intoned like a Dalek.

Sue fell about laughing. 'Oh, Dave! Even after all these years, you do crack me up.'

Lily rolled her eyes. God, she was a horrible person today. She usually loved her mum and Dave's banter. And Dave's robot impression. It was as though a huge, black cloud had settled around Lily's shoulders. She didn't feel like herself at all.

'Shall we go and sit down?' Ivy suggested, slipping her arm through Jamie's.

'Why not?' he said, throwing Lily an awkward glance.

Lily ignored him and headed for the table. Her mum was definitely putting on the glitz today. All the best silver was out, looking suspiciously like it had been polished for the occasion, along with the fancy glass mats her mum normally hated because an entire rib of beef had once slipped off the table. The cat had gorged herself and thrown up spectacularly on the lounge carpet. Sue had scolded the mats as though they were alive and hid them in the back of the cupboard.

'Coming through, coming through,' Dave sang, holding up dishes of broccoli cheese and roast potatoes. He placed them on the table with a flourish.

'Smells good, Dave,' Jamie commented. 'You know how I love a roast potato.'

'I do, I do,' Dave said, touching the side of his nose. 'Also, big secret for your mum, girls,' he added, 'but I've made her a birthday cake.'

'Have you?' Ivy asked with some surprise. 'I thought you hated baking.'

Dave grinned. 'Well. I've had a cake made is what I should have said. It's one of those trendy ones that looks half-done, you know? And it's in purple and white, her favourite colours.'

'Sounds perfect,' Lily smiled at Dave. Dave was a good man. Slightly boring if she was being super-critical, but amusing in his own way and good to her mum. Especially after everything she'd been through all those years ago. Dave, with his white hair, chubby cheeks and garish dress sense was like a cheery, amiable gnome: reliable and always smiley. Most of his comments required an exclamation mark after them because he was so upbeat.

'Dave!' Sue called from the kitchen. 'I need your robot man skills. The pork is rested and ready for carving.'

'Right you are, my love!' he called. Turning away from them, he did his robot dance out of the room.

Jamie laughed. 'He's so great.'

'Isn't he?' Ivy agreed. She turned to him and smiled. 'It feels different that we're here for lunch like this, doesn't it?'

Jamie met Lily's eyes across the table. 'Er...'

'You know, as a couple,' Ivy said, taking his hand.

'Oh.' Jamie nodded vaguely. 'I guess so, yes.'

Ivy turned to Lily. 'Were you OK the other night? You dashed out so quickly.'

Lily really wished Jamie would stop staring at her. Did he think that if he gaped at her enough, her mortifying confession would disappear?

'Yes, I was fine,' Lily assured Ivy, feeling her stomach lurch at the memory. 'I just felt so sick. Too much prosecco.'

Ivy smiled kindly. 'Poor thing. Mind you, we drank loads after Lily left, didn't we?'

'Too much!' Jamie concurred, giving Ivy a cheeky smile. 'I've been hungover ever since.'

'He has.' Ivy stroked his hair. 'I've been his nursemaid. I didn't even go into work yesterday.'

Lily watched her sister. She'd missed work yesterday and played nurse? Ivy was in love. There were no two ways about it. Lily fiddled with her shiny cutlery. She had to be happy for Ivy. She simply had to be. It wasn't her fault she had fallen for Jamie too. It wasn't even Jamie's fault; it was just that he *knew*.

Dave broke the silence as he arrived with the carved pork on a wooden board, accompanied by an impressive pile of crackling. 'Let's get stuck in!' he said, as though it was the best lunch in the whole world.

'Let's not forget the Yorkies!' Sue said, shimmying behind Dave with a large dish of puddings. 'The one thing Dave cooks!'

'It's the least I can do, Sue,' Dave said, kissing her cheek affectionately. 'What a woman, cooking on her own birthday.'

Sue pretended to swat him away, but she clearly loved his attention. 'Well, I couldn't leave you to do it, could I, Dave? You'd have burnt the bottom of the oven and we'd have been ordering a Chinese take away!'

'So true!' Dave chuckled, serving Jamie a heap of juicy-looking pork and a generous serving of crackling.

'Thanks, Dave, but that's enough,' Jamie said, patting his flat stomach. 'Got to keep my figure now I have a girlfriend.'

Lily kept her eyes on her dinner. God, this was awful. How on earth was she going to endure this?

'You two do look lovely together,' Sue commented, sipping her favourite Lambrusco.

'Thanks, Sue,' Jamie put his fork down and slipped his arm around Ivy's shoulder. 'But Ivy would make any man look great.'

Lily's fork clattered onto her plate. 'Sorry,' she said.

Ivy was blushing again. She really did look beautiful today, Lily decided. Aside from her glorious auburn hair cascading down her back and a pretty lilac jumper that brought out the green in her eyes, Ivy had a glow about her. And Jamie looked great too. Uncomfortable, but happy. Even though it pained Lily to admit it.

'Remind me how the two of you got together,' Sue said. 'It's such a lovely story!'

Lily's stomach lurched. She wasn't sure she could handle hearing a blow-by-blow account of Ivy and Jamie getting together. She glanced desperately towards the front door. Could she just make some sort of excuse and leg it?

Ivy smiled happily. 'Oh, you say it, Jamie. You tell it better than me.'

Jamie met Lily's gaze briefly then cast his eyes to the table. He looked rather embarrassed, but he started the tale. 'So, I was sitting in the park near my work one lunchtime, eating some sushi in the sun,' Jamie began, throwing Ivy a glance that looked suspiciously senti-mental. 'When suddenly, just as I was about to devour a California crab and avocado roll, this huge, wet chunk of ham and pickle sandwich landed right in my lap.'

Ivy giggled and nudged him.

'It was Ivy,' Jamie followed up, his expression indulgent. 'She was trying to feed the birds and she got rather carried away, hurling a great lump of bread at some pigeons.'

'My sandwich was awful and I was having this really bad day at work,' Ivy chipped in, looking bashful. 'I kind of hurled my sandwich at those pigeons and I didn't even realise Jamie was there.'

'And then we both looked up and laughed and realised we knew each other.'

Lily felt quite nauseous at this point, even though Dave's Yorkies were delicious. She was cross with herself. She clearly was a horrible person. Because it was a charming story. If it had been anyone else telling the story, Lily would have thought it was delightful and romantic. Serendipitous, even. As it was, Lily couldn't help thinking Ivy and Jamie looked like one of those couples at the end of When Harry Met Sally, talking about their relationship and how they met and finishing each other's sentences and generally being overwhelmingly cute.

Ivy let out a sigh that sounded both wistful and content. 'So anyway, I immediately went over to apologise. Jamie offered me some of his sushi because my sandwich was so terrible and we got chatting and—'

'And we didn't really stop,' Jamie said, looking thoroughly pleased with himself. 'We were both late back from lunch and then I asked Ivy if she'd like to meet up after work. She said yes, so we headed to this bar in Mayfair.'

'It was so swanky,' Ivy remembered, giving Jamie a sweet smile. 'Fancy cocktails and mouth-wateringly delicious canapés…'

Lily choked on a piece of Yorkshire pudding. That was *her* fantasy! She had always wanted Jamie to take her to a posh bar in Mayfair with a cocktail list as long as her arm and tasty, little amuse-bouches to share. Lily felt despondent, guilty and like a bitch all at the same time.

Jamie inclined his head modestly. 'Well, I was trying to impress you, wasn't I?'

Ivy kissed him. 'It worked. And it's worked ever since. And not the expensive, fancy stuff. All the other things.'

'What a lovely thing to say. You've made my day with that.'

Lily really might regurgitate spongey batter all over the table in a minute. Jealousy was an ugly emotion, that was for sure. She sighed.

'I can smell wedding bells in the air!' Dave threw out, clapping a hand over his mouth as soon as the words had been uttered. 'Or am I getting ahead of myself?'

'Dave!' Ivy looked utterly thrilled.

Jamie looked surprised, but not thrilled at the idea? Or maybe Lily had that wrong. She wiped her mouth with a napkin. Enough. This was no way to carry on. She had to get a grip on herself, accept that Jamie and Ivy were probably headed for greatness and change the way she was acting around them. Either that or…

'Anything new with you?' Sue asked Lily, as though she had suddenly realised her youngest daughter was getting left out.

'Me?' Lily took a swig of Lambrusco and tried not to wince. 'I'm…' She lifted her eyes and found Jamie staring at her again. Apologetically. Kindly. Oh God. How mortifying. That was it. In that moment, Lily knew exactly what she was going to do. Something drastic was needed. And listening to Jamie and Ivy gushing like lovesick teenagers as they talked about their delightful, romantic connection had given her just the right impetus.

Lily took a deep breath. 'I'm going to change jobs,' she announced. Crikey, she thought to herself. She had actually just said that out loud.

'Are you?' Sue said, putting her knife and fork down with a clatter.

'Wow!' Dave exclaimed, looking thoroughly excited.

Ivy and Jamie just stared at her. Disbelievingly in the first instance and – yes, shocked in the second.

Lily felt a surge of powerful rightness. This was so the way to go.

'Yes. I'm going to move to France for a few months,' she added airily.

'France?' Dave looked delighted and he turned to Sue, open-mouthed. 'How fantastic. We'll come and visit. Whereabouts?'

'Chamonix,' Lily said, her heart thumping crazily. She was beginning to feel rather thrilled at her announcement. And worried. She didn't even have the job yet. Was she jumping the gun? Imogen seemed to think it was in the bag. Well, she'd said it now so somehow, Lily was going to have to make this happen. Otherwise, she would look like an absolute numpty.

'Well.' Sue visibly put aside her concerns and her expression changed. Looking impressed and rather proud, she smiled warmly at Lily. 'It's not like you to step out of your comfort zone, Lily, but good for you! That job at the spa was boring you senseless, wasn't it? What did they say when you resigned?'

'Erm…' Lily faltered and felt Jamie's eyes on her again. He knew she hadn't resigned yet.

Unexpectedly, Jamie came to her rescue. 'You said they were disappointed you were leaving, but they were pleased for you, weren't they?'

Lily sucked her breath in and nodded gratefully. 'Yes. That's about the size of it.' She had no idea how she was going to pull this whole thing off, but she had jumped off a cliff and she had to go with it. She was seriously fed up with her job at the spa anyway.

'Are you really doing this?' Ivy asked sceptically. 'I'm not being rude, Lily, but you're usually so...'

'Predictable?' Lily finished. 'Yes. That's the whole point.' She felt energised and empowered. 'So I'm doing it. I'm doing something unpredictable. And scary.'

'Will you... be back for Christmas?' Sue asked, as Dave started to clear the plates away.

'I don't know.' Lily felt a bit panicked. She hadn't thought that far ahead. But thinking about it now, Lily knew she didn't want to let her family down. On the other hand, she wondered if she might be needed in Chamonix. Surely it didn't shut down over Christmas. People probably stayed in the hotel and Lily knew Imogen was staying there. Lily loved Christmas, and a lot of what she loved about it was family. She didn't want to ruin it for anyone, especially not her mum and Dave. Or Ivy for that matter. Or Jamie...

'Not to worry,' Sue said, squeezing Lily's hand across the table. 'We can worry about that later.'

'I think we have a couple of things to celebrate now, don't we!' Dave said, coming in with the cake he'd ordered. It was one of those cylinders with icing half-covering the cake in a patchy fashion. It was covered with miniature macarons and fresh flowers and it was met with much oohing and aahing. The candles were lit and blown out to a noisy rendition of 'Happy Birthday'.

After an adequate period of time sitting on the sofa and having to watch Jamie and Ivy cuddling and whispering, Lily told everyone she was heading home. She had a feeling Jamie was going to try and talk to her and she couldn't have that. There was nothing to say.

Waved off by her mum and Dave in the doorway with their arms comfortably wrapped around one another and a romantic silhouette of Jamie and Ivy entangled in a kiss in the front window, Lily headed home in her bright red Mini and phoned Imogen via her Bluetooth.

'Lily.' There was a pause. 'Shall I get Celine to call you tomorrow morning?'

'Yes please!'

'I'm on it,' Imogen said. No cheap shots like 'I told you so' because that was the kind of friend Imogen was. 'Phone me when you're home because I want to know EVERYTHING.'

'Will do,' Lily said. Hearing 'Torn' by Natalie Imbruglia coming on the car stereo, Lily turned it up full blast and surrendered to the angst.

Chapter Four

The next week felt like a whirlwind to Lily. The phone call with Celine on Monday went like this:

'So, Lily,' Celine said in a charming French accent. Lily had never heard her name said so prettily. 'I have read your CV in detail. You have excellent qualifications and you sound perfect for our opportunity here at the Boutique Hotel Devereux.'

'Thank you so much,' Lily had replied.

'Please tell me more about yourself,' Celine had asked. Her English was excellent, even though she didn't seem as bothered about perfecting her accent.

Lily had talked about her passion for massage and her previous jobs. Celine had asked a few questions and Lily had answered to the best of her ability.

'When can you start?' Celine had asked crisply at the end.

'Oh, er. Well…' Lily hadn't been sure what to say.

'I am playing with you. Imogen mentioned that you hadn't resigned yet,' Celine had said, sounding amused. 'Within the month would work for us, though, if you could manage that.'

'I'm sure I can make that happen,' Lily had replied confidently, even though she didn't have a clue how leaving the spa was going to pan out. Immediately afterwards, she spoke to Libby about her plans. Libby was disappointed to lose her, but she was also pleased for her. She liaised with Karen, who ranted and fumed and opposed, but finally, she agreed to let Lily leave after two weeks rather than working the full month.

And so, that week, Lily set about wrapping up her life in London and preparing for Chamonix. She managed to rent her flat out to her close friend Helen, who also took on Lily's red Mini for the time being. Lily sold a designer handbag she wasn't fond of on eBay as well as some clothes and a pair of shoes that had cost the earth and had only been worn once. She bought some new jumpers and got some mismatched ski outfits from friends, deciding she would sort the rest out when she arrived in Chamonix. She had a black puffer jacket that was warm enough to see her through the first few weeks and, according to Imogen, she could rent the rest when she got to Chamonix, especially ski boots and skis.

Not that Lily was suddenly that keen on the idea of skiing. It still seemed like the most ridiculous idea in the world to throw herself down the side of a steep, snowy mountain with slippery things strapped to her feet. But she would worry about that later. All that mattered was that she was doing something daring. It was both terrifying and exhilarating. Lily wasn't allowing herself to stop and think about it, otherwise she might change her mind.

She had also successfully managed to avoid talking at any length to Ivy. She had managed to keep all their chats brief and about her new job opportunity. Lily was also pleased with herself that she had avoided Jamie. He had sent her several texts asking to meet up and chat and he had called her five times. She had politely sent back a response thanking him for his messages and assuring him that she would be in touch soon. Which wasn't a lie. Lily was planning to get in touch, but only once she had sorted out everything for her big move and she was about to leave the country.

Which was right about now, Lily thought to herself, the night before she was due to fly to Geneva, the closest airport to Chamonix. She picked her phone up, biting her lip as she tried to figure out what to say to him, when she heard her doorbell. Pushing past her suitcase and almost tripping over one of Helen's boxes full of 'bedding and plates,' according to the writing scrawled across it.

Squinting through her spyhole, Lily saw Jamie on the other side. Oh, for the love of God. She didn't want to actually *see* him. Speaking on the phone would have been more than enough. Wait. Was Ivy with him? Pausing before opening the door, Lily looked through the spyhole again. No, he was alone. She pulled the door open.

'Jamie.'

She hadn't called him 'J' since she'd found out about him and Ivy. There wasn't a specific reason. It just felt weird.

'Lily.'

And he hadn't called her 'Red' since then either. Maybe he called Ivy 'Red' now. Oh man. How pathetic did that sound? Jamie wasn't that crass. He obviously just felt the same as Lily did about their nickname thing.

Lily's heart clenched as she let Jamie into her flat. Damn. He still looked good. And she still felt all wobbly around him. Her stomach was doing the flip-flop, butterfly thing and she had to fight hard not to touch him.

Lily hardened her heart. She was moving to France for at least three months, which was her agreement with Celine. And it was, she was sure, the best decision she'd ever made.

'Have a seat.' Lily gestured to the sofa and very deliberately sat in the armchair opposite.

Jamie sat down awkwardly, even though he had thrown himself carelessly onto the very same sofa any number of times before.

'What can I do for you?' Lily asked politely, not sure how else to start the conversation.

Jamie rubbed his hands together, something he always did when he was nervous. 'Erm… I'm… I don't know…' he faltered. 'It's… listen, Lily, are you really leaving?'

Lily frowned. 'Yes, I'm really leaving.' She pointed to her suitcase.

Jamie rubbed his hands together again. 'OK. But you're not going… it isn't…'

'Because of you?' She finished, guessing that was where he was going with his questions. She cringed, remembering the lunch at her mum's house a few weeks back. Lily had to keep reminding herself of that because it was what had propelled her into action and into changing her life.

Jamie shrugged. 'I guess.'

Lily sighed. She could tell him how arrogant he sounded, asking her that, but she wasn't sure he was being arrogant. She could deny it. But what was the point? She'd left her dignity behind in a 'funky', flower-covered cocktail bar in Covent Garden a few weeks ago and they both knew it.

'Yes, Jamie,' Lily confirmed, putting her chin in the air in an attempt to feel dignified and in control. 'First and

foremost, I am mostly leaving London because of you.'
She felt sad saying that out loud.

Jamie looked crestfallen. He opened his mouth to speak, then closed it again.

'But I had also had enough of my job, I never do anything outside of my comfort zone, and I miss my best friend. Imogen, that is,' Lily added, in case he thought she meant him. Even though Jamie was almost a best friend and she was going to miss him horrendously. 'So you've done me a favour, really. Not fancying me and all that.' She swallowed, feeling her heart clench. Not being fancied was really quite shit. Especially not being fancied by Jamie.

Jamie leant forward. 'Who said I didn't fancy you?' He flushed slightly, which was unusual. Lily wasn't sure she'd ever seen him blush before and she frowned, feeling puzzled. Jamie was far too confident and self-assured for that kind of thing.

Jamie started again. 'I mean… that's not the point. I just had no idea you had those kinds of feelings for me. We always talk about loser boyfriends and annoying girlfriends together.'

'Right.' Lily couldn't for the life of her figure out why Jamie was here. What did he want from her? Hadn't she been embarrassed enough? And what did it matter that he didn't know she had those feelings for him before now? 'Listen, I have an early start in the morning…'

'I'm sorry about Ivy,' Jamie blurted out suddenly. 'I'm sorry I kept it from you. You must feel betrayed and…'

'Rather stupid?' Lily provided helpfully. 'Yes, something like that.'

Jamie got up and started pacing. 'I just didn't know where it was headed, what it meant. I didn't want to say anything if it was just a silly fling. Ivy seemed keen to keep it under wraps and not mention anything to you, so I went along with it.'

'It honestly doesn't matter,' Lily said, getting to her feet. It did, of course, but she wasn't sure what else to say. They obviously had their reasons for hiding their relationship from her, but none of them made any sense to her. She was surprised when, out of the blue, Jamie took her hand.

'I didn't mean to hurt you and I don't want to lose our friendship.' He looked earnest. Upset.

Lily's mouth twisted as she glanced down at Jamie's hand clasping hers. If only the circumstances were different. His hand felt warm and familiar – even though they didn't hold hands much – and it made her feel even more bleak. She wasn't sure she could bear Jamie being here much longer.

'OK,' she said eventually, feeling that she should respond to Jamie's plea to remain friends.

'OK? As in… you're not hurt and you don't want to lose our friendship either?' Jamie bent his head to make her meet his eyes.

'OK as in… I'm exceptionally hurt and I don't see how we can stay friends. Not the way we were before, anyway.' She removed her hand. 'No more late night calls or any of that. I don't think Ivy would like it.'

Jamie nodded slowly. 'No, I guess not. I just wish I'd known about your feelings. Before—'

'Before what? Before you and Ivy started seeing one another?' Lily was beginning to feel impatient. What on earth was he on about? What difference would it have made if he'd known before he and Ivy started sharing sushi and hanging out in fancy cocktail bars?

Lily's phone buzzed on the coffee table and she grabbed it. 'It's Ivy,' she said, pointedly, holding her phone up. 'Texting to wish me a good journey tomorrow.'

Jamie stared at the phone, then at Lily. And then he turned, decisively. 'Right. OK. Well, I'll leave you to your last-minute packing then.'

'Thanks,' Lily said, feeling relieved. She didn't want him to go; it felt like a horrible wrench. But at the same time, this was too painful. Lily showed Jamie to the door.

'I'll say goodbye then.' Jamie turned around in the doorway.

'Goodbye.' Lily nodded, feeling something splinter in her chest. A hairline fracture that could turn into a full-on crack if she wasn't careful.

'I'll be in touch soon…?'

'Uh-uh,' Lily mumbled.

'Maybe I could… I mean Ivy and I could come and visit?' Jamie offered, his face hopeful. 'I love skiing. I used to go with my family all the time until my dad broke his leg. I'm pretty good. I can still do reds and blacks and off-piste…'

Lily didn't have a clue what that meant, but the main thing was that she wasn't sure she wanted Jamie to come to Chamonix. With or without Ivy. As much as she knew she was going to miss him, wasn't this about going cold turkey?

'We'll see,' she said lamely.

'OK. Well, let me know once you're settled.' Jamie looked crestfallen. 'Bye, Lily.'

'Bye, Jamie.'

Lily closed the door and leant against it. God! Did she want Jamie to stay in touch or would it be easier to not hear from him at all? As for visiting… that was a terrible idea. Lily had to mend her heart and stay away from Jamie. Or rather, he had to stay away from her. It wasn't fair of him to want to stay in touch and visit.

Turning and squinting through the eyehole, she could see Jamie still standing in front of her door as if he wasn't sure if he should knock again. Lily wouldn't open the door if he did. After a few agonising minutes, Jamie obviously thought better of it and, moving hesitantly, he left.

Walking away with her head held high, Lily shut all the lights off in her flat and headed for the bedroom. Throwing the duvet over her head, she pushed Jamie firmly out of her thoughts and forced herself to go to sleep. Tomorrow, she was set for a whole new life and Jamie wasn't going to be in it.

Chapter Five

Sixteen Hours Later

'Wow.' Lily set her case down and took in the view. An hour and a half flight from Stansted airport to Geneva and a coach transfer that had taken just over an hour and she was here. Oh God, what had she done? Suddenly, her brave decision seemed like a ridiculous one. Lily felt anxiety circling in her stomach until it felt like a ball of wool wedged in her gut. She had left her job – and her life in London – for a stay in Chamonix. In a ski resort, even though she had never skied in her life.

'Breathtaking, isn't it?' Imogen agreed, mistaking Lily's expression for one of wonder as she contemplated the snow-capped mountains and the pretty alpine village. 'Although I'm quite blasé about it now, to be honest.'

'I don't think I could ever feel blasé about a view like that,' Lily breathed in genuine awe as she soaked up her surroundings.

The village was quaint without feeling old-fashioned and the streets were lined with typical French shops. There were bakeries displaying exquisite pastries in stiff, monogrammed cardboard, stuffed with fresh cream and topped with exotic fruit or fancy, tempered chocolate garnishes. There were clothes shops displaying unusual lingerie, accessories and stylish ski wear and tabacs dotted in between the shops, their brightly coloured signs typifying France for Lily. Towards the end of the village, there were groups of charming hotels, some angular, and some with curved windows and quirky, turreted roofs, the grey slate just about visible under a fine dusting of snow. A pretty river ran through the centre, the River Arve, if Lily's hurried research was accurate. Despite the cold climate, it still bubbled and flowed with some force.

'Come on, let's get you to the hotel,' Imogen said. She stopped, dropped Lily's luggage and threw her arms around her, her red ski jacket rustling as she hugged her best friend more tightly. 'I'm so happy you're here!' She drew back. 'I mean, I'm really sorry about Jamie and Ivy, but you know what I mean.'

'I do,' Lily gave her a wry smile. 'And I'm happy to be here too.' She had missed Imogen badly. Her best friend since school, Imogen was both reliable and fun. She was a party girl at heart, but she was also caring and kind. Lily pulled back and eyed her fondly. Imogen had dyed black hair which suited her, often wearing it slicked back in a ponytail because it was so thick, and bright blue eyes. She always wore red lipstick and winged black eyeliner. Lily believed she either slept in it or had had her distinctive make-up tattooed on by now to save time.

Pushing aside her apprehension over the hugeness of the move, Lily embraced the moment. She was with her best friend in the whole world and she had done something crazy. It would be good for her. She had said she wanted a challenge.

Imogen picked up Lily's luggage again and started walking. 'A quick overview for you. Mont Blanc is the highest summit in the alps. That's the Aiguille du Midi…' she pointed to a vast mountain above the town, 'and there is also Pointe Helbronner, which is the mountain between France and Italy with immense glacier fields. That one is named after some French dude… Paul, I think, who pioneered… something.'

'Hmm, very informative,' Lily commented sarcastically. 'Some dude called Paul who pioneered something. Now I know all the deets about Mont Blanc.'

'Whatever.' Imogen dismissed the sarcasm.

'What else…?' she continued, nonplussed. 'Chamonix is north of Mont Blanc. It's one of the oldest ski resort towns in France. You probably came via the *Route Blanche*, which is the 'white route,' so-called because of the snow that usually covers it. The cable car you can see in the distance is one of the highest in the world and it was built in the 1920s and re-built in the 1950s. I can name all five ski resorts in the area too,' Imogen added. 'If you want me to.'

'No thank you,' Lily said, carefully stepping around a small pile of snow that had been scraped to the side. It looked like a pile of whipped cream. No, ice cream. All that was missing was the cone. 'OK, OK, I'm impressed, Ims. You know your stuff about the area. Kind of.'

Imogen pointed to a tall hotel with a slanted blue roof on the edge of town. 'That's where we're headed. We're nearly there, actually. It's not as far as it looks.'

'Good,' Lily puffed. God. She'd thought she was fit, as well. God knows if she'd be able to cope with skiing down a high mountain. She felt an internal tremor shudder through her. She still wasn't sure about the skiing lark.

She was here for work, to be a sports masseuse. And to forget about Jamie.

'So what was all that about, Jamie coming over last night?' Imogen asked.

Lily sighed and hoisted her bag onto her shoulder. 'I have no idea! He was rambling on about not realising I had those feelings for him and all that, but I don't know where he was going with it.'

Imogen let out a sound rather like a snort. 'Sounds like he's realised he picked the wrong sister, if you ask me!'

'What?' Lily shook her head and inhaled delicious, cheesy aromas drifting from a nearby restaurant. Fondues and raclette – that distinctive, creamy, salty cheese often melted in little individual grill pans. 'Ooh, we must have a fondue. You've got that wrong about Jamie, Ims. I think it's just that he wants the same friendship we had before, calling me at all hours of the day and night, but he wants to be with Ivy too.'

'Well, that's all kinds of wrong,' Imogen stated, throwing an unimpressed glance over her shoulder. 'I really like Jamie, but he can't expect to be phoning you at midnight anymore. And why does he want to? He should be speaking to Ivy about whatever he speaks to you about. I wouldn't put up with that if he was my boyfriend.'

Lily shrugged. She could see Imogen's point, but regardless, she needed to put Jamie behind her, at least for the next few months. He and Ivy deserved the best chance for their relationship to take off. Even if the mere thought of it made Lily feel heartbroken, sick and angry all at once. God, it was all so confusing. Lily wanted to be happy for them, and on some level she was, but jealousy…

or was it more like envy? Yes, envy was consuming her and making it hard for her to be magnanimous.

'This place is off the hook,' Lily said, breaking into a smile. 'I can't believe I actually took the plunge and did this.'

'I know! It's so out of character, all this bravery.' Imogen smiled back, so that Lily knew she was only teasing. 'We'll have you skiing down a black run before you know it.'

Lily shuddered. 'No way! The skiing thing is a whole other challenge. That might be too far.'

Imogen broke into a gleeful grin. 'We'll get you down a mountain, I'm sure of it.'

Lily said nothing and tried to squash down her inner panic. She wasn't great with heights and she had never understood it, even when Jamie had talked incessantly about it. God. Jamie, Jamie, Jamie. Why did all roads lead to Jamie? Even in Chamonix.

'OK. We're here.'

Lily paused and gazed up at the hotel. It was an old building which looked as though it had been recently renovated. Like a large house, it had seven floors and it was white with pretty blue shutters that matched the roof. There was a smart swimming pool area at the front of the hotel which gave it a modern air and dove-grey loungers and parasols were dotted around the tranquil blue pool.

Lily followed Imogen into a quaint but sleek reception area, which had squashy grey sofas with splashes of scarlet in the cushions and rugs. Wood panelling covered the walls, which gave the hotel that traditional, alpine 'ski' vibe.

'It's lovely,' Lily said.

'Wait until you see the rooms,' Imogen told her. 'All wood panelling and high beams and some of the bathrooms are so fancy. Glass doors, marble tiles and purple up-lighting. Not the servants' quarters, natch.'

'Natch. That's OK. I only like blue up-lighting in my bathrooms.'

'Lucky. Ooh.' Imogen nudged Lily. 'It's Celine. She's coming over to say hello.'

Lily turned to meet Celine, intrigued to put a face to the voice she had spoken to on the phone.

'*Bonjour*,' Celine said, extending a hand. 'Lovely to meet you, Lily.'

Again, the charming, accented version of her name. Lily studied Celine as she answered perfunctory questions about her journey. Celine was a slim woman, verging on skinny, with pronounced cheekbones, blond, curly hair and a large gap between her two front teeth. Her skin was tanned and weather-beaten, with a scattering of freckles across the bridge of her nose. She was wearing a pair of turquoise salopettes and a white polo neck with what looked like hiking boots. Ugly footwear, but Celine was *soignée*, elegant and well-groomed, in every other sense.

'So Imogen will show you to your room,' Celine was saying as she checked her watch. She had a nervous, fidgety manner, as though she was powered by nerves and adrenalin. And probably caffeine. 'And then perhaps after you've settled and showered, you'll join us for dinner?'

'Sounds great.' Nodding at Celine, Lily followed Imogen to the lift. 'She seems nice.'

'She is. A bit neurotic maybe? And ski-obsessed,' Imogen added as she punched the number six inside the small, mirrored lift. 'But then, they all are. Honestly,

Lily. They live, breathe and eat skiing. The whole family is the same. Wait until you meet Pierre! He can't talk about anything else. Marc is the same. And Elodie… well.' Imogen's expression darkened. 'I'll tell you about Elodie another time. This is us. Surprise! I moved so I could share with you.'

Lily entered the room and flopped onto the pristine white sheets of the nearest bed, her feet ending up on the red and white throw that was neatly folded at the end. Letting out a huge sigh of relief, she lay back and stared up at the wooden beams of the ceiling. She was actually in Chamonix! She had moved out of her London flat and she was here, all these miles away, in a hotel in the middle of the Alps. It was exciting. And terrifying.

Lily sat up as Imogen starting unpacking for her. And she wasn't simply hurling things into drawers, she was neatly placing Lily's clothes in empty drawers and shelves. She had left a section of the wardrobe aside for any smart clothes Lily had brought with her. Lily hadn't brought that many as she wasn't sure of the etiquette. Also, Imogen had assured her that it was very 'cas' in the evenings and smart trousers were more or less all she needed. Lily had thrown in a couple of winter dresses just in case because she hated being unprepared.

The room was on the small side, with twin beds, each with their own tiny bedside table and matching lamp, but Imogen assured her that this was normal in a ski chalet-style hotel. There were wooden shelves and luckily, a largish wardrobe for them to share, along with a huge mirror with a set of antlers above it hung over a miniscule desk and chair. Somehow, though, it worked and it was a seriously cute little room.

'We don't have a wood burning stove in this room, more's the pity,' Imogen said, hanging Lily's clothes in the wardrobe. 'Those rooms are so beautiful, but we'd have to be paying guests to stay in one of those. We can do this properly later. I don't want us to be late for dinner.'

'There's a balcony!' Lily exclaimed, rushing across a mock-cow skin rug to open the sliding doors. Stepping out, she observed a low coffee-style table with two very comfortable if tiny chairs. Adorable. She leant on the balcony, taking in the magnificent view of the mountains rising majestically above them.

'I know, I know. Wow,' Imogen said, rolling her eyes cheekily as she joined her. 'I'm joking. It's gorgeous, isn't it? I've been so happy here. I genuinely can't imagine going home. Not for a long time. You wait, Lils. You'll fall in love with this place soon. I know you will.'

'Maybe.' Lily inhaled the cold, clean air. Jamie – and Ivy, for that matter – felt a million miles away right now. Which, with the greatest respect, was exactly how Lily wanted it.

'Right. Shower, change and we'll go down for dinner,' Imogen told her. 'I'm going to re-do my make-up, put on the Bardot top that makes my boobs look gigantic and I'm good to go.'

'I need to text my mum and tell her I've arrived safely,' Lily called, dashing to the shower. 'And I don't know what to wear or what makes my boobs look big or any of that…'

'Leave it to me,' Imogen told her. 'I've just viewed your entire wardrobe. Be ready in ten and I promise I'll make your tits look good.'

Chapter Six

'And here we have *tartiflette*.' The hotel chef, who Imogen informed her was called Sylvan, placed the dish on the table with a flourish. 'Let me serve you… Thursdays we all eat together as there are no guests here.'

Lily smiled. She knew this; this was why she had booked her flight on a Thursday, but she said nothing, so as not to take the wind out of Slyvan's sails.

'*Tartiflette* is a simple dish,' Sylvan informed Lily, loitering by her side of the table, 'using Reblochon cheese, the very best of the French cheeses, in my opinion. It is a typical Savoyard cheese, with lardons, white wine, garlic and shallots. I boil the potatoes for ten minutes in very salty water until tender and I fry the lardons and the garlic, then de-glaze the pan with good, white wine… French, of course.'

'Of course,' Lily murmured, overwhelmed by all the information.

Sylvan wasn't done. 'And then I put all the potatoes in, how you say, layers. Then I add the thick cream… I don't know what you call this in English…'

'We call that double cream,' Lily told him, wondering why Sylvan was going to so much trouble to tell her all the details about *tartiflette*. Short, bald and with a dark goatee, Sylvan wasn't remotely her type. And Lily hoped to God she wasn't his. He was a great chef; there was no doubt about that. His *soupe à l'oignon* starter had been a rich, sumptuous dish of joy, with thick strands of onion steeped in a boozy broth, topped with a garlicky baguette dripping with grated gruyere cheese. It had been filling, luxurious and decadent. Which was no mean feat for a soup starter.

Dickhead, Imogen mouthed across the table, jabbing an indiscreet finger in Sylvan's direction. She gave Lily a huge grin.

Lily supressed a laugh and did her best to not look ill-mannered in front of Sylvan.

'It is then baked in the oven so the Reblochon cheese melts and the top gets… I think you say crisp?' Sylvan said, holding his hands up in way that suggested he thought he was being charming.

'OK, Sylvan, I think she's heard enough,' a handsome guy cut in. It was accurate, but rather rude. He held his hand out and somehow managed to make the gesture haughty. 'Hi, I'm Marc Devereux. Pierre's son.'

Massive dickhead, Imogen mouthed helpfully across the table.

'Hi Marc, I'm Lily,' she said, trying to keep a straight face.

'Yes, I know,' he said in clipped tones. 'My mother hired you a week or so ago. Sports masseuse. I know everything that goes on in this hotel. I practically run it, if you must know.'

His accent was clipped and clear and his command of the English language was impeccable. He had chiselled cheekbones that he had clearly inherited from his mother, with a sleek cap of dark hair rather than the blond curls.

'On the nose,' Lily said, thinking perhaps Imogen was right. Marc might just be a massive dickhead.

'On the nose?' Marc looked confused.

'It's an expression,' Lily explained. 'It means… you're absolutely right. Or, precisely.'

'I see.' Marc looked unimpressed. 'I am not sure that is something I need to add to my repertoire.'

'I shouldn't think so,' Lily said, taking a huge slug of white wine. 'I'm sure your repertoire is *exemplary*.'

Marc inclined his head appreciatively, clearly missing her cheeky sarcasm. 'Ah, there is my father. Papa. This is Lily, *la nouvelle masseuse*.'

'*Bonsoir, bonsoir*,' Pierre said, immediately reminding Lily of Dave. Maybe Pierre would start doing a funny robot dance.

Or maybe not, she revised, studying him more closely. Pierre was tall with dark hair and had obviously had a major hand in Marc's appearance. He was handsome in a similar, snooty, self-important kind of way. Like Celine earlier, who was now nowhere to be seen, Pierre wore black ski salopettes as though they were entirely appropriate dinner wear, teamed with a grey polo neck. He had a skier's tan, with faint sunglasses marks around the eyes and a slightly peeling nose. Lily had no doubt the tan ended at the neck and wrists. Not that she had the slightest interest in anything under Pierre's polo neck.

'Aah, *tartiflette*,' Pierre said, taking a seat near Lily. 'Sylvan, you have surpassed yourself.' He helped himself to a large portion, displaying an appetite that didn't match his svelte physique. Presumably it was all the skiing.

'But of course.' Sylvan inclined his head and left the table to return to the kitchen.

Lily hid a smile. Why were they all so pleased with themselves?

Also dickhead, Imogen mouthed innocently by way of an explanation.

Lily giggled. She couldn't help it. All the white wine and Imogen was being such a bitch.

'So, Lily,' Pierre started. 'Welcome to *Boutique Hotel Devereux.*'

'Thank you,' she replied, raising her glass in his direction because she wasn't sure what else to do. She should probably eat some of Sylvan's *tartiflette*, but all the travel and the fatigue was catching up with her. She didn't want to end up being sick again, especially not in front of all these new people.

'You arrived on the right day,' Pierre told her. 'The guests are eating in the village tonight, but tomorrow, everything is back to normal and we work!'

Lily accepted another glass of wine.

Pierre got to his feet unexpectedly. 'Everyone, please welcome Lily to our team at *Boutique Hotel Devereux!*'

Lily wasn't sure why Pierre kept saying the 'boutique' bit when he mentioned the hotel, but perhaps it was important to him.

'Welcome!' everyone around the table chorused.

'Welcome,' Celine added, joining them. She had a beautiful young woman with her. Lily surmised from Imogen's rather naughty low-down after her shower that this was Elodie, Marc's younger sister. Elodie had Celine's blond hair, but she must spend an awfully long time straightening it because it was like a golden sheet hanging around her shoulders. Her face was angular, with full lips and wide, slanting eyes. She looked like a predatory

Siamese cat, her eyes moving around the table as though she was searching for someone.

Lily met Imogen's eyes across the table and, seeing Imogen's mouth opening, shook her head ferociously. If Elodie was also a massive dickhead, it was probably best left unsaid at this point. Because Lily was going to burst into noisy guffaws and make a show of herself if Imogen carried on.

'Let me introduce you to everyone,' Pierre was saying. He went around the four tables in the room, throwing names at Lily. She heard Kate, Amelia, Ollie, George, Joe… and a whole host of other names that she instantly forgot. She decided she would try to put the names to the faces later if they went out for a drink after dinner, as Imogen had suggested.

Drinking far too much wine, Lily managed some *tartiflette* and pretended to eat some of the vanilla-soaked crème caramel Sylvan produced. She also got the detailed, blow-by-blow account of the recipe, apparently just for her benefit.

'Right. Let's escape,' Imogen said once they had cleared the table and helped Sylvan tidy the kitchen. Lily noticed that the Devereuxs, apart from Elodie, melted away at this point, but that was fair enough. It was their 'Boutique' hotel, after all. Elodie hung back, chatting to the staff and seemed to be part of the gang.

'Let's go to Amnesia!' a guy with dark hair shouted, to which everyone agreed.

On Imogen's insistence, Lily had worn some flattish, lace-up Timberland boots that went with her jeans and cropped black jumper combo because apparently no one wore boots with heels or anything too dressy. And judging by the way everyone else was dressed, this was true – jumpers and flat boots were *de rigeur* in Chamonix. They all trudged through the marginal scattering of crunchy snow to get to the Amnesia bar and Lily looked around, enjoying the sight of families and couples eating and drinking inside the glow of nearby restaurants and bars. People were still in full ski wear, furry headbands included in some cases, as though they had just skied down the mountain moments before and alighted onto the snow-encrusted pavement of the town, skis and poles in tow.

Chamonix looked magical. It was lit up with giant, sparkly snowflakes that were strewn across the streets above their heads. Pretty Christmas decorations could be seen everywhere: in shop windows, in restaurants and even in the squares, where there were giant, illuminated teddy bears and sleighs. Lily let out a sigh of pleasure. She was so glad to be here and away from the heartache of home. And it felt so Christmassy here already!

'This – is Amnesia!' Imogen announced as they ducked through a door into a brightly-lit modern bar. There was a dance area with a low ceiling, teaming with people dancing and laughing. The bar had giant bottles of champagne and vodka lined up on it. There were seated areas with uncomfortable-looking white cubes to perch on and a ski gang headed to one of them.

'Welcome to Chamonix.'

Lily turned to find Elodie at her elbow. Elodie pressed a vodka cranberry into Lily's hand.

'Thank you. Elodie, isn't it?' Lily sipped the drink. She hated vodka-cranberry, but she didn't want to be rude.

'So what brings you here? Awful parents? Terrible job? Broken heart?' Elodie regarded Lily haughtily over the top of her glass.

Lily gulped her vodka down. Wow. Was she that predictable? Elodie's English was as superb as the rest of her family, Lily noted. She had a stronger accent, but her vocabulary was impressive.

'People tend to turn up here for one or all of those reasons,' Elodie said, her voice lacking warmth or emotion. She flipped her hair over her shoulder. 'So I just wondered which applied to you.' It was a clinical statement, which made its motivation obscure.

'I see.' Lily forced a smile onto her face. 'Well. My parents are amazing… mum and step-dad, actually.' She didn't want to think about her dad. Not now, not ever. 'My job was boring rather than terrible. Broken heart… er… tick, I guess.'

'Thought so!' Elodie looked triumphant. She smiled smugly, still managing to look beautiful. 'I said you had that look about you. Like you had been… how do you say it in English? Dumped?'

Lily decided she didn't like Elodie very much. 'I wasn't actually dumped,' she said, not sure why she felt the need to defend herself. 'It was more that I was interested in this guy and he ended up dating my sister and…'

'Oh, well, whatever!' Elodie waved a dismissive hand, clearly not interested in the actual details. She appeared to merely be proving a point to herself. 'I'm telling you it's the same thing over and over here. Shall I introduce you to everyone again? You looked like you didn't take any of them in earlier.'

Elodie was going to get vodka-cranberry in her face in a minute. Although Lily realised she couldn't actually throw a drink in Elodie's face because she was a Devereux. Lily urgently looked around for Imogen, but she was being chatted up by the dark-haired guy who'd suggested the bar.

Elodie finished listing everyone's name's in a monotone, talking down to Lily as if she wasn't capable of taking it all in. 'The only person missing is Luc,' Elodie was saying. 'He's one of the ski instructors, but he's very busy and very attractive, so I'm not sure how much time you'll be spending with him. Me and Luc are... we are very close,' she said suggestively. 'He was a terrible playboy when I first met him.' Elodie gave Lily a pointed smile. 'Not so much now.'

'Right.' Bored senseless and tired of being pleasant to someone who was treating her as if she was a complete and utter moron, Lily got up. 'Thanks for that, Elodie. Very informative.'

Heading off swiftly, she moved through the gang of hotel staff, smiling and nodding at them as they said hi and until she found herself next to Imogen, who was still chatting to the dark-haired guy.

'Oh. My. God. Do not leave me with her again,' Lily said close to Imogen's ear.

'Oh crap! Sorry hun.' Imogen looked mortified. 'She's awful, isn't she?'

Lily rolled her eyes. 'So awful. She was banging on about some guy called Luc. I think she was insinuating that they were an item. Or that he is a complete tart.'

'Luc. Aah yes.' Imogen frowned. 'I don't know if he's a tart as such. I've never seen him with anyone, to be honest.'

'Oh.' Lily was confused. Why had Elodie wanted her to think badly of Luc?

'He is seriously hot,' Imogen commented. She glanced at the dark-haired guy. 'Sorry, Ollie. Just saying. Lily, this is Ollie, by the way.'

'Hi Ollie,' Lily said with a grin. He was nice-looking, tall and with a friendly, open face. 'Nice to meet you. Don't worry, Ims; Elodie told me everyone's names again. Twice.'

'Dickhead,' Imogen replied with feeling. She frowned. 'Lily, are you knackered? We can go back to the hotel if you want.'

'I'll walk you both back,' Ollie offered gallantly, obviously trying to impress Imogen rather than Lily, but it was sweet of him nonetheless.

Lily considered. She was exhausted, but this was her first night here and she was buggered if she was going to look like a killjoy. Especially in front of Elodie. She felt a heart-wrenching pang as she thought of Jamie. God, she missed him! She felt her phone in her pocket, itching to call him, but she pushed the thought away. That would be unfair to Ivy, and it would be like picking a scab. No. Cold turkey was the way to go.

And this bar was amazing! It was bright and loud and trendy and the music was fantastic. Lily suddenly felt brave and brilliant for leaving England the way she had. This was just what she needed! This was so exciting compared to her life back in London. Lily knew in that instant that she had done the right thing.

'Nah… I'm up for a big night out!' Lily held her drink out for another vodka. Without the cranberry. 'Fill me up and let's DANCE!'

'Woohoo!' Imogen yelled, throwing her arms around Lily's neck. 'My bestie is BACK!!!'

Lily whooped and yelled too, downing the single shot of vodka in one. She had several more after that, dancing the night away in Chamonix with her new pals, forgetting all about Jamie and her sister. Almost.

Chapter Seven

'Wake up, sleepy head!' Imogen sang, sitting on the edge of Lily's bed. She was wearing a pair of cosy-looking pyjamas with long trousers and a cropped top. Lily was wearing a bright red silky playsuit and had brought her matching satin kimono to wear over the top. Clearly, she hadn't really thought the whole nightwear thing through.

'My head feels bad,' Lily said in a small voice. In fact, her head felt as though it had been hit by a baseball bat and her entire body ached. What on earth had she been doing last night? No more than drinking far too much and dancing, but Lily felt as though she had been knocked sideways.

But what a night! The bar... club, whatever it was, had been fantastic. It was unlike any club Lily had been to in London. There had been something different and cool about it and Lily had spent the night avoiding the dreadful Elodie, but feeling euphoric with the way she had changed her life. It had been fun and wild. Lily was sure she could remember some of the guys stripping on the dance floor and a hilarious walk home that had involved them staggering around in the same circle four times before someone realised and led them into a bar which sold awesome pizzas that came with tequila shots. But dear God, her head.

'Why did I drink so much?' Lily asked dolefully.

'Aah, that's a question no one can answer. Why do any of us do it?' Imogen said, snuggling into bed with Lily. 'But every Thursday, come hell or high water, we do it.'

Lily rubbed her eyes and sat up. 'What time is it?'

'Five thirty am,' Imogen informed her brightly.

'Whaaaaat?!' Lily flopped down on the bed again. 'Why are you waking me up, you horrible cow?'

Imogen sat her up again. 'No, none of that. It's time to get up, that's why! The day starts bright and early here. We're on breakfast duty. And we're a bit short-staffed at the moment, so we're all mucking in.'

Oh dear God. The mere thought of breakfast made Lily's tummy do a flip flop that threatened to turn into a full-on vomit fest.

Lily waited until her stomach settled. 'What's going on with you and Ollie then?'

Imogen looked coy. 'Not sure yet. He's cute, isn't he? He only arrived last week, otherwise I'd have mentioned him to you. I really like him.'

'Well, it's mutual. He looked like a lovesick puppy,' Lily replied. 'Go easy on him, Ims. You eat those kinds of guys for breakfast. God, I need some food, but I feel so sick…'

'I'll be gentle with him. Not! So I'll have the first shower and then you jump in afterwards.' Imogen leapt off the bed. How she was so chirpy was anyone's guess. But Imogen had always been able to hold her drink better than Lily. 'I'll be quick as we're on one of the higher floors, so we have less hot water, believe it or not. It's all about the timing here!'

Lily groaned and sat up properly. She imagined she must look like death and she hoped a hot shower would revive her. She felt around for her phone and found it in the folds of her sheets. Glancing at it, her heart leapt. Jamie had messaged!

'*Hey there. How's my bestie doing in all that snow? Hope you're settling in and that you're not too homesick x*'

Lily bit her lip. 'Hey there' instead of 'Red'. It hurt, but that was just the way it was now. At least she was still 'bestie'. Jamie had sent the message in the early hours of the morning, the way he always used to. How strange. She felt pleased that he had messaged, but slightly guilty about it being in the early hours like that, as she didn't think Ivy would be happy about it. What should she do? Answer or ignore?

'Shower's free!' Imogen called.

Ignore. Or at the very least, leave it for now. Lily got up and, shivering slightly, headed for the bathroom. She really needed some warm pyjamas. A hot – ending up as lukewarm – shower woke her up sufficiently and she pulled on jeans with the brand-new black sweatshirt with 'Boutique Hotel Devereux' emblazoned across it in purple that Imogen had given her. It wasn't the most flattering of garments, but they all had to wear them, so she was going to have to rock it somehow. Adding trainers and tying her auburn hair up in a ponytail, Lily followed Imogen downstairs quietly, as obviously most guests were still asleep.

Outside, snow was falling heavily. Snowflakes were swirling and dancing outside the hotel windows and Lily could see that it was settling on the ground. Winter was well and truly here and in Chamonix. It looked stunning. Imogen led Lily back into the main dining area they'd had dinner in the night before. Lily hadn't taken much notice of the room last night, but today, she could see that it was beautiful. It had huge windows that let in plenty of light, and the light was bright with all the snow. Fir trees could be seen outside the windows, the fronds of their branches heavy with the fresh bout of snow.

Above an imposing fireplace was a wall-mounted set of antlers and there were plenty of ski pictures in frames dotted around the walls. Mostly they were action shots of the Devereux family skiing like pros down impossibly steep slopes, as well as jokey ski pictures that looked as though they had been lovingly collected over the years. There was even an ancient set of skis mounted on the wall that Lily was certain must have belonged to a Devereux family member back in the day.

'So the main hot breakfast guests have is eggs,' Imogen explained as they started laying out the buffet table. 'We cook those to order – any way they're wanted. Guests can have the full English but it's extra and no one really has it.'

'Shit. I don't even know if I can cook eggs,' Lily said worriedly.

'Don't worry, I'll show you. So here,' Imogen gestured to a vast oak table set up in an L-shape at one end of the dining room, 'is where we lay out the continental breakfast. We need to put out the pastries, bread, butter, jam, cheeses, and cold meats. The big canisters for water, milk and orange juice come in on a trolley so we don't have to worry about those.'

Instructed by Imogen as well as Elodie, who seemed to think she was in charge of everything in the hotel including its staff, Lily carried a tray of freshly baked bread from the kitchen to the dining room and started filling baskets lined with linen cloths with chunks of baguette, croissants, mini *pain-au-chocolates* and finally English bread, which seemed pale and unappetising next to its heavenly-looking French counterparts. The bread was joined by jars of apricot and strawberry jam, laden with thick chunks of fruit and chilled platters of all different kinds of cheese: Swiss cheese, brie and goat's cheese plus a mouth-watering array of hams. There was salty *jambon de Bayonne* and *jambon de Paris*, cooked in its own juices, plus a fancy, layered terrine. There were savoury jams to go with the ham and cheese as well as grapes and slices of apple.

'Sylvan can't put out just ham and cheese,' Imogen explained to Lily as they put out cutlery and plates. 'It's just not in his nature.'

'He's a good chef,' Lily commented.

'Sorry, but he's a boring nob,' Imogen corrected. 'Trust me. Don't stay chatting to him too long, otherwise you'll learn how to make *bouillabaisse* in excruciating detail.' She straightened suddenly and nudged Lily, who hid the slice of gooey terrine she'd been about to sample behind her back as she caught sight of Celine approaching. She quickly put the other hand round to catch anything that might slip through her fingers.

'Good morning,' Celine said crisply. 'I hope you had a fun first night?'

'It was lovely, thank you.' Lily could feel the terrine slipping between her fingers and she felt panicked. Why on earth had she picked that moment to steal a slice?

'Sore head?' Celine inquired, looking amused. 'All the staff look quite pale on Fridays as a rule.'

'Your English is superb,' Lily said, frantically trying to hold onto the slippery terrine.

'Why thank you.' Celine preened slightly, pushing her frizzy hair out of her eyes. 'I had a very strict English teacher when I was a child. I detested him, but I must admit, I can speak English almost as well as I can my mother tongue.'

'Amazing.' The terrine was clinging to Lily's fingers for dear life. But not for much longer.

'I have two massages booked for you today,' Celine said, holding out a booking form to Lily.

Seeing that Lily was struggling with something behind her back, Imogen grabbed the form. 'She er... hurt her hands dancing last night.'

Celine looked worried. 'Her hands? How? Will you be able to work, Lily?'

Lily shot Imogen an anxious glance. God! She was a masseuse, for heaven's sakes! She couldn't have injured hands. She thought rapidly.

'YMCA,' she offered vaguely.

Imogen obligingly showed Celine the moves to the famous song by the Village People, flapping the booking form around as she contorted her body into letter shapes.

Celine's delicate eyebrows lifted. She was clearly baffled. 'Well. I shall leave you to it. Your massages are this morning, Lily, although most tend to be in the afternoon after skiing. You are free to start your skiing lessons this afternoon if you wish. I have lined Matteo up for you, although Luc should be back soon and he often takes on beginners if he has time.'

'Thank you so much,' Lily managed politely. As soon as Celine's back was turned, she whipped round and grabbed a napkin to drop the oozing terrine into just as it was about to plop onto the floor.

'What were you *doing*?' Imogen asked, collapsing with laughter. 'I've just had to do the YMCA dance in front of our boss!'

'I don't know.' Lily pulled a contrite face. 'You know I get hangry or whatever. I needed to eat and the terrine looked good. But my hands are always hot, and it started to disintegrate…'

'You crack me up.' Imogen shook her head. 'We'll eat in a minute before everyone arrives. Or just eat now. I don't want you beating the guests up because you're having a blood sugar dip.'

'Stop it. I'm fine. Well, I do need to eat actually…'

Imogen propelled Lily towards the kitchen and made her some poached eggs on toast with spinach, showing her how to do the eggs. They sat perched on stools, eating at a small table set aside for staff. Ollie and the rest of the breakfast crew were swirling in and out of the kitchen and as the guests started arriving for the first serving, Imogen and Lily hopped off their stools and got to work.

'Tea is on the table by the milk,' Lily said pleasantly, for the tenth time, but she couldn't get annoyed as by and large, the guests were very friendly and upbeat. They were all, bar a few who were wearing normal clothes, wearing ski clothes, ready for their day on the slopes at seven am. They wore salopettes in a variety of different colours, some with braces teamed with long-sleeved, polo neck tops. And slippers or just socks. There were Uggs, moccasins and thick ski socks in a variety of colours and patterns.

'Why aren't they wearing shoes?' Lily whispered to Imogen.

'Because they leave their slippers in the boot room and walk out in their ski boots,' Imogen whispered back.

Skiing. It was like a whole new world. It had its own uniform, its own routine and its own language, it seemed. Lily heard 'whiteout', 'fresh powder', 'carving', 'traverse', and 'bomber' just walking past one table. She wasn't sure if they were talking about drugs at first, but soon realised these must all be skiing terms. Because that was all skiers talked about. All. They. Talked. About. For the entire meal that was breakfast, Lily didn't hear any other conversation topics, not even from couples with young babies and children. There was no mention of lack of sleep or bad eating habits or time outs. It was all ski passes and lessons and helmets and gloves and weird skiing terms.

'Wow. It's an obsession,' Lily said, as she heaved a pile of dirty plates into the kitchen.

'What is?' Elodie asked, strolling in and frowning at the pile of plates. 'You need to scrape all those off before putting them in the dishwasher.'

'Really?' Lily asked with wide eyes. *No shit, Sherlock*, she thought to herself. Elodie sure had a stick up her ass, but she looked stunning. Even with a hangover, if she even had one, Elodie looked groomed to perfection. She wore an expensive-looking lilac ski top tucked into tight black ski trousers and her long hair was twisted up in a neat chignon, while Lily could barely manage a tidy ponytail in her own titian hair. Her make-up was flawless: glossy lips and eyeliner that was so straight that it must have taken an extraordinarily steady hand, even at that time of the morning.

'What's an obsession?' Elodie repeated, watching closely as Lily worked, as if she was waiting to pounce and pick holes in anything she did.

'Skiing. I haven't heard anyone talk about anything else this morning.'

Elodie threw her a withering glance. 'Well, that's what they're all here for, isn't it, Lily? And you don't understand because you've never even skied before.'

Lily gritted her teeth and carried on scraping dishes. God, what was Elodie's problem? She was so patronising. What could Lily possibly have done to annoy this girl? She had only just turned up in Chamonix, for heaven's sakes!

'Are you having a lesson today?' Elodie asked. 'You'll probably understand a bit more about skiing once you've put some skis on and experienced the rush.'

'Probably,' Lily replied wearily. She was too exhausted this morning to deal with Elodie's razor-sharp tongue. What did Elodie do – wake up prickly and ready for battle?

'You have your first massage in a minute,' Imogen informed Lily, coming in with more plates. She dumped them and wiped her hands. 'I'll show you the room downstairs so you can get a feel for it.'

'Thanks,' Lily muttered, following Imogen out of the kitchen gratefully. 'What the hell is wrong with that girl?'

'Stick up her ass.' Imogen shrugged. 'Uptight. Needs a good shag, I think.'

'Well, according to the way she was carrying on last night, she's shagging the very hot Luc, right? So I don't think that can be it.' Lily felt grumpy. She wasn't bothered about her hangover, but she couldn't stand bitchy girls.

Girls like Elodie made her feel as though she was back in the playground.

'I have no idea if she's seeing Luc or not, although they are as thick as thieves,' Imogen mused. 'Always together. Anyway, take no notice. Here's your room. Probably not a patch on your posh spa place in England, but it's not that bad.' She pulled a face to show that she was joking.

'It's lovely, actually,' Lily said, walking around it. 'Cosy and welcoming.'

It was. It was very much in keeping with the ski chalet style, with wooden panelling on the walls, low lighting and a long, plush couch in the centre. There were piles of fluffy black towels stacked in an alcove and scented candles dotted around the room. There was a table covered with bottles of aromatherapy oils and wipes and tissues and everything she needed. The couch was already covered with clean towels, the head hole defined, and the room smelt of lavender and amber – the perfect blend of floral and woody.

'OK, I'll leave you to it,' Imogen said. 'I'm on house-keeping duty today... yawn. Then I'm going skiing with Ollie. I think Celine has booked you in with Matteo after your massages, but you need to collect your skis and boots first in the shop opposite.'

'Matteo? What's he like?'

Imogen laughed. 'He's an older dude, very old-school, with a face like a worn leather glove. He wears an all-in-one ski suit. Not a ski jacket and salopettes, but a full-on body suit with a zip up the front, which will probably have you in fits of giggles. It's super tight. But he's a nice guy and pretty patient.' She gave Lily a map and quickly talked her through how to get to the nursery slope she would start on. 'Have fun!'

After Imogen left, Lily felt suddenly apprehensive. She didn't know anything about skis and boots and mountains or any of it. She was borrowing some of Imogen's ski clothes for the afternoon and she had everything bar the important stuff, but her stomach was churning at the thought of it.

There was a knock on the door and a woman with a bouffant hairstyle put her head around.

'Are you the masseuse?' she asked. 'I'm booked in this morning.'

'Absolutely. Come on in.' Lily immediately went into professional mode.

'I asked for a relaxing massage,' the woman said, coming into the room, with a worried expression. 'Not a sports one... my husband wants one of those after me.'

Lily gave her an easy smile. 'Not a problem. If relaxing is what you're after, relaxing is most definitely what you're going to get.'

Stripping off her hotel sweatshirt so she was just wearing her polo neck and jeans, Lily left her client to get settled on the couch in private, then went back into the room. Picking up an oil that had been one of her favourites to use back home, Lily warmed some in her cupped hands and drizzled it across her client's back.

'This is safflower and jojoba combined and it contains lavender, jasmine and Brazilian rosewood so it's rich and ultra-nourishing. In an hour's time, you're going to feel amazing...'

Chapter Eight

Three hours later, after a quick lunch, Lily was standing in some non-matching, wildly clashing ski clothes at the bottom of a mountain, clutching skis, wearing extremely uncomfortable ski boots that felt too tight and restrictive and weird. She didn't like them at all. She had been measured and weighed and fitted and re-fitted for both her skis and her boots and it had been exciting but kind of scary too.

Lily hadn't wanted to ask if her ski boots could be black and silver like the ones all the female skiers she had seen on her way to the shop were wearing and had instead ended up with ugly navy ones that didn't match anything she was wearing. They also made her stand oddly, as though she was tilted forwards. The bottoms of the boots were at an angle, presumably to fit properly into the skis, but they felt bizarre when standing and walking.

Her skis were white with black tips and they looked fairly stylish, but Lily didn't have a clue; they might scream beginner. And she hated her glossy, white helmet while she was thinking about it. It was absurd. Unattractive, clumsy and annoying. And she was sure she must look silly in it, even though everyone wore them. She felt like a cyclist who'd lost her bicycle.

She was standing at the bottom of *Les Planards*, which according to the map Imogen had given her was one of the larger nursery areas in the centre of Chamonix. The 'green piste' had a 'gentle gradient' apparently, which to Lily looked like a hideously steep slope, as well as another slightly more difficult slope. Both slopes had drag lifts and even they looked challenging to Lily. She felt her hands start to shake in the black, puffy ski gloves she was wearing, and she was of a mind to turn back the way she had come. Except that she had had to walk to this part of town in her ski boots, which involved putting a heel down and clonking down onto her toe and the same on the other foot. It had taken ages, she had felt awkward and silly, and she didn't relish having to do it all over again on the way back.

'Lily?'

She turned to find an extremely hot guy standing in front of her. He had dirty blond hair, dark eyes and a sexy mouth that looked as though it was about to break into a smile. The kind of mouth that instantly made a girl want to kiss it. Lily felt shocked at her own thought. She wasn't prone to thinking that kind of thing about a guy she'd just set eyes on.

Lily blinked at the guy. Was this Matteo? Hadn't Imogen said he was on the old side? This guy was in his early thirties and his face was tanned, but not weathered. And he was wearing black salopettes with the red ski jacket all the instructors wore. He had a pair of sunglasses on top of his head and his helmet and gloves were tucked under his arm.

'I'm Luc,' he said, holding out his hand and smiling in a friendly rather than flirtatious way.

Lily felt a frisson of excitement. So this was the famous Luc. Well. He was certainly hot.

'I think you might have been expecting Matteo, but I had a free space, so here I am.' His eyes met hers again and Lily felt another flicker of something. Wow. Luc was indeed good-looking. It was in a very different way to Jamie, who was all floppy dark hair and laughing eyes, but Luc was attractive. Sexy. Imposing. And very tall. But it wasn't just that he was good-looking. He looked fun and exciting and... different.

Lily shook his hand abruptly, realising she'd left him hanging. His hand was warm and his handshake was firm.

'H-hi,' she replied, annoyed to find her teeth chattering. Was it the chilly air or her nerves? Or because Luc was so... tall...?

'You are the new *masseuse*, I think?'

She nodded.

'I will have to book myself in with you,' Luc said. 'I get very tight here.' He pointed to his shoulders.

'Sure.'

The thought of massaging Luc was rather disturbing for some reason, but Lily couldn't very well turn him away. Nor would she if he booked himself in. She felt rather flustered, but she was sure it was one-sided. Luc must get this reaction from women a lot. He was charming and tall and confident and he looked unfazed, so Lily steeled herself. No more falling for guys who didn't fancy her back.

'So. You haven't skied before, no?' Luc started pulling his gloves on.

His accent was attractive, like Celine's. Seductive, even. He did look like a playboy, though. No wonder Elodie was into him. And from what she'd told Lily last night, she was the one who had tamed him. Lily felt a stab of envy, which she swiftly pushed away. She was sick of feeling envious of people around her; she was sure she would get over her heartache one day and find her own Luc. Jamie. Whoever.

'Er… no. I haven't. Skied before, that is.' Lily pulled her gloves on. Her hands were shaking badly. How embarrassing. She was fumbling around like an idiot. It was obviously nerves and not Luc's handsome face.

'Here.' Luc whipped his gloves off and helped her on with hers, as though she were a child, doing the Velcro straps up for her, tucking the edges into the sleeves of her jacket. She found it oddly endearing.

'You are a little nervous?' Luc asked, raising an eyebrow.

'Very,' Lily admitted, letting out a jerky breath. She liked that James Bond one eyebrow lift, and she and Jamie even used to practise it a lot but to no avail.

Oh, do shut up about Jamie, she berated herself. She was turning into a Jamie-bore. She had to stop thinking about him and referencing everything back to him.

'I don't know what's wrong with me,' she said, glancing at Luc. She looked up at the nursery slope. 'That looks high to me, but it's a low one, right?'

Luc grinned. 'It is a low one, yes.' He pulled his helmet on and helped her with hers, then cocked his head to one side. 'You are scared of heights, maybe?'

Lily shook her head. 'I don't think so. A bit, maybe. I don't know. I've never really been up on anything high before. Maybe once. With my dad.'

Her voice faded. She hated thinking about her dad and any memories relating to him. But she knew she had been somewhere high with him once. A mountain? A tall building? Lily wasn't sure. Maybe she had blocked it out. She thought she had probably blocked out many things to do with her dad.

'OK.' Luc shrugged. 'No matter. Let's get you up there and see what happens.'

'We… we're going up there? Right now?' Lily felt her stomach squelch.

'Yes,' Luc nodded. 'Apart from a short instruction here, we are heading up to the lower level slope.' He put his gloved hand on her arm. 'Do not worry. I am here with you. I won't let anything bad happen.'

'I bet you say that to all the beginners!' Lily quipped out of sheer anxiety. The blood was pumping through her body at a rate of knots. She actually felt light-headed.

'I do. And they believe me. And so should you. Let's go through a few things.'

Luc set about showing Lily how to stamp her boots into her skis whilst they were on a flat plane and went through some basic instruction about her stance, how to control the skis with the tilt of her knees, and where her poles should be held.

'Let's get the button lift,' Luc said, once he was sure Lily had everything clear.

'What's a button lift?' Lily felt her heart start thumping uncontrollably again. Being on flat ground was fine, but going up on any kind of lift was sending her spiralling.

Luc showed her how to step out of her skis by using one to push down on the back guard and her boot for the other. 'A button lift is also known as a drag lift or a "Poma", after the French company who made them.'

'Great.' Lily's teeth were chattering again. 'How do we get on that?'

'We walk to it, first of all,' Luc explained. 'And then we put our skis on, shuffle through the gate and then we tuck the button under us like this.' He demonstrated, looking comical as he gestured with his hands and bent his knees. He was playing with her, wanting her to copy him. 'Come. It's fun.'

Fun? Lily was thinking it might be more fun to shut herself in a hot sauna in her ski clothes this afternoon. With Elodie.

Stomping heel to toe in her ski boots after Luc, Lily felt her entire body flood with trepidation. What on earth was happening to her? Why was she reacting like this? Standing into her skis as Luc held onto her, Lily shuffled after him towards the lift, grateful of the queue. It was mostly formed by children, which was mortifying, but there were a few adults there as well. And some of them looked even more unstable than she felt, which was reassuring, but only momentarily.

'I'll go through first,' Luc told her. 'Where is your ski pass?'

'In my inside pocket,' Lily gestured to her chest. 'Do I need to get it out?'

He shook his head. 'No, but you need to aim it at that machine as we go through. Tomorrow, put it in this side pocket here, yes? It will be easier for you.'

Lily was puzzled, but soon realised what Luc meant. The sensor for the pass was low down and she had to contort herself at a weird angle to get her pass read. Basically, she had to aim her boob at the machine and bend over at the same time. On skis. No mean feat. Certain she must look utterly ridiculous and a total novice, Lily managed to get through the barrier without slipping over, just.

Luc grinned at her again. 'That was funny. Well done for not falling over. So.' He gestured to the button lift, which had round circles on the ends of long, metal arms that swung as they came around a rotating grinder. 'We grab the button like so.' He grabbed it and mimed tucking it between his legs. 'We don't sit on it. We just lean into our skis and let the lift drag us up the slope.'

'Simple,' Lily muttered, squashing down the feeling of panic that was threatening to overwhelm her.

Luc smiled. 'You can do it. Shall I go in front of you or behind you?'

Lily shook her head. 'I don't know. What's worse? Or better?'

'I'll go behind and then I can pick you up if you fall off.'

Fall off? He hadn't said anything about falling off. Lily shuffled forward again and held her left hand out for the lift. One went past her and she tried to grab it and failed.

'No problem,' Luc said, rolling his shoulders expansively. 'Who cares? Try again on the next one. Stay calm. Take your time.'

The next button lift came around and Lily grabbed it, hard. Too hard. Trying to tuck it between her legs, she wobbled and fell, landing sideways in the snow. Another button lift went by, but she hadn't a hope in hell of grabbing it since she was face down in the snow.

'Oh God.' Lily didn't know whether to laugh or cry. She laughed but felt herself cringing inside. Everyone else seemed to be able to do this effortlessly. Why couldn't she? Feeling incredibly stupid, Lily struggled to get up, not even remotely managing it. Is this what it felt like to be a turtle flipped over onto its shell?

'It's OK.' Luc's strong, tanned hands came out and lifted her up. 'Let me help you. Here you go.' He expertly drew the next button lift down and held it between her legs. Lily felt embarrassed and she glanced at Luc. He was grinning, but he said nothing.

'Hold on,' he instructed. 'I am right behind you.'

Lily held on for dear life. Her legs didn't seem to want to do as they were told. She was trying to keep them straight and level as Luc had suggested, but they kept wanting to flare out like Bambi on ice and do their own thing. Like falling over again.

Do not fall off, do not fall off, Lily told herself. Jeez. She sounded like Dave.

'We are getting off soon!' Luc shouted to her from behind. 'Remember what I said. You are going to take the lift out, hold on, point your skis to the right and you are going to let go and let your skis slide across.'

Oh my God, oh my God, oh my God. Lily did as Luc had instructed. Holding on slightly too long, she let the button lift ping away from her with a loud screeching noise and turned onto the slope. Realising she wasn't holding onto anything, she wobbled, straightened, lost her nerve and then fell over again. She shrieked, getting a mouthful of snow.

Luc scooped her up as if she weighed nothing, even though she weighed a considerable amount, even if much of it was muscle, and set her upright.

'OK?' he asked. He looked amused, but sympathetic.

She glanced at him, trying to work out if he was laughing at her. 'I'm OK,' she said moodily. 'I'm bruised and I feel like an idiot, but I'm OK. Thank you for helping me up. Again.'

'*De rien*,' he said, with a shrug of his shoulders. 'It happens. Don't worry about falling over. I fell over seventeen times the first time my dad taught me to ski.'

Lily was sure he hadn't. She wanted to believe him, but wondered if it was just a story he had concocted to make beginners feel better after falling arse over tit.

Luc pointed down the slope. 'That is what we are going to get down. Are you ready?'

Lily kept her skis sideways as he'd taught her and looked down the slope. Oh, dear Lord. This was a nursery slope? It looked horrendous. It looked steep and scary and like an absolute death trap.

'Look at the view,' Luc said, leaning casually on his ski pole. 'Have you ever seen anything like that? How beautiful it is, *oui*?'

Lily swallowed and looked at the view. It was stunning. Snow-capped mountains that were picture-perfect, almost as though the brilliant white snow had been painted on in sweeping strokes. Clear skies in a bright shade of blue that was simply breathtaking. There was not a cloud to be seen; the earlier fall of snow had stopped some hours ago, leaving a thick, powdery finish everywhere. The view aside, the slope still seemed steep and unmanageable.

'I'd quite like to go back to the hotel now,' Lily said in a small voice.

'You can't,' Luc replied cheerfully. 'This is the only way down. The button lifts only go up. They don't go down. We go down.'

Lily stared at him. Holy shit. How was she supposed to get down this stupid mountain when she hadn't skied before? She wanted to sit in the snow and refuse to move. She would give anything to get off this mountain right now by helicopter or any other form of transport, but getting down this slope on these slippery skis? Nope. No thank you. *Non.*

And the height. Where had this fear of heights come from suddenly? Lily couldn't understand it.

Don't be such a baby! Lily heard in the back of her mind. *Stop crying and go to the edge. Everyone else can do it!* She started shaking all over. Her dad. Her dad had said those words to her. A memory rushed into her mind without warning. She had been young, maybe five or six. They had been abroad somewhere up a high mountain. Wherever it was, she hadn't wanted to be there. Panic shot through her. And he had bullied her. He had forced her to go to the edge when she was utterly petrified.

'Lily.' Luc's voice interrupted her thoughts, his voice calm and authoritative. 'What did I say at the bottom of the slope? I am here with you and I will not let anything bad happen. Do as I tell you and I promise it will all be OK. Trust me.'

Lily stared at him, coming out of her reverie. He wasn't her dad. He was trying to help her, not bully her.

'OK,' she said shakily. She didn't know why, but she was going to trust him. Jesus, but she was petrified.

'What do I need to do?'

Chapter Nine

'OK, so we're taking this really slowly.' Luc demonstrated pushing the tips of his skis together, flaring the backs of them out.

'Your arms are *here*, poles in this position.'

Lily copied him, her heart thumping.

'We call this a snow plough,' Luc explained. 'For the kids, we call this a "wedge" or a "pizza". For the adults, a snow plough. Perfect position, by the way.'

The compliment flew over Lily's head. She felt as though she had a wodge of cotton wool in her throat. She felt as though she was about to speak in public in front of thousands of people. Naked. With a pineapple on her head. She felt foolish and gauche and so far out of her comfort zone she didn't know what to do with herself. Lily took hold of herself. She could do this. *She could do this.*

'Shall we make a start?' Luc gave her an encouraging nod.

Not giving herself time to think, Lily nodded back. She pulled her goggles down and gritted her teeth.

'Relax,' Luc said. He pushed away slowly and went into a perfect snow plough. An elegant, effortless snow plough.

Lily hesitated, then followed him. Whoa. Her legs were shaking so much, she was wobbling all over the place. It was hard to stay in the snow plough shape. She put her weight forward as Luc had instructed, but felt herself glide down the slope. Which didn't seem as steep now that she was moving down it.

'You are doing so well!' Luc shouted. He reached the bottom and showed her how to come to a stop by widening the snow plough.

Lily widened it, but her thighs starting screaming and she started to lose her balance, falling over again within seconds. 'Euugh!'

Luc helped her up. 'All part of the fun,' he told her. 'Seriously. Don't worry about falling over. You're going to fall over a lot. I can assure you I still fall over.'

'Now that I would like to see,' Lily said, spitting snow out of her mouth. 'God, I must be covered in bruises. And my mum always told me not to eat snow. Or was that just yellow snow?'

Luc looked confused, then he laughed. 'Ha! Probably just yellow snow. And yes, you'll be a little bruised. But you will be OK.'

Lily raised her eyebrows. She supposed he was right because it was only a few bruises, but she didn't relish the idea of falling over in the snow all the time. Perhaps it was simply par for the course, though. Par for *her* course anyway.

'What now?' she asked.

'Now we go up again.' Luc set off on his skis. 'You will need to use your arms to get you to the lift this time!' he shouted over his shoulder.

Puffing as she used her poles to stab the snow and push herself forward, Lily wished she'd gone to the gym more when she worked at the spa back home. She'd had no idea skiing was such a physical sport!

This time she didn't fall on the button lift. She managed to grab one, tuck it between her legs and go up the slope without issues. She didn't even fall over when she got off. She was still petrified at the top, however, the height thing still causing issues. Over the next hour, as she and Luc went down the mountain doing excruciatingly slow snow plough turns, Lily estimated that she fell over approximately twenty-three times. Which was particularly galling when five-year-olds were snow ploughing past her without so much as a wobble, shrieking at the sheer fun and fabulousness of it all.

'So I've beaten your record then,' Lily panted, refusing Luc's hand because she knew she needed to get herself upright without him. 'Thank you, but God! It's so hard getting up with skis on.'

'It gets easier,' Luc held his hand out again as she slipped again. 'OK. I think we should leave it there for today. You need to grab a hot chocolate or a mulled wine, and you need to relax. And I want you to know that you have done very well today.'

'Oh, Luc.' Lily took off her goggles and pulled a face. 'You are a true gentleman. But I think falling over that many times makes me a pretty bad student.' She put a hand to her face. She was pretty sure she must have red goggle marks all around her eyes, but she couldn't look any sillier than she had all afternoon, so it really wasn't an issue.

Lily sighed. She hadn't exactly made a great first impression. Not that it mattered, of course. She was here to get over Jamie, not fall for someone else, however attractive Luc was. Lily remembered Elodie. She could imagine these two as a couple – good-looking and sexy, skiing superbly down a mountain together. How depressing. Lily felt totally inadequate all of a sudden.

Luc stepped expertly out of his skis and helped her out of hers. 'Falling over doesn't mean you are a bad student, or that you won't be able to do this once you've had a good set of lessons. Falling over means that you are trying hard.'

Oh, he was sweet! Falling over meant that she was trying hard. What a lovely way to look at it. All Lily knew was that she was exhausted. And sore. And she felt somewhat humiliated. She didn't enjoy looking silly and she wasn't used to not being able to do something well. In fact, she had always prided herself on turning her hand to most things, especially when it came to sport. Lily knew she couldn't be good at everything and she had no idea why it suddenly mattered to her, but she wanted to be good at this.

Luc glanced up the mountain. 'There is Elodie, I think,' he said, pointing to a figure in black much higher up doing the most superbly stylish parallel turns.

'How can you tell?' Lily squinted into the distance.

'It's the bright pink helmet,' Luc told her. 'She had it made specially and she always wears it.'

Lily watched Elodie enviously. She was an amazing skier. Elodie had that effortless, almost laid-back style that only the most natural of skiers could achieve.

'She has been skiing since she could walk,' Luc informed Lily, seemingly reading her mind.

'It shows,' Lily said, in awe. She watched Elodie weave skilfully down the mountain without missing a single turn.

Her body moved fluidly like poetry in motion, her blond ponytail flicking out from side to side as she turned. As she reached the lower part of the mountain, Elodie performed an almost languid 360 turn on her skis before zig-zagging towards them.

Show off, thought Lily, wishing more than anything that she could manage a three sixty turn. Or just stay upright for more than five seconds.

Elodie headed for them at a speed that made Lily nervous. It looked like Elodie was going to crash into them, but right at the last minute, she executed a side turn that brought her to an abrupt standstill and which showered a light spray of snow over Lily.

Lily gasped and held her arms up as she glanced down at her snow-spattered ski clothes.

'Elodie!' Luc sounded cross. 'Stop showing off.' Now he sounded indulgent.

Dusting herself off, Lily watched them discreetly, wondering idly what the deal was with the two of them.

'Sorry. I didn't mean to get snow all over you.' Sounding unrepentant, Elodie lifted her goggles. She turned to Luc and treated him to a wide smile. Her teeth were very white and very straight. 'Wonderful powder today.'

'Yes.'

'Powder?' Lily asked. 'Does that mean fresh snow?'

Elodie tore her eyes away from Luc long enough to shoot Lily a withering glance. 'Of course. How was your first ski lesson?'

'Oh, well...' Lily paused, about to describe her hilarious attempts at staying upright, let alone her snow plough turns.

'She did very well,' Luc cut in, his dark eyes flashing at Lily, as if warning her to stay quiet. 'Especially since she has a terrible fear of heights.'

'Really?' Elodie threw Lily an unsympathetic glance. 'That won't help your skiing one bit. If this,' she gestured to the low plain of the nursery run, 'has caused you issues, I doubt you'll get much higher or be able to progress much further with your technique.'

Luc dusted some snow from Lily's shoulder. 'Not true at all. I think I can help Lily with her height issue. And the skiing will come.'

Elodie shrugged, looking bored. 'Well, I must get back. I assume I will see you at dinner?' This was directed at Luc. It was incredible the way she could somehow freeze one person out whilst focusing her entire attention on the other person. It was rather impressive, if exceptionally ill-mannered.

'Possibly not.' Luc inclined his head politely. 'I might be seeing my parents.'

Elodie smirked and snapped her boots smartly out of her skis. 'OK,' she said, as though she didn't believe him. 'I'll see you later either way.' With barely a nod in Lily's direction, Elodie strode away, somehow even making the heel to toe motion of walking in her snow boots seem elegant.

'Let's go,' Luc said, looking tight-lipped for the first time that day.

Lily followed Luc off the slope, knowing her clonking strides were far less elegant than Elodie's, but she was so tired, she was past caring. Glancing at his face as they walked side by side, Lily couldn't read it and she was dying to ask him about Elodie. What was the story between the two of them? Lily sensed something. Chemistry, perhaps? Conflict of some kind? A clash of personality? History? Maybe Imogen knew more than she was letting on. Lily would grill her later. She was fascinated by their dynamic and she wanted to know more. Just out of curiosity, of course.

Gallantly taking her skis from her and carrying them on his shoulder, Luc chatted to Lily about skiing and about a restaurant in town he really liked which apparently did the best fondue he'd ever had. For her part, she quizzed him about the skiing terms she'd heard that morning and laughed as he de-mystified the slang for her.

'Carving? That is turning whilst on the edge of the skis, moving from one side to the other,' Luc explained as they neared the hotel.

'Doubt I'll ever do that,' Lily tried to take her skis back, but Luc refused. 'A bomber?'

Luc frowned. 'I think that is a skier or a snowboarder coming down the mountain in a way that is out of control.'

'OK, how about traverse?'

'Going across the mountain rather than down. Zig-zag, do you call it?'

'Yes. And what was the other one?' Lily thought for a second. 'A whiteout.'

'A whiteout is when you can't see because of heavy snow or fog.' Luc set their skis down as they arrived outside the boot room.

'Crikey. I hope I never experience that. I'd be petrified.'

Lily followed Luc into the boot room. It was a large, chalet-style area with straight prods sticking out of one of the walls, some with wet ski boots hanging from them, the others bare or with slippers on. The other walls were sectioned off to hold skis.

'So your skis go in here,' Luc slotted them in for her and removed his helmet. His dirty blond hair was squashed down onto his head, but he ran a hand through and it looked all sexy-messy again. 'And your boots there.' He started removing his boots quickly. 'Shall I remove yours for you?'

'My boots? Oh no, don't be silly.' Lily sat down, wincing as her bruised bum came in contact with the solid wooden bench in the middle of the room. 'I can do it.' Bending over, she struggled with the straps and bindings, her fingers numb from the cold.

'Wait. I'll show you.'

Luc hung his boots up and went down on one knee and undid her bindings. As he released the catches on her boots, Lily let out a joyful squeak. My God, but those boots were uncomfortable! Her feet felt swollen now that the tight boots were off. It was as though the blood supply had been cut off. Lily was sure she would have marks all over her legs where the straps had been. She couldn't wait to take her thick ski socks off – even they felt restrictive.

'Oh wow, thank you,' Lily breathed. She caught a whiff of Luc's aftershave and couldn't help inhaling deeply. It was woody and masculine. She suddenly realised his head was right by her feet – which must be horribly sweaty after all those hours stuck in tight boots. And what if – God forbid – they smelt?

'Right, I'd better go,' Lily said, anxious to get her sweaty feet away from Luc's nose.

Luc stood up. 'Me too. A long bath would be good. Relax your muscles.' He looked at her face and laughed.

'What am I saying? You are a *masseuse*. You know all this.' He paused. 'Nice to meet you, Lily.'

'And you,' Lily said, still enjoying the way he said her name. She'd better not be blushing. 'Thank you for your patience today. I know I wasn't the easiest of students.'

Luc shook his head. 'No apologies. I think you were very brave today. I have some thoughts about your fear of heights, but leave it with me.'

'Oh OK. Thank you.'

'I'll see you later.' With that, Luc left.

Lily stood up and let out a yelp. Her legs were killing her. Her bum was killing her. Her arms were killing her. Her feet felt as though they had been pushed through a mangle. A hot bubble bath was definitely in order. And then Lily wanted a hot chocolate followed by a huge glass of mulled wine. Preferably followed by another one.

Chapter Ten

Lily sank into the bath and let out a contented sigh. Hot, bubbly water had never felt so good. She'd quickly washed her hair in the shower before filling the tub with scented bubble bath, keen to grab some hot water before it all disappeared. She clipped her wet, auburn hair up and laid back.

'So how was it?' Imogen came bounding in, still in her ski clothes. She sat on the edge of the bath.

'Pants,' Lily replied dramatically. She sank lower into the tub. 'Well. I was terrible, let's put it that way. Pathetic. I fell over so many times, it was cringeworthy. I'm covered in bruises and look like I've done ten rounds with Anthony Joshua. And thanks for not mentioning that I shouldn't put my ski pass next to my tits. I looked like a right wally aiming my boobs at the machine. Luc was lovely though, so it wasn't all bad.'

'Isn't he?' Imogen shot her a mischievous glance. 'Did you fancy him? And sorry about the ski pass thing.'

Lily swatted a handful of bubbles her way. 'No. Yes. I mean, who wouldn't? He's seriously hot. But I didn't actually fancy him, if you get my drift.'

'That's because you're still in a Jamie bubble.' Imogen removed her ski socks with a hiss of pleasure. 'Oh, thank God. Isn't it amazing taking your ski socks off?'

Lily grinned ruefully. 'Yes, except that mine were rank and Luc took my boots off for me. Face. Feet. Not great.'

'Luc took your boots off for you?' Imogen looked surprised. 'He's a gent, make no mistake, but I'm not sure I've seen him do that before. He must like you.'

'He likes Elodie,' Lily retorted, soaping herself down. 'Or Elodie likes him. Any goss about the two of them?' she added casually.

Imogen narrowed her eyes, as if she suspected Lily had an ulterior motive for asking, but then focused on the question. 'Hmm. There's something between them for sure, but I don't know. I don't think he seems overly interested in her if I'm honest. They're close, but I don't think it's a sex thing.' Imogen took down her ponytail, allowing her thick, ebony hair to hang freely. 'I could be wrong, of course.'

'Oh well.' Lily shrugged nonchalantly, not sure why she was even asking. Jamie had been in her thoughts on and off all day and her heart kept pinging because she missed him so badly.

'Everyone fancies Luc,' Imogen said, standing up and starting to clean her teeth. 'Because he's lovely as well as hot. But I haven't seen him with anyone since I got here.'

Lily thought about that then dismissed it. 'Am I on dinner duty again?'

'Yes. While we're still short staffed. Sylvan's made his famous duck dish tonight. All the guests love it. Do you have any massages booked for later?' Imogen finished cleaning her teeth.

'No, but I noticed that Sylvan has booked a few in.' Lily pulled a face and shuffled down deeper into the bath.

'I'm guessing he always has massages, though? Working in a kitchen?'

'No!' Imogen burst out laughing. 'He hasn't booked any massages before as far as I know. Sylvan fancies you!'

Lily shuddered. Sylvan wasn't her type and the last thing she needed was someone trying it on with her. Especially during a massage.

'Sylvan is hot on your trail. I'll have to see you and Luc together to know if you have chemistry, but I would love it if you two got it on.' Imogen.

Lily threw bubbles at Imogen. 'Shut up, Ims! I'm not here for that. And Luc is a playboy. He must be. No one looks like that and doesn't play about.'

'He's in his thirties, though,' Imogen commented reasonably. 'He's probably been a player, but I don't know if he is now. As I say, I've not seen him with a member of staff or a guest since I've been here.'

'Probably got some secret girlfriend stashed away somewhere,' Lily commented.

'Probably. Did you get back to Jamie?' Imogen pushed her dark hair out of her face.

'Not yet. I will do, though. I don't want to be rude, but I also need to totally friend-zone him.'

'Hell yes. That's absolutely the way to go.'

'How was your skiing today?' Lily asked.

'Perfection,' Imogen said, climbing out of the tub. She wrapped a towel around her and handed one to Lily. 'Once you get the hang of it and get the bug, it really is incredible. Ollie is really good, actually. He'd said he'd teach you if you want. Luc will be teaching lessons most of the time,' she added.

'Of course.' Lily got out of the bath gingerly. 'Oh man, I ache all over. That's really lovely of Ollie. I just hope he's patient. I am seriously bad.'

Imogen waved a hand. 'So was I at the start. Don't worry. Come on, we'll be late, Lils. We're on a strict timeline in this place and Celine will be on our case if we're not on time.'

'I'm on it.'

Lily hurried out of the bathroom to get dressed and blow dry her hair with the terrible hotel dryer. She still hadn't gotten back to Jamie and she was desperate to talk to him, but she simply didn't have the time.

—

Sylvan's duck dish was indeed a triumph.

Confit of duck with a cassoulet of haricot beans, pancetta and Toulouse sausage, served with duchesse potatoes according to the menu Sylvan had displayed prominently in the lounge area. Handwritten in swirly, barely legible handwriting, each course was thoroughly described. Before the main course of duck with golden swirls of baked and piped mashed potatoes, the guests had enjoyed salmon mousse choux pastries in the shape of fish. And the dessert was *Poire belle Hélène* – pears poached in a sugar syrup, served with a chocolate sauce and homemade vanilla ice cream, creamy and pale, flecked with fragrant vanilla. Quite simply, the entire menu was superb. Lily couldn't help thinking Sylvan was rather wasted in this tiny, if lovely, hotel. He could certainly work somewhere more high profile if he wanted.

Sylvan swept self-importantly through the restaurant in the manner of a Michelin-starred chef, stopping to speak graciously to guests and to discuss his culinary skills, pausing occasionally to make sure the staff had served his dishes with the leg bone facing *downwards*.

'I have booked a massage with you for Monday,' Sylvan told Lily as she walked past carrying two plates laden with duck.

'Yes, I saw that,' she replied in a civil tone, sighing inside. 'I hope you enjoy it.'

'Oh, I'm sure I will,' he replied, giving her a meaningful look.

Lily pulled a mock-horror face at Imogen as they swirled past each other in the dining area. The Devereuxs were not present, but Pierre had called a meeting in the staff area after dinner for all but a few staff who would man the bar for the guests.

'OK, time to clear away!' Sylvan clapped his hands as the last of the guests left the dining area and headed into the bar. The staff got to work, mumbling under their breath about Sylvan and his clapping.

Elodie arrived at the end to do her usual directing of staff and just generally being condescending and rude.

'Lily, if you could please make sure the tables are wiped down *properly*. And I do mean properly. There were crumbs left on the table this morning.' She threw Lily and Imogen a stern glance as if they were the culprits, even though they had been on plate duty earlier. 'Ollie, George and Joe, if you can rearrange the tables in preparation for the breakfast buffet. Amelia, Kate, you're on dish washing.'

'Who put her in charge?' Lily whispered to Imogen as they scrubbed the wooden tables down thoroughly. 'Or is she actually in charge and I'm being impolite?'

'Nope.' Imogen scrubbed a crusty spot of duchesse potato from the table. 'In the absence of Celine, Elodie thinks she's the best woman for the job. Between her and Sylvan, it's hard to get a word in edgeways.' She held her hands up and pulled her 'hey, chill' face. 'Listen, I certainly don't want to be in charge, and I doubt you do. So I can't say I'm fussed either way.'

Lily could see Imogen's point. Someone had to run the show if Celine and Pierre weren't around and maybe she was just narked because Elodie kept being obnoxious to her. But she was obnoxious towards to everyone, wasn't she? Lily wondered if Elodie had it in for her specifically, however, and she said as much to Imogen as they finished cleaning the tables.

'Have you ever thought that it might be because you're exceptionally pretty, Lily?' Imogen answered as the boys started moving the buffet tables around them. 'All new girls are a threat to the other girls and ditto the boys for the boys. I'm not saying it's exactly like that TV show *Love Island* here, but… it's basically like *Love Island*.'

'Don't be daft! I thought I'd done something to offend her.'

'No, she's genuinely just a bitch, Lils.' Imogen finished her table. 'Are you done? We'd better get off to this meeting.'

'I'm done.'

They put all the cleaning stuff away and headed to the staff area. It was a cosy room tucked away at the back of the hotel with sofas and armchairs, a large TV and a table tennis table. When they arrived, most of the sofas and armchairs had been taken and the room was practically full. All the instructors were there, including Luc, who was leaning against the wall at the far end. He smiled when he caught sight of her, then carried on chatting to whom Lily assumed must be Matteo, judging by the chamois leather complexion and the snug-fitting, turquoise all-in-one ski suit.

There was a slight hush in the chatter as the Devereuxs entered the room together. Celine, Pierre and Marc were still sporting ski gear, but Elodie had changed and she looked radiant in a pair of tight jeans and a black polo neck jumper, her golden hair around her shoulders in a straight sheet as though it had been professionally ironed.

'Thank you all for coming to this meeting,' Pierre said, taking residence at the front of the room. Celine stood by his side, with Marc and Elodie standing back slightly. Elodie seemed to be making a point of shimmying closer to Luc, but Lily might have been mistaken. Imogen clearly agreed, however, because she gave Lily an unsubtle shove in her already bruised ribs.

'I wanted to speak to you all about some issues we have been experiencing at Boutique Hotel Devereux,' Pierre was saying, his tone grave. 'This is confidential information and it is to go no further than this room. Is that understood?'

The staff looked at one another, shocked. This sounded serious.

'There have been some administrative errors,' Pierre continued. 'Mistakes with bookings, such as rooms being double-booked and overcharging for rooms with set rates. Also a few other things that haven't gone unnoticed, but are more minor compared to those offences.'

There was now a hush across the room. Lily glanced around quickly to see if anyone looked uncomfortable or guilty, but everyone just looked shocked. Elodie was watching everyone like a hawk, presumably also trying to work out who might be behind the errors.

Pierre cleared his throat and carried on. 'The Devereux family take many of these bookings, but obviously you are all on rotation and run the desk at one time or another. It hasn't been possible to ascertain who is responsible as some of these bookings were telephone bookings and I can't say for sure who was on the rota each time. On a more serious note, money has gone missing.'

There was a collective gasp. Lily was taken aback. She glanced at Imogen, who looked equally stunned. Administrative errors were one thing, but missing money was another.

Pierre looked grave. 'It saddens me to have to tell you all that, but it's happened more than once, and I am sharing this with you all in the hope that the culprit will come and see me privately and own up.'

Ollie put his hand up. 'How has money gone missing, if you don't mind me asking?'

Celine stepped forward, pushing her frizzy hair out of her eyes. 'Money has gone missing in various ways. Some from the cash box in the main office. Extra money from overcharging has been syphoned from the main account and anyone could have done that because you all leave your login information in the desk drawer.' She stared at all of them pointedly. 'Because we trust you. And because we need you to all take turns manning the desk.'

'That's terrible,' Imogen breathed. She looked around the room. 'I just don't understand how any of us could be capable of that.'

Ollie and a few others shook their heads, while other staff members looked indignant or upset.

Pierre took over again. His body language was rigid and disapproving. 'Well, I'm glad you all feel that way, but unfortunately, one of you isn't telling the truth. I will be in my office for the next three hours. I invite the person responsible to come and see me privately and I promise to be as fair as possible. I will listen to any reasons and we will work together to find a solution.' He looked saddened, his shoulders sagging briefly. 'I hope the person steps forward so we can resolve this. That's all, everyone.'

Everyone stood and looked at each other for a second and then slowly they began to melt away and leave the room. Lily and Imogen left with Ollie and headed upstairs to Lily and Imogen's room.

'Wow.' Ollie threw himself onto Imogen's bed. 'Shocking or what?'

'Defo.' Imogen joined him on the bed. 'Who do we think it is?'

Lily sat on the edge of the tiny desk. 'God knows. You know them all better than I do.'

Imogen shook her head. 'I can't imagine any of the staff doing this.'

'Even the ski instructors have access to the office,' Ollie said. 'It could be anyone. It could even be one of the family,' he added darkly.

Lily pulled a face. 'One of the Devereuxs stealing from the Devereuxs? What would be the point of that?'

Ollie looked crestfallen. 'I don't know. I was just playing Inspector Gadget.'

Imogen supressed a laugh and caught Lily's eye as if to say 'bless'. 'Anyway, let's change the subject. We know it's not us. Have you gotten back to Jamie yet?'

Lily clapped a hand to her mouth. 'God, no, I haven't! What should I say?'

'Show me what he said.' Imogen took Lily's phone. 'Hmm... I would just go back and go on about how gorgeous it is here and say that you've started skiing. Friend-zone him completely.'

'OK, good call.' Lily quickly typed a message back to that effect. 'Oh, how weird. Ivy has just sent me a message.' She looked up worriedly. 'Do you think she's with him?'

Imogen shrugged. 'Doesn't matter if she is. You just friend-zoned him so it won't look odd anyway. What did Ivy say?'

'That she misses me and hopes I've settled in.' Lily frowned. 'A very Ivy-ish text, but I'm surprised she hasn't mentioned Jamie.'

'Ask how things are going,' Imogen urged.

Lily grinned. Imogen was uber-nosy, but Lily wanted to know as well. She sent a message back and received a response from Ivy seconds later. 'It's all wonderful with Jamie!' followed by a big red heart.

Lily felt herself plummet immediately, then felt terrible. This was her sister. She should feel pleased for her.

Imogen put her hand on Lily's. 'Ouch. Sorry I made you ask.'

'That's OK.'

Ollie pretended to roll his eyes. 'Men!' he said amiably. 'We're all bastards, aren't we?'

Lily decided she rather liked Ollie. She hoped Imogen wouldn't swallow him up and spit him out the way she had with others.

'You need a distraction,' Imogen announced, sitting up.

'Oh God.' Lily cringed. 'Don't go on about Sylvan or other men please.'

Imogen tutted. 'Not men! Skiing. You need to get into skiing. Once you get the bug, you'll be totally distracted and want to do that all day long. When you're not working, that is. Ollie, we need to help her.'

Ollie sat up and saluted. 'At your service, ma'am. Tomorrow, we hit the slopes!'

As sweet as Ollie was, Lily felt her stomach churn all over again. Maybe she wasn't cut out for this skiing lark. And for some reason, she wasn't sure she was going to trust Ollie on the slopes the way she had Luc. But maybe she needed to give him a chance. Maybe skiing with Ollie would be even better.

Not believing it for a second, Lily put skiing out of her mind and carried on gossiping about who the thief might be.

Chapter Eleven

'Oh, that feels *formidable*...' Sylvan breathed happily.

Lily rolled her eyes and carried on massaging Sylvan's back with firm, professional strokes. He had requested a relaxing massage, but for some reason, using slow strokes felt inappropriate, so Lily had opted for a more breezy, impersonal approach.

'And what is that oil? It smells *delicieux*!'

'It's just sweet almond with lavender and chamomile,' Lily replied in a low voice, hoping to encourage Sylvan to not talk too much. She had lit several candles and dimmed the lights so the room was dark, but she was now worried Sylvan had mis-read the atmosphere. Perhaps he thought she had been trying to create a romantic vibe.

Lily shuddered. Hopefully not.

'Mmmm... I love the smell of lavender.'

Lily couldn't help smiling. This was the second massage Sylvan had had in as many days. And both times, he had talked enthusiastically throughout.

He had a good body, Lily observed, more from a clinical perspective than anything else. He clearly worked out in addition to being a prolific snowboarder, and he had well-defined back muscles and his arms bulged impressively. That aside, Lily felt completely unmoved by Sylvan's physique – and his effusive compliments. He simply wasn't her type.

Lily sighed. Sylvan was her third massage this morning and her mind had wandered each time. The trouble was, she really missed Jamie. She wished she didn't, but she did. She missed their chats and jokey messages and the hugs and the way he made her feel. He hadn't messaged her since the other night and even though Lily was firmly going cold turkey, she felt disappointed. But it was for the best. This was why she had come to Chamonix, after all. To get over Jamie. To put some distance between them. To let Jamie and Ivy get on with their relationship. Her heart sank at the thought. She longed for the time when she wouldn't feel that way and would be happy to hear how fabulous things were between them.

'You are helping put up all the Christmas decorations after this, yes?' Sylvan asked, lifting his head from the face hole. He had red creases all over his face.

'Er, yes. Head back down, please. I need to do your neck.'

Lily concentrated on the massage. The last thing she wanted to do was put up Christmas decorations when she still ached all over, but Celine had asked her to do it. And to be fair, she wouldn't have to clean the guest's bathrooms if she put the deccies up. She was also skiing with Ollie and Imogen later, which was making her feel horribly anxious. Lily had managed to avoid skiing over the past few days because she had so many massages with non-skiing guests, mostly women, who had them at prime skiing time: first thing in the morning during lessons and in the afternoon when lessons were over and everyone was skiing together in groups.

'There you go,' Lily said, finishing up and covering Sylvan's body with a towel. 'Take your time and I'll go and get you some iced water.'

Sylvan nodded but didn't move. Typical. The only time Sylvan relaxed and didn't speak or move was when he was due to leave. Lily stepped over the predictable little puddles of water dotted throughout the corridor – the boot room was a few doors down and snow fell off the bottom of guests' and instructors' trousers as they traipsed back to their rooms. She grabbed Sylvan's water, and as she turned back, Lily crashed straight into Luc.

'Ooh!' she shrieked, her face in his chest.

'Sorry.' Luc grinned and grabbed her elbows. He was wearing salopettes and a tight black ski top. 'I didn't mean to scare you.'

'That's OK.' Lily took a breath and released herself from his grasp. Reluctantly. 'I was miles away.'

Luc frowned, the furrow in his brow doing nothing to take away from his attractiveness. 'Miles away?'

'It's an expression. It just means I was thinking about something else.'

'Ah.' Luc's brow cleared. 'I see. Are you OK?'

'Oh yes. About to put up some Christmas decorations.'

'That's nice. Better than cleaning the toilets.'

Lily smiled. 'I guess so. And I do love Christmas.'

A shadow passed across Luc's face, but it was so fleeting, Lily wasn't sure if she was mistaken.

'You don't like Christmas?'

Luc's face closed up. So she hadn't imagined the shadow.

'No,' he said shortly.

'Oh, OK.' Lily shrugged, having the feeling there was more to it than Luc just not liking Christmas. She hadn't seen him look this serious since they had met. His face always looked on the brink of laugher. 'Not your bag.'

Luc frowned again.

'I don't know why I keep speaking to you in English idioms,' Lily sighed. 'Not your bag means... it's not your thing. You don't enjoy it.'

'Oh right. No.' Luc glanced at the floor. 'I don't enjoy it.'

'Fair enough.' Lily was intrigued. She had assumed Luc was a charming playboy, but he looked agonised right now, as though some memory was tearing him apart.

'My grandparents try to make Christmas special,' Luc commented. 'But my parents... *non*. And for me, no. I try to ignore it.'

'That's a shame,' Lily said lightly. 'Maybe I can get you to change your mind about that.'

Luc shook his head. 'I'm afraid not. But it's very nice of you to think that.'

Lily was puzzled. Luc seemed resolute. What could be so terrible about Christmas that he felt this way?

'Luc,' Sylvan appeared in the doorway of the massage room, fully dressed and glowing from his massage. He gave Luc a curt nod.

'Sylvan,' Luc said, nodding with equal seriousness, although Lily had a feeling Luc's was more of a tongue-in-cheek kind of nod. 'Good massage?'

'Amazing,' Sylvan replied rather smugly. 'Haven't you had one yet?'

'No,' Luc inclined his head, seemingly back to normal after his dark mood moments earlier. 'I'd love one soon, though. I'm hearing such good reports from everyone.'

Lily didn't know if Luc was just being polite, but if he wasn't, that was music to her ears. She prided herself on being good at her job. She wanted to ask him what he thought about Pierre and Celine's speech the other night and who he thought might be involved, but she wasn't sure Luc was the gossiping type.

Sylvan loitered for a while, then realising he was superfluous to requirements, he left, accidentally stepping in a melting snow puddle. He let out a violent, comical 'Merde!' then disappeared around the corner.

Luc looked amused, then he turned back to Lily. 'I'm glad I found you. I have this card for you.' He handed her an old-fashioned business card. It was covered in little ivy leaves and curly writing. 'A friend of the family is a hypnotherapist. She is excellent and I thought she might be able to help with your fear of heights.'

'Right...' Lily stared at the card doubtfully. She wasn't sure she believed in such things. Massage was as holistic as she got, usually. 'I suppose it couldn't hurt,' she said out loud. 'Thank you.'

'I can see that you're sceptical,' Luc said astutely. 'So maybe it's not for you. But if you really want to get past it and move on with your skiing, it might be worth a try.'

'No, you're right,' Lily said, realising she had nothing to lose. She tucked the card into her pocket. 'And I do want to get better at skiing. I have to go upstairs and find Celine. Walk with me?'

'Sure.' Luc fell into step beside her. 'Have you been skiing since our lesson?'

'No.' Lily shook her head as she climbed the stairs. 'But I'm going with Ollie this afternoon.'

'OK…' Luc's face was unreadable, but Lily had the impression he was concerned. 'Ollie is a good skier, but he's not an instructor.'

'Of course. But you guys are so busy. I can't expect you to babysit me.'

'Babysit you? I don't see it that way.' Luc climbed the stairs easily and paused at the top. 'I would like to help you. Let me check my schedule and see what I can do.'

'Thank you, but don't worry too much.' Lily had no idea why she had just said that. She wanted Luc to teach her to ski; despite her fear, she had felt at ease with him immediately and she trusted him.

'Don't let them take you higher than a green run today,' Luc warned her seriously. 'And I mean that, Lily.'

Lily loved the way he said her name. Like 'Lill-lee'.

'No higher than a green run. OK.'

Luc touched her arm. 'I am not joking. Someone with a fear of heights like you have… that will set you back weeks. I have seen this happen many times before. You need to master skiing on the nursery slopes and then you will feel confident of your ability before going up to higher, more difficult runs.'

'I'll take that on board,' Lily said. Seeing Luc hold his hands up in confusion again, she smiled contritely. 'I mean, I've heard you and I'll make sure I take your advice.'

Luc sighed, a smile making his eyes crinkle up at the edges. 'I thought my English was good before you came along. And now I realise I know nothing. *Nothing. Sacre bleu!*'

Lily laughed. She decided there was something rather cute about Luc. If a man of his height and appearance could be considered 'cute'.

'Luc. Are you keeping my new member of staff from her Christmas decorating duties?' Celine appeared next to them, giving Luc the benefit of her rather gappy smile. She was in ski clothes again, even though it didn't look as though she had been out on the slopes yet today. Lily wondered if she ever wore anything else. Celine would probably look incongruous in a dress. Or fabulous, possibly. She had the kind of model-esque figure that would probably look fantastic in anything.

'Yes,' Luc said, as if he wasn't about to apologise for it. Celine looked as though she hadn't noticed. Lily couldn't help thinking Celine always seemed distracted. Lily wondered if she was worried about the business, or about the thief in their midst. Lily knew if she'd been in Celine's shoes, she would be.

'Well, we need to get started in the reception area,' Celine said, pointing to a large plastic box. 'And then we'll move on to the restaurant.'

'I'll leave you to it,' Luc said. 'I'll be in touch, Lily. About massages and about skiing.'

'Cool.' Lily felt a bit flustered again at the thought of massaging Luc, but she decided to worry about it if he actually booked one in. She was certain he was simply being kind to her and that he didn't fancy her or anything like that.

'Let's get on with it,' Celine said in a firm voice. 'It takes ages to decorate the whole hotel.'

The whole hotel? Lily's heart sank. She loved Christmas, but this sounded like a Herculean task.

It took three and a half hours to put all the decorations up. By the end of it, Lily was Christmased-out. She and Celine and a few other helpers had decorated the reception area with traditional French decorations, including little nativity scenes and wreathes made from green foliage and little ribbons. A huge tree – a *Sapin de Noel*, according to Celine, which translated as a Christmas fir – had been erected that reminded Lily of the one in the London spa, but only in terms of its size. It was decorated with ribbons, candles, something frothy and white called 'angel hair,' and an array of pretty lights. Lily was confused when Celine placed tiny children's shoes around the bottom of the tree as well as some fake presents, but was informed that French children left their shoes there instead of stockings for Father Christmas.

'It's not something people do these days,' Celine had told Lily. 'But I like it. It's sweet, *oui*?'

'*Oui*,' Lily agreed, finding it all rather charming.

The restaurant was decked out in an alpine theme with wooden stags. Larger ones were hung from the walls and smaller ones were placed on windowsills and around the mantlepiece. More little shoes were put in and around the fireplace. They then moved on to other parts of the hotel, placing ornaments and clusters of baubles on the windowsills on the landing and tables along the corridors. Mirrors were decorated with more garlands. It seemed that the French didn't particularly favour tinsel. Not in this hotel, at any rate.

'What do you think?' Celine asked, once they had finished.

Lily took a long look around. 'It looks stunning,' she said. '*Boutique Hotel Devereux* looks ready for Christmas to arrive.'

Celine looked pleased. 'Elodie hates Christmas,' she said as they packed the boxes away to go back into storage.

Lily frowned. So Elodie and Luc had that in common. 'Oh really? Why's that?'

Celine shook her head of frizzy curls, her expression evasive. 'Aah, that's her business, but she does struggle with it every year. Are you going skiing today?'

Lily checked her phone and saw that she had a few missed messages from Imogen, telling her where she and Ollie were. 'Looks that way.'

'You don't enjoy skiing?' Celine looked as though such a concept was a pure anathema to her. For someone who lived, breathed, ate and slept skiing, it was clear that Celine had become unaccustomed to anyone who didn't do the same.

'I've only had one lesson,' Lily confessed, feeling defensive. 'And I... I don't like heights.'

Celine looked horrified. 'That's terrible! Have you tried hypnotherapy?'

'Luc gave me a card.'

'Good.' Celine looked relieved. 'You need to lose that fear, Lily. Otherwise you'll never be a good skier.'

Lily wasn't sure she wanted to be a good skier because her stomach was turning somersaults at the thought of going up a mountain again. Urged by Celine to get a move on, Lily quickly got changed, did up her excruciating ski boots (where was Luc when she needed him?) and hurried out to meet Ollie and Imogen, awkwardly carrying her skis and poles. Imogen was waiting for her at the bottom of the mountain, looking rather impatient.

'Ollie's up there somewhere, so I'll take you up in the cable car.'

'Up there? Cable car?' Lily wanted to turn and run back to the hotel. 'I don't like the sound of either of those. Why are we going in a cable car? The nursery run is over there. I haven't been any higher than that before. Luc said I shouldn't go higher than the nursery run today.'

Imogen gave her a reassuring hug, almost causing Lily to drop her skis. 'You'll be fine, I promise. I'll look after you. You're going to love it and nursery runs are only for the first day. I'm sure Luc would have taken you to this next run if he'd been skiing with you today. It's only a little blue one.'

A little blue one.

What had Luc said? No higher than a green run. Was blue harder than green? She asked Imogen, who waved an airy hand.

'Blues and greens are really similar. You could have a green that's harder than a blue, you know? It's all about the twists and the turns and the steepness.'

The twists and the turns and the steepness.

If Lily could have run in the opposite direction in her ski boots at that point, she would have done. She had barely been able to handle a nursery run a few days ago. How on earth was she supposed to handle a blue run? She was a total novice. Lily knew she'd sound like an idiot if she said that she was getting a really bad feeling about skiing today, but she was.

Imogen led the way through a turnstile and Lily was glad she had re-positioned her ski pass so she wasn't presenting her boob to the machine. Stepping heavily into the cable car, she held on for dear life as it started to move.

'Oh God,' Lily breathed. 'I am literally petrified.'

'What?' Imogen pulled a face, obviously surprised. 'I've never seen you scared in your life!'

'You've never seen me on a mountain before, that's why. Or in a cable car.' Lily leant against the window and stole a glance outside. Oh good God. How high was this thing going? Catching sight of the snowy ground disappearing beneath them, Lily closed her eyes. This was horrific. She had waves of nausea coursing through her body and she quite simply didn't want to be here. In this cable car or anywhere near a mountain.

'Lily, are you really feeling that bad?' Imogen looked worried. 'I thought you were exaggerating when you said you had this height thing going on.'

'No,' Lily muttered, wondering if her complexion was as green as she felt. 'I'm really not, Ims.'

'Oh Gawd.' Imogen looked guilty. 'Look, Ollie is such a strong skier. I know he'll be able to reassure you and get you down.'

Lily found that she couldn't speak at that point. Her mouth felt parched, as though it were full of cotton wool. As the cable car alighted at the top of the mountain, Lily caught sight of the view. Stunning. But Jesus, they were high up. She stepped out of the cable car, almost slipping because she was so nervous. Ollie was waiting for them, surrounded by some of the other chalet staff. Including Elodie.

'Lily,' Elodie said, eyeing Lily's random selection of ski clothes scathingly. 'I didn't realise you were joining us today.'

Lily opened her mouth to speak, then closed it again. Without a gallon of water, she wasn't going to be able to articulate anything because this felt like the worst case of dehydration.

'She's not,' Imogen told Elodie smartly. 'She has a private lesson with Ollie today.'

Elodie sneered. 'I didn't realise Ollie was a qualified instructor.'

Imogen narrowed her eyes and was about to retaliate, but Ollie stepped in. Not literally, because he was on skis, but figuratively.

'I'm not a qualified instructor,' he said agreeably. 'But I am pretty good at this and I think I can help Lily.'

'We can *all* help Lily,' Elodie said, clearly wanting to see Lily skiing and failing miserably at it. 'Luc said she did very well the other day.'

'Yes,' chorused the rest of the staff, sounding far kinder than Elodie.

'We'll get you down,' Amelia said.

'We will,' Joe nodded.

Knowing that everyone apart from Elodie was being genuinely encouraging and supportive, Lily suddenly found herself trembling all over. The thought of skiing in front of all of these people was utterly terrifying. The thought of skiing itself was terrifying, let alone doing it in front of people she didn't know who were most likely superb at it.

'We're not skiing with them,' Imogen assured her quietly.

'Good, because I can't… I simply can't…'

Lily clutched her poles, not sure what to do with herself. Her heart was pounding, she was sweating and aside from it being chilly, she was feeling cold all over. She desperately wanted a helicopter to descend onto the top of the snow-capped mountain and fly her away. Or to be whisked away on a skidoo, or whatever the things were that looked like jet skis on ice. Or to strap on a parachute if anyone had one and just... no, maybe not that one. Lily would still have to confront her fear that way. Looking around, she could see everyone watching her eagerly, wanting her to enjoy this sport they were passionate about. Wanting her to love it as much as they did. The pressure felt suffocating and the sense of panic was overwhelming.

'I think we should all leave Lily alone,' Amelia said, out of the blue, sliding closer to Lily. 'I have this horrible fear of cats and it makes me go like that – all shaky and weird and like I could faint.'

'Yes,' Lily whispered, swallowing repeatedly to try and get some saliva into her mouth. 'That.'

'I'm telling you, I couldn't even *stroke* a cat,' Amelia said vehemently. 'If one walked up to me now...' She shuddered. 'God! Even the thought of it is making me freak out. So if you feel anything like that, Lily...'

'That's exactly how I feel,' Lily managed, wishing she could squash down her feelings of panic. How had Luc managed to do this with her the other day? Lily was sure she had felt just as bad as she did now.

'Right.' Amelia took control and Lily could have hugged her. If she could have achieved that on skis. 'We're going and we're leaving Lily, Ollie and Imogen here.' She pushed her poles into the snow and started to move away. 'Follow me, guys...'

Looking affronted that she wasn't in charge because she was a Devereux and clearly thought she was the best skier, Elodie followed Amelia and everyone else waved and followed them. They soon disappeared down the mountain, dropping down one after another like brightly coloured lemmings.

'Right.' Ollie looked at Lily sympathetically. 'Let's get started. I know you're scared, but sometimes being thrown into the deep end a little can make you overcome anything.'

Lily started to shake again. Being thrown into the deep end? No way. That was the last thing she wanted.

'I'm assuming you can do snow plough turns,' Ollie said, snapping his goggles down over his eyes. 'So that's all we're going to do here. It's the same thing, just down a slightly steeper slope.'

Shit, shit, shit. Lily wanted to throw up. Why on earth was she up here on a blue run? The nursery slope had scared the living daylights out of her.

'Trust him,' Imogen pleaded, putting her hand on Lily's arm. 'It'll be OK...'

Not trusting herself to speak in case a barrage of swear words came out, Lily pulled her goggles down and gritted her teeth. She would rather be anywhere but here. Literally *anywhere* but here.

'We're heading for that restaurant down there.' Ollie pointed with his pole to a pretty chalet-style building covered with Christmas fairy lights.

'OK,' Lily said with teeth that were chattering. Not from the cold, but from sheer terror.

'We're going to shuffle over to the edge here.'

The edge. Even the expression made Lily feel panicked. She shuffled closer, her legs wobbling, and she was grateful when Imogen held on to her.

'You're doing great,' Imogen assured her.

Lily couldn't even speak at this point. Fear was consuming her like a cold, snowy blanket and she wanted to vomit.

'Lily, if you want to go back down in the cable car, I'll take you,' Imogen said suddenly, grabbing Lily's pole anxiously. 'Ollie, I don't think she should go down there.'

'Ims.' Ollie threw her a confident smile. 'I can do this. Lily. We are going to head across the mountain. OK? Not down, across. All we have to do is get from side to side. I'll go first, you follow and then Imogen can go behind you.'

Lily nodded. She could hear the blood thumping in her ears. As she looked over the edge of the mountain, she felt her legs go slightly out from under her.

'We're going across like this.' Ollie set off sideways, snow ploughing across the steep, snowy mountain face. He made it look so easy, gliding across and flaring one ski out to the side to turn. 'It's all about the weight distribution. Lean from side to side and then you'll…'

His voice was lost as he travelled further down. Where the hell was he? Luc had stayed with her the whole time. Lily felt her entire body tense as she set off, which Luc had told her was the worst possible thing to do because skiing was about being relaxed and just allowing the body to glide and turn with controlled but graceful movements.

Lily felt herself shaking all over as she crossed the mountain. She tried to remember everything Luc had taught her a few days ago, but her mind had gone blank.

Ollie was miles away and Imogen was behind her. The slope was so steep! Horribly steep. Nothing like the nursery run. It was as though she had gone from flat to vertical. Lily had never felt so out of control in her life.

She managed to do a clumsy snow plough turn and started talking to herself as she crossed the mountain. *You can do this. You just have to get across and turn. That's all you need to do. Don't look down. Do. Not. Look. Down.*

Another voice popped into her head. '*Don't be such a BABY, Lily! So what if it's high? Don't be so weak. Why can't you do this? Everyone else can do this. It's EASY. You must be so stupid…*'

With that, Lily lost her nerve completely. She was flailing about all over the place, her skis doing their own thing, her poles stabbing desperately at the air as if it might somehow help her. Lily gathered speed and momentum and found her skis pointing downwards, rather than across. She was going down the mountain. Fast. She thought her pounding heart might burst right out of her chest. Imogen was screaming to Ollie to help her and out of the corner of her eye, she could see Ollie turning around and doing some weird sliding thing with his skis to get to her.

But Lily couldn't seem to stop. She could hear Ollie yelling at her to slow down, to turn. To point her skis together at the front and hold them in a triangle. Lily could hear him, but she couldn't seem to do anything. Fear had taken hold and she was a gibbering mess. As she hurtled down the mountain faster than most of the competent skiers alongside her, Lily had no time to think. She could barely breathe. She sensed Ollie nearby but still couldn't seem to steer herself. She was petrified that if she lost her balance, she might break every bone in her body.

'Slow down!' Ollie shouted next to her. 'Snow plough, SNOW PLOUGH!'

Lily did her best to angle her legs, but her skis seemed to have a mind of their own. She could see the lights from the pretty chalet they were headed for getting closer and closer and closer and the panic in her chest was almost painful. How was she going to stop? She tore down the mountain, heading for the chalet. Should she just fall over?

Lily was seconds away from the chalet. Imogen had caught up and Lily could hear her screaming commands to her, but she couldn't make sense of them. Lily careered off to one side suddenly, managing to slow down. She turned her skis into a snow plough and skidded towards a wooden shack. Then smacked into it. Hard.

Lily's poles went through in the air, she lost her skis and fell in a heap.

'Oh my God, Lily!' Imogen snapped herself out of her skis and dropped to her knees. 'Are you OK? Did you hit your head?'

Ollie sent up a spray of snow as he stopped and leapt out of his skis. 'Lily. Shit. Are you all right?' He took his goggles off. 'I'm so, so sorry. I had no idea you were that scared.'

Lily stared at both of them, dazed. 'I think I hit my head,' she mumbled. And then everything went black.

Chapter Twelve

Twelve Hours Later

Lily groggily opened her eyes. Where the hell was she? And sweet Jesus, why did her head hurt so much? She ached all over. Her arms, her legs, her stomach. But especially her head.

'Lily? Can you hear me?'

With difficulty, Lily turned her head to the side and saw Imogen sitting on the bed, staring at her worriedly. She had tears in her eyes and looked as though she'd been sitting there for ages; her black hair was in disarray and there were sooty lines of eyeliner streaking her cheeks.

'Where am I?'

'You're in your bed. In the hotel room. *Boutique Hotel Devereux*,' Imogen added, clutching Lily's hand.

'I know the name of the hotel, Ims.' Lily tried to sit up but couldn't. She wanted to say something about the fact that they all kept saying 'Boutique' in front of the Hotel Devereux bit, but she couldn't seem to form the words properly.

'We thought you had a concussion,' Imogen said tearfully. 'You've been into hospital and brought back again after lots of tests. And since then, you've been asleep and I've been so scared, but they told me it was fine and not to worry…'

She started to cry again, rubbing at her face like a child. It reminded Lily of how Imogen used to look when she got royally pissed and they'd stumble out of nightclubs together when they were younger. She was always crying wretchedly over some man and looking wrecked afterwards.

Lily touched her head gingerly. There was a large bandage that had tape all around it and she could feel a lump like an egg underneath it.

'Wowzers. That's a big bump. Do I have bruises?'

Imogen let out a distressed squeak. 'Oh, Lils. I don't even want to show you.'

Lily felt alarmed. What did Imogen mean? 'Get me a mirror. Please,' she asked, feeling anxious.

Imogen looked upset, but she grabbed her make-up bag and took out a compact. 'Brace yourself,' she said, wincing as she handed the mirror over.

Lily swallowed and opened the compact. Holding it to her face, she gasped. She had two black eyes. Great, big circles of black around her eyes like a panda. But definitely nowhere near as cute as a panda.

'Bloody hell,' she said, wanting to cry.

'I know,' Imogen nodded. 'But I have make-up. Really good make-up. The kind that covers up tattoos, remember? The way I cover my arm up when I go and see my mum?'

Lily smiled, but even that hurt. 'Wow. I don't even know if your tattoo make-up will cover this up. I look *ridiculous*. And I am in so much pain.'

'Poor Ollie is so upset,' Imogen told her. 'He brought those for you this morning.' She pointed to a large bouquet of pink and white flowers displayed in a vase. 'He's been beside himself.'

'It's OK,' Lily said, struggling to sit up but managing it with Imogen's help. 'It's not his fault. I shouldn't have gone down that blue run. Luc said not to. But I just wanted to do it, you know? I wanted to see if I could overcome my fear.'

Imogen pushed her hair out of her face. 'It was terrifying, Lils. I was so scared you were going to break your neck.'

'Yeah, me too,' Lily said ruefully.

'Everyone has been into see you, even the Devereuxs.'

'Not Luc, I hope?' For some strange reason, Lily felt mortified at the thought of Luc seeing her like this.

'Not Luc, no, but he has asked after you several times and those flowers are from him.' Imogen pointed to a vase of beautiful yellow roses.

Lily broke into a smile, then made her face sober again when she realised Imogen was watching her with great interest. 'What? I like roses.'

About to say something, Imogen was distracted by Lily's phone ringing. 'It's your mum,' she said, handing it over. 'Celine phoned them about your accident.'

'Lordy.' Lily answered the phone. 'Hey.'

'Lily!' Sue sounded distraught. 'Are you all right?'

'We've been so worried about you! *So* worried about you!' Dave called out.

'I'm all right,' Lily assured them. 'I look like I've been boxing and I think I hate skiing, but I'm OK.'

'Lily, what happened?' It was Ivy. She sounded calm and in control, but Ivy could appear as cool as a cucumber even when she was in the throes of a panic attack.

Lily gave them a quick rundown of her accident. 'And then I don't remember anything after that,' she finished. 'I think I passed out.'

'She had a mild concussion,' Imogen explained, taking the phone, 'but she's recovering well.' She prudently didn't mention Lily's bruises.

'Was someone with you? Like, an instructor?'

Lily caught Imogen's eye. It was Jamie's voice.

'Not an instructor, no. Imogen's friend Ollie was teaching me.'

'What kind of run were you on?' Jamie sounded frantic.

Lily wasn't sure why he sounded so freaked out. 'A blue.'

'A blue?' Jamie was practically shrieking now. 'You shouldn't be on a blue this early on! What was this Ollie thinking? No wonder you had a tumble! Blues can have moguls and jumps and oh my GOD. That's absurd!'

'Calm down, Jamie!' Ivy sounded cross. 'It's done now. It's not Lily's fault. She's new to all this.'

Sue interrupted. 'Darling, do you want to come home? I could look after you here. Dave could come and collect you.'

'Of course, of course,' Dave called out.

'I'm fine,' Lily said firmly. 'I don't need to come home. I'll need to rest up a bit and then I just want to get back to work.'

'And no more skiing without an instructor,' Jamie cut in. 'People who ski always think they can teach and they can't and it's so *bloody* dangerous.'

'OK, Dad,' Lily said, rolling her eyes at Imogen.

'Sorry.' Jamie went quiet. 'I'm just worried about you. We all are. Maybe I should come and check the place out. I hate the thought of you having accidents.'

'Jamie.' It was Ivy. 'Go over if you want to, but only to ski! Lily is a grown woman. She can take care of herself.'

'Absolutely,' Lily agreed. 'It's all fine. I have an excellent instructor called Luc who will be teaching me from now on.' Lily had no idea if she was ever setting foot on a mountain again, but she felt that she had to reassure everyone. 'And Ollie is absolutely lovely; he just didn't realise I had this terrible fear of heights.'

'Let's let her rest,' Dave said. Even he sounded jolted and not his usual cheery self. 'Lily needs rest.'

'He's right,' Sue said, still sounding upset. 'We all love you, Lily, and if you want to come home, we are here for you.'

'Love you all. Bye,' Lily said, ending the call. 'Crikey. What a fuss.'

'So Jamie sounded all cut up,' Imogen commented, clearly intrigued. 'I wonder how Ivy felt about that?'

'No idea.'

Lily didn't want to think about Jamie. All she could think about was being up and about and covering up her awful bruises. But Lily felt a pang in her chest. She missed Jamie. She really, really missed Jamie. He was her friend, a close friend who had almost been a best friend. And not talking to him like they used to – almost on a daily basis – was excruciating. Hearing his voice like that had been heaven. But horrible too.

Imogen gave her a sympathetic smile. 'I know. It's shit. Especially since he obviously really cares about you. But you're going to be all right. You'll look like a panda for a while, but you'll be all right.'

'Yeah.' Lily let out a weighty sigh. 'I'll be fine. Gotta stop mooning after him, haven't I? That's why I came here, after all.'

'That and to head butt a ski shack,' Imogen responded. 'Well, at least you won't have to be on breakfast duty for a while,' she added innocently. 'Not with a face like that.'

'Every cloud,' Lily said, feeling drowsy again. 'God, I think I need to sleep again.'

'Go to sleep. I'm not going anywhere,' Imogen said, taking up her position on the bed again.

And with that, Lily fell into another long, deep sleep.

–

A few days later, Lily was feeling much more with it. Her headache was gone, the lump on her head had gone down and she was moving about and feeling fairly normal. The only problem now was that the bruises on her face had gone from black to a rainbow of colours ranging from pale green to lemon and brown. And she was due downstairs for some Christmas cocktail party for the guests. She was wearing a cream jumper dress, with black tights and little black ankle boots – but it all clashed with her face. Or her face clashed with her outfit. One of the two.

'Do not stress,' Imogen said. 'I am here with my make-up palette. Sit back and let me get your face back to its best.' She got to work with brushes and sponges, blending away furiously, every so often taking a step back to assess her work.

'There,' she said, giving Lily's face a final dab. 'Check you out.'

Lily looked in the mirror and her mouth fell open. She looked almost normal! Not completely normal, because it was noticeable that she had a fair amount of make-up on and she was normally fairly fresh-faced, but still. She had left her auburn hair loose in the hope it would cover her face, but she could definitely be seen in public.

'It's a miracle! Thank you.'

'Least I can do,' Imogen said, looking shame faced. 'I'm still having nightmares about you hurtling down that mountain and so is Ollie.'

Lily shook her head. 'Stop. Let's go. I need to get out of this hotel room. What's a Christmas cocktail party anyway? A cocktail party with a Christmas theme or a party with Christmas cocktails?'

'Good point! Not a clue. Let's go.'

They headed downstairs and Lily even enjoyed seeing different walls and views out of the window. She had been going stir-crazy shut away for days like that. Various staff members – even Elodie, who looked as though she might snigger at the state of Lily's face – had taken it in turns to bring her food. She had dined on *daube provençale* (braised beef stew with vegetables, wine and garlic), baked salmon fillet with a mouth-watering salsa containing fresh herbs and a tangy vinaigrette, and a clam spaghetti drenched with garlic and chilli that had been to die for. But eating in bed had never been her thing and Lily couldn't wait to get back to what had become her new normal.

The hotel looked extremely Christmassy with all the decorations up and pretty snowflakes drifting past the vast windows on each floor. Even the air smelt Christmassy, like fir cones and gingerbread. Lily realised it was coming from the candles that had been placed around the hotel, their lights glowing warmly in dark corners.

Downstairs in the reception area, guests and staff were milling around, holding cocktails and chatting. Christmas music played in the background. It was mostly English pop music – Wham's Last Christmas and the like. Lily felt strange, even homesick for a moment, but maybe it was just that she missed Jamie.

Celine, in ski clothes as always, was talking loudly and passionately about skiing and she smiled brightly at Lily when she caught sight of her. Elodie – and Luc, for that matter – were noticeably absent. Which probably meant something, but Lily didn't care to think about it.

Pierre came over immediately, looking like the Milk Tray man in an all-black outfit. His face was concerned, but as ever, there was a level of detachment in his expression. 'Lily. You poor girl. I do hope you're feeling better?'

'Much better, thanks,' she said, touching her face self-consciously.

Marc, looking equally suave in a smart blue shirt and jeans, joined his father and gave Lily a funny little bow. 'Sorry to hear of your accident. That particular blue run can be exceptionally fast when it's icy.'

A crestfallen Ollie rushed over to give her a hug. 'I'm so sorry,' he said, squeezing her. 'I feel so awful. I should never have—'

'It's OK.' Lily brushed his apology off with a smile, mostly because he looked so crushed and she didn't want him to feel bad.

'They've told me off,' Ollie said, hanging his head in Pierre and Marc's direction. 'Apparently I did the classic move of taking a beginner up to a slope that was too high too soon.'

Pierre nodded, throwing Ollie a stern glance. 'Even without a fear of heights, it can destroy someone's confidence. That's often it for the beginner for the entire week of skiing.'

Marc shook his head disparagingly and Lily immediately felt the need to defend Ollie. 'It's my fault, not his. I went down it and I shouldn't have done. Lesson learnt.'

'Hmm.' Looking unimpressed, Pierre left them to it and started chatting to some nearby guests. Marc also took his leave.

'So it's a party with Christmas cocktails,' Imogen informed Lily, pressing a glass into her hand. 'This is a champagne cocktail with *fraise de bois*. That's wild strawberry liqueur to you and me.'

'Wow.' Lily stared at the cocktail. It was served in a champagne flute, half with champagne and half with a pink-red liquid. Cranberries dipped in sugar, meant to look like snow, hung from the side of the glass. It looked exquisite. And it tasted divine.

'Sylvan has his uses,' Imogen agreed. She and Lily had always loved cocktails, even when they were young. Dave used to serve them snowballs when they were too young to drink, in cocktail glasses, with a maraschino cherry bobbing in the frothy yellow liquid. When he ran out of Advocaat, he would allow them a tiny drop of Babycham, the bubbles tickling their noses and making them giggle.

'That's *delicious*, Lils. There's a winter spiced pear cocktail with star anise on top and a really alcoholic one with Aperol and chocolate bitters in it with orange rind on the side and a chocolate ball on top. A real chocolate ball!'

'He's a genius,' Lily exclaimed. 'Creating incredible food is one thing, but these are things of great beauty...'

'You like?' Sylvan suddenly appeared at Lily's elbow.

'Very much. They are so beautiful too. Really.'

'Your face looks better,' Sylvan said, getting rather too close.

Lily took a discreet step backwards. 'Er... don't get too close. I look terrible under all this make-up.'

'Not possible,' Sylvan said gallantly. 'I hope you will be ready to give me another massage soon?'

'Yes, of course,' Lily said, adopting a professional tone.

'Here, try one of these,' Sylvan suggested, pressing a delectable-looking pastry into her hands. 'It's called a *bouchée à la reine*. It's chicken and morel mushrooms in a white wine sauce.'

It's a vol-au-vent, Imogen mouthed behind Sylvan's back, sniggering like a naughty schoolgirl.

'It's amazing,' Lily commented, shoving Imogen discreetly. And it was. Regardless of it being a *vol-au-vent*, it was a fancy one, worthy of far more than being show-cased in a hotel next to a ski resort. Stealing another glance at Sylvan, Lily frowned inwardly. No, she still didn't fancy him. What a shame. Such a fantastic chef. And any man who could make cocktails like that...

She looked up as Luc arrived, closely followed by Elodie. Lily felt a thud of disappointment, but she didn't really know why. Luc was wearing a puffer brown jacket with a fur hood and slouchy jeans with boots and Elodie wore a similar puffer jacket in black with black jeans and a sleek, cream jumper with long silver chains around her neck.

Luc came straight over. 'Lily. How are you feeling? I'm so sorry I haven't visited. Imogen wouldn't allow me in the room.'

Lily suppressed a smile. Good old Ims. She knew Lily wouldn't have wanted Luc to visit her with all her horrible bruises.

'That's OK. Thank you for the roses.'

'*De rien*,' Luc waved a hand. 'You are very welcome. How do you feel about skiing now?'

'Terrified. Like, even more than I was before.' Lily was grateful that Luc wasn't saying 'I told you so' about her going down a blue run when she shouldn't have done. 'But oddly, I don't want to give up on it.'

'Good. Good for you.' Luc rubbed his chin. 'If you want to sort the hypnotherapy out, I'll come with you. If you want me to?'

Lily found herself grinning at him. 'That's so nice of you. Yes, OK. I'm definitely willing to give it a go. If I can get my fear of heights under control, I hope I can learn to ski, even if it's only on green runs.'

'I'm confident we can get you beyond green runs,' Luc told her.

'I'll owe you a free massage if you do,' Lily said without thinking. Since when had she offered massages out as payment for anything?

Luc's dark eyes were fixed upon her and Lily felt herself squirming slightly. Was he laughing at her? If she didn't know better, she might have thought he was *smouldering* at her. But surely not. Lily must be mistaken.

'I may well take you up on that,' he replied finally, not taking his eyes off hers. It was disconcerting and rather delicious at the same time.

At that point, Elodie joined them and slipped her arm through Luc's. 'Aah Lily. I heard about your accident. Poor you. Your face looks really, really bad.'

Lily wanted to laugh out loud. Elodie looked stunning tonight, but she was so bloody offensive.

Luc frowned at Elodie. 'Her face looks great. She skied into a shack, Elodie.'

Elodie shrugged, pursing her beautiful mouth and tightening her grip on Luc's arm. 'Will you try to ski again?' she asked Lily, managing to look completely disinterested.

'Yes,' Lily replied firmly. 'Definitely.'

And in fact, Elodie was spurring her on to do it – and to do it well. So maybe it wasn't a bad thing that she was a bit of a bitch. She watched Luc and Elodie, trying to work out their body language. Elodie fancied Luc; that much was clear. What Lily couldn't work out was whether or not Luc fancied Elodie. Equally, it wouldn't surprise her if they were an item, because there was a relaxed closeness between them which could mean anything from deep friendship to something far more. Not that any of it mattered, of course. Lily was just intrigued.

'Let's sort out that hypnotherapy,' Luc said to Lily as Elodie dragged him away. 'We'll catch up soon.'

She nodded and watched them as Elodie forced what looked like an espresso martini with a festive crumb around the rim – gingerbread maybe? – on him and helped herself to a winter spiced pear cocktail. Elodie glanced over at Lily then leant into Luc and whispered something in his ear. She giggled prettily and Luc laughed and shook his head.

Were they laughing at her? Lily suddenly felt incredibly tired and rather embarrassed. Maybe Luc wasn't the great guy she thought he was. Maybe he was under Elodie's spell far more than she had imagined. In fact, Lily wasn't sure she was attracted to Luc after all.

'Do you wanna split?' Imogen said. 'Celine said we can duck out if you've had enough.'

'Yes please,' Lily said gratefully. 'I feel as though I've had the stuffing completely knocked out of me for some reason.'

'Totes understand,' Imogen said, tucking her arm though Lily's the way Elodie had with Luc. 'Let's go back to our room. Netflix and chill.'

'What? That means something else, you silly woman.'

'It's OK,' Imogen told her comfortably. 'We don't have Netflix.'

'Phew,' Lily said. Luc gave her a lovely smile as they left the reception area and Lily managed a small one in return, perplexed. The smile had seemed genuine, but hadn't he and Elodie been sneering at her just now? Lily wasn't sure if she could trust Luc at all now.

Chapter Thirteen

A few days later, Lily was sitting in a café in central Chamonix in the main square, drinking a spectacular hot chocolate that made her yearn for a Terry's chocolate orange. It was the kind of hot chocolate that came in a big glass mug filled with melted chocolate that was laced with orange liqueur. It was topped with cream, mini marshmallows and a flake. There were also mini gingerbread men around the base of the mug. It had cost an arm and a leg, but it was worth it. It was like Christmassy heaven in a cup.

Sitting in front of her was the card Luc had given her for the hypnotherapist. She still hadn't made the call and she hadn't been anywhere near a mountain. She was looking out onto a Christmas market with lots of little wooden huts strung with fairy lights, selling Christmas decorations, festive drinks, wooden ornaments, cookies and much more. Lily loved markets like this. Such a lovely, busy atmosphere and it all looked so festive.

'Lily?'

Lily looked up to find Luc standing in front of her. He was wearing his red ski instructor's jacket and had clearly just come off the slopes. Lily couldn't help thinking about the way he and Elodie were laughing at her the other night and she stiffened slightly.

'Hey. Good lesson?'

'Great lesson.' Luc gestured to the seat opposite. 'May I?'

Lily nodded and watched as he ordered himself a coffee after checking if she wanted another hot chocolate.

'God, no thanks. Delicious, but calorific, I should imagine.'

Luc pointed to the card in her hand. 'Do you have an appointment?'

Lily bit her lip. 'Not yet.'

Luc leant forward, putting his tanned hands on the table. 'Listen. What happened to you on that slope must have been terrifying. And it's totally understandable. But if you want to overcome this, I truly believe hypnotherapy will help you.'

'I've totally lost my nerve,' Lily confessed, twisting her hands in front of her. 'I want to conquer this, but I don't know if I can bring myself to confront it, you know?'

Luc sipped his coffee. 'Yes, of course. But the hypnotherapy will calm you down and prepare you. Why don't you phone now? What do you have to lose?'

Lily swallowed, feeling her hot chocolate churning in her stomach. What *did* she have to lose? Maybe she'd have the hypno and she wouldn't feel any different, but at least she would have tried.

'And I will teach you to ski,' Luc told her. 'I will arrange for you to have lessons with me once I have completed my ones for the hotel.'

Lily stared at him. Why was he being so nice to her? Especially if he was seeing Elodie? But if anyone was going to teach her to ski, Lily knew she would choose Luc.

'OK.' She made a decision. 'I'm calling the hypnotherapist now.' She took out her phone and made the call, Within seconds, she was speaking to a kindly-sounding lady who spoke excellent English. Her name was Bernadette.

'I have two appointments free tomorrow, and…' There was a pause. 'I actually have a cancellation today. But it's in ten minutes' time. Could you do that?'

'In ten minutes.' Lily gulped. Talk about being thrown into the deep end. She met Luc's eyes and he gave her an encouraging smile. He mouthed something to her. 'OK. Ten minutes. I'll see you then. No, Luc says he'll take me there so I don't need the address.'

Lily ended the call and realised her hands were shaking. 'God, what's wrong with me? It's only hypnotherapy.'

'About something you're petrified of.' Luc paid the bill and led the way out of the cafe.

'This market is so pretty, isn't it?' Lily commented as they strolled through the square. 'So Christmassy…'

Luc shrugged. 'I suppose.'

Lily could have kicked herself. 'Sorry, I forgot you hate Christmas.'

'That's ok. It's not your fault.' Luc gave her a brief smile.

'Maybe one day you'll tell me why,' Lily said daringly.

Luc glanced at her, seeming surprised. 'Maybe,' he replied.

Lily didn't know why she'd even said that to Luc. They were hardly close. She really didn't even know him. She was sure she was the last person he would confide in. She walked alongside him, pleased to be in normal boots rather than ski boots. Luc clonked along beside her, but somehow seemed to make the motion natural rather than awkward. He led her through some narrow lanes and across a bridge and then, suddenly, they were there.

'Here.' He rang the doorbell. There was a small pause and then a petite elderly lady with short coiffed hair and a neat outfit of tailored trousers and a thin jumper opened the door. She had dark eyes, like juicy currants, and she looked kind.

'Luc.' She held her powdered cheek out to him and he kissed it, then kissed the other. 'And this is Lily,' he said, standing aside politely.

Not sure if she should kiss or shake hands, Lily was glad when Bernadette leant over and kissed both cheeks.

'Lovely to meet you,' Bernadette said. 'Come inside. Luc, will you wait?'

'Oh, you don't need to do that…' Lily started.

'I won't wait, actually,' Luc replied, checking his watch.

Lily felt disappointed and berated herself silently. Why on earth would he wait? An initial session lasted for two hours.

'I'll get changed, sort some work out at the hotel and come back,' Luc said.

Lily was about to protest, but then she realised she didn't have a clue how to get back to the hotel. She hadn't been paying any attention as they were walking to Bernadette's house, so she'd have a nightmare finding her way alone.

Yes, that's why I want him to come back and collect me, Lily told herself wryly, not sure she believed her own thoughts at this point. Nonetheless, she was going with it.

'*Bon.*' Bernadette gave Luc an affectionate smile and showed him out. 'Come this way, Lily.' Bernadette led the way through a cottage-style property with cute little windows and uneven floors. They passed through a sitting room, a large kitchen and out into a sunny dining area at the back. Each room was decorated with pretty Christmas lights and dark green garlands and in the dining area there was a lovely real fir tree with green, white and red decorations on every branch.

'It's such a pretty house,' Lily commented, taking a seat on the squashy grey couch Bernadette had offered her. There was a little table nearby with water in a carafe, glasses and a box of tissues. Two ginger cats were curled up under a dresser in a basket. They were so intertwined that it was impossible to see where one head began and where the other one's tail ended. There was a fire burning in the hearth behind Bernadette's chair and it danced and roared gently in the background, the logs letting out the odd hiss as they moved.

'Thank you. I've lived here all my life, believe it or not.' Bernadette settled herself in a nearby armchair. 'I hope the cats don't bother you?'

'I love cats. It's so Christmassy in here,' Lily said, starting to feel apprehensive about the hypnotherapy. It felt very real now and she wasn't sure she was going to like it. 'Luc hates Christmas,' she blurted out, even though she wasn't sure why she had brought him up.

'Yes, he does,' Bernadette agreed. She regarded Lily with interest, her eyes lighting up. 'How well do you know Luc?'

'Oh, not at all,' Lily said, tugging a cushion onto her lap and pleating the folds absent-mindedly. 'I've only just met him. He mentioned it the other day when he was teaching me to ski and I… was intrigued, I guess. I love Christmas. And I've never met someone so violently opposed to it.'

Lily glanced out the window. 'It must be tough for him here with Christmas around every corner.'

Bernadette nodded slowly. 'I see. Well. Luc has his reasons when it comes to Christmas and maybe he'll tell you about them when he gets to know you better.' She smiled at Lily. 'Let's get to your fear of heights and see if we can understand what the issues are. And then I can see if I can help you.'

'Sounds good.' Lily fidgeted. She felt uncomfortable and she couldn't put her finger on why. She felt exposed, but deep down, she knew that this was probably going to help her.

'So, tell me about skiing with Luc the other day,' Bernadette started writing on a notepad. 'What did you feel? What memories did it bring up?'

Lily took a deep breath. 'I felt petrified. I thought I was going to die. I felt panicked because… because I think I felt as though I might not be able to do it.'

'Why?'

'Because… because… I thought I wasn't going to be any good at it, perhaps?' Lily met Bernadette's kind eyes and chewed her lip. 'Because my fear of the height, being that high up, I just fell apart.'

'What memories came to mind when you were at the top of the mountain?' Bernadette asked, her pen poised over her notepad.

Lily started to feel panicked again. She felt the fear and dread rising inside her the way it had at the top of the mountain and, once again, she could hear her dad's voice playing inside her head.

'*Why can't you do that? Everyone else can do it. What are you scared of? Why are you being a sissy? You're such a BABY...*'

Lily felt tears choking in her throat.

'Talk to me,' Bernadette said gently. 'If you can.'

Lily hesitated, then began to relay the voice to Bernadette the way she could hear it in her head. She talked about being up high with her dad and about the way he had treated her. How it had affected her. What it had made her feel. There was something about Bernadette's sympathetic eyes and compassionate nature that made her easy to confide in.

Bernadette put her notepad down. 'Aah. So this makes sense now.'

'And then I had this awful fall.' Lily touched the bump on her head as she talked about careering down the blue run and crashing into the ski shack. 'I blacked out, but it was so painful. And I was aching and hurting for days afterwards.'

'That must have been so frightening for you.' Bernadette shook her head. 'I can't imagine how terrifying. You're very brave even talking about it now. You've been through some serious trauma. How do you feel when talking about your dad?'

'I hate talking about him.' Lily felt her stomach tighten.

Bernadette said nothing. She waited.

Lily swallowed. Her mouth felt dry again, the way it had at the top of the mountain with Luc. 'It's... he was... he was a bully,' she stated finally. 'To me and to my mum. Not so much to my sister, for some reason. But he used to pick on me constantly.'

'Is he still in your life?'

'No.' Lily shook her head. 'He left when I was ten. He left us with absolutely nothing to go start a new life with his mistress, who became his third wife. He really hurt my mum. He used to hit her and I couldn't do a thing about it.'

Bernadette's face softened. 'That must have been very hard for you. Especially as a child.'

Lily shrugged. 'It was horrible for a while. We had no money and my dad really messed things up for us.' She stopped, not sure she wanted to go into more details. She touched her face. It was wet from tears she hadn't even been aware she'd been shedding. 'My mum is fine now. She's married to Dave, who is very kind and sweet and he adores her. And she adores him. They're very happy.'

'That's good. I'm so glad she has met a lovely man and has a solid, caring relationship. But you have been very damaged by this.' Bernadette put her head on one side thoughtfully. 'And you probably don't think about him that much if you can help it, but up that mountain, all of those feelings came rushing back. The bullying, the pain of how he treated your mum. Briefly, you became a child again – in pain, terrified. I think this is all tied up in your fear of heights.'

Lily stared at Bernadette. That made so much sense. Why hadn't she seen that? Why hadn't she realised that it wasn't so much the heights, it was the bullying that had come with it, that had triggered her fear in the first place?

'Yes. Yes, I think that's it. I haven't been up anywhere high since that incident. Not until now.'

'I'm not surprised.' Bernadette asked a few more questions, then set her notepad aside. 'OK, I think I have the full picture now. Or almost. And I think I know how we need to deal with the fear of heights and its associations. Are you ready for us to find some appropriate mantras and feelings for your hypnotherapy?'

'I think so.' Lily let out a slow breath. She felt better. Lighter. As though something heavy had lifted off of her shoulders. She still felt pain inside, but it didn't feel as burdensome.

Bernadette ran through a series of sentences and feelings, all of which were positive, about heights and about skiing. About Lily feeling in control, doing everything at her own pace, and knowing that nothing bad was going to happen to her. She was safe.

'I'm going to play some soothing music,' Bernadette said, turning a CD player on.

It reminded Lily of the music she often played during her massages and she instantly relaxed.

'And I'm going to talk you through the hypnotherapy. Don't worry if you don't feel as though you are "going under", I think you would say in English. All you need to do is relax and let me talk to your subconscious.' Bernadette carried on speaking, her voice sounding mesmerizing and absorbing.

Lily suddenly felt extremely tired. It was as though the past few weeks had caught up with her and washed over her like a heavy, crashing wave. Jamie. Jamie and Ivy. Chamonix. Heights, skiing, her dad. The accident. She could hear Bernadette's voice in the background, almost as though she was far away.

Lily felt as though she'd gone into a deep sleep. Her arms felt heavy and she was vaguely aware of Bernadette's voice in the background, telling her to raise her hand or her fingers. Something like that. Lily was certain she hadn't done that; her hands and arms had remained by her side on the sofa – dull, heavy and immoveable. There were no other sounds in the room other than Bernadette's voice and the soft lullaby of the music. Or was that a crackle from the fire? Lily wasn't sure.

'And three, you're feeling more alert,' Bernadette was saying. 'Your eyes are still closed, but you're aware of the sounds in the room and of my voice. Two, you can feel the sofa underneath your legs and you are opening your eyes…'

Lily opened her eyes and frowned. She felt supremely relaxed but alert at the same time, but she was also confused.

'And one, you're fully in the room, feeling calm and confident and ready to carry on with your day.'

Lily pushed her hair out of her face. 'But that only felt like…'

'A few minutes?' Bernadette smiled. 'I know. You were under very deeply. You lifted one arm and wriggled the fingers on your other hand when I asked you to. Did you feel that?'

Lily shook her head. 'I didn't. Not at all.' She felt sceptical, but deep down, she knew something had just happened to her. She trusted Bernadette and Lily felt far better than she had when she had arrived. Calm, confident, secure. She thought about skiing and didn't feel anything much. Not excitement, but also not fear. She felt calm.

'Do you remember me reciting the phrases we agreed on?' Bernadette said, gesturing for Lily to drink some water.

'I don't remember a single thing,' Lily said, feeling rather strange about that. 'I remember the chat before it, about my dad and the heights but after you put that music on... not much at all.'

'That's very normal,' Bernadette explained, getting to her feet. 'And you did very well. I would say that you would need a few more sessions for the heights and maybe, if you want to, to talk about your dad, but it's entirely up to you.'

Lily wasn't sure what she wanted to do. She stood up and her legs felt a little wobbly. Not the way they had at the top of the mountain, but they were still quite jelly-like.

'How much do I owe you?' she said, following Bernadette through the house.

'Nothing,' Bernadette told her with a smile. 'That was a favour for Luc. He looks after me in many ways because I am a friend of the family.'

Lily was taken aback. 'Oh no, I couldn't possibly let him... you...'

'Yes, you can,' Bernadette told her, giving her a sweet smile. 'We call it an "energetic exchange" in this business. Luc and his family are loyal to me and I am loyal to them.'

Lily wasn't sure what to say. 'I'm paying for any other sessions I have,' she insisted as Bernadette opened the front door. A gust of chilly air blew in, along with a few snowflakes.

'That is very acceptable to me,' Bernadette said, letting out a chuckle. 'It is only the first session that is free.'

Lily laughed. 'OK. That works for me. Thank you and I'll be in touch soon, I'm sure.' Stepping outside, she looked around for Luc.

'Hey.'

She turned and there he was. Wearing the brown fur-edged ski jacket he'd been wearing the other night with jeans and some matching brown Moon Boots that only certain men could pull off.

'How did it go?'

'I don't know.' Lily pulled a face. 'I don't even know if anything happened.'

Luc laughed. 'I know. I felt the same when Bernadette hypnotised me.' He started walking and Lily fell into step with him.

'What did you have hypnotherapy for?'

Luc's face closed over. 'Aah well. I don't like to talk about that.'

'I don't like to talk about the stuff that came up in my session either,' Lily said, mildly irritated by Luc shutting her out, which was totally irrational because they barely knew one another. Luc was entitled to his privacy.

'Oh.' Luc gave her a sideways glance. 'Aren't we both... what is the word I have heard the English use? Precious. Is that it?'

Lily thought for a second. 'Precious? Yes. Maybe. You definitely are. I'm just private. And you didn't tell me it was free either.'

'You are uncomfortable with that?' Luc looked surprised. 'I didn't mean to offend you. But if you don't feel OK with it, you could always buy me dinner.'

Lily let out a laugh. Cheeky sod!

'OK,' she said. 'Let me know when you want me to do that.'

'Now?' Luc suggested, his face deadpan.

'Fondue?' Lily offered, remembering Luc waxing lyrical about it the other day. It was early, but she could always eat. Especially as the last thing she had had was an orange liqueur hot chocolate.

'You had me at fondue.' Luc pulled a face at his shit joke. 'I mean, that sounds great. I know the best place, if you'll allow me to show you.'

Lily followed him, feeling her stomach fizzing slightly. What on earth was happening here? She had barely thought about Jamie and she felt absurdly over-excited about a silly lunch with Luc. And she shouldn't. He was just being friendly and he was in love with Elodie. They had probably been laughing at her the other day at the Christmas cocktail party.

Lily climbed the steps to the restaurant, glad she had reminded herself of those things. Now she felt more in control. As attractive as Luc was, he probably just felt sorry for her. If blondes with big lips and size eight figures were his bag, it was unlikely Luc was going to be attracted to a size ten (twelve on a fat day) redhead.

Good to know, Lily thought to herself as she tore her eyes away from his backside, which looked pretty fantastic in those tight jeans.

Chapter Fourteen

They were sitting in a chalet-style restaurant with wood on the floor and walls and the low glow of lamps and candles on every surface. The aroma of the cheese was tantalizing and, tucked inside the restaurant, it felt much later in the day with the dim lights and the cosy atmosphere. The restaurant was very busy, teeming with a lunchtime crowd of skiers and a gaggle of noisy children. It was festive, too, decked out with pretty Christmas lights and decorations with a large tree dominating one corner. It was covered with surprisingly trashy-looking baubles and gaudy tinsel.

'Forgive the décor,' Luc commented. 'They don't like the subtle look in here.'

'I don't mind it,' Lily said with a smile. 'But I love Christmas, as you know.'

Luc said nothing but took a menu from a waitress. The waitress said hi to Luc in a flirtatious way, as though she knew him. Lily wasn't sure why that bothered her; Luc was a playboy. He had probably made his way around most of the girls in the village, according to Elodie.

'I thought I owed you a massage, not dinner,' she said rather snippily.

Luc pushed his dirty blond hair back and eyed her with some amusement. 'That was for skiing lessons, not for hypnotherapy.'

'I've only had one lesson,' Lily returned. She had no idea why she was acting like she had ferocious PMT.

'That's not my fault,' Luc protested mildly. He regarded her with some confusion. 'I said I would help you, but then you had that accident with Ollie.'

'Sorry,' Lily said shortly. 'I'm being a bitch. The hypnotherapy brought up a few things.'

'Such as?' Luc leant forward with interest. 'Oh, I'll have a beer,' he told the waitress with a pleasant, but not overly friendly smile. 'And for you, Lily?'

'I'll have the house wine, please,' she decided. 'A big one.' She closed the wine list.

'What colour?' Luc enquired politely.

'Oh yes.' Lily cringed. 'White please. I don't discriminate based on colour when it comes to wine.'

The waitress looked confused.

'It's OK,' Luc told her. 'She's making a joke.'

The waitress shrugged and left. Luc grinned at Lily. 'You've confused her, I think. Her name is Claudette. She went to my school, but she's a few years younger than me.'

'Oh, right.' Lily hadn't considered Luc's place in Chamonix, in the community, as it were, but she guessed he had grown up here. 'Where did you go to school then?'

Luc told her the name of his school and where it was. 'I used to be a waiter in this place too, years ago.'

'You?' Lily pretended to be shocked. 'Waiting on tables?'

Luc laughed. 'I know. I wasn't very good. I dropped four bottles of wine and at least three fondues.'

'No, you didn't!'

Luc rolled his shoulders modestly. 'OK. So it was only one bottle of wine and two fondues.'

Lily couldn't help smiling, but she wasn't sure if he was pulling her leg. She couldn't imagine Luc as a teenager, gauche and clumsy. She wondered if he was handsome as a boy or if he'd grown into his looks.

'Luc.' An older woman with curly bobbed hair and wide eyes walked over to the table. 'So lovely to see you.'

They did the double cheek kiss and she smiled at Lily. 'And who is this?'

'This is Lily. Lily, this is Francine. Lily works at the hotel as a *masseuse*. I am teaching her to ski,' Luc added.

'Aah lucky girl.' Francine nodded. 'He is the best. At skiing. Not at carrying fondues.' She rolled her eyes and hurried over to another table.

So Luc had dropped a fondue!

Luc's face became more serious. 'Can you tell me about the hypnotherapy?'

Lily gave him a clinical overview, describing how it had felt like five minutes, not an hour, and that she wasn't convinced she had lifted her arm or fingers. And she didn't remember anything Bernadette had said except when she had been 'going under' and as she had come out of it.

'All sounds fairly standard,' Luc said, munching on some complimentary olives that had been brought over. 'I felt the same. But it made all the difference for me. What I mean was not so much the hypnotherapy itself, but what it brought up for you.'

Lily sat back and took a swig of wine to buy some time. Did she trust him? She had thought she did when she had first met him, despite all the warnings Elodie had given

160

her. Normally, Lily always trusted her gut, but there was something about the way Elodie talked about Luc…

'Hey.' Luc shrugged easily. 'If it's private, it's private. I just thought maybe it might help you to talk about it.'

'Why do you hate Christmas so much?' Lily blurted out. 'Why won't you talk about that?' She took another gulp of wine.

Luc's lip tightened, but then he relaxed again. 'That's a fair question, I guess. Especially as I'm asking you to open up about something very personal.'

'I was just being silly,' Lily went into damage limitation mode. 'It doesn't matter.'

'No, that's OK.' Luc drained his beer and asked for another one, getting Lily another wine at the same time. 'OK. I do have a good reason for hating Christmas. Well, not Christmas itself, but the time of year. Something happened one Christmas that has affected me ever since.'

Lily watched Luc's troubled face as he appeared to grapple with himself. What on earth had happened to him?

Before he could speak, the fondue arrived. It came in a large pot with a stove underneath it, a tealight keeping the fondue warm.

'This is called a *caquelon*,' Luc told her, pointing to the pot.

'It smells divine,' Lily said, inhaling the mouth-watering aroma of cheese, white wine and just the faint whiff of garlic. 'Wow. I mean, that's literally just calories in a pot, isn't it?'

'Yes, but it tastes *so* good. Tomorrow we will ski and you won't even remember that you ate all this cheese.'

'God, I hope so.' Lily took one of the long-stemmed forks and speared a cube of bread with it. Dipping it into the fondue, she twirled the bread around in the unctuous mixture. Christmas tunes started playing loudly in the background, an interesting mix of English and French. The French didn't quite cut it with the traditional English pop tunes.

'This is comté and reblochon,' Luc informed her, tipping his head back to put a cheese-soaked cube of bread into his mouth. 'Mmm. That is amazing. The Swiss version has gruyere and emmental, but I think this one, with the stronger tasting cheese is better, *non*?'

Lily was in cheese heaven. She couldn't even speak. She just wanted to enjoy the exquisite flavour of the melted cheeses and the wine and the bread.

'When this is finished, there is usually a crust of toasted cheese in the bottom of the dish,' Luc told her. 'It's not burnt – it's toasted. You can scrape it out and eat it. It's superb.'

'I think I'll probably have had enough by then,' Lily said, loving how her wine complimented the cheesy taste in her mouth.

'You might be surprised. It's incredible, isn't it? It's essentially just garlic rubbed on the bottom of the dish, wine and grated cheese. But it is heaven.' Luc's phone rang and he took a glance at it, then turned it to silent, placing it on the table between them. 'Where was I?'

'You were talking about Christmas and why you hate it,' Lily prompted. She didn't want him to lose his train of thought because the food had arrived, however fantastic it was.

'Oh yes.' Luc's face fell again. But within a few seconds, he was speaking again. 'OK. I had a younger sister, Anais. There were four years between us. She was very different than me. Not as happy, always troubled. We never knew why.'

Lily stopped eating, listening with rapt attention, trying to ignore the jolly Christmas music in the background.

'She made some strange friends,' Luc said, wiping his mouth with his napkin as he took a break from the fondue. 'Started to behave… erratically, I think the word is. My parents, me, we knew there was something wrong. We tried to help her. They sent her for therapy and we asked her college to talk to her. But nothing seemed to help.'

'How worrying.' Lily knew she would feel sick if she had to watch Ivy going through something like that.

'We found out she was taking drugs. Heavy use. Different types.' Luc looked devastated.

Lily stared at Luc. He was clearly carrying a terrible pain around with him.

'One December, five days before Christmas, she disappeared. We couldn't find her or reach her by phone and none of her friends knew where she was. Not even the people she took drugs with knew.' Luc gazed at Lily, his dark eyes haunted. 'I looked everywhere for her. I searched Chamonix and all the surrounding villages for five days. I knocked on doors, went to all the places she liked. And all the places she hated.' Luc paused, his hands twisted on the table.

'Go on,' Lily said gently. 'If you can. If you want to.'

Luc nodded slowly. 'This is the hard part. I finally found her. Well, not me exactly. The day before Christmas Day.'

'You found her on Christmas Eve?' Lily felt deeply upset for Luc. 'Where? What had happened to her?'

'Yes. We were due to have our *réveillon*, our big dinner on the night before Christmas, but none of us wanted to. My grandparents were hosting the dinner and just before it, we received a call from Bernadette.'

'Bernadette?'

'Yes. She found Anais down by the river when she went out to get extra chestnuts for my grandparents' dinner.'

'Was she...' Lily's voice came out as a whisper.

'She was dead,' Luc admitted painfully. 'A drug overdose.'

'Oh no.' Lily felt immeasurably sad and suddenly wanted to call Ivy and tell her she loved her.

'We don't know if it was an accident or if she did it on purpose. There was no note, but it may have been washed away by the river. I think that is what hurt my parents the most... not knowing. Not knowing if it was an accident or if Anais was so desperate and unhappy that she took her own life.'

Lily felt tears pricking at her eyelids. How awful for Anais to die that way, all alone. And how horrible for the family.

'I don't even know what to say,' she managed, feeling a sob in her throat. 'I'm so sorry, Luc. So very sorry.'

Luc reached out and touched her hand. 'It's OK. And I'm sorry... it's a tragic story, I know.'

'Don't apologise.' Lily dabbed at her eyes with her napkin, streaking it with eyeliner and mascara. 'Thank you for trusting me. I must look a mess. I have an older sister, Ivy. The thought of her getting involved with drugs like that and dying all alone… it's a hideous thought. Your poor family.'

Luc nodded. 'My parents have never gotten over it. It was twelve years ago, but it often feels as though it happened yesterday, especially at this time of year. She would have been thirty-two this year.'

'So sad.' Lily took a shaky swig of wine. 'No wonder you hate this time of year. And here I was, trying to get you to appreciate the tinsel and the bloody trees and all that nonsense. I can only apologise.'

Luc let out a laugh. 'Don't be silly! How could you know I had a story like that? I know I must sound like… who is that character in English literature who hates Christmas?'

'Scrooge?' Lily offered, blowing her nose into her napkin. 'Oh dear. How rude of me. You're nothing like Scrooge.'

'Well, hopefully not. I would love to enjoy Christmas again, if I'm honest. I think my parents would too. I think we always feel too sad and guilty and we cannot seem to break out of that pattern.'

'Understandable.' Lily gazed at the fondue. 'I'm not sure we did the fondue justice.'

Luc peered into it. 'Aah well. Another time, perhaps?'

'Perhaps.'

Lily eyed Luc over the rim of her wine glass. She was seeing him in a totally different light now. She had imagined him as some shallow playboy – amusing and surprisingly kind, but maybe without much depth under his good looks and amiable manner. However, there was Elodie to think about and the last thing Lily wanted to do was fall for someone else the way she had with Jamie. She was supposed to be getting over someone, not getting on top of someone else.

'So. I've shown you mine… now you show me yours,' Luc said, relaxing back into his chair.

'S-sorry?'

Luc smiled. 'I just meant that I have opened up to you. So maybe you feel you can with me as well.'

'Oh, right.' Lily wasn't sure she could after hearing all of that. Her childhood had had its moments, but no one had died. 'Another time if that's OK? I promise I will, but not right now.'

Luc shrugged, but in a friendly fashion. 'No problem. A phone is ringing, though, and it's not mine.'

'It's me.' Lily took her phone out. It was Jamie. Shit. She didn't want to talk to him now. Not right now, anyway. There were also three missed calls from Imogen. She had been so engrossed that she hadn't even heard her phone.

'Do you need to take it?'

Lily shook her head and turned the phone to silent, the way Luc had earlier. 'No. It's not someone I want to talk to right now.'

'Ex-boyfriend?' Luc inquired, while asking for the bill.

'Ha. No. Far from it.' Lily turned her phone over in her hands. 'Ex-best friend, sort of, who is dating my sister.'

'Ohhh,' Luc said, managing to make the word sound long and drawn-out. 'That's not great.'

'No, it's not. I want them to be happy, obviously. But still…'

'That's a hard situation. When did you find out about that?'

'A few weeks before I came here.'

'Really?' Luc looked taken aback. 'You had deep feelings for this guy then. To have come all this way to get away from him.'

Lily thought about that. She did have deep feelings for Jamie, but it was more about confessing her own feelings and being deceived by the two of them. She was sure Luc didn't want to hear all the gory details.

'Well, there was more to it than that, if I'm honest. I told him—'

Luc finished his beer. 'You don't have to defend yourself. We've all been in love before.'

Had she been in love with Jamie? Lily had thought she was. She missed him like crazy on some levels, and she had come all this way to get away from him. Or was it to get away from the cringeworthy embarrassment of offloading her feelings only to have them rejected?

Was it possible she just missed Jamie's friendship? Lily had a feeling that much of her reason for leaving England had been about the betrayal and the fact that it was Ivy whom Jamie was seeing that had made her feel foolish, making her want to disappear. She wanted to articulate these feelings to Luc for some reason, but before she got a chance to do so, Luc's phone lit up again on the table. Before he picked it up, Lily saw that it was Elodie. And by the looks of it, it was Elodie who had phoned the first time. Luc frowned and didn't answer.

'She has phoned twice,' he commented.

'Is that normal?' Lily said, gathering up her jacket and handbag. 'Imogen has phoned three times as well, but we're in touch on and off all day long so it's not necessarily weird.'

Luc pulled his ski jacket on and he seemed to have shut down. His face was now unreadable. 'It depends. I'll call Elodie on the way back to the hotel. Shall we go?'

'Yes, of course.' Lily felt disappointed. They had connected so much over the fondue and Luc had seemed to really trust her to have told her such intimate details about his life. But the spell appeared to have been broken and Lily wasn't sure if it was because of the Jamie conversation or if it had been Elodie's phone call.

They stepped outside into a swirl of falling snow that was settling on top of the snow already on the ground. It was starting to get dark and the view through Chamonix, filled with fairy lights everywhere, looked simply magical. Lily couldn't help thinking that even these sorts of sights must set Luc off and remind him of Anais.

Luc put a call into Elodie on the way back to the hotel, but there was no answer.

'Let's just get back,' Luc said, his long legs taking great big strides through the town.

Lily hurried alongside him, trying to keep up and feeling a flash of trepidation about what might be waiting for them at the hotel.

Chapter Fifteen

Back at the hotel, drama was indeed taking place. Staff were milling around, agitated, in the reception area even though it was almost time for the dinner service.

'What is going on?' Luc asked Imogen as they came through the main doors, bringing a whirl of snowflakes and chilly air with them.

'Seems you're not the only one having accidents,' Imogen said, giving Lily a wry smile. She was dressed in the hotel sweatshirt, ready for dinner service. 'Pierre had a horrific fall today. Oddly, it was when he was teaching on a green run and he's broken his leg in three places. He's been taken to the local hospital for surgery. They're saying he might never ski again.'

'*Merde*.' Luc looked upset. 'That is terrible news.'

Imogen agreed. 'He was demonstrating some parallel turns and his ski got caught on a lump of ice. His ski went one way and his leg went the other way.'

Luc winced.

Imogen continued. 'Celine is at the hospital with Pierre and Marc has been put in charge.' Her expression suggested that this was a terrible idea, but she refrained from further comment in front of Luc. 'Elodie is around somewhere, but I'm not sure where.'

'Thank you, Imogen.' Luc gave her a brief nod. 'I need to make calls. Lily, I will speak to you soon.' He turned away, already dialling.

'Will Pierre really never ski again?' Lily felt awful for him. She might not have taken to skiing yet, but she couldn't imagine loving something with the passion that Pierre did and it being taken away.

'That's what everyone is saying. It's a really bad break. They've had to completely re-set his leg.'

'Ouch. Poor Pierre. Makes my banged head seem rather silly now, doesn't it?'

'Nah. That was still bad.' Imogen nudged Lily. 'Where have you been all afternoon, you minx?'

'Hypnotherapy,' Lily explained. 'I wasn't going to go. It was all rather unexpected.'

'How did it go? What happened? Did you eat a lemon thinking it was a chocolate muffin and pretend to hump a lamp you thought was the sexiest thing you'd ever seen?'

'Shut up! No, nothing like that.' Lily gave her a nudge back. 'It was weird, but not in that way. I just can't remember the middle part of it.' She gave Imogen a quick rundown of her time with Bernadette, including all the stuff that had come up about her dad.

'Sounds strange, but you never know. Maybe it will do the trick for you. How are you about the dad stuff?' Imogen knew all about it, having nursed Lily through much of the fallout. There were many nights when they had stayed up until the early hours at Lily's house, whispering about Lily's dad and everything that was hurting her.

'Not great. I was going to tell Luc about it, but he told me about his sister and I didn't really want to go there.'

'Luc has a sister?'

'Not anymore, but I don't think I should say more than that.'

'Crikey. Fair enough. And where were you the rest of the day?' Imogen demanded, pointedly checking her watch. 'You've been gone for ages.'

Lily shrugged in an off-hand manner. 'Luc and I went for a fondue.'

'*Luc and I went for a fondue*,' Imogen mimicked. 'You're saying that as if it's not a big deal, Lily.'

'Why is it a big deal?' Lily took her coat off. 'God, it's always boiling in here.'

'It's like a sauna,' Imogen agreed. 'But anyway. Stop changing the subject. It's a big deal because Luc is only the hottest ski instructor here. And he never takes anyone out for lunch. He's very private.'

'Actually, I took him out for lunch to say thank you for my free hypnotherapy and yes, he is very private, but he did open up to me over the fondue. Big time. And then Jamie phoned.'

'What?' Imogen was almost beside herself with excitement. 'I need to hear all about this, but we need to do dinner service. Sylvan has cooked *coquilles St Jacques* – seriously good by the way – followed by *blanquette de veau*. I hate veal so it's pizza for me later, but don't tell Sylvan.'

'And dessert is a *Paris-Brest*,' Ollie grinned, joining them. 'Sounds naughty, but it isn't. A cream puff, by all accounts. Full of whipped cream.'

'Saucy,' Imogen said, giving him a juicy kiss. 'Come on. We have hundreds of guests to feed and none of them will particularly care that Pierre has his leg hoisted up in the air in plaster.'

'And might not ski again,' Ollie added glumly. 'Poor guy. He has a stick up his ass, but I wouldn't wish that on anyone.'

Putting the drama to one side for the moment, they all got on with dinner service.

–

Hours later, Lily sat in the room alone, staring at her phone. Since Jamie had called her, she had been in a quandary. What should she do? Should she continue to ignore him, or should she call him back? Maybe a text message. That was more distant, not as personal.

But it was so tempting to hear Jamie's voice. She hadn't spoken to him in days, no, weeks. That wasn't normal for them. Lily missed his voice and his jokes and just everything.

Not sure she was doing the right thing, Lily sat down on the bed and dialled his number. As soon as she had dialled, she regretted it. What if Ivy was with him? How bad would that look? About to end the call, Lily started when Jamie answered.

'Lily! Thanks for calling me back.'

Jamie sounded delighted to hear from her.

'Oh, hi,' Lily said tentatively. He sounded close, but also far away. She felt half-upset and half-elated to be speaking to him. 'I wasn't sure if I should call or not.'

'Why not?' Jamie sounded genuinely surprised. 'We talk all the time.'

'No, we *used* to talk all the time,' Lily corrected him. She paused. She had sounded sharp. And she didn't want to sound like some bitter old biddy who'd been rejected.

'It's just that I don't want to upset Ivy. You know, if she saw my number coming up on your phone or whatever.'

'But we're friends!' Jamie protested. 'Don't be silly. Listen, I know you were upset about me and Ivy, but I really want us to still be friends. Can we talk more? Please?'

Lily hesitated. She didn't want to encourage Jamie to call more and she wasn't sure if it was healthy for them to go back to chatting all the time.

'Where is Ivy now?' she asked, laying back on her bed. She felt deeply relaxed and she wasn't sure if it was the hypnotherapy or not. Or maybe it was speaking to Jamie again. She loved the hotel room she shared with Imogen; it had become their little sanctuary. They had all their personal touches like photos and ornaments dotted around the room and Lily had recently received a parcel from her mum with some extra bits like the fluffy pale blue fleece she used to have on her bed and her skanky old stuffed bunny, the one she had cuddled for years. Both of them smelt achingly of home.

'Ivy's working late,' Jamie said, sounding as though he was also settling down on his bed. 'Hang on, I'm just getting comfy. She works late a lot, your sister.'

'Are you living together?' Lily asked cautiously, not sure if she wanted to hear the answer.

Jamie scoffed. 'Living together? No way. Don't get ahead of yourself, Red.' There was a pause while they both digested the fact that he had used his nickname for her for the first time in weeks.

'What do you mean? Don't you want to live with Ivy?' Lily wasn't sure if she liked Jamie scoffing like that. Ivy was still her sister.

'Yes, of course. In the future,' Jamie said smoothly. 'But not now. Not yet. It's early days. And Ivy is kind of married to her job.'

'You feel neglected,' Lily guessed, wondering if this was why Jamie had gotten in touch.

'God, no! I don't feel neglected. You know me. I'm super sociable and super independent.'

That was true, to be fair. Jamie had always done his own thing and whenever he had a girlfriend, he didn't tend to live in their pocket. Actually, Jamie hadn't moved in with any girl yet. He did like his own space.

'So enough about me and Ivy,' Jamie said comfortably. 'What's happening there? How are you after your accident? I've been worried sick about you.'

Lily couldn't help the leap of pleasure his comment gave her, but she berated herself. *Oh, do stop it*, she told herself. *Idiot*. 'Oh, it's all happening here. I've had hypnotherapy for my fear of heights, which bought up all sorts of horrible memories about my dad. Today the owner of the hotel broke his leg in three places and might never ski again.'

'No way,' Jamie breathed.

'Yes way. Poor bloke is being operated on as we speak.'

'Wow. That's hardcore. Fancy never being able to ski again. I get arsey when I know I'm not going again for another year. But if I could never ski again, I think it would kill me.' There was a pause. 'So how do you feel after all the stuff about your dad coming up today?'

'Sad. Upset. Angry,' Lily mused, rolling over and tucking her arm under her pillow.

'I'm not surprised.' Jamie sounded compassionate. 'Every time it comes up, it's like re-living the trauma, isn't it?'

'Yes, exactly that.' Lily let out a sigh. This was the thing with Jamie. He always understood and he always made her feel better.

'That was so brave of you, though,' Jamie said. 'To talk about that. And with the height thing. He was such a nasty bully.'

'I just didn't think it would affect me the way it has. To think that the horrible things he said to me all those years ago could stop me from learning to ski. I've honestly never been so petrified in my life.'

They chatted for another ten minutes, talking about Lily's dad and skiing and what was going on at Jamie's work.

'So, I'm still coming to visit,' Jamie said towards the end of the call. 'If that's all right with you.'

Lily felt a tremor of excitement at the thought of seeing Jamie again, but she pushed it down because she knew it was inappropriate. It might not actually happen anyway. Lily decided to put it to one side until it did.

'It's fine with me. Maybe Ivy might want to come?' Lily felt that she should invite her sister as well.

Jamie scoffed again. 'I don't think she'd step away from work for long enough to visit, Red. I can't even get her to agree to a holiday next year.'

Lily felt a flash of jealousy at the thought of Jamie and Ivy on holiday together, the two of them stretched out on loungers in shorts and bikinis, sipping Aperol spritzes as they laughed and tanned together. God. What on earth was wrong with her? She was such a horrible person.

There she had been, thinking she had grown up and moved on from all this envy.

'Aah well. Let's see what happens. Nice talking to you, J.' His old nickname slipped out accidentally, but it felt like the most natural thing in the world.

'And you. Night, Red.' Jamie sounded contented.

Lily ended the call. How did she feel about Jamie now? The same? Different? Lily got up from the bed and thought about it. She had definitely missed talking to him. She loved the jokey tone and the way he made sense of everything. They had been friends for so long, he knew everything about her and that just made things so incredibly easy. There was history between them. It was as though Lily didn't need to explain herself to Jamie because he already knew what had happened and how she felt about her past or whatever else might come up when they chatted. That was it. Jamie felt like home.

Lily wandered over to the window. She wasn't sure how she felt about Jamie coming over to Chamonix. It almost made her escape pointless. Well, not exactly. There was still the experience of it and hopefully the skiing and seeing Imogen and meeting everyone. Like Luc. But still, she had come to Chamonix to get over Jamie and here he was, talking about coming to see her. Maybe she should insist that he didn't come? Maybe it would just set her back months and she would wish she hadn't seen him?

Feeling as though she needed some air, Lily grabbed her pale blue fleece from home and popped her slippers on. She opened the doors to the balcony and stepped out, breathing in the chill, sharp air. It was an extremely clear night; the sky looked dark navy and it was dotted with a gazillion tiny stars that Lily was sure made up many constellations, but she had no idea what any of them were. She wasn't sure what a clear night meant for the following day in a ski resort. Lots more snow? No more snow? She would have to see in the morning.

Lily realised she could hear low voices talking beneath her and she carefully leant over the balcony to see who it was. It was Luc and Elodie. Lily could tell it was Elodie from the bright blond of her hair and the other one had to be Luc with all that messy, dirty blond hair and the brown ski jacket. Lily pulled back, not wanting to eavesdrop, but not before she saw Luc draw Elodie into his arms. He pressed a kiss to Elodie's forehead, then gave her a proper hug, tucking her head under his chin.

Lily pulled her fleece around her more tightly. There had to be something between them. Simply had to be. Who kissed someone that tenderly if they didn't have feelings for them? And hugged them in that 'I'd do anything for you' kind of way?

Not sure why she even cared what was going on between Elodie and Luc, Lily left them to it and went back indoors. She was going to crash out asleep and replay the phone call with Jamie in her head. Not her afternoon with Luc having chats over fondue, but Jamie.

Chapter Sixteen

The Following Day

Luc turned to Lily. 'Are you ready?'

'I think so.'

Lily gritted her teeth. Luc had finished his formal lessons and she had completed breakfast service, two massages and a hurried lunch with Imogen in the local patisserie. Well, not so much lunch as a hot chocolate and an exquisite pastry called a *religieuse*, which was made of two choux pastry cases filled with *crème pâtissière*, covered in ganache, with more whipped cream piped on top. My god, it had been incredible. Lily couldn't wait to get skiing, if only to do her thighs a favour.

She was standing in central Chamonix at the entrance to the cable car Imogen had told her was one of the highest in the world. They had left their skis, poles and boots in a locker.

'OK, so today, I am testing out Bernadette's hypnotherapy. Using the cable car *Aiguille du Midi*.'

'Right.' Lily felt a mixture of calm settling upon her and anxiety coursing through her and she wasn't sure which one was going to win.

'We're going up inside that,' Luc pointed to the cable car. 'Before we even ski. We're going up and we're coming back down and depending on how you feel after that, we'll stick to a low slope and we'll ski.'

'Right,' Lily said again. Luc looked suave in his red ski jacket, his tan giving him a healthy glow. But since seeing him with Elodie last night, Lily felt detached from him again, almost as if their intimate chat the day before hadn't taken place. She wasn't sure if it was some kind of defence mechanism that she had deliberately put in place or if it was something that had occurred naturally.

Luc was different today too. Was it because he had confided in her and he felt that he had opened up too much? Or maybe it just came down to Elodie. Maybe the tender hug and kiss had put him back in that headspace and that was why he was being rather coolly professional towards her.

'How do you feel about going in the cable car?'

Lily realised Luc was talking to her. 'I'm not sure. I feel OK, but every so often my legs go wobbly.'

'OK, that's not too bad. Anything else?'

Lily frowned. 'I'm having these really weird thoughts and I don't know where they're coming from.'

'Weird. What do you mean?'

Luc gave her his full attention, which unnerved Lily. Sometimes Luc had this way of focusing his dark eyes on her as though he could see nothing else and didn't want to. It was intense. Lily tried to get hold of her thoughts.

'Things like… nothing bad is going to happen to me. I have nothing to be afraid of here. I'm in complete control. I'm calm and I can do this.' She glanced at him. 'Stuff like that.'

Luc looked pleased. 'That is Bernadette. Trust me. Those are the kinds of phrases she would use during the hypnotherapy.'

'But why don't I remember her saying any of that?' Lily still felt sceptical, but maybe this stuff did actually work. To be fair, she did feel relatively calm. Anxious on the inside, but it was under control, rather than spiralling into something chronic.

'Let's get in it and see how you feel.' Luc led the way. 'I'm afraid we can't get off apart from the official stop off points obviously, but we are going all the way round and back down again without attempting to get out higher up the mountain.'

'OK.' Obediently, Lily followed Luc to the queue and shuffled forwards in line. Soon enough, they were at one of the cable cars. It was a rectangular box with red edges and floor to ceiling windows. The kind that usually gave Lily nightmares.

The doors opened and they got in. Lily felt a moment of extreme panic, but she was able to squash it down. It subsided without much effort and she found herself saying the same phrases over and over again in her head.

Nothing bad is going to happen to me. I have nothing to be afraid of here. I'm in complete control. I'm calm and I can do this...

'Do you want to stand in the centre of the car?' Luc asked.

Lily shook her head. 'No. Let's do this properly. I'm standing next to the windows. And I'm looking down.'

'Good for you.'

Luc talked her through points of interest as the cable car climbed. Lily was half-listening because it distracted her and half checking in with her feelings because she wanted to understand how she was reacting to the views.

The views were breathtaking and that was a fact, she thought as she gazed through the window. Snow-capped mountains were everywhere. Lily could hear Luc telling her the names of the summits and peaks and she was conscious of wanting to look down to see how high they were, which she had never wanted to do before. Maybe the hypnotherapy had worked. The thought of skiing was still giving Lily a bad case of nerves, though.

'There are a few cool restaurants and bars up here,' Luc was saying. 'At the North Tower, there is a cafe and a snack bar and in the summer, the "3842" is open. That's the restaurant that's at an altitude of 3842 metres.'

'Wow. That's high.'

'The *Aiguille du Midi* has its own postage stamp and a letterbox too,' Luc commented, grinning. 'Weird, *oui*?'

'*Oui*. But quite cute if you think about it.'

'Cute?' Luc threw her a glance. 'Maybe.' He turned away, but Lily thought he was smiling. 'There is a Central Tower as well and it has a galleried walkway that connects the Rebuffat terrace with the Mont-Blanc terrace. You can view a few glaciers from here.' Luc talked to her about a cave carved into the rock with a museum displaying climbing and mountaineering memorabilia. 'And the view of the Alps from the Top Terrace is incredible. There is a wonderful panoramic viewing platform. It's called "Step into the Void". It's literally like stepping out into nothing with the Alps underneath you.'

'Sounds great,' Lily said, pulling a mock-horrified face. She broke into a smile. 'Just kidding. Are we getting out there?'

Luc let out a sudden laugh. 'Are you serious? I'm game if you are.'

Lily shrugged. 'Why not?'

God. What the hell was she thinking? This terrace sounded *hideous*. They got out and queued up. Lily started to feel sick, but told herself that she could do this. *She could do this.* They were given funny grey slippers to wear and before they knew it, it was their turn. They stood in front of 'Step into the Void' and Lily took a breath.

It was a glass box. *Glass.*

'It's glass, but it's built around a metal frame,' Luc said soothingly. 'It's totally safe. There are three layers of glass bound together. It can withstand high winds and temperatures. Are you ready?' Luc grabbed her hand.

Lily didn't stop to think. Wearing the grey slippers, she and Luc stepped out onto the glass platform.

'Oh my God,' Lily breathed. She looked down. 'Oh. My. God. That is insane!'

It was like floating above the Alps, standing over the snow with the ground falling away beneath them. Lily felt panic flooding through her, then euphoria. She was doing this. She was scared still, but it felt like a case of mind over matter, and she was working hard at it, but she was doing it. She might vomit, but she was doing it.

'Well done,' Luc cried, squeezing her hand. 'I can't believe you did this!'

Lily couldn't either. And she was jolted by Luc holding her hand, even though he was just being supportive. They took some funny selfies because Lily was certain she wouldn't believe she'd actually achieved this.

'You are a rock star,' Luc said as they left the viewing platform. 'That is more than I thought you could do today.'

'Ye of little faith…'

'What?' Luc looked confused. 'You speak in riddles.'

'Idioms, my friend, idioms.'

Buoyed up by the success of her walk out onto Step into the Void, Lily felt she could afford to be cocky for a moment.

'Let's go skiing,' Luc said.

And with that, Lily felt herself deflate. And she couldn't understand it. If she could walk out onto that platform, why was skiing making her nervous? They travelled back down in the cable car, with Lily conscious of Luc chatting away in the background, but not really listening. Her stomach was doing somersaults. And she couldn't make any sense of it. She had just conquered something incredible up there. She truly thought she had conquered her fear of heights. But now that they were about to ski, Lily was getting anxious and panicky again.

On autopilot, she followed Luc out to get her skis and poles and after Luc had helped her do up her ski boots, they headed over to a different green run. This one was called *Les Planards*, which was across the road from the Mer de Glace railway station.

Lily snapped into her skis and felt surprisingly comfortable in them. Using her poles to propel herself forwards and feeling her muscles scream a little in return, she followed Luc, shuffling forwards, getting up slight speed on the sloped parts. This green run had a button lift like the one the other day and Lily managed to get on and dismount without too many problems.

'This is the bigger of the two nursery slopes, but it's a gentle gradient,' Luc told her. 'And well done. You looked very calm and confident on the lift just then. It's the shorter one, and there is a long one we can try another time, but you looked in control.'

'It felt all right,' Lily admitted. 'That chair lift looks a bit scary.' She pointed upwards.

'That goes to a blue run and I think a red run. Let's not worry about that for now. I love chair lifts, actually. You get such great views. A bit like the cable car.'

'But outdoors and dangling from not much.' Lily shivered. 'Oh Luc. I feel as though I've lost my nerve completely.' She wasn't shivering, she was shaking. 'I think it must have to do with my dad.'

Luc squeezed her shoulder. 'You still need to tell me about that. But for now, let's focus on skiing.' He bent down slightly to make proper eye contact with her. 'You can snow plough very well. You can snow plough turn very well. If you fall on this slope, you will bruise your ego, but not much else, *oui*?'

'*Oui*.' Lily took a deep breath and focused on the thoughts forming in her brain methodically, as though they had been planted there. Which they probably had.

I can do this. Nothing is going to hurt me. There is nothing to be scared of. I'm braver than I think I am. I can ski. There is no reason why I can't do this.

'Bernadette in your head again?' Luc guessed, pulling her goggles down for her. 'Let's build on that and go down this slope. Follow me.'

Lily did as she was told. Her dad's voice came into her head, telling her she couldn't do it and that she wasn't good enough, but she pushed it away.

I'm braver than I think I am…

She followed Luc down the slope. It was busier than the other one, but Lily did her best to block everyone else out. Again, it felt like a mind over matter situation. Luc started to put in some snow plough turns and she copied him. They were wobbly, they weren't perfect, but she was doing it. Luc stopped and watched her snow plough turn on her own, whooping encouragement from the side lines. He then skied after her and met her at the bottom.

'So much better!' he said, seeming absurdly pleased. 'I am so happy for you. Shall we go again?'

'Doh. What else?'

Lily grinned and felt herself relax inside. She didn't fancy going higher than they were for now, but a calm snow plough down this green one was doing her confidence no end of good. They went up again and this time, Lily really focused on getting her body to relax and just glide. It was still an effort to block out the negative voice in her head, but the other voice, the 'cheerleader' as she had decided to call it, was louder. And way more convincing.

'You look amazing!' Luc shouted on their tenth turn down the green run. 'Keep going, keep going!'

Lily allowed her body to do what Luc had repeatedly trained it to do. She relaxed into her turns and a couple of times even felt her skis turning as though they were going parallel. That scared her too much, so she flared them out into the snow plough position again.

'You nearly parallel skied.' Luc skied up alongside her, his face literally beaming. 'I am so proud of you. So proud!' He leant towards her and Lily felt her breath suck in. Was he going to kiss her?!

Luc pulled himself up. There was a moment where they stared at each other and time stood still. It actually stood still. It was like being in a snow globe, with everything else melting into the background – people, noises, sights. As if the two of them were suspended in something together. A moment. Like an icicle dangling from a fir tree. And then the icicle dropped.

What was that? Lily was poleaxed. She had never experienced anything like that before. Not with anyone. Not even with Jamie. She swallowed, feeling that she had dry mouth again.

'Do… do we go up again?'

Luc seemed to retreat within himself. 'No, I think that's enough for today. But you should be so pleased with yourself. You didn't once let your nerves get the better of you.'

'That's not me, that's Bernadette,' Lily said, still rocked by that weird moment between them.

'It's both. And you did very well to get back into the right headspace after coming down in the cable car. You shut down at that point. I could see the fear taking hold again.'

'Me too.' Lily shivered again at the memory. 'It was like this horrible cold feeling and I couldn't shake it off. It was crawling all over me.'

Luc helped her out of her skis. 'Sounds nasty. As I say, you did well.'

Lily watched him hoist her skis onto his shoulder and she trudged after him. She wanted to ask about Elodie, but she wasn't sure how to get her into the conversation. Luc inadvertently provided her with the perfect opening as they headed back to the hotel.

'Pierre has had his operation,' Luc told her. 'The family is still very upset about it all.'

'Poor Pierre.' Lily couldn't wait to get her ski boots off. 'And… how is Elodie?' She couldn't look at Luc, but she felt him glance at her and stared steadfastly ahead.

'Elodie? She is upset, naturally. She adores her father and it's hard when someone you love hurts themselves so badly. Marc is fine, too,' Luc added, sounding rather tongue in cheek. 'In case you are wondering.'

'Oh good.' Lily felt her cheeks flush slightly. Had she been that obvious? 'I really like it here,' she threw out, mostly to change the subject.

'Really?' Luc looked amused. 'I'm glad to hear it. Are you thinking of staying beyond Christmas?'

Lily thought about that. She hadn't given herself a chance to think beyond each day, given the drama that had ensued since her arrival, but she knew she would have to start thinking about that soon. She missed home; that was a given. She missed her mum and Dave, and Ivy of course. And Jamie. Maybe she would feel differently once Jamie had visited. If Jamie visited.

'Did you hear from your friend again?' Luc asked. His face was the picture of innocence.

'Jamie?' Lily wondered why on earth Luc would be asking her such a thing. 'I did, actually. He's thinking of coming to visit. He loves skiing,' she added, to clarify.

'Does he?' Luc raised an eyebrow. 'Is he good?'

'Not as good as you, I'm sure,' Lily said, with a half-smile.

Truthfully, she had no idea how good Jamie was at skiing. He talked about it incessantly whenever he returned from a trip, but Lily had worked out that everyone who was into skiing was *really into skiing*. It was a sport to be passionate about – apathy had no place in the world of skis and mountains. But Luc was an instructor, after all; Lily imagined his technique would be far more honed.

'Well, it would be lovely to meet one of your… friends,' Luc said, heavy emphasis on the 'friends' part. He sounded sarcastic, which, in her limited experience, was unusual for him.

'I'll be sure to introduce you if he comes,' Lily said, feeling herself stiffen. Why was Luc acting like a dickhead? Surely he didn't feel threatened by Jamie? She stepped into the boot room and sank down onto the bench. She wouldn't let Luc undo her ski boots for her. Not after being so silly about Jamie. She bent over and struggled with the straps and bindings. Why did they always feel so tight?

'Shall I help?' Luc stood over her, his face impassive.

'No. That's fine,' she snapped, irritated by his presence suddenly. 'I can do it myself.'

'Fair enough,' Luc said, but he frowned. 'I'm happy to help, but if you insist…' He left her to it and Lily felt like an idiot. And it took her a good twenty minutes to undo her boots without Luc's help because her fingers were cold and the bindings were tight and, well, it was just harder.

Huffing to herself, Lily finally managed to yank her boots off and release her sweaty feet. Taking stock of her day, she decided that it had been a good one. She and Luc had achieved a lot. Well, she had achieved a lot with Luc. Stepping into the Void, all the perfect (or near perfect) snow plough turns. Overcoming her nerves. Not allowing Luc to have his face next to her smelly feet.

Lily frowned. Did Luc like her? She really wasn't sure. They got on so well and it seemed as though there was a connection between them, even sizzling chemistry at times. There were moments when Lily was convinced Luc was really into her. There was the way he had leant into her earlier, as though he was going to kiss her. He hadn't, but it had been a magic moment.

Lily stood up, feeling a welcome ache in her legs. Wowzers. Was she beginning to enjoy the post-ski burn they all talked about? Lily couldn't wait to lower herself into a warm bubble bath. She shuffled her way upstairs, feeling her legs seize up slightly and, once in her room, sat on the edge of the bath and started to run the hot water.

As she poured amber-scented bubble bath into it, Lily thought about Elodie. Did she have some kind of hold over Luc? She acted as though she had a claim to Luc, but Lily had no idea what it was. She wanted to find out, but Imogen didn't seem to know anything and Celine hadn't mentioned any connection between Luc and Elodie. Bernadette clearly knew an awful lot, if not everything, but she was intensely loyal to Luc and Lily knew she wouldn't breathe a word unless she felt it was right to do so.

Lily wasn't sure how she was going to find out what the link between Luc and Elodie was, she just knew that she wanted to understand it. It suddenly seemed incredibly important. Because she kind of liked Luc and she wasn't sure if Luc kind of liked her. Trailing her hand distractedly in the warm, soapy bubbles, Lily felt confused but excited.

Chapter Seventeen

A Few Days Later

Lily had just finished a massage with a gushing Sylvan followed by an energetic sports massage for Signor Santorini, who by all accounts popped over from Italy via the tripoint of France-Italy-Switzerland at the top of Mont Dolent whenever he could to ski his socks off. He would leave his wife behind, thus rendering her a 'ski widow'. It was rather like a golf widow, but with poles instead of clubs.

Lily was due in a staff meeting and was running a little late since Signor Santorini adored chatting. When he started talking in ski language, he could not be stopped. Although he would have been better off speaking in Italian than in ski language because Lily had no idea what a 'mogul field' was or what it meant to 'drop off a crest'. Equally, she wasn't sure she even wanted to know what a 'big dump' was. All Lily knew was that, like everyone else in Chamonix, Signor Santorini was obsessed with all things ski.

Washing her hands and making sure her room was set up for her next client, Lily made her way to the staff area. Everyone was already there, including Luc, so she slipped in the back quietly. Marc was up front, talking through a list in his hand and Elodie stood at his side, looking slender and modelesque in tapered black ski pants and a pale pink jumper that made the most of her slender curves.

'As I was saying, my mother is taking some time off, partly for herself and partly to be with my father in hospital,' Marc said, his expression grave. He looked dapper as ever, but exhausted, with dark shadows under his eyes and a weary expression.

Imogen threw Lily an intrigued glance. Why would Celine need time out for herself?

Marc carried on. 'Thank you to those who have asked after him. He is doing as well as can be expected. He's fine, but obviously devastated by the accident and very worried about his skiing career going forward, both as an instructor and at a competitive level.'

A murmur of sympathy rippled through the group of staff. They could all understand how awful it would be to not be able to ski ever again and not one of them would wish such a thing on their worst enemy, let alone their boss, who was so passionate about teaching and competing.

'Onto other issues,' Marc continued. He ran through some social events and the work schedule for the following week. He praised a few individuals for specific achievements, then moved on. 'The Christmas cocktail event the other week was very successful. We used it as a networking event as well as a social gathering and made several repeat bookings for next year. We plan to have another drinks event closer to Christmas. Elodie will be in charge of it. Elodie?'

Elodie stepped forward. 'Yes, I'll be organising an event for staff and guests, and staff attendance is compulsory.

Sylvan, could you please submit some new canapé and cocktails suggestions to me by tomorrow evening?'

Sylvan frowned, presumably at the short notice request, but gave a little bow of agreement.

'Good,' Elodie said crisply. 'I thought we might have a more Christmassy theme for this event, so some of you will be asked to dress in costumes for the evening.'

There was a collective groan this time. Lily sighed. She imagined she would be one of Elodie's costume victims. And Lily had no doubt the costume would be along the lines of a big, fat snowman or a star with her arms stretched out all night long. There would be no sexy elves or Mrs Santa for her if Elodie was in charge. Lily was certain of that.

'I'll let you all know nearer the time about your outfits.' Elodie consulted her fluffy white notepad. 'I am also arranging a staff Christmas lunch. No guests.'

Everyone visibly brightened at this news.

'It will take place at *Le 3842* on the *Sommet de l'Aiguille du Midi*. Stunning views, delicious food and they have a special Christmas menu.'

'It's lovely there,' Imogen whispered to Lily. 'You'll love the food.'

Lily bit her lip. This was the restaurant attached to 'Step into the Void' where she and Luc had been the other day. It could only be reached by cable car, but Lily had a bad feeling about the way Elodie was smirking. Mostly in her direction.

Elodie continued. 'We will obviously reach the restaurant by cable car, but we will ski most of the way back down. For anyone who is brave enough, do not drink too much! The plan is to hike 150 metres across the ridge line.

This takes you directly to the *Vallée Blanche*. Not for the faint-hearted! It is very, very high and there are ropes to hang onto, but it's a sheer drop. Once we've taken a group photo – I have my selfie stick ready – we will put our skis and snowboards on and off we go. It's an off-piste, unmarked route, but it's not that difficult.' She threw a glance at Lily. 'So if you have a fear of heights, you have two weeks to get over it.'

'Cool!' Ollie said enthusiastically. 'Can't wait.'

He wasn't alone. All the seasoned skiers and snow-boarders in the room – i.e. all of the staff – looked as though Christmas had come early.

Lily gulped. Then seethed inwardly. Why on earth had Elodie arranged something so challenging? Lily didn't want to be arrogant about this because maybe it had nothing whatsoever to do with her, but she couldn't help thinking that Elodie had arranged this Christmas lunch to alienate her. It felt like it was meant to exclude her from a social event that she would desperately love to attend, either because her skiing wouldn't be up to it or her fear of heights might hold her back.

She felt Luc's gaze on her and even though he looked concerned, she stuck her chin in the air. For all she knew, Luc and Elodie had arranged this together. Lily felt close to tears, but maybe she was wrong. Maybe Elodie wasn't bullying her, but it did feel that way. Lily told herself she was being silly. This was probably what the staff always did and she was taking it personally. Surely Elodie must have far better things to do than organise a lunch designed to exclude or humiliate Lily.

'One other thing,' Elodie lowered her notepad. 'Marc has some updates on the issues my father mentioned at the last staff meeting before his accident. But I have one other complaint to bring up.'

Everyone waited.

'A guest has complained about a massage they had.'

Lily looked at Imogen, who seemed equally flabbergasted. No way. She had never had a complaint from a client in her life. She was professional to the hilt at all times and she loved her job. Lily felt her cheeks flaming. And why on earth wasn't Elodie speaking to her about this in private? Why was she belittling her in front of everyone?

Lily steeled herself. 'Who made the complaint?' she asked, hoping to God her voice sounded steady.

'Madame Argent,' Elodie said, staring Lily down.

Madame Argent. Lily stared back at Elodie, not shying away for a second. Madame Argent was a kindly old lady from Biarritz who had come with her husband to Chamonix so that he could ski and she could shop, go on a few walks and have spa treatments. They came once a year together and made the most of it.

Madame Argent had waxed lyrical about Lily's massages, effusive in her open and frequent praise. She had booked a massage every single morning for the entire week and a half they had been there. Madame Argent had also presented Lily with a gift of some beautiful hand creams when they had left, kissing both her cheeks warmly. They wouldn't be back until the following December, either, making it a very difficult accusation to prove.

Lily knew in her heart of hearts that Madame Argent hadn't made a complaint. She had genuinely enjoyed her massages and Lily knew if a client wasn't happy with what she was doing, because she checked throughout. Pressure, the type of massage, even the oil. Lily often got clients to smell the aroma of the oils before she even applied them, as some clients had an aversion to certain scents like ylang-ylang. Madame Argent liked gentle strokes, except on her shoulders where she carried all her tension, a lavender-based oil and, randomly, but because she was a very cool sixty-year-old – Ibiza classics in the background by request.

'What did she say?' Lily asked frostily, knowing she needed to stand her ground.

'Apparently, the pressure wasn't right, and you rushed her through her massages,' Elodie said, without referring to her notepad.

'That's ridiculous!' Imogen cried, unable to help herself. 'Absolutely ridiculous. Lily never rushes a massage and she always asks if the pressure is right. Madame Argent *loved* Lily. She gave her a present when she left and she—'

'Are you calling me a liar?' Elodie gave Imogen an odious glare.

Imogen stared back as if to say 'if the cap fits, wear it'.

'Madame Argent loved her massages,' Lily stated simply. 'I would know if my client wasn't happy. Perhaps there has been some mistake.' She sounded sane and calm, but inside, she wanted to cry with frustration and outrage. What was Elodie trying to achieve with this? It was unprofessional. She glanced at Luc. He looked furious, but Lily had no idea why. Was he cross with Elodie? Or did he think it was right for Lily to be punished?

'Well, I can assure you that she did complain,' Elodie snapped. 'I have it in writing if you'd like to see it.'

'Yes please,' Lily said confident, that no letter of complaint would ever be produced. 'Photocopy it and hand one out to everyone. Then let's call Madame Argent and ask her too.'

'I think perhaps this should be discussed in private,' Marc interjected, bringing the talk to a close. 'Elodie, Lily, book a meeting to discuss this later please.' He frowned, looking extremely displeased with the confrontation. 'To update you on the other unpleasant matters my father brought up, I'm pleased to say that no more money has been taken recently.'

Everyone brightened. Some good news after Elodie's horrible accusation.

'All the bookings are going through efficiently. I am taking care to check every single one of them and man the desk more or less at all times now.' Marc ran his hand through his hair distractedly, making it look uncharacteristically dishevelled. 'But everything looks good. No one stepped forward and owned up, by the way.' He eyed them carefully. 'But I am taking it that being found out formally was enough. I hope that we can leave it there and I am happy to say no more about it assuming that it ends here.'

There was a muffled silence, with a few whispers and comments, then everyone became quiet again.

'That will be all,' Marc said, taking his leave. Elodie shot out of the room after him, closely followed by Luc.

Everyone gathered around Lily.

'She has a bloody cheek,' Imogen said furiously. 'How dare she accuse you of that, Lil. And in front of everyone!'

'What a bitch!' Ollie agreed.

'If she had picked anyone else,' Lily said, 'but not Madame Argent. She really loved her massages and gave me so much praise. I know she didn't complain.'

Imogen nodded. 'I think she only picked Madame Argent because she comes once a year. Any other client might pop back in February or March for the next season, but not those two. They're creatures of habit.'

'Not nice to say it in front of everyone,' Amelia commented with feeling. 'She must have it in for you.'

'I did think that with the staff lunch,' Ollie offered. 'That's an ambitious route, even for the more advanced skiers and snowboarders. I'd offer to get you down, but after last time...' He tailed off ruefully.

'That's OK,' Lily told him, appreciating his loyalty. 'I guess I'll just have to miss out. Two weeks isn't enough for me to overcome my fear, or to learn to ski to that level. I'll just have to miss it.'

Imogen looked upset. 'Oh Lily, no! Surely we can get you down that slope between us. Luc won't let you be left out. I'm sure of it. Surely you could take the cable car back down again?'

Lily didn't know for sure. But she knew she would feel like a terrible failure if she had to do that when everyone skied down.

'Where is Luc?' Joe asked.

'He ran after Elodie,' Imogen said darkly. 'Hopefully to slap her. Or kick her off a mountain.'

Lily's phone rang. It was Ivy. Lily was relieved to take the call and get out of the oppressive atmosphere of the staff room. Grabbing one of the staff jackets, Lily headed outside and sat on one of the benches outside the hotel. It overlooked the pool, which wasn't being used much at this time of year, but the view of the pool with all the fairy lights around the fences and the backdrop of the mountains was absolutely breathtaking.

'Ivy. How are you?'

'Not too bad.' Ivy sounded tinny, as though she was at home in her flat.

Lily glanced at her watch. Ivy should be at work now. 'Where are you?'

'At home. Tummy ache.'

Lily's brow knitted. Ivy was never sick.

'How are you? What's happening in Chamonix?'

'Ha. Not much.' Lily gave her sister a quick rundown of the skiing, the hypnotherapy and everything else, ending with the recent staff meeting.

'Oh dear. Sounds as though you've made an enemy in Elodie,' Ivy commented. 'Are her and this Luc an item?'

'Probably,' Lily commented gloomily. 'There's definitely something between them.'

'Stay out of it then,' Ivy said. 'It'll only cause you trouble otherwise.'

'Yep.' Lily's heart sank, but she knew Ivy was right. There was nothing to be gained by getting close to Luc. As well as they got on, Elodie had clearly marked her territory and Lily wasn't going to gain anything by stirring it up. It wasn't as if Luc had made any kind of move on her anyway.

'You like him.' Ivy stated the fact.

'I don't know what I think of him.'

'Yes, you do.' Ivy sighed. 'Oh Lily. Just be careful.'

'I will.' Thinking that she couldn't feel much worse than she did right now, Lily bit the bullet. 'How are things with you and Jamie?'

There was a pause. 'I'm not really sure.' Ivy sounded miserable. Lily was certain Ivy's tummy ache was more about Jamie than anything else. 'I think he thinks I work too much.'

'And do you?'

'Probably, but we're going through a really busy time at the moment. I have to be there all the time and it's so hard juggling everything.' Ivy sighed. 'But I really like him.'

'I know you do.' Lily felt sorry for Ivy. She knew she was trying to have everything and was having a hard time pulling it off, but maybe she needed to think about what was important to her. If Lily had Jamie, she wouldn't put work in front of him.

'Have you… have you spoken to him?'

Lily hesitated, but only for a second. 'Yes, but only once. We text occasionally.' That was stretching the truth a tad. They texted most days now, but Lily did her best to keep it brief.

'Did he say anything about me? About us?'

Lily pulled a face. How awkward. She didn't want to lie, but she didn't want to get involved. 'Erm… kind of. Just that he doesn't see you as much as he'd like to, I suppose.'

'Oh God!' Ivy sounded like she was going to cry. 'I'm trying so hard, Lily. I really am. Maybe I'm just not cut out for a relationship.'

'Don't be daft. Of course you are. You're amazing. And Jamie knows that.' He must know that, Lily reasoned to herself. He wasn't dumb or blind. Ivy was a catch. Maybe they weren't suited for each other, but only time would tell on that front. And actually, for the first time, Lily wasn't sure she wanted them to break up. Well, if they weren't happy, of course, but not for her own personal gain.

Lily sat and thought for a moment. How about that? How had that happened? She certainly hadn't felt that way when she'd arrived in Chamonix. The change had clearly done her good. And it had nothing whatsoever to do with Luc. No. Yes. Maybe. Oh God.

'I have to go. I have a work call coming through,' Ivy said. 'Sorry, Lily. I'll call another time, but I'm glad you're loving Chamonix.'

'Bye, Ivy.' Lily ended the call and sat for a moment watching her breath come out in little white puffs.

So today she had learnt that Elodie was gunning for her and wasn't afraid to show it, and that something had shifted in the way Lily felt about Jamie, but she wasn't sure what. As for Luc… no, Lily was still none the wiser.

Chapter Eighteen

'And two, you're aware of the room and you want to open your eyes…' Bernadette brought Lily back from the hypnotherapy. 'How do you feel?'

'I feel OK,' Lily said, stretching her fingers. She liked being in Bernadette's room; it felt comfortable and calm and she liked the crackle of the roaring fire. 'I still don't feel myself lifting my arms or anything like that, but I believe you. If you say I'm doing it, I'm doing it.'

'Sometimes it's just a flicker of your little finger when I ask your subconscious for permission to talk to it.'

Lily shook her head. She still didn't understand how it all worked – all she knew was that it was working. She felt generally calmer, but especially on the slopes. The fear and anxiety hadn't completely subsided, but it was manageable.

'And how is the skiing?' Bernadette asked. She went and fetched some of her special hot chocolate for Lily. It was indulgent and delicious, and it had become a little ritual of theirs after Lily's hypnotherapy. As soon as Bernadette sat back down again, one of her cats jumped onto her lap and curled up in a fluffy, ginger ball.

'The skiing is going well,' Lily nodded. 'I feel so much more confident. We've stuck to green runs so far, but we're going higher and I feel OK with that.'

'You can do it. You are lucky you have Luc helping you.' Bernadette said this with an innocent face, but Lily was sure there was more to the statement.

'He… told me about Anais,' she said, feeling it was safe to bring up Luc's sister with Bernadette.

Bernadette's eyebrows raised. 'Did he? Such a sad business. I still miss her to this day. Well, Luc certainly trusts you, doesn't he? He really doesn't talk about her much. And certainly not with people he doesn't know very well. Hasn't known for that long,' she corrected herself.

'Maybe that's why he felt he could talk to me,' Lily wondered out loud. 'Maybe it's because I'm not involved in any way.'

Bernadette disagreed. 'No, Luc's not really like that. He tends to only trust a few people, and the whole issue around Anais is very hard for him to talk about. He felt so responsible, as though he should have been able to stop it from happening. But of course, he couldn't. When people take drugs…' Bernadette tutted. 'They are out of control sometimes. And only they can stop themselves from repeating those patterns.'

'Yes. It's such a shame that it's affected his ability to enjoy Christmas too. But I totally understand.'

'Perhaps it's time for that to change?' Bernadette suggested, stroking her ginger cat. He was called Jez. Luc had named him, apparently.

'What, the Christmas thing?' Lily was confused. 'I'm not sure how.'

'I think if Luc could see Christmas through someone else's eyes, perhaps he could enjoy it again. And not think of Anais every time it gets to this time of year.'

'Really?' Lily sat up, feeling excited. 'I mean, I love Christmas! Absolutely love it. I could... well, I don't know anything about Christmas in France. There must be lots of traditions?'

Bernadette smiled. 'There are. But I can help you with those.'

Lily took another sip of hot chocolate. 'Shall we do it? Is it worth a try?' Her face fell. 'There is always a chance that it might not work out, I guess. We might go to all this trouble and then it falls flat.'

'Falls flat?' Bernadette looked flummoxed. 'Is that to do with skiing?'

'No!' Lily got up. 'Falls flat means it didn't work. Or the plan failed.'

'Right.' Bernadette lifted Jez up and put him on the sofa, still curled up in a ball. 'I see. Well. I think we should get our heads together and see what we can come up with. Maybe it would do Luc's parents good to step out of this horrible depression at Christmas time too. But we shall see. Maybe our plan will... fall flat, as you say.'

Bernadette showed Lily out, arranging a time for their final hypnotherapy session as she did so.

Lily stepped outside, as ever, feeling the sharp contrast of Bernadette's warm, cosy home compared to the chilly air outside, as delicate snowflakes spiralled through the air. She was due back at the hotel shortly for a massage with Celine, oddly, but she was going to take her time strolling through Chamonix.

It truly was picture-postcard pretty. Christmas card pretty, in fact. Every tree and monument was adorned with fairy lights that twinkled and shone and each shop had bright lights above it and more festive lights and decorations. The ground had a thick layer of snow on it and every surface had a good sprinkling as well, even the little street signs advertising shops and restaurants. The Christmas market was out in full force, the little huts dusted with snow, each one giving off a warm glow from the small heaters all the sellers used.

How could she help Luc see the beauty of Christmas again? More to the point, how to do it without dismissing the terrible tragedy that had blighted it? It was going to be difficult and Lily wasn't even sure she was doing the right thing, but if Bernadette – who knew Luc exceptionally well – thought it was a good idea, then Lily was going to trust her. Her phone rang; it was Jamie.

'Red!'

'J!'

The old nicknames came naturally again now.

'What's happening, dude?'

Jamie sounded like a rapper at times, but it was always tongue in cheek.

'Are you down with the kids?'

'No. Not at all. Not. At. All. In fact, all the kids think I'm sad and geeky.'

'Ha!' Lily smiled. 'Not much happening really. I have another skiing lesson this afternoon and I might attempt some parallels.'

'Woohoo! You go, girlfriend!' Jamie laughed. 'No, seriously. Good for you.'

'I know. Get me. It remains to be seen if I can manage them or not. Luc's a good teacher though.'

There was a pause. 'You're spending a lot of time with this Luc, by the sounds of things. I hope he's old and ugly. And fat.'

Lily frowned, not sure why Jamie was interested in what Luc looked like. 'Er... no, actually. He's pretty... hot.'

There was another pause. 'Well. Lucky you,' Jamie said, finally.

'Yes indeed. Anyway.' Lily changed the subject slightly. 'Luc hates Christmas, so I'm going to try and sort out a proper one for him this year. If I can.'

'So you're not back for Christmas then?' Jamie sounded disappointed. 'I'm definitely visiting then.'

Lily chewed the finger of her glove. 'Umm. Maybe not. I haven't properly decided yet.'

And I haven't even spoken to Mum and Dave about it, Lily thought to herself.

'Have you spoken to your mum and Dave about it yet?' Jamie asked, echoing her thoughts.

'No, but I will,' Lily said, resolving to call them later.

'They'll be gutted. Did you say Luc hates Christmas?'

'Yes.'

Jamie let out a derisive snort. 'What sort of wally hates Christmas?'

Lily felt a rush of irritation. 'The sort of wally whose sister took an overdose a few days before.'

'Oh.' Jamie fell silent. 'Fair dos, Lil. I didn't know that.'

Lily immediately felt contrite. 'Of course you didn't. How could you? Anyhoo. It's a sad time for him and I'm just trying to cheer him up a bit. Repay him for all the free ski lessons and the absurd amount of patience he's had to show me.'

'Well that is because you are a very awesome person,' Jamie said warmly. 'And I wouldn't expect anything less from you. Listen, I have to dash, but I'll be in touch soon to let you know dates for me to pop over and see you. We can ski together! That is… if you want me to come?'

'Do bears shit in the woods?' Lily asked, smiling.

'Great. Speak soon, Red. And even better, see you soon.' Jamie signed off.

And not once did he mention Ivy, Lily said to herself.

—

'And how about this one?' Lily wafted another oil under Celine's nose.

'Oh, that one, definitely. I love that.'

'Me too. It's my favourite. It's Indian Moringa oil, with cinnamon, bergamot, myrrh and sweet honey.'

Celine tucked her arms by her side, laying her head down. 'It sounds wonderful. Whatever you can do to get rid of all these knots in my back and shoulders.' She lifted an arm to flip her frizzy blond hair out of the way, then relaxed again.

Lily set her music up. No Ibiza cool classic hits for Celine. She was more of a 'sounds of nature' type of personality. All her candles were lit and there was a lovely, warm glow in the room. She warmed some oil in a burner she had taken to using, mixing it with some cold oil in her hands. Drizzling it along Celine's spine, Lily got to work.

'Mmm, that feels good,' Celine murmured.

Lily worked on Celine's shoulders. There were many knots and lumps in Celine's shoulders and all around her shoulder blades. Lily had to work hard to pummel them out, which she did as gently as possible, but occasionally, she had to be firm. Celine was slender, verging on skinny if Lily was going to be critical about it. 'Under-nourished' they had called it at college, but despite her weathered-looking face, she had good skin elsewhere. Youthful and smooth. And Lily suspected that it wasn't so much that Celine didn't eat, so much as she was one of life's worriers.

'You are very good,' Celine said, lifting her head as Lily worked on her calves.

'Thank you. I love my job.' Lily rolled her thumbs up the back of Celine's legs.

'I can tell.' Celine half-lifted herself from the couch. 'Lily. I wanted to apologise for the recent incident with Elodie.'

'Oh?' Lily didn't realise Celine even knew about it.

'I think it was a case of crossed wires,' Celine said apologetically. 'Elodie… sometimes gets things wrong.'

Lily inclined her head. It must have taken a lot for Celine to apologise and openly say that she thought Elodie was in the wrong.

'Thank you. It's fine. We don't need to mention it again.'

Lily still felt mortified each time she thought about Elodie embarrassing her in front of everyone like that, but there was no point in worrying about it now. Everyone had jumped to her defence, apart from Luc, who had trotted after Elodie like a little lap dog, which Lily still couldn't understand. But still. Everyone else had leapt to her defence and that had been enough for Lily to feel vindicated. Even if the Luc thing still stung when she thought about it.

'You are very gracious,' Celine said.

'It's fine.' Lily paused. 'I just… Elodie doesn't seem to like me very much, I'm afraid.'

Celine let out a sound that was rather like a snort. 'Elodie doesn't like anyone much, Lily! Not girls, anyway.'

Lily quite agreed, but she still thought there was more to it as far as she was personally concerned. She hadn't seen Elodie show the same level of animosity towards Imogen or any of the other girls there.

'Does it have something to do with Luc?' Lily blurted out suddenly. She immediately regretted speaking up. How unprofessional. She focused on her massage, hoping Celine would ignore her comment.

She didn't, but she seemed unfazed by it. 'Luc? No, I wouldn't think so. They are very close, of course.'

Lily bit her lip. Could she follow that comment up? Was it appropriate? 'Erm… yes, they are very close, aren't they? But I guess they would be.' She left the comment hanging.

Celine relaxed more deeply into the couch. 'Why?'

Lily pulled an agonised face. God, what had she started? And why was Celine acting this way? If Luc and Elodie were an item, surely she would know. 'Oh, I don't know. Just their… chemistry…' she finished lamely.

'Chemistry?' Celine sounded vague. She didn't comment further.

Lily sighed. Whatever digging she did about Luc and Elodie, she wasn't ever able to come up with anything concrete. She couldn't understand it.

Abruptly, Celine sat up properly and wrapped the towel from the couch around her body. She burst into tears.

'Oh no, are you OK? Hang on…' Lily grabbed her box of tissues and thrust them into Celine's hands.

'*Merci*.' Celine tugged several tissues out and wept into them.

Nonplussed, Lily watched and waited, occasionally patting Celine's towel-clad knee. What on earth was wrong? Celine must be worried about Pierre, Lily decided. Of course, that's what it was. Unless it was her comments about Elodie and Luc for some reason…?

'I am so sorry.' Celine sniffed. Then she started shredding the tissues in her hands, as though she wasn't aware she was doing it.

'It's OK.' Lily shook her head. 'Please don't worry. It must be very stressful for you with Pierre being in hospital.'

'Pierre?' Celine lifted her head. 'Oh, yes. I suppose so. I am worried he will not be able to ski again. Pierre lives to ski.' She let out a laugh that sounded suspiciously bitter.

'Doesn't everyone here?' Lily asked blithely. 'I was taken aback when I first arrived here with the focus on skiing, the obsession. The constant chat about skiing, skiing, skiing.'

Celine gave her a watery smile. 'I love skiing as much as the next person. I adore it, in fact. I feel so alive when I ski.'

Lily nodded, wiping her hands on a towel. 'I do understand that.'

Celine dabbed the shredded tissues to her eyes. 'I'm glad you're enjoying it after your difficult start.'

'Is there anything I can do to help?' Lily asked, not sure if she was overstepping the mark. Celine was her boss, after all.

Celine shook her head, looking desolate. 'You are a very sweet girl. No, I'm afraid not. It's me and my marriage. I feel so neglected and so…' She stopped abruptly. 'I am talking too much. Ignore me. It's just the stress of… Pierre.'

Lily put the towel she'd been using into a linen basket. Celine wasn't stressed about Pierre. She might be unhappy with him and Lily could well believe that she felt sidelined by Pierre's obsession with skiing and with work, but Celine had something else on her mind, something that was troubling her deeply.

She continued the massage, warming some more oil in her burner. Celine seemed calmer after her tears and Lily made sure the massage was one that would boost her well-being. When she returned at the end of the massage with some iced water, Celine had dressed herself and she was sitting on the couch.

'I must apologise for my tears earlier.' She looked uncomfortable.

'You really mustn't.' Lily swiftly changed the subject. 'I was thinking that the staff could do a little collection for Pierre. Buy him a card and some chocolates, maybe?' She was winging it and that was the best she could do on the spot.

'That's very kind. I am sure Pierre would appreciate that.' Celine stood up. 'Thank you again for a wonderful massage. We are lucky to have you here. Have you thought anymore about staying after Christmas?'

Lily chewed her lip. 'I don't know yet. I think I'll be here for Christmas, but I don't know after that.'

'I hope you stay,' Celine said, squeezing Lily's arm briefly.

I hope I do too, Lily thought to herself. She had a lot of decisions to make.

Chapter Nineteen

'You might stay there for Christmas?' Sue's usually cheery voice sounded flat, but not disappointed.

'I don't know yet. Maybe not.' Lily didn't know what was the best thing to do. She was sitting on the edge of a wall near the *Musée Alpin* in her ski wear, waiting for Luc. She hadn't been sure her mum and Dave would be in as they usually played bowls on a Tuesday, but she had got lucky.

'Is it OK if I put you on speaker?' Sue was asking. 'Dave wants to talk to you too.'

Dave came on. 'Lily? Are you staying in France for Christmas?'

'I don't know,' Lily repeated. 'I mean, I want to come home because I miss you so much, but there are things going on here and oh, I feel so awful about it. I LOVE Christmas with you guys.'

'We love it too, we love it too.' Dave agreed. 'But. What a wonderful opportunity for her, Sue. Don't you agree? Christmas in France… in Chamonix! All that snow and they must have some lovely decorations up, Lily?'

'Stunning,' Lily said, loving the way Dave always put a positive spin on everything. They were so lucky to have him in their lives.

'Oh yes, Dave. An amazing opportunity.' Sue sounded more upbeat. 'I do see that. I do.'

'Could you... come out here?' Lily suggested, the idea suddenly coming to her. 'I mean, I know that's a bit mental because it would be so much easier if I came back to you, because that's just me travelling and not all of you, but...'

'What do you think, Sue?'

'I don't know, Dave. It's a bit crazy, isn't it?' Sue sounded quite keen. 'A bit of an adventure for both of us, though, do you think? We'd have to look into it properly...'

'We would, we would.'

'I mean, where would we stay? At the *Boutique Hotel Devereux*?' Sue asked. 'Does it stay open at Christmas time? Or would we stay somewhere else? Is there a nice, family-owned type hotel nearby? Or perhaps we could stay in town, Dave. We wouldn't need to learn to ski, would we, Lily?'

Lily started laughing. 'No!'

'We need to get the laptop out, Sue,' Dave was saying. 'I'll get onto it right away. Bye, Lily. Speak soon!'

Dave was obviously off to fire up the laptop and get onto Trivago quick smart.

'Leave it with us, love,' Sue trilled. 'But I'm sure we can find a way to make this happen! Dave, what's the laptop saying...?'

With that, they both signed off. Lily smiled, then felt a huge pang. She missed them badly. Chamonix was beautiful, but it didn't feel like home because the people she loved were missing. Thank God Jamie was coming to visit. It was a start, at least. Lily missed Ivy, too, even though they weren't super close, but she was still used to having Ivy half an hour away if she wanted to chat or have dinner. And Ivy had been distant recently. It was ever since Lily had left for Chamonix, in fact.

'What's up?'

Luc was standing over her, grinning. He was wearing his brown puffer jacket rather than his red ski instructor's coat and he looked good.

'Aah. I miss my family.' Lily held her phone up as if that might articulate the depth of her feelings to Luc somehow. 'I just spoke to them and… I just miss them, you know? My mum is… she's just a great mum. And my stepdad is so funny. He's very positive and happy and he makes my mum feel good. He makes us all feel good.'

'You have a stepdad?'

'Yes.' Lily realised Luc didn't know her back story. Because she hadn't told him any of it.

'Would meeting my parents make you feel better?' Luc asked out of the blue.

Lily met his eyes. 'Your parents? I'd love to meet them. Where are they?'

'In that cafe.' Luc pointed to a quaint little place across the road. 'I just met them for coffee, but they would have another one if you come back with me.'

'Sure.'

Lily stood up and started walking with Luc. They left their skis and poles outside and went into the little cafe together. It was called 'Côtés Macarons'. Lily hadn't been there before, but the window looked enticing; a multi-coloured macaron pyramid took pride of place in the centre of the window and it was surrounded by macarons of every colour and flavour imaginable:

coconut, peach and blackcurrant, vanilla, pistachio, salted caramel, rhubarb. The colours were vibrant, punchy and unapologetic. There was also an array of delectable-looking pastries and cakes on offer. Inside, the *salon du thé* was like a swanky lounge with wooden tables and hot-pink furnishings.

Luc led the way to a table with a smartly-dressed couple.

'*Tu es de retour!*' The woman said, looking pleased.

'Yes, I'm back.' Luc kissed her cheeks. 'This is Lily. Lily, this is my mother, Violetta.'

Violetta stood up. Wearing her blond hair in a neat chignon, she was rocking a cropped puffer jacket in emerald green with a fur collar that looked suspiciously like real rabbit with black trousers and little ankle boots with fur edges.

'Aah, Lily.' Giving Luc a little wink, Violetta stood up and embraced Lily warmly. ''ow lovely to meet you. Luc… 'e 'as talked about you.'

Lily blushed. 'Oh, how nice. I'm very pleased to meet you, Violetta. And what a pretty name.'

Violetta smiled. 'Thank you. I also like yours. This is Raymond.' She gestured to her husband.

Raymond was somewhat of a hottie. Tall, blond and with a good physique for a man of his age, he stood up and kissed Lily's cheeks. He had a moustache and it tickled her cheeks.

'*Enchanté*,' he said with a broad smile. 'Please, sit. Some tea?'

'Yes, please.' Lily sat down at the next table with Luc. Cups of tea soon arrived, accompanied by a plate containing a selection of macarons.

'So. You enjoy the skiing now?' Violetta asked.

'A little,' Lily replied. 'Thanks to Luc, I can actually stay upright now.'

Violetta smiled proudly. 'My son is a very good instructor.'

'He is.'

Lily noticed that despite Violetta's smile reaching her eyes, her eyes were sad. The pain of losing Anais was clearly never too far away. Raymond hid it better, but there was a melancholy droop to his moustache that gave him away.

They chatted about skiing as Lily munched on the delicious macarons. She realized she would have to tell Imogen about this place if she hadn't been there yet, since Imogen was addicted to macarons. Lily talked about her work, probably talking too much about it as she was so passionate about being a masseuse and about her home life. Violetta and Raymond seemed to listen keenly, even if they might have missed the odd word here and there.

'And where will you go for Christmas?' Violetta asked. Even saying the word seemed to cause her a little wince of pain. 'Will you go 'ome?'

'I was thinking of going home,' Lily said slowly. 'But now I think I might stay here.'

'*Vraiment?*' Luc looked surprised. 'Really?'

'Yes. I'm hoping my parents might join us, but I don't know what's happening with that yet.'

'And after Christmas?' Raymond asked.

Lily held her hands up. 'I don't know about that yet either. I have many decisions to make.'

Luc checked his watch and stood up. 'We should get up on the mountain. It's getting late.'

'OK.' Lily stood up. 'It was so lovely to meet you both.'

There was much kissing and hugging, and then she and Luc left. They quickly grabbed their skis and headed towards the ski centre.

'Green?' Luc enquired, pulling his helmet over his blond hair.

'Blue,' Lily said bravely. She had been thinking about this since her last visit to see Bernadette and she thought she was ready.

'Good girl,' Luc grinned. 'Let's go. Somewhere different, though. *Les Grands Montets*. There is a blue run there called *Marmottons* that will be perfect. It's a good place to practice.'

'OK.' Already feeling nervous about her decision, Lily followed Luc. They got a chair lift, which in itself was a feat of precision and skill.

'Sit down!' Luc cried as the lift came up and bumped their legs.

Sitting down quickly, Lily put her skis over the footrest as instructed and let Luc pull the bar down.

'Oh God,' she breathed, looking down. 'We're high, Luc. And our skis are dangling in the air.'

'Good, isn't it?' Luc high-fived her. 'Look at you,' he added more quietly. 'I am so proud of you. You decided you wanted to do this and now you have done it.'

'We're not down the blue yet,' Lily warned. 'And it's a bit windy, isn't it?' The chairlift wasn't as bad as she had thought it would be, but she wasn't enjoying the way it was swinging around in the gusts of wind.

Luc said nothing but looked ahead. 'Check out the view.'

It was incredible. Dark green fir trees studded the steep-looking slopes. Naked Christmas trees, Jamie had always called them, and snow stretched out before them and behind them.

'This lift was replaced a few years ago,' Luc informed her.

'Please don't say it broke,' Lily pleaded, feeling her stomach turning somersaults. 'I can't even think about stuff like that.'

Luc laughed. 'Fair enough. OK, to get off, we stand and let our skis glide down the slope.'

Lily felt a tremor of fear again, but she did as she was told. She wobbled as she let her skis glide down the slope, but she managed it.

'Well done.' Luc directed her to the side. 'So. A blue run is like a green run with a slightly steeper slope, but we do not care about that. We are going to cross from side to side the way we did on the nursery slopes and not take any notice of the slope itself. OK?'

'OK.' Lily followed Luc slowly across the slope.

'Snow ploughs for now so you feel comfortable,' Luc shouted. 'And then we will start to draw one ski close to the other one.' He demonstrated, making the move look smooth and easy.

Lily took a gulp of cold air and did her best to copy Luc. Her leg felt as heavy as lead as she tried to draw it round. It simply would not do as it was told!

'Why can't I do it?' she shouted to Luc in frustration.

'Do it again!' he yelled back.

Lily tried again. Her leg still felt like a dead weight, but this time, she managed to bring it in more sharply.

'And the other way!'

Lily did as she was told.

'And again!' Luc called.

Lily did it again. And again and again. Buoyed up with her success, Lily lost concentration and then control, and her skis went one way and her body the other.

'Ouuff.' She landed with her face in the snow. She spat it out. 'Not the face, not the face,' she joked, as Luc pulled her up. 'Am I bleeding?'

'No.' Luc sternly brushed snow from her helmet. 'So that is a lesson in keeping your focus.'

'Yes, sir,' Lily said meekly. He was right, of course.

'But apart from that... I am so proud of you!'

Luc scooped her up into his arms. Lily's face ended up in Luc's neck and she caught the full force of his aftershave. It was delicious. And his body was all warm and sexy and firm and...

'Bloody hell,' she said as he released her.

'What?' Luc was confused.

Not as confused as Lily. The only person who had made her feel all wibbly like that before was Jamie. And the wibbliness she had just felt with Luc had been completely different. It was hotter, more disorientating, more disturbing and just... hotter.

'Nothing,' she mumbled, adjusting her goggles. 'What now? More of the same?'

Luc looked up towards the sky. '*Merde*,' he muttered under his breath.

'What's wrong?' Lily felt panicked. When Luc looked worried, she knew she needed to worry.

'Whiteout,' Luc said to her, pointing.

'Oh my God.' Lily felt herself go pale. Not a whiteout. That was the thing she had always dreaded. All around them and descending from above was a white cloud like thick, snowy fog that wound itself around them. Within seconds, they could barely see more than a few metres in front of them.

'Do not panic,' Luc instructed her calmly. 'We are going to stick to the sides and follow the flags. We are going to do smaller parallel turns or snow plough turns. Worst case, I will ski in front of you in a snow plough and you will hold my poles. I will get you down.' He touched her chin. 'Do you trust me?'

'Y-yes.' Lily was shaking all over. This was terrifying. They were on a blue run and she couldn't see a thing. She wasn't confident with her parallels and this was steeper than anything she'd ever been on before.

'Follow me. My parents have a little place down here. Let's aim for that. I wanted to take you there anyway.'

Luc's authoritative tone reassured her, and Lily had no choice but to do as she was told. Her legs were wobbly, her hands were gripping her poles way too tight, and Lily knew that fear had hunched her entire body up. It was the worst thing she could possibly do when skiing. Lily struggled to parallel turn in such a narrow space and being near the edge was putting the fear of God in her. She couldn't see the edge. What if she skied off it into the abyss? She didn't know what was on the other side. Was it more snow, a steeper slope, trees… nothing?

'Luc, stop,' she shouted, coming to a clumsy stop. She could barely see him and she wished he was wearing his red jacket today. 'I can't do that. I'm too scared.'

'Tuck in behind me,' he instructed firmly, getting into a snow plough position. He grabbed her poles and tucked his in under his arms so the ends were sticking out behind him. Lily grabbed the ends and positioned her skis inside Luc's. She wobbled as they started to move, but she held her stance and let him guide her. Finally, she felt safe. Luc did little turns where he could, but mainly, he controlled his snow plough for a while, which must have killed his thighs almost as much as it killed Lily's.

The whiteout was still in full force, hanging like a snowy fog over and around them. It was eerily quiet with only the occasional noise of another skier slowly passing them. Lily and Luc didn't speak as they descended. Luc was no doubt concentrating, and Lily… well, basically she didn't want to die.

We must be near the bottom, Lily thought to herself, her thighs screaming. *We simply must be. And how long do these bloody whiteouts last?*

Just when she thought she couldn't possibly ski any more, Luc took a gentle turn to the right. How he could see in this heavy white smog was anyone's guess, but maybe he was more used to it. Lily gripped Luc's poles for dear life and did her best to match the movement of his skis with hers. They slowed to a halt and Lily realised they were by some kind of log cabin.

Luc wiggled away from her skis and, turning, pointed at the log cabin. He shuffled over to it and took his skis off. He helped Lily with hers, then fumbled around in his jacket. Finding something – a key? – he unlocked the door to the cabin and pushed it open. Lily almost fell through the door she was so grateful to have cover.

Leaving their skis and poles outside, Luc came in and closed the door. Lily took her goggles and helmet off, panting with the effort of the skiing.

'Oh my God,' she said. 'That was…'

'That was a bad one,' Luc agreed. 'My legs are killing me.'

'Me too.' Lily glanced around. They were in the cutest log cabin. It was small, but well-equipped and very cosy. Wooden beams, cream and fern-green furnishings and lots of personal touches, presumably courtesy of Violetta. It was a romantic little hideaway. She took out her phone, tutting as she realised that it was dead.

'Well.' Luc glanced out the window. 'Looks like this is our home for the next couple of hours. That whiteout is not shifting at all.'

'Right.' Lily stared at him. Her heart started to hammer slightly in her chest. Stuck in a romantic log cabin with Luc? She could think of worse things.

'There is a hot tub,' Luc said, starting to take his boots off. He shot a glance in her direction, but Lily couldn't read his eyes. 'I will go and get it started. We... need to warm up after that.'

'Right,' Lily repeated dumbly. A hot tub. Were they sharing? Taking it in turns? And just a small thing, but they didn't have bathing costumes.

Lily gulped and wished she could phone Imogen. She needed to send out an SOS.

Chapter Twenty

Lily removed her boots and wandered around the log cabin, looking around while Luc was fiddling around with the hot tub. The whiteout wasn't letting up and nothing but white fog could be seen through every window. Lily imagined that the view from this little cabin would be fantastic on a clear day.

There was an adorable little kitchen with wooden units, dark blue touches dotted about and a large oak table in the centre. Little navy curtains the size of tea towels had even been put up in the window and, in opening a few cupboards, Lily could see that it was complete with everything anyone would need.

Luc was back, checking his phone. 'I have service,' he said, focusing on the screen. 'I'll let everyone know where we are.'

'Great.'

Luc sent a couple of texts and then dropped to his knees, piling logs into the fireplace.

'We need to get warm,' he was saying as he set fire to the logs and some firelighters.

'Perfect,' Lily said, feeling an odd mixture of excitement and calm at being in the log cabin with Luc. She was actually quite warm already; the skiing had made her work up a sweat and it was surprisingly toasty in the little hut. She felt rather sweaty, though, so she removed her jacket and hung it on one of the hooks by the front door.

'I love this place,' she commented, drinking in the ambiance. 'It's lovely.'

'It is,' Luc agreed. 'My parents don't use it so much now, but I like it as a...' he paused.

'Bolthole?' Lily offered. 'That's what we would say in English. Somewhere to escape to.'

'Yes, that.' Luc sat back, satisfied with his fire-making skills. 'There should be some food. Are you hungry?' He padded past her to the kitchen.

'A little,' Lily admitted. She was rather taken aback at how his proximity was affecting her. She had just caught a waft of his aftershave and it was messing with her head. She hoped she smelt of perfume and loveliness, not pongy sweat.

'What can I do?'

'See if there is a bottle of mulled wine in that cupboard.' Luc pointed as he opened another cupboard. 'Here is some of my mother's fruit cake.'

'Sounds delicious. Is this it?' Lily held up a large glass bottle with a flip lid like some bottles of beer and cider have.

'Yes. Let's warm it up.' Luc poured it into a saucepan and put the gas on. 'It's homemade,' he explained. 'My mother would not buy something like that from the shops. She thinks it's too sugary.'

'It smells wonderful.' Lily inhaled. It smelt of vanilla and cloves, nutmeg and cinnamon. It was a proper mulled wine.

'It is very alcoholic. That has brandy in it too,' Luc grinned.

'Lordy. I'll never get down the rest of the mountain.'

'Some people ski better after a few drinks, you know.'

Lily peered into her glass. 'I don't know. I always feel as though I need to have my wits about me when I'm skiing.'

Luc looked up, puzzled. 'Your what about you?'

'Oh right. I feel that I need to be… on the ball.' Lily tutted at herself. 'God! That's no better. I feel that I need to—'

'Concentrate?' Luc offered, hacking the fruit cake up rather roughly.

'Yes. That.' Lily laughed. 'Your English is so good I often forget myself and use funny expressions I assume you'll understand.'

'I've noticed,' Luc said drily. 'But my vocabulary is improving a lot around you. I need to have my wits about me. I've got it.'

Lily cheered. 'Well done, you. I can teach you loads of English swear words too, if you want.'

Luc raised his eyebrow, James Bond-style. 'I think I know them all, but do give it a try.'

They feasted on the cake, which was rich and stuffed full of candied orange peel and nuts, and they drank the warm wine sitting by the fire. Luc was right; the mulled wine was very strong, but Lily decided it might help her relax. Soon she was trotting out some of her favourite swear words and expressions. Shocking Luc, even, by the look on his face.

She'd worry about the skiing later. The whiteout was still going strong, so Lily had no idea when they were going to venture out of the log cabin. It felt like a cosy, safe cocoon, almost as though real life had been suspended, regardless of whatever might be going on outside.

'How long do these whiteouts last usually?' Lily said, watching the swirling cloud from the front window. She couldn't even see any other skiers at this point. Or much of anything else, to be honest. The log cabin was enveloped by thick, white mist.

'They can last for twenty seconds or they can last for hours. It depends on how long it takes the cloud to pass over. This is a bad one,' Luc admitted.

Lily shuddered at the memory of the cold cloud descending on them. 'Thank you for getting me down,' she told Luc. 'My hero and all that.'

'Anytime,' Luc said with a grin. 'You did well to hold your nerve. And my poles.'

Lily swallowed. Why had that sounded suggestive? She was being ridiculous. Luc was always a gentleman and he wasn't prone to making crude comments. Lily frowned. She really needed Imogen right now. She was all over the show imagining things and maybe even wanting to imagine things.

'Good parallels earlier too.' Luc got up and topped up their wine. Clearly, he hadn't meant to be suggestive in any way; his mind was focused on her skiing technique. 'We must keep working on those. Not necessarily today, but when we ski together next. I'm booked into some other private lessons over the next few days as the Devereuxs have three English families arriving, but we can ski again after that.'

'I understand.' Lily felt a thud of disappointment and berated herself. *Silly woman*, she scolded. *He does have an actual job to do*. 'I like all the photos,' she commented, pointing to a collection of black and white postcard-sized photographs arranged artistically on the wall.

'My dad is a good photographer. There are a few of Anais in the bedroom.'

'Can I look at them?'

'Of course.' Luc stood up and led the way to a tiny bedroom. It had a double bed, a miniscule wardrobe and a cute white dresser with dark blue flowers painted all over it. 'Here.' He gestured to a cluster of colour photos that had been arranged together in one frame.

Lily studied the photos. Anais had been pretty. Very pretty. She had Raymond's height by the looks of things and Violetta's blond hair. Hers was long and tangled in all the photos, as if being neat and tidy had been an anathema to her, but the wild, untamed look suited her. Her dark eyes, so like Luc's, danced with fun and unspoken laughter in the pictures, making her seem very real and alive. Except that she wasn't.

Lily felt immeasurably sad. 'She was so pretty. And she looked full of life. How sad for you all.'

Luc nodded, but said nothing. He touched one of the photos with his finger. 'I wish you could have met her. She was so full of fun. So funny. She could always laugh at herself, you know? She played the clown, if that is how you say it.'

'Something like that.' Oddly, Lily liked it when Luc got something slightly wrong in English. It always sounded rather endearing.

'Shall we sit in the hot tub?' Luc suggested, tearing himself away from the photos of Anais.

'Er... well, I don't have a swimsuit and I'm not sure we should...'

'What? Sit in it naked? Together?' Luc stared back at her innocently. 'That's a shame. I was hoping for that when we came here.'

'Oh. Well. That's rather…' Lily felt herself blushing and she wasn't sure she liked this cocky version of Luc.

'I arranged the whole whiteout just to lure you here. Even if it hurt my thighs,' he added wryly.

'Oh.' Lily suddenly felt silly. Luc was poking fun at her. Of course he didn't mean for them to sit in the hot tub naked. Lily reminded herself that this little interlude had been accidental. Obviously Luc hadn't planned any of this, although he had mentioned earlier that he had wanted to show her the log cabin earlier.

Stop it, she berated herself. She just wished she had some idea of how Luc felt about her. Or if he even liked her. Surely he liked her? They were spending an awful lot of time together and he seemed to really enjoy—

'Lily. Please.' Luc interrupted her thoughts and opened the door of the miniscule wardrobe. It was full of clothes hanging from the rail, but there were also stacks of clothes to the side. Ski layers, t-shirts, and… swimsuits. 'If you would like to choose one, I'll meet you in there.' He grabbed a pair of bright red shorts and left her to it.

Lily felt embarrassed. Why did she keep making a tit of herself in front of Luc? He was the consummate gentleman, so why was she acting as though he was about to leap on her and ravish the hell out of her? Maybe that was just secretly what she wanted…

No. NO. Lily squashed that thought down as she sorted through some swimsuits. It was time to remind herself of anything that would turn her off when it came to Luc.

That was the best option when she was about to sit in a hot tub, half-naked, with the man. Gulp.

So, Luc and Elodie were an item. Surely they were an item? They were absurdly close, and they had either some kind of hold over each other or they were connected on some level. It was as though they had an unbreakable bond. No one had been able to shed any light on it, despite subtle and unsubtle digging. Imogen was none the wiser, and not even the brief chat with Celine during the massage had given her more of an insight. It was so frustrating.

OK, so what else did she have to go on? Right, well, Luc had laughed at her that time with Elodie at the Christmas drinks and made her feel like a total wally. And he hadn't defended her when Elodie had made her fake accusation. He had simply run off after Elodie as if he was going to comfort her and he hadn't exactly backed Lily up.

And, more importantly, Lily still had feelings for Jamie. He was her close friend and he was fun and lovely and Lily wasn't going to act on it because of Ivy, but she had feelings for him. For Jamie. Not Luc, Jamie. There. Lily felt in control again. She was back on top and ready to sit in a hot tub with Luc with his top off and those thighs.

Pulling out a black swimsuit with a plunging front and white piping, Lily decided to give it a whirl. Was it Elodie's? Had she worn it here with Luc? Lily found the thought upsetting for some reason, so she was relieved when she realised the swimsuit still had the tags on. She slipped out of her ski clothes and laid them out to dry, wriggling into the swimsuit. Her bikini line was all good because she'd had it lasered for months at the spa she used to work at in England, and it was one of the best things she'd ever done. The swimsuit fitted her but didn't do much to hide her cleavage, which was bursting out of the thin material as though it had a mind of its own.

Tugging it up desperately, Lily grabbed a towel and wrapped it around herself for good measure. She found a hair band in the dresser and tied her red hair up so it was in a big messy bun on top of her head.

Heading out to the bathroom at the back, she found Luc sitting in the tub with his arms stretched out. He'd brought their glasses of mulled wine in and had set them on the side. Steam rose from the tub and Luc had obviously pushed his blond hair out of his face because it hung wet and comically skew-whiff. It looked dark when it was wet, and he looked different, but still hot. Oh man.

'Wow. This is lovely.' Lily fiddled with her towel, wishing Luc would look away. *Now would be a really good time to act like a gentleman*, she thought to herself. It was to no avail, though, because for once, Luc wasn't behaving himself. He had his dark eyes fixed on her with amusement.

Sod you then, she thought, whipping her towel off. Climbing the steps with as much dignity as she could muster with legs that were still pink from the cold and maybe also the fire, Lily sank into the warm, bubbly water.

'Oh, that is heaven,' she murmured, luxuriating in the warm bubbles. The hot tub felt like the best place to be. Especially with… no, it was just the hot tub. The hot tub felt great. 'Mulled wine too. A rather perfect day,' she added, meeting Luc's eyes rather daringly and forgetting her good intentions from a few moments ago.

'Isn't it?' Luc raised his glass at her, giving her a cheeky smile. 'I organised the whiteout especially, and on the slope where the cabin was.'

'Oh, do shut up,' Lily said, closing her eyes as she sank more deeply into the tub. 'Stop taking the piss.'

'The piss? Oh, you mean laughing at you, *oui*?'

'*Oui*.'

'Actually, I did want to show you the cabin,' Luc admitted, pulling a 'so shoot me' face. 'I thought you would like it. I just thought we might arrive with more style. You know, with proper vision and side by side, skiing smoothly to the door.'

Lily laughed. 'Oh really? I think a tandem snow plough is the most elegant way to travel. Apart from the horrific pain in the thighs, that is.'

Luc laughed too. They sat in the tub for another half hour, chatting about nothing in particular. Lily enjoyed Luc's company. He had relaxed and let his guard down and he was charming. Very funny and very likeable. Fanciable, in fact. Very, very fanciable. Yum, yum, bubble gum, as Imogen would say.

Lily fanned her flushed cheeks. Damned hot tub…

At one point, Luc stopped talking and stared at her quizzically. 'Hey. You said you were going to talk to me about your dad at some point.'

Lily was taken aback. She hadn't even thought Luc would remember to ask.

Luc held a hand up. 'You don't have to talk about it if you don't want to.'

'No, it's OK.' Lily took a deep breath. Luc had told her all about Anais and, according to Bernadette, he didn't talk to anyone about his sister. 'My dad was… he was a bully,' she said, letting out a jerky breath. 'He put my mum through hell. And me, I guess. He used to pick on me all the time. Tell me I wasn't good enough.'

Luc watched her intently, but said nothing.

'I felt so stupid around him.' Lily was shocked to feel tears pricking at her eyelids. 'I couldn't seem to do anything right. And the way he treated my mum… God, Luc. It was awful. He… he hit her. In front of me. He cheated on her. He had children by loads of other women all over the world, and then he left one day and left us with nothing.'

'That is terrible.' Luc looked genuinely traumatised by her story.

'It was.' Lily fought the urge to burst into tears. 'We had no money. We had to sell our house and live in a council flat because my dad hid all his money away offshore. He sold his company to a friend for a pound so he could buy it back later.'

Lily felt a stab of fury as she remembered what her dad had put them through.

Luc reached out and touched her hand. 'I am so very sorry you had to go through that.' He shook his head, his eyes brimming with sympathy. 'I find it hard to understand any man being that way towards his children. My father… he is such a kind, gentle man.'

'He is.' Lily swallowed. 'Raymond seemed like a lovely man. A lovely dad. He is very proud of you.' Luc was still holding her hand. She wanted him to.

'I hope he is proud of me,' Luc commented. 'He is the man I measure myself by, so I want to be like him and for him to be happy with my choices.' He paused. 'Your mum is with someone else now, I think you said?'

Lily nodded. 'Oh yes. An amazing man named Dave. My stepdad. He's brilliant. You'd love him. I mean, that sounded weird. You know, if you ever get to meet him.'

Luc gave her a wide smile. 'That is good to hear. I would love to meet both of your parents.'

She stared at his hand, still clasped around hers.

'Sorry,' Luc said. He left his hand where it was for a while. Then he removed it. 'I suppose we should check on the weather?' He lifted himself out of the water, displaying a smooth, sculpted chest and good thighs. The red shorts made him look even more tanned and Lily buried her face in her mulled wine. Luc wrapped a towel around himself and gallantly put Lily's towel closer to the steps.

'Thank you for trusting me,' he said, still looking moved by her story. 'It must have been hard for you to talk to me about your dad.'

Lily nodded, not trusting herself to speak.

Luc wandered into the other room and Lily let out a breath, realising she had been holding it as Luc left the room.

Lordy. That had been an intimate moment and for some reason, it had really shaken Lily up. She rarely talked about her dad to anyone other than Imogen or Jamie – and with Bernadette, it had felt detached and professional to a degree – but with Luc, Lily couldn't explain it. She felt exposed and vulnerable. But on another level, she was glad she had spoken to him about her childhood. It felt as though they were even, but in a positive way.

'The whiteout is clearing,' Luc called.

'Great,' Lily said, her heart sinking. Oh bugger. Now it would be time to go. And she had been enjoying herself too. Emerging from the warm water, she wrapped her towel around herself and joined Luc in the lounge. He had tucked his towel around his waist and he was rotating his arm and shoulder, wincing painfully.

'God, is that from lugging me behind you?' Lily asked, feeling guilty.

'Maybe, but not because you are heavy.' Luc rolled his shoulder again. 'I have an injury – bad accident on a black run years ago. Certain things aggravate it.'

'Let me see.' Lily got Luc to sit down and pushed her fingers into the muscles around his shoulder blade. 'Aah! Here.' She pushed a little deeper and felt him stiffen. 'I can help with that. Least I can do. Lie down,' she instructed. 'Either on the sofa or the floor.'

Luc opted for the sofa, laying down with his arms by his side. Lily got to work, rotating the shoulder gently before going into the muscles with practised fingers, manipulating and massaging.

'Oh, that is good,' Luc groaned.

Lily smiled. 'Well, I owed you a massage for the ski lessons.'

'Er, I'm expecting more than ten minutes in return for the lessons,' Luc retorted, his voice muffled from the cushion.

'OK, well this is a down payment,' Lily told him. His back and shoulders were also tanned, but not as tanned as his face. He was in incredible shape – toned, with good definition. Lily gulped. She shouldn't be this attracted to someone other than Jamie, although she wasn't sure which was worse: Jamie was taken and Luc probably was too. And Elodie was already her enemy.

'OK, that's you done for now,' Lily said, standing up. 'We'd better get back.'

Luc turned over and pulled an exaggerated disappointed face. 'A short down payment, but it was good. Thank you. I look forward to the rest of it.'

Lily busied herself getting dressed again in the other room. Luc had told her to leave all the wet things by the hot tub as a cleaner came in once a week. She strapped herself into her ski boots again, groaning as the boots cut into her calves. She wiggled her legs around to get them more comfortable. Luc tidied up and put the fire out safely, pulling his brown jacket on again.

'Ready?'

'Yep.' They stepped outside. The view, as Lily had predicted, was glorious. The whiteout had fully cleared, leaving a blue sky and, astonishingly, no cloud whatsoever. There was a view of unnamed mountains stretching out in front of them, as well as a rather steep slope.

Lily gulped and steeled her nerves. God, this was going to be a challenge, but she was going to have to trust Luc. And herself. She followed Luc down slowly, haltingly, but as soon as she found her feet again, she worked on the parallel turns. When she looked down, she felt sick and all the familiar fear shot to the surface. But when she ignored the down part of the slope and just moved across it, she was fine. It took a while to get down, but she made it.

At the bottom, there was a restaurant with a bar area that was full of skiers who had obviously camped out there during the whiteout. They had all been drinking and there was a loud, happy atmosphere across the decked area.

'You did very well,' Luc told her as they stepped out of their skis. 'Very well. Especially now I know about your dad. Good for you.' He put his arm round her and drew her in.

Why did that feel so right? Lily relaxed into his embrace, enjoying every second of it. Luc pulled back and stared at her mouth.

He's going to kiss me, Lily thought, her heart thumping in her chest. *And I bloody well want him to.*

One of their phones rang between their bodies, making them both jump.

'It's me,' Luc said, touching his jacket. 'It's Elodie.'

Of course it was. Elodie was never far away from them, was she?

'She's saying we need to get back.' Luc frowned. 'I guess we'd better go.'

'Yes, we better had.'

They walked back to the hotel in silence, both deep in thought. When they entered the reception area, Elodie rushed up to them.

'Luc, Marc wants to see you in his office.'

'OK. I will see you later, Lily.' Giving Lily a lingering glance, Luc headed off to the office area.

Elodie looked at Lily with a tight smile on her face. 'Did you enjoy the whiteout?'

'I wouldn't say I *enjoyed* it as such,' Lily replied, wondering why Elodie was looking so pleased with herself.

'You spent some time with Luc at his parents' cute log cabin,' Elodie said, stating it as fact.

Of course she knew! And of course she'd been there before. Lily felt narked, and a bit sick at the thought of Elodie and Luc in the hot tub together, stretched out on the fur rug in front of the roaring fire…

'He is so kind, isn't he,' Elodie said.

Not sure where Elodie was going with this, but knowing it was nowhere good, Lily watched her warily.

'Kind? Yes. Yes, he is.'

'He has taken you under his wing and he is looking after you.' Elodie's face twisted spitefully. 'But that is Luc all over. He feels sorry for people and he knows a broken-hearted girl when he sees one.'

Lily fought an urge to slap her. Oh, for the love of God! What was this girl's problem? Elodie definitely had it in for Lily. There was no doubt about it.

'What is your point, Elodie?'

'He is so easy to fall in love with, isn't he?' Elodie sat on the edge of one of the sofas, flicking one of her slender legs in agitation. 'As he well knows.'

Lily started to have a horrible creeping feeling. Was Elodie suggesting that Luc had deliberately made her fall for him? If so, that was a very cruel game he was playing. Or was Elodie just messing with her head? Lily knew she wasn't remotely trustworthy. After all, she had made up a complaint in front of everyone just to make Lily look like an idiot.

'Ask him yourself,' Elodie shrugged, knowing full well that Lily wouldn't dream of doing such a thing. She had, however, succeeded in placing a very large seed of doubt in Lily's head. 'But in the meantime, I have a surprise for you.'

'Great.' Lily felt that she would rather ski up that blue run backwards in a whiteout than see what kind of twisted surprise Elodie might come up with.

Elodie turned and waved at something – someone – behind her. The person turned and got up. A person with messy, floppy dark hair and flirty eyes.

Lily gasped and clapped her hands to her face. 'Jamie!'

'Lily! Red.' Jamie strode towards her and pulled her into a hug.

Lily hugged him back, shocked to the core. She breathed in his familiar smell, the woody aftershave and the washing powder, and closed her eyes. He was a piece of home. Was it the same as Luc hugging her and the way she had felt then? Lily wasn't sure. But this was Jamie. Lovely, lovely Jamie. Lily squeezed him harder.

Lily opened her eyes and found herself staring right back at Luc, who had just come back from his catch up with Marc. They stared at one another. Luc's expression was inscrutable, but she knew what she was thinking. She was thinking that she had been played, good and proper. Luc had felt sorry for her, and playboy that he was, he had flirted and befriended her and made her fall for him. He couldn't be that callous, though, could he? Maybe he was just a playboy at heart and all his chat had been calculated. Meeting his parents, opening up about Anais, all of it.

Lily felt horribly upset at the thought of it. But Elodie was a bitch, she reminded herself. Maybe, just maybe, it wasn't true.

'This is Jamie,' Lily said, untangling herself from Jamie's arms.

'Jamie, the one Lily talks about all the time,' Elodie interjected, the picture of innocence.

Lily shot her an evil look. She hardly talked about Jamie at all. And certainly not to Elodie, of all people.

Looking stoked at that news, Jamie turned and held his hand out to Luc. 'Luc? You're the one who's looked after Red so well since she's been here. Thank you.'

Luc hesitated then shook Jamie's hand. 'Red… right.' He said Lily's nickname as if he didn't like it. Lily cringed slightly.

'We must ski together,' Jamie said to Luc. 'I hear you're almost as good as me,' he deadpanned and then broke into a smile. 'Jokes. I know you're fantastic. You'll have to show me all the good off-piste.'

'Of course.' Luc smiled politely. 'I have some private lessons booked in, but will have some time in a few days, if you are still here.'

Jamie pulled his 'flying by the seat of my pants' face. It was one Lily was very familiar with. 'Open ticket, but it all depends on work too. I have a conference to attend here in town. Red, you'll have to show me around.'

'Definitely.'

Lily suddenly felt even more delighted that Jamie was here. Thank God. She needed an ally, Jamie was her good friend, and she needed him. Lily glanced at Elodie. She was watching everything with a smug smile, her arms folded. God, she was odious! One of the most horrible people Lily had ever met in her life.

'Well. I will leave you both to it,' Luc said, inclining his head in their general direction. His eyes met Lily's briefly, then slid away.

'See you at dinner?' she said, hating how distant he was being. The intimacy of the log cabin suddenly felt like a million years ago.

'I'm eating with my parents,' he told her shortly. His expression softened. 'But I'm sure I'll see you around.'

'Right.'

Lily felt herself plummet slightly as Luc left and Elodie hurried after him. What had just happened? She was cross with Luc if he was playing her, but he had no reason to be cross with her! What had she done wrong?

'Red.' Jamie turned back to Lily. 'You look great. I'm so pleased to see you. Are you pleased to see me?'

'Yes, of course,' Lily gave him a warm smile. 'We must go and find Imogen. She'll be delighted to see you. Are you all settled in your room?'

'Yes, it's up on the second floor, with a balcony and a hot tub. Well, a bath with jets.'

'You have one of the posh rooms,' Lily told him, feeling his arm snake around her shoulders. It felt natural and normal. They were often that way with one another. 'Lucky you.'

'Lucky me indeed,' Jamie said, smiling down at her. 'Lucky me.'

Lily walked out of the lobby in a daze. What was all that about? They headed for the staff room and Imogen got all excited when she saw Jamie. She introduced him to Ollie and all the other staff while Lily sat on the edge of the sofa and caught her breath.

Watching Jamie flicking his floppy hair out of his eyes and shaking hands with everyone on the hotel staff, Lily tried to make sense of her feelings. She was over the moon that Jamie was here. Looking at his face brought home right back into the room and it made Lily realise that as much as she loved it here in Chamonix, there were things she missed about home. Mostly friends and family, if truth be known, but still. Lily had been rather concerned that she wasn't missing home more, but she had left so abruptly that maybe that was normal.

And what about Luc? Lily twirled a lock of red hair around her finger. She liked Luc. There. She had admitted it. And she shouldn't like him because Elodie clearly had some kind of claim on him. Also, if Elodie was correct, Luc was an arrogant player who got his kicks from making heartbroken girls fall in love with him. Lily frowned. Did she believe that of him? She had thought he was a player when she had first met him. Or had Elodie told her that?

Lily felt confused by the whole situation. She badly needed a girly catch up with Imogen to chew it all over and make sense of it. But for now, Jamie was here and Lily owed it to him to make his trip fun.

'Are we all out on the beers tonight?' Jamie asked, looking thoroughly excited.

'Yes!' Lily said. 'Of course we are.'

'Brilliant! After dinner, you can show me the sights of Chamonix,' Jamie said to Lily, coming back to stand by her side.

Sylvan shimmied over, clearly jealous that Jamie had turned up. 'Dinner is mini *croque monsieur*, followed by *confit* of chicken.'

'Ooh,' Jamie cooed, clearly realising that Sylvan needed some kind of applause after his announcement. 'That sounds yummy.'

Sylvan flinched at the use of the word 'yummy', obviously not feeling that it was extravagant enough to describe his superb cooking.

'I will see you at dinner, Lily,' he said, walking off.

'He fancies you,' Jamie said, openly laughing.

'Shut up,' Lily said, nudging him. 'He books massages with me every other day.'

'Dirty monkey.' Jamie pulled a face. 'I hope he's not one of your hairy clients.'

Lily giggled then sobered up. 'I wish Ivy was here,' she said, meaning it. 'Don't you?'

Jamie's face became impassive. 'Yes, of course,' he answered smoothly. 'That would have been lovely. But she's working. Naturally.' He turned away and started chatting to Ollie about skiing and where all the best runs were.

Lily chewed her fingernail as she watched him. He still gave her those feelings and he shouldn't, because of Ivy, but thoughts of Luc kept popping into her head as well. Lily no longer knew who she liked, who she trusted and where she wanted to be. And she didn't even know if she had any control whatsoever over what was going to happen. Jamie represented home and familiarity and Luc represented something new and different and exciting. Not in the sense that she would ever end up with him, of course, but just in the way that he represented her new life in Chamonix.

As everyone made post-dinner arrangements to go to two trendy bars and an insanely loud nightclub, Lily wished she could just hibernate in Luc's parents' log cabin on her own for a few days. Her life had suddenly gotten really complicated and she had no idea how she felt about anything.

Chapter Twenty-One

Imogen's alarm went off at five thirty. She reached out sleepily and turned it off.

'Oh dear,' she groaned. 'My head.' She struggled to sit up, her black hair flopping over her face. 'Lil. Who's that on our floor?'

Lily sat up with slightly more ease. 'That's Ollie and that's Jamie,' she said in a low voice. 'They wouldn't leave last night so we tossed our fleeces over them and they slept there.'

'Bloody hell.' Imogen managed to get out of bed. 'Why do you look fresh as a bloody daisy, woman?'

'I didn't drink the shots,' Lily told her with a wicked smile. It was true. Everyone had gotten in on the shots last night and Lily had refused them. Shots made her exceptionally drunk and, for some reason, she had felt that she needed to have her wits about her. As it turned out, it had been a really fun evening and she needn't have worried. Jamie had been hilarious and as playful as a puppy and everyone had adored him. Still, Lily was glad she hadn't overdone it because she hated doing breakfast duty on a hangover. The smell of the eggs always made her want to barf.

Lily had been plagued by images of Luc and Elodie together, especially since the two of them had been noticeable by their absence. Images of Luc's tanned body writhing all over Elodie's beautiful, slender frame, her super-flat hair being tossed around with gay abandon, had caused her to feel quite nauseous. Was it just the principle of the thing? Was it because she liked Luc and thought of him as a *very* attractive friend, while she thought Elodie was a harpy with horns and a devil's tail?

Lily grinned as she watched Jamie turn over under her baby blue fleece, repositioning the 'I Heart Skiing' cushion under his head so his dark hair flopped all over it. He had the best face, Lily thought, feeling her heart clench slightly. Well, not the *best* face. Luc's was pretty hot too.

Oh, do shut up, she scolded herself. There is more to life than these two men, neither of whom were actually hers. They both belonged to other people – one of them Lily's sister, and the other a harpy with horns and a devil's tail. All she could do was enjoy Jamie's company and try to figure out if Luc was a manipulative playboy with a black heart.

Easy peasy. Shouldn't be too hard to work out, Lily told herself, shaking her head at the ridiculousness of it all.

'What's happening?' Ollie said, lifting his head from the pillow. 'Oh no. Who hit me with skis last night?'

'Porn Star Martini did that,' Imogen told him smartly as she emerged from the shower room. 'And her pal B52.'

'Oh dearie me,' Ollie flopped down again. 'I'm not on breakfast duty, am I?'

'Yes, you are, lover boy,' Imogen said, laughing. 'You'd better get up.'

'Wass happening?' Jamie sat bolt upright. 'And where the fricking hell am I?'

Lily got out of bed. 'What's happening is you're hungover and so are we. We have to go and serve breakfast to everyone and you don't.'

'Sweet!' Jamie said, flopping back down on the floor. 'What time is my conference? Does anyone know?'

'I think you said midday yesterday,' Lily said, stepping over him. 'And you can have my bed now if you want.'

'Brilliant!' Jamie said, heaving himself up and throwing himself into the warm space Lily had left. 'Someone please set an alarm for five to twelve and then I'll…' Before he finished talking, he was fast asleep again.

Lily, Imogen and Ollie got themselves up and dressed and downstairs. With very sore heads, they started the breakfast service, completing their tasks like clockwork because they had such a good routine now. Elodie was nowhere to be seen and Lily had a horrible feeling she had stayed with Luc. Not that it was any of her business.

Lily assessed her day. She had two massages first thing, one with Sylvan and one with a guest, followed by her last appointment with Bernadette. She had promised to show Jamie around Chamonix before his conference, but perhaps it would be after if he was sleeping off his hangover until then. She set an alarm on her phone to go and wake him after Sylvan. After breakfast service, she hurried down to the room. Sylvan was only seconds behind her, always keen. He spent the entire massage talking, asking her very unsubtle questions about Jamie and when he was done with that, he wanted to know all her Christmas plans. At that point, he moved on to talk about one of the new chalet girls, Charlotte, perhaps signalling the end of his infatuation with Lily.

With any luck, she thought to herself.

Lily suddenly remembered that she had been planning to make Luc fall in love with Christmas again. Did she still want to do that if he was the massive dickhead Elodie had made him out to be? Lily finished Sylvan's massage and made a pact with herself. She loved Christmas and it was such a shame that Luc didn't anymore. If she could get him to enjoy even a modicum of the festive season and see it as something fun for the first time in years, she was all for it. So she was going to go ahead with her plans and she would speak to Bernadette about it later.

Ushering a still-keen Sylvan out of the room, Lily nipped upstairs to wake Jamie up.

'Conference in two hours,' she told him, shaking his bare shoulder gently. He had removed his shirt from the night before.

'Oh jeez,' he groaned, rolling onto his back. 'Why on earth did I drink all those shots?'

'Because they taste good. Get up. I have to go back to work and then I have hypnotherapy. Shall I meet you in town?'

'Perfect,' Jamie said, putting his legs over the side of the bed, then forcing himself to sit up. 'Bloody, bloody hell.' He checked his phone. 'Oops, messages from Ivy. I'd better give her a call.'

'I'll leave you to it,' Lily told him, feeling a pang, but pushing it away. Heading back downstairs to her massage room, Lily got on with her day.

—

'So how do you feel after your last session?' Bernadette asking, placing Lily's hot chocolate on the table beside her.

'Thank you. Pretty good actually. I mean, that whiteout was shocking, but I wasn't as scared as I thought I would be.'

Lily had told Bernadette all about it earlier. She felt good that she hadn't frozen or cried; she had simply gotten on with getting down the mountain. With Luc's help of course.

'My friend Jamie arrived yesterday, too,' Lily informed Bernadette.

Bernadette eyed her shrewdly. 'Oh yes? And he is a friend or a special friend?'

Lily smiled and sipped her hot chocolate. 'Well. I have feelings for him, but he doesn't have them for me. He's dating my sister.'

'That's complicated.' Bernadette stroked Jez's brother, Charles, as he strolled past haughtily. 'But is it nice to have him here?'

'Definitely. He's a bit of home, if you know what I mean.'

'I do. And do you feel the same about him now that he's here?' Bernadette asked.

Lily thought for a moment. 'I don't know, if I'm honest. He's my friend, but I came here to get away from him and it's been good for me to have that break.'

Bernadette smiled at Lily. 'But did all those feelings come rushing back when you saw him?'

'I don't know,' Lily admitted. 'There were feelings for sure, but I don't know. Maybe... maybe not... I don't know!'

'OK, OK.' Bernadette laughed. 'And how is Luc?'

Lily felt her body stiffen slightly. 'Elodie told me he was trying to make me fall in love with him. That he knew I was broken-hearted and he was trying to distract me.'

Bernadette stared at her for a moment, then burst out laughing. 'What? There is no way Luc would waste his time acting like that, I can assure you. He doesn't need to make girls fall in love with him. They just do.'

'I'm sure,' Lily said, sounding snippy to her own ears. 'Is he… a playboy, Bernadette?'

'A what? Like Hugh Hefner?' Bernadette's face was a picture.

'Well, kind of. I mean, does he have a bad reputation? With girls.' Lily could feel herself flushing.

'Oh, that.' Bernadette smiled mischievously. 'I think he used to have that reputation,' she said honestly. 'I think he used to have lots of fun. But he's grown up now. He's wary of messing around too much with chalet girls and the like because they often come for a season and then they're off. Perfect for him back in the day, but not so much now when he's of an age to want to settle down.'

'Hmm.' Lily wasn't sure what to make of that. Did a leopard ever change its spots? Or did it just grow up, as Bernadette was suggesting? Maybe it just didn't matter if Luc was dating Elodie.

'What do you think of Elodie Devereux?' Lily asked before she could stop herself.

'Elodie Devereux.' Bernadette's expression became grave. 'She is a very mixed up girl, in my opinion. She used to be Anais's best friend. Did you know that?'

'No, I didn't know that.' Lily was stunned. Why had no one mentioned that before? Why hadn't Luc mentioned that?

'I'll leave Luc to talk to you more about that one,' Bernadette said with a wise nod of her head. 'Now I have made you a list of everything Christmas-related that we do here in France. You know it's all mostly about Christmas Eve?'

Lily took the list and tried to read Bernadette's tiny, curly writing. 'Yes, I've heard that. You have a big dinner, I think? But how can I go about organising that?'

'You can't, but I can,' Bernadette replied triumphantly. 'I thought we would play it like this. I will invite Raymond and Violetta. You will invite Luc. We will do all the cooking together and organise all the Christmas things.' She shrugged. 'Worst case, you and I have the most enormous meal on our own and we eat leftovers for days afterwards.'

'Deal.'

Clutching her list, Lily popped her shoes in a rucksack and pulled her ski boots on. Saying goodbye to Bernadette, she grabbed her skis and poles from the hallway and left to meet Jamie. He was waiting for her outside one of the bars in the centre of town. He had changed into his ski clothes, wearing a fairly loud turquoise jacket with orange trousers, but they suited him. And at least she wouldn't lose him on the slopes.

'I've asked this guy if he'll stash our skis for us as long as we come back for hair of the dog,' Jamie said, gesturing to a nearby bar. 'Do you fancy showing me around?'

'Sure.'

They tucked their skis next to each other in the special area by the bar – 'his and hers', Jamie quipped – and set off through the town. Lily showed Jamie her favourite haunts, including the fondue restaurant she and Luc had eaten in and a few funky bars. She showed him the macaron tea shop where she had met Luc's parents and they wandered through the Christmas market, buying pretzels and hot chocolate.

Lily suggested that Jamie buy Ivy some pretty earrings for Christmas. They were definitely her style, and he did so, but rather reluctantly.

'OK, so I need a beer before we ski,' Jamie said. 'I need something to perk me up. My head is thumping.'

They sat outside under a heated lamp and Lily ordered a mulled wine, while Jamie got a beer. Lily idly wondered where Luc was, then remembered he had lots of private lessons over the next few days.

'How was your conference?' Lily asked, thinking the mulled wine wasn't half as good as Violetta's.

'Dull as shit,' Jamie replied, flicking his hair out of his eyes. 'They brought it forward by three days, hence my early arrival, by the way. I was going to tell you and then I thought I would just surprise you.'

'I was definitely surprised,' Lily said with a smile. 'How was Ivy when you spoke to her earlier?'

'She was fine,' Jamie said. He let out an almost indiscernible sigh. 'Busy with work, as usual.' He met Lily's eyes. 'To be honest, I don't know if it's working out, Red. I really like her, but I think we want different things.'

'Maybe,' Lily said sadly. She hated the thought of Ivy getting hurt. Ivy had been so excited about the two of them getting together, but now it all seemed to have fallen rather flat. Lily was pleased that she didn't feel angry or upset about it anymore. And she wasn't sure what that meant. Was she over Jamie? She eyed him over her mulled wine. She wasn't sure she was really over him, but perhaps the feelings weren't as strong and painful as before. It was a dull ache rather than a sharp pang.

'Shall we ski?' Jamie said, draining his beer.

'Yes.' Lily was excited. She would show Jamie her newfound skills and hopefully he would be impressed. 'I can't do anything more than a blue, I'm afraid.'

'Really?' Jamie looked disappointed. 'I thought we'd tackle a red today.'

Lily felt herself have palpitations and she knew she had to stand her ground. 'I'm really sorry, but that will just send me into a tailspin. I need to work up to a red. But if you want to go off on one without me, feel free. I'd hate to hold you back, especially on your first day here.'

'Don't be daft!' Jamie shrugged off his earlier comment. 'I'm here to see you, apart from my conference, so a blue run it is.'

Feeling pleased that it was more important to ski with her than dash off down the difficult runs by himself, Lily took him to the run she and Luc had gone down the other day. She soon found out that skiing with Jamie was a whole new ball game compared to skiing with Luc.

'Let's go!' Jamie cried excitedly at the top of the mountain. He set off at a high speed, not even looking behind him to see where Lily was.

Lily took a deep breath. She reminded herself about all the basic skills Luc had taught her and Bernadette's words rang in her ears as usual. Her dad's voice had been drowned out by all the hypnotherapy and Lily was over the moon about that. But where the hell was Jamie?

Lily took her time and started with some good, strong snow plough turns. She then tried to parallel, reminding herself of Luc's instructions as she did so. Something didn't feel quite right today, though, and Lily wasn't sure what it was. Was it because Luc was absent? Was it because she was effectively alone, since Jamie had bombed off without her? Lily was rather peeved about that, truth be told. She fell over a couple of times, but picked herself up and carried on. When she got further down, she found Jamie waiting for her at the side, easy to spot in his bright jacket and salopette combo.

'Where did you get to?' he asked her. 'I totally lost you.'

'I'm not that speedy at the moment,' Lily said, feeling rather foolish. 'I'm only just perfecting my parallels.'

'Really?' Jamie looked flabbergasted and quite unimpressed. 'But I thought Luc the wonder instructor was teaching you? I thought he'd been teaching you for weeks.'

Lily felt vexed. 'He has. It's just been a labour of love. I was petrified, Jamie. Literally petrified. I couldn't even move off the top of the nursery slope on the first day. I've come so far...' Her voice petered out and she stopped talking, worried she might start to cry.

'OK, OK,' Jamie put his arm round her. 'I'm sorry. I just thought this Luc had turned you into the most magnificent skier, that's all. I didn't realise you were still at this very basic level.'

Lily frowned. Was Jamie being a wanker on purpose? Or did he just not realise how nobbish he sounded?

'I've been so looking forward to skiing with you,' Jamie said, looking dejected, and once again, Lily felt annoyed. Was she supposed to feel guilty for not being a better skier? She had done her very best since she had been here and quite frankly, she thought some good parallels on a fairly challenging blue run deserved a medal. Where was patient, encouraging Luc when she needed him?

'I tell you what,' Jamie said, squeezing her shoulder. 'I'll teach you to ski properly. I'll get you doing parallel turns to die for. In a matter of minutes.'

Lily shook her head. 'I have to go at my own pace. I get too nervous otherwise.' She could feel the horrible, cold, curling panic rearing up inside her again.

'We'll go super-slow,' Jamie told her. 'I promise.' He demonstrated a perfect parallel. 'See. It's as easy as that! Copy me.' He did another one. 'Go on. I'm watching you.'

Feeling edgy, Lily did her best. It felt OK, but she knew it wasn't perfect.

'No, not like that. You're not watching. I'll go again.' Jamie did another turn, his skis flicking snow up.

Lily gritted her teeth. She could feel her entire body tensing up again in just the way it shouldn't. She felt as if she was leaning the wrong way and putting her weight on the wrong leg. She was and Jamie told her as much. In very critical terms.

'I'm telling you how to do it,' Jamie finished, looked irked. 'I don't get how your body is doing something different.'

'Because you've been skiing for fifteen years and I've been doing it for five weeks. With a horrific fear of heights to battle as well!'

Lily felt tearful on the slope for the first time since she had set off that day with Luc. She felt stupid and useless and as though she wasn't going to be able to get down the mountain at all.

'Oh well, looks like your knight in shining armour has just arrived,' Jamie snapped.

Lily turned and saw Luc skiing towards her. She couldn't help but feel her spirits soar. He *was* her knight in shining armour. On the slopes, at any rate. And all of a sudden, Lily realised how incredible he was as an instructor and how patient. He hadn't once made her feel stupid or inept.

'How is the skiing?' Luc asked, popping his goggles up.

'Not great,' Lily admitted. 'I seem to have fallen apart again.'

'I don't know how you do it, mate,' Jamie told Luc, looking exasperated. 'I just can't ski that slowly. And her parallels...'

'Her parallels are excellent,' Luc said smoothly. 'When she is relaxed.'

Lily could have kissed him. No, she really could have kissed him. He was an instructor, so it was his job to be patient and kind. But he had just defended her and she felt immeasurably grateful, especially after Jamie's near-bullying style of teaching.

'I can take over here if you like?' Luc offered. 'I have half an hour before my next private lesson. And you can go and get a really good ski in on your first day.'

Jamie didn't need telling twice. 'Thanks, mate. I appreciate that. I'll see you back at the hotel, Red.'

Wordlessly, Lily watched Jamie ski away from them. Well, that was a side of him she hadn't seen before. It wasn't a pretty one, that was for sure.

Luc had a strange expression on his face as he watched Jamie ski away at high speed, doing razor-sharp turns before disappearing from sight. 'Right. Let's get back to your parallels. If you remember, this is all about drawing that ski round and shifting your weight. See...'

Lily copied Luc, feeling her breathing begin to regulate. This was better, this was how she felt good. They got to the bottom in good time, probably ten minutes or so.

'Again?' Luc asked.

'Actually, I think I should go on my own,' Lily said, knowing she was doing the right thing. 'You were amazing rescuing me like that, but I have to be able to do this on my own. Right?'

'Right. I'm impressed.' Luc gave her a smile. 'Good for you.'

'See if you can find Jamie on the red runs or the blacks,' Lily suggested innocently. 'Out-ski him.'

Luc laughed. 'I'm due on a red for my lesson, anyway. And I'll do my best if I see him. Just for you. Remember everything I have taught you and... have fun.' He skied off and Lily took a deep breath. She was doing this blue run. Alone. She went up in the chair lift and she set off from the top without giving herself time to think. She worked on her turns, bringing her ski in to the other one, maintaining her balance, using her core. She wobbled, she fell, she resorted to the odd snow plough when it felt steep or fast. But she got down the blue run. Alone. And in pretty good time and in pretty good shape. The odd bruise here and there, but nothing lasting.

At the bottom, she took her skis off and bumped into Imogen, who was standing in the outside section of the bar clutching an Aperol spritz.

'Hey! I saw you come down that blue on your own. You go, girl!' Imogen jumped about, no mean feat in her ski boots.

'Don't fall over,' Lily laughed. 'And give me a swig of that. I bloody need it.' She took a huge gulp of Imogen's drink and went inside to buy them another round.

'So what's the deal?' Imogen asked, settling down at a table, plonking her helmet and gloves down next to her.

'The deal?'

'Luc or Jamie, Luc or Jamie?' Imogen looked like a naughty schoolgirl, all excited about the prospect of a good man gossip.

'Oh God. Stop it. It's not as simple as that, is it?' Lily got onto a stool with difficulty. 'These bastard boots. I do hate them still.'

'Sods, aren't they?' Imogen took a healthy swig of her orange-hued drink. 'Why isn't it as simple as that?'

'Because Jamie is with Ivy and Luc is probably with Elodie.'

'Well.' Imogen took stock. 'I don't think Jamie is very happy with Ivy, do you? I think she's all about her work and he's a social butterfly who is impatient about everything.'

'He certainly is about skiing,' Lily said. She told Imogen what had happened on the blue run earlier.

'Oh dear. What a wally. That's not attractive.'

'No. It's not.'

'So maybe it's a one player game then!' Imogen raised her glass. 'Much easier.'

'Well, that's the issue, isn't it?' Lily said gloomily. 'Is Luc just a player?' She told Imogen what Elodie had said the other night.

'Poppycock!' Imogen spluttered. 'That is such a pathetic attempt to get you to go off him.'

'Why though?' Lily wanted to know. 'They must be an item. Or Elodie wants them to be.'

'Well, that's possible. But apart from that, I don't see it. They are good friends, for sure. And Luc indulges her, but it's like… it's like he sees her as his little sister or something.'

Lily narrowed her eyes. Was that it? Did Luc see Elodie as a replacement sister now that Anais had gone? Especially since Anais and Elodie were best friends?

'Oh, I don't know, Ims,' Lily said, feeling tired all of a sudden. 'Maybe it doesn't matter. I'm just going to focus on doing this Christmas thing for Luc.' Then she outlined her and Bernadette's plan.

'That sounds amazing. They do a lunch thing at the hotel on Christmas Day, I think, but the Devereuxs do their own thing Christmas Eve and Ollie wants to take me out to dinner that night. He's booked somewhere already.' She looked all heart-eyed and Lily couldn't help laughing. Imogen never really fell in love, but this time, she clearly had.

'Hang on. Isn't that Luc bombing down that black run?' Imogen said, squinting into the distance. 'And is that…'

'Jamie hot on his tail? Yes it is!'

Lily watched them avidly. They were both excellent skiers, to be fair. Jamie was kamikaze in style, throwing himself down every twist and turn, whereas Luc was more precise – fast, elegant and skilful. Though he was still demonstrating a huge amount of daring.

'Jamie might beat him on speed,' Imogen guessed, watching them. 'But Luc is amazing! I've never actually seen him ski that way before. Wow. I mean, that!' She stopped and gasped. 'I would have stacked it doing that. And so would Ollie! He's sensational!'

Lily pulled a face at Imogen. 'Easy tiger!'

Imogen elbowed her. 'Shut up, you silly moo. I don't fancy him! I only have eyes for Ollie, you know that. But seeing Luc skiing like that... it is rather hot.' She giggled.

Lily grinned. She hadn't seen Luc ski like that before either. He had always been taking it slowly with her and stopping in front of her. But watching him parallel at high speed like that was impressive to say the least. Not to mention as sexy as hell...

Lily watched Luc weave down the steep mountain face, barely losing a beat, maintaining his poise and control throughout. The speed he was travelling at was breath-taking! And Jamie was hot on his heels.

'My money's on Jamie,' Imogen stated enthusiastically.

'Whaat? No way! I'm rooting for Luc all the way.'

Imogen raised an eyebrow. 'Of course you are! And so am I, deep down. But someone has to root for Jamie, don't they?' She winked.

Their eyes went back to the slope and they watched avidly, feeling mounting excitement as the two guys zig-zagged down the treacherous run.

'Luc's ahead!' Lily said breathlessly.

'Hang on, Jamie's catching up — now he's ahead!' Imogen was jumping around on her stool, almost falling off in her excitement. 'This is brilliant, Lils! It's like they're having a duel over you!'

Lily tutted, but felt an undeniable stab of pleasure at Imogen's words. 'Don't be daft! They don't even know we're watching!'

Imogen slapped her arm. 'I know that, you silly woman. I mean they're only doing this because of you.'

Lily shook her head disbelievingly. 'No, you're wrong.' This wasn't about her! This was about boys pissing in the snow. As it were.

Imogen sighed. 'You're so, so dumb when it comes to men, Lily. Listen. Why is Jamie here?'

'He had a conference.' Lily kept her eyes on the mountain. 'Oh God, I thought Luc was going to fall!'

'He organises the conferences,' Imogen replied. 'And he can host those anywhere. Come on, Lily.'

'He loves skiing!' Lily frowned and pointed to the mountain. 'Where did they go?'

Imogen squinted. 'They might have gone off-piste for a bit, but they'd have to re-join it there. See? Anyway, Jamie could have gone anywhere for his conference. He's here to see you.'

'We're friends,' Lily protested.

'You have loads of friends. Where are the rest of them? They're not here visiting. Not even your sister.'

Lily bit her lip. Imogen had a point, especially about Ivy. Why hadn't Jamie said anything? If he had feelings of some kind, he'd have spoken up, wouldn't he? She said as much to Imogen.

Imogen shrugged. 'It's a tricky situation, hun. He's dating your sister. I said it from the start – I think he picked the wrong sister. He assumed you weren't interested and he moved on to Ivy. That's my honest assessment and I haven't deviated from it.'

Lily cringed. It sounded horrible for Ivy. Lily hated the thought of Ivy being second best to anyone. She was worth far more than that, and Lily wasn't convinced that Imogen was right on this front anyway.

'And Luc. Luc is another reason Jamie is here.' Imogen winked knowingly and helped herself to some savoury bar snacks they had been given, shovelling a handful into her mouth.

'Now you *are* being silly.'

'Trust me, I'm right about this. You told Jamie about Luc giving you skiing lessons. You've probably mentioned Luc far more than you realise, because that's what people do when they like someone.'

Lily felt herself blushing. Oh, this was all so embarrassing. She didn't mention Luc a lot, did she?

'Oh yes,' Imogen nodded knowingly. 'Yes, Lily. It's like me. I talk about Ollie all the time. When I really don't need to be talking about him. It's a thing.'

'Oh bloody hell…' Lily felt about fifteen. This was mortifying. Had she really fallen that badly for Luc? She fancied him and she wasn't going to deny that, but did she feel more for him than just basic… well, animal attraction?

Imogen triumphantly brought out her trump card. 'Anyway, for boys, this stuff is a red rag to a bull. They can't bear someone else being your hero, because *they* want to be your hero.'

'I wouldn't have said he was my hero on the slopes earlier,' Lily retorted. She combed out her helmet hair. 'He just wanted to go and ski and me being so slow was annoying the hell out of him.'

Imogen shovelled more snacks into her mouth. 'Yes, he didn't do himself any favours there, did he? He didn't do the gentlemanly thing, but in his defence, skiing is such a bug. And he hasn't skied in, what, three years, you said? It's like a drug to some people.'

'Yes, maybe.' Lily wasn't sure what to think. And this was all supposition on Imogen's part. Jamie hadn't said a word to her about having feelings – and neither had Luc. So this was probably all academic and nothing she needed to worry about. Jamie might not be happy with Ivy, but he hadn't made any overtures to her. And with Luc, who knew? There was Elodie to think about, and again, no one had said anything to Lily, so she was going to disregard it.

'Ooh! There they are.'

Imogen pointed as two figures appeared from between the trees. Luc and Jamie! Neck and neck, matching each other parallel for parallel and, on occasion, just going straight down without any turns – which looked horrifically dangerous to Lily.

'They're going to kill themselves,' she said worriedly to Imogen.

'Who would you run to if they both fell?' Imogen shot at her, pointing her finger for good measure. 'Quick! No overthinking!'

'Luc!' Lily cried.

'Ha!' Imogen clapped her hands. 'There you go!'

Lily put her hands to her face. 'Oh no! Poor Jamie. No, Jamie. Jamie definitely. He's my friend and I've known him for much longer…'

'You're overthinking!' Imogen sang. 'Too late. You said Luc first. So that's who you'd run to.'

'*Merde!*' Lily said, shocked at herself. Or was she? She and Luc had become very close, but every time they got close, Elodie popped up and stirred the pot somehow.

Imogen cupped her hands, pretending to be a commentator. 'And they're coming down the black run at high speed – breakneck speed! They're neck and neck and it's not clear who the winner is going to be. Ooh and Jamie takes the lead but Luc has caught up again. Jamie is taking some serious risks, which might cost him dearly...'

'Knobhead,' Lily said, laughing.

'And Jamie has cut Luc up.' Imogen stopped and frowned. 'Now that – was not good at all. That was actually bang out of order. Did you see that, Lily?'

Lily's nodded. 'I did. Oh my God. Jamie.'

Lily's mouth fell open as she watched Luc pull up sharply. He almost fell and the slope was so steep, Lily was amazed that he managed to hold himself. She couldn't believe Jamie had played dirty like that! How ungentlemanly. How unsporting! She watched Jamie carry on down the last of the slope, while Luc shook his head furiously. He took a moment and then he swiftly got himself going again.

'Bloody hell!' Imogen was agog. 'That was terrible! He knew he was losing, so he did that. What a sore loser!'

'Tell me about it!' Lily was upset. She had known Jamie for years and she had never seen this side of him before. Or hang on. Had she? Lily remembered a time at school on Sport's Day. Jamie had been on the relay team and he always ran number four. His team was losing and there was no way they could win. Then the person in the lane next to him had mysteriously fallen. It was very sudden, almost as though he'd been pushed. Or tripped. And maybe there had been other incidents. There was something weird at Jamie's work when he hadn't got a promotion, but the person who did get it had left mysteriously.

Looking back, Lily realised that she may have excused Jamie's behaviour in the past. Because they were friends and none of it had ever mattered or affected Lily directly. Jamie had always relayed these incidents to her as though they were simply fun, inconsequential things that had happened.

'All's fair in love and war, eh?' Imogen commented.

'But it's not, is it?' Lily said, feeling her mood plummet. She felt idiotic. It wasn't that she had changed – or even that Jamie had changed. It was that, for some reason, Lily had just started seeing Jamie for exactly who he was. Before that, she had been blind to his faults because they were such good mates and because the silly things he glossed over had always seemed, well, silly. But cutting Luc up the way he had didn't seem silly. It seemed a little sinister, and it showed a streak to Jamie's personality that Lily wasn't that keen on.

Jamie skied over to them, out of breath and looking victorious. 'Did you see us? What a race!'

Imogen gaped at him. 'Yes, we saw you!' She wasn't going to let it pass. 'You totally cut Luc up. So I'm not sure why you look so triumphant.'

Jamie shrugged, not even having the grace to show remorse. 'Well, there was an icy bit and I had to scoot round it. It was just unfortunate that he was in the way.'

Lily stared at him and shook her head. God. He really was a numpty. He sounded like a child! A child who couldn't get his own way, so he had employed a dirty tactic in order to get what he wanted.

'Er, no, you were losing, so you played dirty,' Imogen corrected. 'That's what happened, Jamie!'

Luc was approaching them, and Lily had no idea what he was going to say or do. He stopped next to Jamie and removed his goggles. Imogen and Lily waited with bated breath.

'Great race,' Luc said finally, extending a hand.

Lily and Imogen glanced at each other.

'Thanks,' Jamie said, nonplussed. He had clearly expected Luc to either ski past in a strop or rock up and make a dig about his poor sportsmanship. Instead, Luc had played the gentleman to the hilt and he had gone on a charm offensive.

Lily met Luc's eyes. His face was impassive, but she could see it in his eyes. He thought Jamie was a massive dickhead. And if she wasn't mistaken, he thought Lily was just as bad. Presumably because he thought they were an item or that there were feelings.

But there were no feelings now. Of that, Lily was sure. As Lily was watching them both on those slopes, Lily knew she was rooting for Luc. She was appalled by Jamie's behaviour. It wasn't major in any sense, it was just crap, and after leaving Lily on the slopes earlier and making her feel terrible about her skiing, cutting Luc up like that had finished Lily off completely. The strong feelings for him that had faded since she had come to Chamonix anyway seemed to have evaporated. Jamie just wasn't who she thought he was. Or rather, she'd always ignored his bad qualities, and now it was as though they were being blared out over a stereo.

'I must get back,' Luc said politely. 'I will see you all later. Thanks again for a good ski off.' He gave Jamie a nod and then turned and skied away from them.

Imogen glanced at Lily and pulled a face.

'Well, I guess I'd better get back too,' Jamie said. He looked confused, as though he realised he'd been outplayed. 'Are you coming, Lily?'

Lily swallowed but raised her chin decisively. 'No. I think I'll stay here for a bit.'

Jamie looked disappointed – sulky, even. 'Fair enough. See you at dinner then.' And off he went.

'He's a *massive* dickhead,' Imogen commented. 'I've gone right off him!'

Lily nodded. How much of her time had she wasted mooning around after Jamie when he was clearly an idiot? Why hadn't she realised what he was like? Had she been so infatuated with him that she had missed these characteristics? She must have been. Perhaps it was seeing him in a different context, or because of Luc. Lily wasn't sure.

'Lily, stop beating yourself up.' Imogen interrupted her thoughts. 'I know you and I know what you're doing. It's just that Jamie has always been your friend. You've never seen him in a relationship before – not really. And sometimes you see someone's true colours when they're under pressure.'

'I guess so. I just feel like an idiot.'

'Nah. We've all been there,' Imogen said. 'We've all fallen for someone who has turned out to be a big knob-head. It's just disappointing when that person is a friend as well.'

Lily finished her drink. 'True. But it's Ivy too. I just don't think Jamie cares about her and I don't want her to get hurt.'

'That's for her to sort out,' Imogen said gently. 'Come on, let's get back. It's dinner time soon and we're serving.'

They got off their stools and collected their skis.

'What about Luc?' Lily asked. 'I'm confused about him too. Everything Elodie has said…'

'She's lying,' Imogen scoffed. 'You just need to speak to him.'

Lily fell silent as they made their way back to the hotel. What a day. She'd realised that the guy she thought was amazing and who she'd had feelings for was actually an idiot, and she realised that she'd fallen head over heels in love with a guy who might be dating Lily's biggest enemy.

I've really messed up this time, Lily thought to herself.

Chapter Twenty-Two

The following day, Lily was in the office looking for the notebook she used for booking her massages. Usually she kept it in the top drawer of the cabinet, but it wasn't there. She had slept badly, tossing and turning as she thought about Jamie and Luc and Ivy. Every hour, almost on the hour, she had seen the time, and she felt bleary-eyed and exhausted today. She had dark shadows under her eyes. It had to be said that she didn't really look her best.

Where was this bloody book? No one else would find any use for it; it was only for her massages. She huffed and sorted through the drawers. She knew she was going to have to speak to Jamie today as well. They needed to clear the air and Lily was going to be as honest as possible with him, even if the thought of it made her want to curl up and die.

Lily opened the bottom drawer of the cabinet and rummaged through it. Perhaps she had left her book in her massage room? She flipped through the paperwork and other notebooks and sighed. Then she frowned, tugging at something at the back of the drawer. It was a brown envelope, pristine and neatly folded. Lily peered inside. What were all these little slips? She took them out and leafed through them. They were from a casino – losses from a casino, more specifically, and there were a lot of them. Lily checked the dates. They were old, from a month or so ago, and they were from a casino some miles away, not the one in Chamonix Mont-Blanc. That one was a smart, glamorous building adorned with fairy lights and little bushes standing outside.

Lily closed the envelope thoughtfully. Was this where the missing money was going? Someone had a gambling problem. It could be anyone, since they were all in and out of the office all the time. Or was the more obvious answer that these slips belonged to someone in the Devereux family?

Lily's brow knitted. Why hadn't the person destroyed the slips? Put them through the shredder? These slips weren't from the past week or so, and could therefore belong to Pierre. He could he be the one with the gambling habit, and could have forgotten about these slips before he broke his leg. Or what about Marc? He always seemed so together, but who knew what was going on behind closed doors. Elodie? As much as she wanted to think it was her, Lily wasn't convinced. She could see Elodie floating around a casino in a designer gown looking fabulous, but she couldn't see her sneaking off to gamble in secret.

Celine? Lily paused. Again, could she really see it? Celine was highly-strung, but a gambler?

'Oh hi.'

Lily jumped out of her skin. Luc was standing right behind her. 'Good God, man. You made me jump.'

Luc looked amused for a moment before his expression became distant. 'What are they?' He turned his head to look. 'Oh.'

'I know.' Lily put everything away and looked around to make sure no one else was approaching. 'I just found them in there when I was looking for my massage book. Who do you think they belong to?'

'I have no idea. Would you like me to take them? I'll try and get to the bottom of it. Speak to the casino, maybe.'

'Good idea,' Lily nodded, handing the envelope over. 'I won't say anything to anyone.'

'That's good. I think we should try to keep this quiet.'

Lily observed Luc discreetly as he had a quick look through the contents of the envelope. He looked tired, with dark shadows under his eyes that were almost as bad as hers. She kind of wanted to hug him, but he wasn't giving off a vibe that encouraged any sort of contact whatsoever. In fact, for Luc, he looked positively unfriendly.

'Listen, about Jamie yesterday,' she started.

'You don't need to say anything,' Luc said, shutting her down.

'But I do,' Lily insisted. 'The way he was with me, definitely the way he was with you—'

Luc raised his eyebrows. 'He is your… friend. There is nothing to say.'

'There is a lot to say,' Lily said hotly, wanting to say her piece. 'I couldn't believe the way he acted towards you. That was so unacceptable. You would have beaten him hands down if he hadn't cut you up like that.'

'It doesn't matter,' Luc said, looking bored. 'I haven't given it a moment's thought. It was just a silly race. As for this,' he held the envelope up. 'Leave this with me and I will get it sorted.' He left the office without another word.

'OK.' Lily felt small and embarrassed and completely hopeless. Whatever spark had been between her and Luc in the past, if there even had been any kind of spark, had completely disappeared now. Whatever they may or may not have had, Luc was clearly over it.

Later That Day

Lily was Christmas shopping. She had been out skiing with Ollie and Imogen, on blue runs only, and had thoroughly enjoyed it, even though she had a heavy heart. She had completed her massage duties for the day: four guests and no Sylvan. He was in hot pursuit of Charlotte, the new girl, which was a huge relief.

In one of the more upmarket shops in Chamonix, Lily found a beautiful woollen scarf in emerald green for her mum, who had a scarf for every occasion, but always loved to receive a new one. She bought a funny kitchen gadget for Dave, which she knew he would love. Dave was easy to buy for. He liked to receive books or gadgets or new shirts or funky socks. He just appreciated any gift, really. He was that kind of guy.

Next, Lily looked for something for Jamie. She wasn't massively feeling the love for him right now, but they always bought each other token gifts. She found a pair of ski gloves that were similar to the ones he had, but a bit more stylish. Perfect. As she wandered to another department, Lily thought about Luc. Should she get him a present? She wasn't sure. She didn't even know what was going on between them. But they were friends at least, right? He probably wouldn't buy her a gift, though, and then she'd feel like a moron and it would be all embarrassing.

Lily caught sight of something. It wasn't expensive, but it was a good one. It was also impersonal, but kind of personal, because Luc would understand why she'd bought it for him. Perfect! And if he didn't get anything for her, she'd keep it for herself and pretend that she hadn't thought about him either.

She was nearly done, but then she found a sexy going out top for Imogen and a jokey book about skiing for Ollie. And finally, Ivy. Lily considered earrings for Ivy, but remembered she had encouraged Jamie to buy some. She opted instead for a beautiful slippery cream silk shirt that was suitable for both work and play, with gold buttons and elongated cuffs.

Just at that moment, Ivy rang. Lily paused and composed herself, then answered the call.

'Did you know I was buying your Christmas present just then?' she asked.

'No,' Ivy chuckled. 'I just thought I would call you.'

'I'm joking. I know it wasn't some sort of psychic moment.' Lily finished paying and left the store. 'How are you?'

'Not too bad.' Ivy sounded rather upbeat. 'I have this amazing new contract and I've been working on it for months. It's kind of a big deal.'

'Good for you!' Lily loved Ivy's work ethic. She might not have time for a relationship right now, but she was devoted to her work. That's what made her heart sing.

'How's Jamie?'

'Haven't you heard from him?' Jamie was going down in Lily's estimation by the minute.

'On and off, but to be honest, I've been way too busy to worry about his level of contact.' Ivy sounded detached and Lily was glad.

'I haven't been that impressed with him since he's been here, if I'm honest.' Lily found herself outside the casino and it reminded her of her chat with Luc earlier. Fighting the dark mood that threatened to descend, Lily sat down on a nearby wall and dumped her bags next to her. She told Ivy what had happened on the ski slopes the day before.

'Doesn't surprise me,' Ivy replied. 'I've seen this side of Jamie a few times before. He's super competitive and I think just a bit immature. I'm not sure he knows what he wants. I... did think he had the hots for you, to be honest.'

'Oh God, really?' Lily felt horribly guilty. 'Listen, Ivy. I have a confession to make.'

'Oh. I don't like the sound of that.' Ivy sounded flat.

'No, no, don't be silly. Nothing has happened. It's me. I used to have feelings for Jamie.' Lily came out with the words in a rush. 'I don't now, but I did for a while. For around six months or so.'

There was a pause. 'Oh, Lily! He was the guy you liked. You tried to tell me about him, but didn't say who it was.'

'That's right. I wasn't sure if I should say anything and then you two told me you were seeing each other that night.' It felt so good to be honest with Ivy.

'That must have been so horrible for you. No wonder you left abruptly. And, oh God, me and Jamie all over each other at Mum and Dave's too!'

Lily wanted to reassure her. 'It's not your fault. I did come here to get away from Jamie. Over him, I guess, but it's been the best thing for me. The skiing, the people I've met…' Her voice tailed off.

'You've met someone!' Ivy sounded pleased and Lily was fairly certain it didn't have to do with her not having feelings for Jamie anymore.

'It's complicated,' Lily said, laughing at her use of that immortal line.

'Isn't it always?' Ivy fell silent. 'I'm going to end it with Jamie when I get back anyway. We're just not suited. I need someone more… mature. More work-focused, I think.'

Lily sighed. God, it was all such a mess. But she was glad that the feelings – or lack thereof – were mutual between Ivy and Jamie. She had been so worried about Jamie finishing with Ivy and Ivy being devastated when, actually, Ivy was already on the case and she sounded clear, calm and happy.

'Go sort this complicated thing out with whoever this guy is,' Ivy told her. 'You deserve to be happy, Lily.'

'Thanks, you too. I just don't think it's as easy as that.'

'It's as easy or as hard as you make it, Lil. And that's enough wisdom for me. I need to get back to work.' Ivy signed off and Lily let out a sigh. She felt better already. She guessed she needed to speak to Jamie next.

'Fancy a drink?'

Lily jumped. This time it was Jamie. What was it with everyone today? Jamie was wearing the coat and trousers he had turned up in and Lily had a feeling he was leaving.

'Yes, OK.' Lily stood up and smiled as Jamie gathered up her bags. Well, at least he hadn't completely lost his manners. They walked to a nearby patisserie and found a table. It was very Christmassy, with the window full of festive-looking pastries and cakes. There were little red macarons with reindeer faces and Lily ordered some to go with her coffee.

Jamie looked uncomfortable. 'I think I owe you an apology,' he started. 'For yesterday.'

'Which part?' Lily asked as their coffee arrived.

'Leaving you on the mountain like that.' Jamie shook his head and looked thoroughly awkward. 'I got the skiing bug again and all I could think about was the powder and how I wanted to get back into it. I was a sod to you. I'm really sorry.'

Lily squeezed his hand across the table. 'It's OK. I didn't like you much at the time, I have to admit, but since I've been in Chamonix, I've seen what skiing does to people.'

'And the way I cut Luc up.' Jamie lifted his eyes sheepishly to meet Lily's. 'What a prat! I just wanted to beat him, and he was better than me and I had to stop him.'

'Wow.' Lily was impressed at his honesty but turned off by his words. She was also annoyed at herself because she knew there had been other times when Jamie had behaved like this and she'd ignored it.

'I was jealous,' Jamie admitted. 'You and he have this chemistry and I thought you liked him. Well, you do, and he definitely likes you.'

'He doesn't,' Lily replied in a dull voice.

'Er, yes he does,' Jamie insisted. 'The two of you are just being total idiots. But anyway. I came here to tell you how I felt about you.'

Lily bit her lip and said nothing. Oh God.

'It's OK.' Jamie held his hands up. 'I realise now it was just stupid. As in… I liked you for ages and you didn't like me, and we were just friends. Then I got over it and fell for Ivy, and then you said you had feelings. It threw me all over the show.'

Lily shook her head at the silliness of it all.

'And then I tried to make it work, but we're not suited, and I thought it was because I wanted to be with you.' Jamie wrapped his hands around his coffee. 'But I realise now that it's not about you or about Ivy. I just don't really want to be in a relationship right now.' He looked coyly at her. 'And I can't compete with a dude like Luc. He's high end. Top drawer. And I'm a prat who cuts a guy up on a black because I treated it like a pissing contest.'

Lily couldn't help laughing. At least Jamie could admit that he'd been a massive dickhead. He had redeemed himself on that front.

'Aah well,' she said. 'Lots of good things have come out of this. You've done lots of skiing. I moved here and it has been the best thing I have ever done.' *And Ivy is – and will be fine*, Lily thought to herself.

'And you've met a great guy,' Jamie said, asking for the bill. 'You just need to sort that out now. And I need to catch my plane.'

'You're off?' Lily did feel a stab of sadness, but she knew it was for the best.

'I'm off. I have stuff to sort out at home.' Jamie met her eyes and unspoken words passed between them. He and Ivy were over – they just needed to say the words to one another. It would be amicable, though, and that had to be a good thing.

They got up and left the patisserie. They started walking back to the hotel together.

'It's a great place,' Jamie said. 'Will you stay here?'

'I don't know yet.' Lily still hadn't decided. 'I don't know what to do in the summer months.'

'There will be a job,' Jamie said confidently. 'You'll be fine. It suits you here. You're flourishing.' He gave her a sideways glance. 'Sorry I was such a dick about your skiing. I should have realised what an achievement it was for you to get down that blue run.'

'You really should have,' Lily agreed, giving him a shove. 'But I forgive you.'

'That's because you're awesome,' Jamie told her. They were at the hotel now. 'Luc is a lucky guy.'

'Do stop saying that,' Lily said crossly. 'I can assure you, Luc doesn't think he's lucky at all.'

Jamie smiled. 'Nah. That's just because you two need to admit your feelings to one another and get it on. Trust me. I'm a guy and I can read him like a book.' He handed her bags over. 'I'm going to say goodbye here. My bags are in the lobby.' He hugged her. 'Bye, Red. I'll speak to you soon.'

Lily watched him walk into the lobby, feeling sad. She didn't think Jamie would be in touch for a while. Their relationship, or rather, their friendship, had shifted. They weren't going to be as close now, which was gutting, but that was how it had to be.

Imogen came into the lobby as Lily walked in.

'We're due in a staff meeting,' she told Lily. 'Elodie is on the warpath. Again.'

'Oh crap.'

Lily's mood turned darker. A staff meeting with Elodie was the last thing she needed. She followed Imogen into the staff area and dumped her bags in the corner. Luc was present, but apart from a brief glance in her direction, he didn't acknowledge her. Lily felt even sadder.

Everyone had been wrong about Luc having feelings about her, that was for sure. Marc and Elodie stood at the front of the room with Celine. They all looked serious.

'First of all, my father is due home soon,' Marc started. 'We are all looking forward to welcoming him back.'

Everyone clapped politely.

'Any news on his skiing?' Ollie asked.

Marc nodded. 'They think he'll be OK, but he's going to need a few more operations.'

'Thank God for that,' Ollie said, voicing what everyone else was thinking.

'I have the schedule for the week here and I will pin it on the noticeboard. Guests, skiing lessons, etc,' Celine said. 'We also have the social evening for guests this week, so you will all need to attend.'

'Do we still need to wear stupid costumes?' Imogen asked, giving Elodie an evil stare.

Elodie narrowed her eyes at Imogen.

Celine shook her head. 'No, we're not doing that now. We're just having a little Christmas social for the guests.'

'And that's the only reason it's going ahead, by the way,' Elodie announced snippily. 'Because it's for guests.'

Everyone stared at her, confused. Lily glanced at Luc, but he was resolutely looking ahead.

'More money has gone missing,' Elodie said, scrutinising them all as if she might be able to pick out the culprit by glaring. 'We thought it had all stopped, but it hasn't. So as of now, apart from the social evening, all Christmas events are cancelled. Including the lunch at the 3842.'

There was a collective groan.

'Forgive me, but every cloud,' Lily whispered to Imogen. 'I was shitting my pants about going up there.'

Imogen nodded. 'We can go there anytime,' she whispered back. 'She was only doing that to be a bitch to you.'

'Merry bloody Christmas,' Ollie muttered. 'She's such a cow.'

Elodie was in full vitriolic flow. 'So for the time being, Christmas is cancelled. There will be no special lunch here, and no trip up to the 3842. Unless the person who is doing this steps forward by the end of today, nothing will go ahead. And that person – whoever you are, whoever is doing this to my family's company and hotel – you will be responsible for everyone missing out.'

There was silence in the room. People exchanged glances, but no one said a word.

Elodie shrugged. 'So be it. You have until the end of today. Meeting adjourned.' With that, she swept out and Marc and Celine, both looking extremely upset, followed.

'Wow,' Imogen said, sitting down heavily on a nearby sofa. 'Talk about dramatic!'

'Definitely.'

Lily strained her neck to see where Luc was, but there were too many people milling about. She had to speak to him, though, to see what he'd found out about the casino slips. What if he knew who the culprit was? He'd have to tell the Devereuxs so the staff didn't miss out on their Christmas lunches and everything else.

Lily looked up. 'Hang on. They're coming back in.'

'What?' Imogen got up.

Marc, Elodie, Celine and Luc came back into the room.

Marc hushed everyone with his hands and the loud gaggle of noise came to an abrupt halt.

'Luc has some information he would like to share with us all,' he said.

They all stood to attention. Lily felt sick. Luc must know who was responsible, or maybe he was just going to talk about the casino slips.

Luc stepped forward. He raked his hand through his dirty blond hair and cleared his throat. 'Right. I have something to say to you all. And that is... sorry.'

There was a hushed gasp. What did Luc mean? Lily found that she had that cotton wool in her mouth, the kind she used to get at the top of mountains.

Luc was talking again. He looked calm. 'There is nothing I can say to defend myself, but I can't let everyone else suffer because of my actions.'

Lily started to shake her head. No way. Luc wasn't the thief. He couldn't be! He didn't have a gambling problem! This was ridiculous. Lily tried to catch his eye, but he wouldn't look at her. Lily felt sick. This couldn't be happening. She felt Imogen take her hand.

Marc and Elodie looked shocked to the core. All staff members looked poleaxed.

'So it is with regret that I tender my resignation,' Luc said finally.

Lily felt like crying. Was anyone who she thought they were? Jamie had turned out to be someone she hadn't really known and now Luc was revealing himself as a thief with a gambling problem.

'No.'

Everyone looked up to see who had said no.

It was Celine. She stepped forward. 'No, Luc. I cannot let you do that.'

'Celine,' Luc said, sounding as though he was warning her.

'It's OK,' she told him gently. 'Everyone. Marc, Elodie. I am so sorry. Luc was trying to do a noble thing, but I cannot let him. I am the thief.' She hung her head.

'What?' Elodie looked astonished. '*Maman*, no! If it's Luc, let him take the blame.'

Imogen stared at Lily pointedly, as if to say, 'Is she for effing real?'

'It's not Luc. He's being the ultimate gentleman.' Celine gave him a watery smile. 'In English, you would call it "falling on his sword". But I have to be brave and I have to own up to this.'

Luc gave her a sympathetic smile.

'I've had this gambling problem for some time now,' Celine said, wringing her hands. 'It has just been my personal hell, but then I got desperate. And I stole from the family business.'

Marc looked horrified, but he moved forward and put his arm around his mother. Celine almost crumpled, then she bravely lifted her head.

'All I can say is I am very sorry to have put suspicion onto all of you. I feel so ashamed.'

'I think we will leave it there,' Marc said, holding Celine up. She looked close to collapse. 'Elodie, get the door please. We need to get *maman* some water.'

For a second, Elodie looked like a rabbit caught in the headlights, then she suddenly moved into action and opened the door. Marc helped a stumbling Celine out and Elodie shot out after him.

'Bloody hell!' Imogen let out a jerky breath. 'That was hardcore! Fancy Celine having a gambling problem. And stealing from her own business? That's madness!'

'Luc's the man, though, isn't he?' Ollie said. 'He was fully prepared to take the blame for Celine. I'm assuming he must have known it was her.'

Lily thought so too. People had gathered around Luc asking him questions, but she desperately wanted to get to him.

'I'm opening the bar,' Joe called. 'If you want – or need – a drink after that, follow me.'

Imogen nudged Lily. 'Go and talk to Luc. Go on! You need to talk.'

Lily squared her shoulders. They did need to talk. He didn't look as though he wanted to talk to her, but she was going to give it a go anyway.

'Luc?' She walked up to him.

'Lily.'

'Can we talk?'

Luc stared at her. 'OK. Yes, of course.' He checked his watch. 'Shall we go for a walk?'

Lily nodded. She followed him out, giving Imogen a helpless glance as she left. She had no idea how this chat was going to go, but Lily had to know how he felt. Or tell him how she felt. One way or another, they needed to sort things out.

Chapter Twenty-Three

Luc and Lily headed out of the hotel. Nothing was said for several minutes as they trudged through the snow and into the twinkling lights of central Chamonix.

'How about the fondue restaurant?' Lily suggested.

'They have a nice bar,' Luc agreed. They took the side road to the restaurant and went in. It was roasting inside like last time and they immediately took their coats off. Lily enjoyed the gaudy Christmas decorations of the place once more, admiring the statement tree and all the bold baubles.

Luc ordered some drinks and they got onto high, uncomfortable bar stools. They loved a bar stool in Chamonix.

'Well,' Lily said.

'Well,' Luc said. His dark eyes met hers, but they were impenetrable. He was wearing a smart black jumper that showed off his physique, but it didn't do it justice. Not from what she remembered seeing at the log cabin, anyway. She fanned her face to get rid of that memory.

'Hot in here, isn't it?'

Luc watched her in amusement. 'Er... yes, I suppose so.'

'Where shall we start?' Lily asked, wanting to get the conversation away from her disturbing thoughts. 'How about Jamie?'

'Jamie?' Luc frowned, as if Jamie was the last person he wanted to talk about.

'He's a tool,' Lily explained, holding on to the stem of her mulled wine glass. 'The way he left me up the mountain and cutting you up like that.'

'A tool...' Luc pondered the word.

'A twat. An idiot. A moron.'

Luc's brow cleared. 'Oh right! Yes. Yes, he is a tool. For any number of reasons.'

'I don't have feelings for him,' Lily blurted out. She felt her cheeks flush. 'I just need to say that.'

Luc contemplated her. 'But you did?'

'I did.' Lily winced. 'For a while. He has been my friend for a long time and he's fun and I just started to think maybe there was a chance we were something else. But we won't ever be. I don't even think we'll talk much now.'

Luc almost drained his beer in one go. 'And that makes you sad?'

'Losing Jamie as a friend?' Lily nodded. 'That, yes, but nothing else. I didn't realise who he was, that's all.'

'What about your sister?'

'She doesn't want him either,' Lily said with a short laugh. 'But he'll be fine, I'm sure. He's not ready for a relationship. He's... immature.'

'A tool,' Luc said again, clearly liking the new expression he'd learnt.

Lily grinned. 'So, Celine.'

Luc raised his eyebrows and ordered more drinks. 'I went to the casino and asked about those slips. They told me it was her. I was shocked and wasn't sure what to do about it. I was going to speak to her, but before I could, Elodie decided to cancel everything.'

'So you thought you'd take the blame?' Lily was perplexed.

'For the time being. As a public thing, you know? To get Elodie to lift her ban on everything and so I could speak to Celine privately.' Luc shrugged expressively. 'I thought maybe they could reinstate me later on. I don't know, I just thought I should do it. I didn't really think further ahead than that.'

'It was a very noble gesture,' Lily told him. 'Really sweet.'

'I don't know about sweet.' Luc dismissed the compliment. 'I just did it in the moment, yes?'

'Yes. Poor Celine though. She looked so broken. I don't think she's very happy with Pierre.'

Luc nodded in agreement. 'I think maybe you are right. She certainly has a few demons.'

Lily swallowed and took another gulp of mulled wine. She wanted to talk about Elodie, but she wasn't sure how to broach the subject.

'Can I talk to you about Elodie?' Luc said.

'Er, yes. Of course.' Unexpected, but handy. Lily waited.

'She's a mixed-up kid,' Luc commented.

'Kid?' Lily knew she probably looked disbelieving, but Elodie wasn't a child. Mind you, neither was Jamie, but he had sure acted like one.

'Yes.' Luc gave her a very direct stare. 'She is the same age as Anais would have been. In fact, she was her best friend.'

'Right.' Lily didn't want to let on that she already knew. She wanted Luc to talk and Imogen had always taught her that if you want a guy to talk, don't ask questions. Just listen and wait. It worked.

'Yes. She was distraught when Anais died. Absolutely inconsolable. She and Anais were very close. Elodie dabbled – is that what you say? Dabbled in drugs as well, but not like Anais, who became terribly addicted. Since Anais died, Elodie hasn't touched drugs. Not once.'

'That's good. I guess having a close friend die like that must shock a person into changing. If anything happened to Imogen…' Lily shuddered. 'No, I can't even think about it.'

Luc nodded. 'Elodie almost became my little sister, you know? Not replacing Anais, because no one could, but Elodie is very… young at heart, if you know what I mean? She thinks she's sophisticated and grown up, but she's young and vulnerable. Like Anais.'

'Kind of.' Did this mean that Luc's feelings for Elodie were purely platonic? Lily vehemently hoped so.

'There is nothing between us,' Luc said suddenly. He put his hand near hers on the bar. 'Elodie and I are just friends. Like you and Jamie.'

What?! Lily pulled a face. One of them must have fancied the other one at some point.

'Not like that!' Luc frowned, guessing what she was thinking. 'I don't see Elodie that way. I get that she's attractive, but she feels like family to me. We almost fell out recently anyway. Over you.'

'Over me?'

'Yes. She's very protective of me.'

'I've noticed,' Lily said dryly.

'Yes, well. She has her reasons. I fell for a couple of girls here before and they left. It was years ago,' he added hurriedly. 'But Elodie dislikes beautiful girls who turn up.'

Lily flushed at that. Beautiful?

'She thinks I'm going to get hurt again, but it's not for her to say. She's my friend, not my mother. I have one of those already.'

'And a very fabulous one too.'

Luc smiled. 'I can only agree. Elodie tries to protect me,' he added softly. 'She thought you were another girl here to hurt me. Another girl who will stay for a bit, then leave and take a piece of my heart with her.'

Ouch. That sounded painful. That was the last thing Lily wanted. As for leaving, she still hadn't decided what to do about that. She missed her family, but she didn't want to be away from Luc either.

'That's why she tried to discredit you that day,' Luc added. 'To scare you away, I suppose. I told her off. We rowed and it wasn't pleasant.'

'Oh.' Lily wasn't sure what to say to that. She wasn't pleased they had rowed, but if Luc stuck up for her, she had to feel chuffed about that.

'We're all right now, but she did take against you.' Luc eyed her carefully. 'I think, like me, she could see that you were different.'

Lily bit her lip. Luc thought she was different?

'Yes, I think you are different.' Luc smiled at her. 'I have been upset with you. Over Jamie, maybe. I thought you wanted to be with him and when he turned up, he was a tool.'

Lily let out a laugh. She wanted to tell Luc what Elodie had said about him, but it didn't really matter. Now Lily knew what Elodie had been trying to do. It was certainly misguided, but at least it was because Elodie cared so deeply about Luc.

'I really enjoyed our stay in the log cabin,' she said, not sure how to lead the conversation that way.

'Me too.' He met her eyes again and, this time, there was deep intent within them.

Lily shivered slightly. Good God, the man was sexy. He took her breath away.

'We – we should go back there,' Lily offered.

'We definitely should,' Luc agreed. He put his hand on hers and linked his fingers through hers.

Lily loved the feel of his warm fingers in hers. It felt so intimate. God, she wanted to kiss him. He was so gorgeous. And an amazing person.

Luc took her chin in his other hand and angled her head to one side. Lily could barely breathe. She closed her eyes and… Luc's phone rang.

'*Merde!*' Luc checked it. 'It's Elodie. She's sent texts saying I am needed back at the hotel. *Merde,*' he said again.

'Go,' Lily said, putting aside her crushing disappointment. 'It must be about the money thing. Or Pierre.'

'Yes.' He squeezed her hand again. 'To be continued?'

'Definitely,' Lily said, feeling everything in her body react to his touch. She could only imagine what it would be like to put her hands all over that sexy, hard body.

'I will call you later. And maybe we can go skiing tomorrow? Not a lesson. Just for fun.'

'Perfect.' That was a lovely idea. They always had lessons, so to just ski for the sake of skiing would be amazing.

Lily watched Luc throw his jacket on and leave. Just as she was relaxing and drinking her mulled wine, he strode back in, took her face in his hands and kissed her. He really kissed her. It was the kind of kiss that had her heart melting, her back arching and all her senses tingling. His hands were in her hair, his body was curved into hers and it felt intimate and incredible and like the best thing she had ever touched or tasted.

Luc pulled back. 'I couldn't wait any longer to do that. Not even for the Devereuxs.'

Lily was too busy panting to be able to speak.

Suddenly everyone in the fondue restaurant burst into a noisy round of applause. Lily went bright red while Luc smiled ruefully and held a hand up. This time he left the restaurant and he didn't come back.

Lily finished her drink and decided to head over to Bernadette's. They only had a few days to sort this Christmas Eve dinner and she needed a proper update.

Bernadette opened the door and broke into a smile. 'You look as though you have been kissed a lot!'

Lily squealed. 'No way! Do I? How can you tell?'

'You look dishevelled,' Bernadette told her. 'Your cheeks are pink and your eyes are sparkling. Your hair...' She stroked it into place. 'Come in. I need to talk to you about the meal. Mind the mistletoe above the door!'

Lily smiled at the large bunch of green stalks and milky-white berries hanging above her.

Bernadette showed Lily the table, which had already been prepared.

'That looks amazing!'

Bernadette had opened her table up so it could easily seat eight people and had even laid out all the silver cutlery and silver and gold mats. Even the plates had been laid out – white with a delicate beaded design. There were candles and in the middle there was a huge floral display of white Christmas roses and green foliage. Lily imagined that the table would look superb with all the candles on. None of it matched, but it didn't matter. The table had a green and red tablecloth with the corners tied up.

'That is so the devil can't get in,' Bernadette explained. 'An old tradition. The three candlesticks represent the trinity.'

'What are these?' Lily touched some gold-fringed paper parcels which were laid out by each place.

'They are called *les papillotes*. They contain candied fruits or chocolates. Just a little gift for everyone.'

'They are so pretty.'

'For the food, we will have oysters and smoked salmon,' Bernadette said, leading Lily to the kitchen. She showed her the big crate of oysters she had somehow managed to squeeze into her fridge.

'I adore oysters.'

'Then foie gras. I know, I know. Some people think it is naughty. But it's traditional and I will do something delicious with it. Then we will have pheasant with truffles and chestnuts. And if you can help me make a *bûche de Noël*?'

'Of course. Isn't there some tradition where you eat thirteen desserts?'

Bernadette rolled her eyes. 'Yes, but we're not doing that! There's no time and it's a Provençal thing, not something that is done all over France. Anyway, we have superb wines for each course. Look. And the best champagne from Reims.'

'Wonderful!' Lily felt excited. She needed to check with her parents about coming. She had phoned them four times since the other day and they were being very coy about it all. Dave got all silly and started talking about something else.

'So, about the meal. Have you invited Luc yet?'

'No. I meant to earlier, but I got distracted.' She went pink again.

Bernadette chuckled. 'I see. Well, Luc doesn't do much on Christmas Eve, so I doubt he'll be busy. He prefers to stay indoors. Violetta and Raymond are coming. They think I am having a little drinks ceremony.'

'Do you think they'll be cross when they see all this?' Lily asked worriedly.

'I don't know,' Bernadette answered honestly. 'All we can do is hope that they see it in the right way.'

Lily felt anxious. 'Do you think they will?'

Bernadette held up two fingers, crossed.

'And how will we mark Anais' passing without making it melancholy?'

'That is the part I am worried about,' Bernadette mused. 'I have been thinking and thinking, but I don't know what to do about it. It is so tricky.'

Lily thought for a minute. The one person who might know how to do something to honour Anais, aside from Luc and his parents, was Elodie. Was there even a chance that Lily could speak to her and get her on side for this meal? She had no idea, but it might be the only way to get the idea right.

'Leave that with me,' Lily said. 'I have an idea.'

'OK, good, good. Shall we make this *bûche de Noël*? It's like a…'

'Yule log?' Lily suggested.

'Yes, I think so. Grab those eggs, will you?'

Lily took down a box of fresh eggs from the counter and she and Bernadette got to work.

Chapter Twenty-Four

'Elodie? Can we talk please?'

Elodie turned around, her sheet of golden hair swinging over her shoulder. She gave Lily a hostile stare, then shrugged.

'OK,' she said. She was wearing tight jeans and an off-the-shoulder cream jumper that made the most of her gorgeous figure.

Lily gestured to a sofa in the staff area, wondering if she would stop feeling intimidated by Elodie's sleek and stylish appearance. The staff area was empty, and it felt calm and tranquil, the large window at the end framing a Christmas-perfect view of staggered fir trees, a ripple of ice-capped mountains and a heavy fall of snow. The snowflakes danced and spiralled down past the window like the start of a Christmas movie and it all looked magical. Lily didn't think it would ever stop taking her breath away and she hoped she would always appreciate the beauty of her surroundings.

'Listen, I know you don't trust me yet and you're worried I'll hurt Luc,' Lily started, pushing her auburn hair out of her eyes. 'Please know that I have feelings for him, and I'm not planning to go anywhere for a while. If at all,' she added.

Lily still wasn't sure what she was going to do in the summer months if she stayed and she knew she would make frequent trips home to see her family, but she also felt as though her new friends had become her extended family in Chamonix.

Elodie eyed her suspiciously. 'Really?' Her tone was one of disbelief.

'Really,' Lily answered firmly. 'I'm not planning to hurt Luc. Far from it. If anything, I'm worried I might get hurt.'

'Luc is a very good man!' Elodie told her sharply.

'You told me he was a player who enjoyed making girls fall in love with him,' Lily reminded her mildly.

Elodie had the grace to wince. 'Yes, well. I said that to put you off him because I thought you were just another girl.'

'And do you still think that?'

'Maybe not,' Elodie conceded. 'He told me off about the complaint thing, by the way,' she offered grudgingly.

'Did he?' Lily was stunned that Elodie had confessed such a thing. 'I had no idea. I thought he ran after you to see if you were OK or something.'

'No way!' Elodie laughed. She actually laughed! 'He told me off and told me to stop targeting you. I think that was the word he used. He was so angry.' She looked at Lily properly. 'I am sorry about that, OK?'

Lily stared at her. She wanted to slap Elodie for doing it in the first place, but at the same time, it felt like it was already water under the bridge. Lily felt good that they had cleared the air, even though she imagined Elodie might always be edgy around her because of how protective she was of Luc. 'I wanted to ask for your help with something, actually.'

'Oh?' Elodie raised a perfectly shaped eyebrow.

Lily told Elodie about the dinner planned for Luc and his parents at Bernadette's. 'And the thing is, we really want to mark Anais' passing, but we don't want to bring the mood down because the idea is to somehow, if we can, help Luc and his family feel good about Christmas again.'

'That is a really lovely idea.' Elodie looked down and when she lifted her eyes again, there were tears in them.

'You must still miss Anais very much,' Lily said, feeling for Elodie. How painful it must have been to lose her best friend like that.

Elodie nodded and dabbed at her eyes with her fingers. 'I hate crying. But yes, I do miss her. Very much. There isn't a day that goes by that I don't think about her. And I feel so sad that I couldn't stop her.'

'I don't think there is anything you could have done,' Lily told her. 'I know you feel responsible in some way, but when drugs take hold of someone...'

Elodie took a deep breath. 'Yes. It is so horrible.' She paused. 'Can you leave this with me? The idea for Anais? I need to think about it.'

'Of course.' Lily wondered if she could ask about Celine, but she wasn't sure if she would be overstepping. She and Elodie had only just started talking, but she needn't have worried.

'I'm so worried about my mother!' Elodie blurted out, putting her hands to her face. 'Why do people get addicted to things? Anais with the drugs, my mother with gambling?' She wiped more tears away.

'I don't know,' Lily said, feeling sorry for Elodie. 'I think sometimes it's because there's other sadness going on below the surface, you know? And something needs to fill that void. And then that good feeling – if that's what it is – that good feeling becomes the addictive thing.'

Elodie let out a heavy sigh. 'It's just hard to think that my mother has been that sad and that she needed to find something else to make her feel better. We have this business and she has my father. She has Marc and I…'

It seemed that Elodie was unaware of her parents' marital problems, and it certainly wasn't her place to mention what Celine had confided.

'My father is due back any minute,' Elodie said, checking her watch. 'He knows about my mother and we are going to get her some help.'

'That's good.' Lily turned her head to the door. 'Could that be him now?'

Elodie got up. 'Let's see. I hope so. It has not been the same here without him.'

Lily followed her. It was Pierre. He was being brought home by Marc as he was still in a wheelchair. His bad leg was stuck out on a stand and it was bandaged and set. His dark hair was immaculate, and he still looked suave in a pair of grey trousers with the leg snipped off and a black jumper, but he looked worried. Lily suspected that Pierre wasn't anxious for himself as much as he was for Celine. Marc was pushing him and he looked pale and worried.

Celine came out of the office to greet Pierre.

'Pierre!' She looked pleased to see him as she walked over and took his hands. 'You look good. Healthy.'

Pierre squeezed her hands, looking agonised. 'Do not worry about me. It's you we need to look after now. My leg will mend.' He pulled her closer to him and the gesture was tender, even poignant. 'Please let me help you.'

Marc looked distressed and his eyes met Elodie's.

'I'm so sorry.' Celine was openly weeping. She had lost all her composure and her shoulders dropped as though she couldn't keep pretending anymore.

Lily could see that Elodie was struggling as she watched her parents. Not sure if she was doing the right thing, she reached out her hand and took Elodie's. Elodie held Lily's hand tightly.

Celine wiped her eyes. 'I can't believe I took money from the business, Pierre. I am so, so sorry...'

'No, no, *cherie*. It's OK.' Pierre shook his head. 'There is no need to be sorry. The money is nothing. I just hate that you have felt this way. I promise to spend more time with you and to work on us more.'

Elodie's face crumpled as she realized that her parents had been having marriage trouble.

Marc swallowed. '*Papa*. We are so happy to have you back.' He leant over and hugged Pierre.

Pierre clasped Marc to him. 'Thank you for collecting me. And for looking after the *Boutique Hotel Devereux* in my absence.'

Lily hid a smile. She had no idea why Pierre talked about the hotel in this way, but it always made her chuckle. She let go of Elodie's hand, sensing that Elodie wanted to appear unruffled.

Marc turned to her. 'Oh, Lily. Earlier today, a friend of mine mentioned he'd need a sports masseuse this summer, if you're interested and if we don't have full time work for you here. If you're thinking of staying.'

'I am.' Lily beamed. That was exactly what she had needed.

'We'll still have plenty of guests over the summer,' Marc told her. 'They come here for walking and cycling and all the summer sports. It's just as busy, but I wanted to let you know about this other work.'

'That's great, thank you.' Lily decided it was time to leave the Devereuxs to sort themselves out as a family. 'I'll leave you all to it and, Elodie, if you could let me know about any ideas?'

'Yes, of course.' Elodie gave her a grateful smile.

Lily called Luc as she walked down to the boot room. 'Ready for our fun ski?'

'Definitely,' he said. 'Meet you in town?'

'I'm on it.'

—

'So how are you feeling?' Luc asked, repositioning her goggles for her.

'A bit scared, but I'm OK,' Lily said. She tightened her gloves. 'I don't know why this feels different! We've skied together so many times.'

Luc pulled his goggles down. 'Yes, but I am always stopping and waiting for you. This time, we are skiing together. I'll take it slow, OK? But if we can, we need to get some more speed today.'

Lily stared out at the horizon for a moment. It was a bright day, but it was still snowing. It made visibility harder, but Lily steeled her nerves. Nothing could be worse than the whiteout. They were on a top to bottom blue called Aillouds. It would take them from the top of the Prarion gondola all the way down to the bottom of either the Bellevue or the Prarion lifts.

'It is 900 metres,' Luc explained. 'It's a long run, tree-lined, and it has some lovely cafés and restaurants. We can stop for lunch somewhere maybe?'

'Sounds great.' Lily felt her stomach flip over at the thought of skiing normally without much stopping and starting, but she had to do this. It would be empowering and it was about time she skied properly.

'There are a few moguls halfway down,' Luc warned her. 'You can either give them a go or slow right down and go around them.'

'OK.' Lily felt her body tense up, but she was going to do her best to stay calm and enjoy skiing with Luc.

'Let's go!'

Luc set off. He took it slowly and he kept turning around and checking on her. Lily focused and relaxed her body. She tried to parallel as much as possible and then, every so often when she felt out of control with her speed, she fell back on a snow plough and then she immediately felt back in control again. After a while, Luc picked up the speed a little and Lily did her best to match it. She felt scared, especially since the slope was steeper than she was used to, but she held it together and she was proud of herself.

'Moguls!' Luc shouted over his shoulder. He slowed down and showed her how to go over them.

Lily baulked at that and avoided five on the trot. Then she decided to go for it. And over she went! She didn't stack it, she held her poise and she carried on.

'*Très bien!*' Luc cried.

Lily grinned. She loved how encouraging he was.

Further down the run, Luc gestured with his pole to a restaurant tucked away to the side and they both pulled up there. It was a cute, chalet-style restaurant with a bar overlooking the rest of the fir tree-lined run.

They ordered drinks and sat in the bar area, taking in the view.

'You are doing so well with your skiing now,' Luc commented. 'Your confidence is up.'

'I have to focus all the time on relaxing!' Lily said. 'Which feels weird, but I know it's the right thing to do.'

'Definitely.'

They ordered some of the usual Savoyard fare – cold meats and cheeses and some delicious bread.

'I have something to ask you,' Lily started nervously.

Luc looked at her with raised eyebrows. 'I don't know if I like the sound of that. You look very serious.'

'I know.' Lily swallowed. 'Bernadette and I have a… Christmas dinner planned for you and your parents. Well, drinks and some food.' She decided to play it down. 'It's on Christmas Eve.'

Luc avoided her eyes. 'You know how I feel about the whole Christmas thing…'

'Yes, and I promise I'm not forcing you to love it the way I do or anything like that.' Lily was earnest. 'We don't want to ignore what's happened, either, so we want to honour Anais as well. But Christmas can be such a magical time, especially with friends and family.'

Luc sighed. 'OK. I'll go, for you, Lily, but please don't expect me to see it the way you do or suddenly feel differently. Anais left such a hole in our lives.'

'I understand.' Lily's stomach unknotted itself. At least he had agreed to come!

'Shall we ski?' Luc said.

Lily nodded. 'Can't wait. Wow! Who would have thought I would ever say that?'

Luc laughed. 'You love it now. It's amazing.'

Mostly, Lily adored skiing so much because of Luc. She also hoped that Luc might learn to love Christmas again mostly thanks to her.

Chapter Twenty-Five

Christmas Eve

'Are you off?' Imogen asked, emerging from under the duvet.

It was late afternoon. The night before had been a great night out and they had slept in ridiculously late, but it was time for Lily to get moving.

'I am.' Lily smiled at her as she brushed her auburn hair. 'Don't look like that,' she added as Imogen pulled a pouty face. 'I'll see you tomorrow. And you and Ollie are having your big romantic Christmas Eve thingy later.'

'We are,' Ollie's head appeared next to Imogen's from under the duvet. 'I have lots of lovely things planned.'

'Do you?' Imogen's eyes lit up. 'You are a very good boyfriend.'

'I am,' he replied, giving her a heartfelt kiss. 'But I need to sleep now. Have a lovely day, Lily. Hope it all goes well with Luc.' With that, he disappeared under the duvet again.

Imogen tutted and got up. She motioned for them to go to the bathroom. 'Lazy sod,' she said, not meaning it for a second. 'Love him,' she added quietly, once inside the bathroom. She looked bashful.

'What?' Lily nearly dropped her bag of presents. 'Did you just say that?'

'I said that,' Imogen said, looking terrified. 'And I said it out loud.' She put a finger to her lips. 'Shhh. He doesn't know yet. I'm telling him later.'

'Oh, Ims!' Lily gave her a hug. 'That's so cute. You and Ollie make such a great couple.'

Imogen pretended to puff herself up. 'Thank you kindly.' She smiled at Lily. 'So what about you?'

'Me?' Lily forced herself to look vague. 'Not sure what you mean.'

'Oh, stop it.' Imogen nudged her. 'What time is kick off?'

'Not until later, but Bernadette and I have so much to do, so I'm heading over there shortly.'

Lily felt excited, but she was also nervous. She had no idea how Luc was going to react. As for her parents... she wasn't entirely sure what they were doing or when they were arriving. They were being very evasive every time Lily called them to discuss it.

'It will be fine,' Imogen assured her. 'Go for it, bestie. I can't wait to see you and Luc as a proper couple. You really deserve to be happy.'

Lily felt a rush of emotion. She had come such a long way since she'd arrived in Chamonix. She had been so broken and now she felt whole again. It had been cathartic to come here and to conquer her fear of heights and, yes, confront how she felt about her dad. She had made new friends and she was spending quality time with her best and oldest friend. And meeting Luc had been the best thing of all.

'Are your mum and Dave going to get here today or tomorrow?' Imogen asked.

'Tomorrow, I think,' Lily said, her face falling slightly. 'They tried to get flights today, but they were booked up. They did manage to find some for tomorrow morning, though, so they'll turn up then. I'm gutted, but tomorrow is Christmas Day, so that's the important day, isn't it? For us, anyway.'

Imogen frowned. 'I guess so. I get why you're gutted about today, though, as it's such a big deal in this country.' Her expression brightened. 'But hey. Maybe today is about Luc and his family? Maybe it will be easier that way.'

'That's how I'm trying to think of it,' Lily said. 'Anyway. You and Ollie have your gifts, yes?'

'Yes. They're under our little tree out there. You have your presents from us?'

Lily caught Imogen's eye at the use of the word 'us'. Imogen had never used that word about herself and a boyfriend before, and Lily found it deeply touching that her best friend was so happy.

'Are you wearing that?' Imogen stared at Lily's outfit.

Lily glanced down at her jeans and black jumper. 'No, Ims. I have a fantastic emerald green dress that I'm going to put on later when I'm done with all the cooking at Bernadette's.'

'That will be a knockout with your red hair,' Imogen told her. 'Go!' She pointed to the door. 'Have an amazing day and I'll call later to find out how it went.'

'Enjoy your day too. Love you! Happy Christmas.'

Lily hoisted her bag of Christmas presents over her shoulder and headed downstairs. She saw Marc behind reception, on the phone, his pen poised over a notepad. Elodie was nowhere to be seen. Sylvan and Charlotte

– his new girlfriend – shimmied through in matching Christmas jumpers. His had a fluffy penguin on the front, while hers sported a sequinned polar bear wearing a Christmas hat. They were as well-suited as their owners.

'Lily.' Celine stopped her by the doorway. 'Are you heading off for your Christmas Eve dinner?'

'Yes. Do you have a family dinner planned here?' Lily noticed how much happier and healthier Celine looked. And – shock – she was wearing a dress! It was black and tight-fitting, and it had a high neck. It made Celine looked feminine and soft.

'We do. It's a tradition for Sylvan to cook us a superb dinner every year.' Celine smiled. 'We eat so much! But his food is so delicious.'

Pierre joined Celine and slid his arm around her waist. 'We are very glad you are staying with us over the Christmas period, Lily,' he said. 'We have a wonderful lunch planned tomorrow. We hope you can join us?'

'I'll definitely swing by,' Lily said. They looked back at her, puzzled. 'Sorry – that means I'll be there at some point. I'll let you know about the time, but my parents are arriving tomorrow and I have no idea when.'

Pierre and Celine exchanged a quick glance.

'We are easy with the times,' Celine said, clearing her throat. 'Their rooms are ready, so whatever time they get here works for us. Marc will be on reception 24/7.'

Pierre nodded, his sleek, dark hair not moving even one centimetre out of place. 'We look forward to meeting them.'

Celine nodded along in agreement.

'Thank you. Enjoy your dinner!'

Lily wasn't sure why they were acting so strange, but she didn't have time to think about it. She and Bernadette still had some last bits of cooking to do and Lily had promised to pick up some final groceries. On the way, she caught sight of a pretty brooch shaped like a peacock and bought it for Bernadette on impulse, knowing it would look fabulous with the sort of eccentric clothes she wore.

Chamonix looked glorious, Lily thought, juggling the box of groceries she was carrying as she paused to take in the breath-taking view. The magnificent range of mountains in the background, capped by snow, looked vast and unreachable. Keen skiers, getting their last ski before Christmas, were zig-zagging down the mountains in brightly coloured ski coats. For a moment they resembled shiny Christmas tree baubles as they bobbed and dived amongst the deep green fir trees.

The village itself looked beautiful. Dusted with a heavy shake of snow like icing sugar from a giant sieve, some of the chalets and restaurants looked rather like edible gingerbread houses. The village was buzzing and lively as inhabitants and ski enthusiasts bustled around carrying presents and doing last-minute shopping.

Lily inhaled the air, breathing in the tantalising aroma of warm, doughy pretzels and mulled wine. The village of Chamonix felt alive with Christmas cheer and expectation and Lily felt a rush of happiness. At Bernadette's house, she found the door ajar and pushed it open. Inside, the house smelt sensational – there was meat cooking in the oven and the smell of cinnamon and chestnuts in the air. Jez the cat strolled up to Lily and wound his way through her ankles.

'Do you have everything?' Bernadette asked. She came and took the box of groceries from Lily's arms.

'Yes, it's all there. The house looks – and smells – amazing,' Lily commented.

'Come through,' Bernadette called.

Lily followed her. The table looked magical. There were even more candles set out and they were all lit, giving off Christmassy scents. Bernadette had twisted the cream and silver napkins into beautiful shapes on each plate and there was a huge centrepiece dominating the table. It was a glass bowl containing an assortment of fresh white flowers, deep green foliage and branches that were sprayed with silver glitter spray. It looked gorgeous. Bernadette had Christmas music playing in the background and the whole place looked, felt and smelt fantastically festive.

'We don't have long.' Bernadette poked her head out of the kitchen. 'I need to check the pheasant and we need to plate up the foie gras.'

'Coming!' Lily emptied her bag of presents under the tree and headed into the kitchen.

She and Bernadette worked tirelessly for the next two hours. They got everything ready, finished the table and prepared all the food. They were so engrossed that they didn't even hear their first guests arriving.

'Bernadette?' Violetta's blond chignon appeared in the doorway.

'Violetta!' Bernadette wiped her hands on a tea towel and embraced her friend warmly. 'You look wonderful. Come in, come in.' She reverted to French briefly and spoke to Violetta before Bernadette turned to Raymond. They hugged, holding on to one another, and Lily knew they were remembering that terrible Christmas.

'Thank you for this,' Raymond said, his voice steeped in emotion. 'We weren't sure we were going to be able to make it today, but we think it's time.'

'I'm so glad,' Bernadette said. 'So glad. Not only because I would be eating pheasant and oysters for the foreseeable future if you hadn't turned up.'

Raymond chuckled. 'You know how much I love oysters.' He looked handsome in a soft jumper and jacket over some formal trousers. His blond hair and moustache looked as though they had been coiffed into place, but Lily wasn't sure Raymond was that vain.

'I do.' Bernadette checked her watch. 'And where is Luc? He said he wouldn't be late?'

On cue, Luc arrived. He looked slightly dishevelled as if he had been rushing, which was unlike him, but he still managed to pull it off. He removed his brown puffer jacket to reveal a chunky cream jumper and jeans. Seriously hot. Lily met his eyes and glanced down at herself.

'Oh God. I'm still wearing my scruffy outfit!'

Mortified, Lily dove into a nearby bathroom with her bag, already tearing off her jumper, which reeked of cooking. She took a breath and changed into the emerald green dress she had bought in town that week. It was an impulse buy and Lily wasn't entirely sure it was the right thing to wear as it was very snug-fitting and low at the back. However, when she emerged, she received admiring glances from both Luc and Raymond, and Violetta went into raptures over it. Bernadette winked at her.

There was a knock at the door.

'Who else are we expecting?' Lily asked, looking up from pouring glasses of champagne.

'I'll go,' Luc offered, throwing Bernadette a smile.

Lily had no idea why everyone was acting so strange around her. They were being so secretive and it was driving her nuts.

'Who was—'

Lily almost dropped the glasses of champagne she was carrying.

Standing in front of her was her mum. And Dave. And Ivy. Lily was gobsmacked. She was delighted and emotional all at the same time.

'Oh my goodness!' Lily was pretty sure she was going to cry.

'Shall we take those from you?' Sue beamed, taking the champagne flutes out of Lily's hands.

Lily threw her arms clumsily around her mum's shoulders, slopping the drinks everywhere. 'I can't believe you're all here! You said you couldn't get here until tomorrow!'

'Lily!' Sue scolded. 'You've covered me in champagne!'

Lily didn't care. She hadn't seen her family in months and she was going to hold onto them and make the most of it. She breathed in her mum's familiar coconut shampoo and the spicy, woody scent of her favourite Youth Dew perfume.

Finally, Lily reluctantly pulled back. Ivy was wearing a classic white ski jacket over a pair of smart black trousers, her red hair hanging loosely around her shoulders and her cheeks pink from the cold. Sue and Dave were wearing wildly clashing colours with trousers, hats and coats in bright blues and reds and greens all fighting against each other. Dave, in particular, looked as though he was about to head off to Antarctica – he was trussed up in an enormous turquoise coat with a big, furry hood and he was wearing oversized green mittens and some bizarre trousers that looked as though they were three sizes too big for his sturdy frame. All he needed was a rucksack and a pick axe, and he could be off hiking the side of a glacier. Clearly Dave thought Chamonix was forty degrees below zero with mountains to climb before dinner.

'Lily!' he said, holding his arms open wide, his chubby cheeks rosy and gnome-like.

Lily fell into Dave's arms, giving him the biggest hug.

'We've missed you, we've missed you,' Dave murmured into the top of her head.

'I have missed you too,' Lily replied, feeling choked up. There was something so solid and dependable about Dave. Unlike her real father, Dave had always made Lily feel safe. She met Luc's eyes over Dave's shoulder and he gave her the kind of understanding smile that melted her heart.

Violetta and Raymond looked on, their arms around one another. Lily wasn't sure if they were upset or happy but realised it was the latter when they smiled and nodded at her. Lily marvelled at their ability to be pleased for her when they must still feel heartbroken over Anais.

'I'm so happy you've arrived today!' Lily commented, finding she had to wipe a tear from her eye when she pulled away.

'Surprise!' Dave said, spreading his arms wide again. 'We told you a little white lie so we could turn up a day early. Everyone but you knew about it! Celine and Pierre Devereux at the hotel and Bernadette. Luc, of course, since he just picked us up from the airport. He had to get up super early.'

Lily caught his eye again. Luc gave her a shrug, but said nothing.

'It's a brilliant surprise, just brilliant,' Lily said, hugging Ivy. 'Are you OK?' she asked her as an aside. 'About Jamie, I mean?'

Ivy nodded and looked unperturbed. 'I'm absolutely fine, Lily. Don't worry, I've never been better. I was upset, but I can assure you, I'm not now. Between you and me, Jamie is a bit of a dickhead,' she said quietly.

'Yes, I realised that recently too,' Lily murmured.

Ivy smiled at Bernadette. 'But Chamonix is beautiful. Jamie wasn't wrong about that. It looks like a Christmas card!'

Bernadette started pouring more champagne as she chatted away happily to Ivy about her home town. Lily felt so warm and fuzzy inside, she thought she might burst. She watched as her mum and Dave introduced themselves to Bernadette and then to Violetta and Raymond by shaking hands and cheek-kissing. Ivy did the same and soon they were all chatting about the travel and the snow and the skiing and Christmas and anything else that came up, as though they had all known one another for ages.

'Look at that beautiful table!' Sue exclaimed. 'How did you get the centrepiece to look like that, Bernadette?'

'Oh, I won't be skiing,' Dave was saying to Raymond vehemently. 'No, no, no. I'm sorry, Raymond, but I have two left feet. Two left feet! I can't dance for toffee. Sue will tell you.'

'Toffee?' Raymond asked, bewildered. 'Toffee is a sweet, *non*?'

'Oh, he *really* can't dance,' Sue agreed, turning to Violetta to ask where she had purchased her trouser suit. 'Two left feet, Raymond! That's why he's good at the robot but nothing else. Don't even *think* about getting that man to do a tango.'

Dave pulled an 'I told you so' expression and shook his head. 'Me and skiing… not going to happen, Raymond. Not going to happen.'

Raymond laughed. 'I think anyone can ski. Even someone with two left feet. And toffee.' He shrugged. 'I will teach you if you like? Or Luc. He is a very good instructor.'

'I've heard,' Dave said genially. 'Looked after our girl properly, hasn't he? Good man, good man.' He clapped Luc on the shoulder, which was some sight, considering how short Dave was compared to Luc.

'You are very welcome,' Luc said. 'Shall I help you out of that jacket?' he offered. 'You must be very hot in here.'

Dave started unzipping his gigantic coat, revealing a garish red and green Star Wars-themed Christmas jumper with Yoda, which said 'This season jolly it is' on the front.

Thank you, Lily mouthed at Luc.

De rien, he mouthed back.

Lily felt her stomach flip over. She was getting some serious feelings for Luc and there was nothing she could do about it. She loved that he had picked up her mum, sister and Dave from the airport without even telling her. What a lovely Christmas present.

'Shall we eat?' Bernadette suggested. 'We have oysters to start and then we have some foie gras with cherries.'

'Ooh!' Sue looked thrilled. 'Oysters, foie gras – this is such a treat! You're spoiling us, Bernadette, and it's wonderful.'

Soon, the room became a hive of activity with Sue, Dave and Ivy putting down their things and Lily and

Bernadette serving the food. Luc made sure his parents were seated in the right places with drinks in their hands. Everyone exclaimed over the oysters, some of which were served uncooked with shallot vinegar and a squeeze of lemon, while others were baked with butter, garlic, cheese and pepper. There were plump rolls of smoked salmon and fresh baguettes and Bernadette served the oysters with a crisp, dry Muscadet.

The next, mouth-watering course featured thick slices – or 'lobes', as they were known – of foie gras that Bernadette had seared earlier with Armagnac and had warmed again at a low heat. Lily spooned a generous serving of sour cherries onto everyone's plates, which Bernadette said was to 'cut through the fat'. This was paired with a good St Emilion, because Bernadette believed foie gras needed a gentle red wine to help it down.

'Oh, that is divine,' Dave said, savouring his mouthful. 'I know it's naughty, but it does taste good.'

Raymond nodded in agreement. '*Superbe*,' he said to Bernadette, stealing some of Violetta's.

Lily looked up and found Luc's eyes on her. She couldn't help feeling a flash of lust as his eyes communicated that he wanted to be alone with her. Unless she was mistaken, but no. Luc wanted to be alone with her and she wanted that too. For now, though, Lily was enjoying being around her family. She threw Luc a smile that she hoped said 'all in good time'.

'Leave some room,' Bernadette warned Raymond as she whisked his plate away. 'We have a few more courses.'

Later, after much chat and louder Christmas music, Bernadette and Lily served pheasant with a truffle and chestnut cake, roast potatoes and a selection of fresh seasonal vegetables, which was served with Bernadette's favourite wine, a Cabernet Sauvignon blend from Bordeaux, all of which was followed by a cheese platter. The cheese had been out for hours and it was oozing unctuously all over the platter. There was roquefort, Sainte-Maure de Touraine (a goat cheese log dusted with ash), a pungent, orange-rind Maroilles and a camembert with truffles. Dave was completely in his element. He tucked his napkin comically into the neck of his Star Wars jumper and got stuck in.

As they sat fat, replete and content, the doorbell rang. Bernadette answered it and they all looked up as Elodie came into the room. She looked divine in a cropped red ski jacket and white trousers that were so tight and unforgiving that it would have had the average woman running for Mont Blanc, but of course, they looked splendid on Elodie.

Lily sat up and glanced at Luc, who got up and greeted Elodie with a hug.

'I hope it is OK that I am here,' Elodie started. 'Lily asked if I could help mark today in some way. For Anais.'

Violetta looked overcome and she reached for Raymond's hand. 'How lovely of you, Lily. And Elodie. Thank you.'

Raymond nodded without saying a word.

Luc took Elodie's coat and she stood awkwardly in the middle of the room. 'I wasn't sure how to mark today,' she said haltingly. 'But when Luc told me that your family was coming, Lily, I thought of Anais's favourite Christmas song. It's an English song. A very popular one, I think. It always makes me think of her. I brought it with me on a CD.'

Bernadette got her CD player working and put the song on. It was 'Last Christmas' by Wham. Lily broke into a smile. She loved this song. Violetta smiled and met Raymond's eyes. He clutched her hand and they held onto one another as they remembered Anais. Luc squeezed Elodie's arm as silent tears rolled down her cheeks. Lily stood up, not sure what to do, but Luc reached for her and she ended up in a clumsy three-way hug with him and Elodie. Oddly, it felt right, even though Elodie had been vile to Lily and Lily hadn't known Anais.

'Oh, what a lovely way to remember her,' Sue murmured, leaning into Dave.

Dave, thoroughly affected by the weight of the moment, was only able to nod his head as he listened to George Michael's smooth tones.

As the song faded away, Luc cleared his throat and raised his glass. 'To Anais,' he said, his voice thick with emotion.

'To Anais,' they all chorused, raising their glasses.

'I will leave you to it now,' Elodie said, slipping her coat back on. 'I am due back at my family dinner, but it was lovely to see you all.' She hugged Violetta and Raymond tightly and said goodbye to everyone else. She gave Lily a fleeting nod that felt like a seal of approval before she left.

'And now, let's have some dessert,' Bernadette suggested gently. 'And some more champagne.'

'I'll help you,' Dave said, getting to his feet, wiping his eyes on the sleeve of his jumper.

'Let's all help,' Sue said, joining in.

Soon, everyone was involved in tidying up and clearing the table and the sombre mood lifted again. Lily found herself alone with Luc.

'Your mum and Dave are good people,' he commented. 'They are kind and genuine. I can tell that my parents adore them.'

Lily smiled. 'I think it's mutual,' she said, watching Dave and Raymond communicating in a bizarre Franglaise, but somehow understanding one another. 'Are you OK?' she said, searching his face. 'That was a lovely moment. Who would have thought it? Wham.'

'Anais did love that song. And it was great to remember her. This has been so special, seeing my parents enjoying Christmas for the first time in years. Your family being here. You...' He took her hand. 'Listen. I don't think we'll get to be alone tonight.'

Lily's face fell. She wanted that so badly.

'Because tonight is about family,' Luc told her firmly. 'But tomorrow, I have something special planned for us. Will you meet me in the morning?'

Lily nodded, trying to control the thrill of anticipation about meeting Luc on Christmas Day.

'Shall we open some presents?' Ivy suggested, looking like an excitable child as she eyed the shiny gifts under Bernadette's tree.

They started exchanging gifts, Dave yelping loudly with delight as he always did when he opened presents. Ivy loved her silk shirt, and she and Lily laughed as Lily opened an almost identical gift from Ivy. It was a silk shirt the same colour as Lily's emerald green dress.

Lily decided to give Luc his present, regardless of whether he had bought her a gift or not. Watching his face as he unwrapped it, she grinned when he broke into a smile.

'It's a—'

'*Caquelon*,' Luc finished. 'A fondue pot. I love it! We can make our own fondue.'

Lily felt absurdly happy about the 'we' part of that sentence. 'It's just a silly thing.'

'Not at all. Here.' Luc took a small present wrapped in silver paper with a bow from under the tree. 'This is for you.'

Lily opened it, all fingers and thumbs. It was a rose gold drinks flask shaped like a bracelet.

'It's just a silly thing.' Luc grinned.

'I love it!' Lily exclaimed, slipping it onto her wrist. 'I can put mulled wine in it in case I get caught in another whiteout. Then I'll stop and have a quick sip whilst looking awesome in my jewellery on the slopes.'

'Exactly.'

More champagne was drunk, and more of Bernadette's rich chocolate *bûche de Noël* was consumed. They all staggered out into the snow late at night, enjoying the Christmas lights and the crunch of snow underfoot. Luc gave Lily a brief head-spinning kiss then headed toward home with his parents as his flat was nearby. Lily led her family back to the *Boutique Hotel Devereux*, where they enjoyed a nightcap with Imogen and Ollie and the rest of the staff before crashing out in bed.

A perfect Christmas Eve, Lily thought to herself seconds before her head hit the pillow and she fell into a deep, contented sleep.

The following morning, Lily was up early. She got dressed and tiptoed out of the room, leaving Imogen and Ollie wrapped round one another in festive onesies. She headed down to the boot room and strapped her boots on, pulled on her helmet and made sure she had her gloves. She was the only person in the boot room, which felt weird, and she grabbed her skis and poles because Luc had said she would need them. She stepped outside, her breath white and ragged in the chilly air.

Trudging through an extremely quiet and utterly magical Chamonix, on Christmas Day no less, Lily caught sight of Luc waiting for her by the lift. She was amazed it was working on Christmas Day, but she guessed it was necessary for all the ski enthusiasts.

'Happy Christmas,' Luc said, drawing her in for a kiss. 'This will sound silly, but I missed you last night.'

'That doesn't sound silly at all,' Lily said, feeling her stomach flip over again. God, he was gorgeous. And kind and funny and… Lily stopped herself. She sounded like an idiot, but as people always said: when you knew, you knew.

'Where are we going?' she asked.

'To the log cabin,' Luc told her.

Lily broke into a wide smile. The log cabin. Of course. Where else?

'This time, without a whiteout,' Luc said. 'Wait until you see the view.'

They went up in the lift and snapped into their skis at the top of the slope. Lily followed Luc down, feeling thrilled whenever she managed to perfect a parallel here and there. They were the only two people on the mountain and it felt amazing. It was still and quiet and the mountain views were magnificent. It was incredible to be able to see in front of her this time, and Lily could finally see what Luc was talking about with the views. She caught sight of the log cabin on the right and started to steer herself in that direction as Luc swooped towards it.

They pulled up together, Lily coming to a clumsier stop than Luc.

'I need to work on that!' she puffed, pulling her goggles up.

'Think how far you have come,' Luc reminded her. 'You couldn't even stop without falling over on day one.'

'Don't.' Lily cringed as she remembered the way she had slipped and slid all over the nursery slope.

'Let's go in,' Luc said, unlocking the door.

Lily stepped inside and gasped. Luc had gone to the log cabin and had put fairy lights up everywhere and put unlit candles all around. There was also a Christmas tree and food laid out on the table with bottles of champagne. Luc quickly went around lighting all the candles, then he lit the fire before turning to Lily.

'Alone at last,' he murmured, pulling her closer.

'Alone at last,' she echoed, feeling another bolt of lust. And something far deeper and more meaningful.

'I want to devour you,' he said, taking her face in his hands. 'And...' He told her the rest in her ear as Lily blushed and squirmed and loved every second of it. 'But most importantly, I just want to be with you today. And all the other days. And get to know and find out everything about you.'

'What – what you just said,' Lily managed. 'I'll give you a proper massage and we'll… cuddle on that rug and we'll…'

'Sounds perfect.' Luc kissed her thoroughly and Lily felt herself melt into his arms. She had never been kissed like this in her life, as though the world might end.

Luc smoothed her hair out of her eyes. 'Even though my heart aches because of Anais, I have fallen in love with Christmas again, Lily. Because of you.'

'I wasn't sure it was possible after Anais.' Lily felt knocked sideways that she had managed to make Luc feel that way.

'Me neither.' Luc bit his lip. 'And it's not just Christmas, Lily. I've fallen in love with you as well.'

Lily swallowed. She wanted to say so much, but what came out was: 'Yes. That. What – what you just said.'

She faltered. No, that was a cop out. She couldn't keep saying stuff like that – she sounded like Sam in the movie Ghost saying 'Ditto' because he couldn't tell Molly he loved her properly. Lily took a deep breath. She could do this. If she could ski down a blue run without falling over, she could do this.

'I've fallen in love with you too,' Lily managed finally. She felt his warm, safe arms around her and felt her entire body respond to his touch.

'Is it time to… cuddle on that rug?' Luc suggested, throwing it a mischievous glance.

'I think it probably is,' Lily agreed gravely. 'That is a rug that is crying out for cuddles.'

'Happy Christmas,' Luc said, unzipping Lily's ski jacket.

'Happy Christmas,' Lily sighed.

They laid on the rug together in front of the roaring fire as snow started to fall heavily outside, with Mont Blanc framed in the window of the log cabin.

Christmas in Chamonix with Luc, Lily thought to herself happily. *What could be more perfect than that?*

Acknowledgements

Thanks to Darren and Alex Blackburn, Carla and John Hopwood, Nikki and Taff, Louise and Johnny, Mark and Mel and all the skiing gang for the inspiration for this novel and for all the skiing fun and technical info. To Phoebe and Daisy, as always, for being my world and for filling my heart every day. To my amazing Mum and to my absent, much missed Dad… for everything. To Claire, Kate, Jane and Jo (Up North) for all the lovely friendship, the support and the sanity.